'Sara Paretsky's V.I. Warshawski remains the most distinctive female private investigator in US crime fiction, and her continuing survival – after numerous pummellings   plausible and very welcome . . . Paretsky's sleuth manages to rile even more people in *Brush Back* than usual, and remains as bloody-minded as ever . . .
immensely entertaining.'
Independent

'Paretsky, who plots more conscientiously than anyone else in the field, digs deep, then deeper, into past and present until all is revealed.'
Kirkus Reviews

'Snappy dialogue, tight plotting and realistic situations make Paretsky's unapologetically politicised thrillers a pleasure to read,
whatever your viewpoint.'
Daily Mail

'With the creation of V.I. Warshawski, Sara Paretsky did more than anyone to change the face of contemporary women's fiction.'
Express on Sunday

'Paretsky has been putting her private investigator through her paces since 1982, changing perceptions of women in crime fiction through the creation of a fiercely independent female detective . . . Paretsky is firing on all cylinders.'
Metro

Also by Sara Paretsky

Critical Mass
Breakdown
Body Work
Hardball
Bleeding Kansas
Fire Sale
Blacklist
Total Recall
Hard Time
Ghost Country
V.I. for Short
Tunnel Vision
Guardian Angel
Burn Marks
Blood Shot
Bitter Medicine
Killing Orders
Deadlock
Indemnity Only

About the author

Sara Paretsky was named 2011 Grand Master by the Mystery Writers of America and is the winner of many awards, including the Cartier Diamond Dagger Award for lifetime achievement from the British Crime Writers' Association and the CWA Gold Dagger for *Blacklist*. Most recently Sara received the Theakstons Old Peculier Outstanding Contribution to Crime Fiction Award. She lives on Chicago's south side with her husband.

Visit Sara's website, www.saraparetsky.com,
Facebook page, www.facebook.com/SaraParetsky,
and follow her on Twitter at @SaraParetsky.

Sara
Paretsky

BRUSH BACK

HODDER

First published in the United States of America in 2015 by The Penguin Group
First published in Great Britain in 2015 by Hodder & Stoughton
An Hachette UK company

This paperback edition published 2016

1

Copyright © Sara Paretsky 2015

A CIP catalogue record for this title is available from the British Library

A format paperback ISBN 978 1 444 75876 4
B format paperback ISBN 978 1 444 75875 7
Ebook ISBN 978 1 444 75874 0

Printed and bound by Clays Ltd, St Ives plc

Hodder & Stoughton policy is to use papers that are natural, renewable and recyclable
products and made from wood grown in sustainable forests. The logging and
manufacturing processes are expected to conform to the environmental regulations of the
country of origin.

Hodder & Stoughton Ltd
Carmelite House
50 Victoria Embankment
London EC4Y 0DZ

www.hodder.co.uk

For Jeremy

He had but little gold within his suitcase;
But all that he might borrow from a friend
On books and learning he would swiftly spend,
. . . And gladly would he learn and gladly teach.
—Geoffrey Chaucer, *The Canterbury Tales*

AUTHOR'S NOTE

While some places and locations in this book may be real, their descriptions are entirely fictitious, as are the events that take place there and the characters who are connected to those places and events.

CONTENTS

SHORTSTOP

I didn't recognize him at first. He came into my office unannounced, a jowly man whose hairline had receded to a fringe of dark curls. Too much sun had baked his skin the color of brick, although maybe it had been too much beer, judging by those ill-named love handles poking over the sides of his jeans. The seams in the faded corduroy jacket strained when he moved his arms; he must not often dress for business.

"Hey, girl, you doing okay for yourself up here, aren't you?"

I stared at him, astonished and annoyed by the familiarity.

"Tori Warshawski, don't you know me? I guess Red U turned you into a snob after all."

Tori. The only people who called me that had been my father and my cousin Boom-Boom, both of them dead a lot of years now. And Boom-Boom's boyhood friends—who were also the only people who still thought the University of Chicago was a leftist hideout.

"It's not Frank Guzzo, is it?" I finally said. When I'd known him thirty years and forty pounds ago, he'd had a full head of red-gold hair, but I could still see something of him around the eyes and mouth.

"All of him." He patted his abdomen. "You look good, Tori, I'll give you that. You didn't turn into some yoga nut or a vegan or something?"

"Nope. I play a little basketball, but mostly I run the lakefront. You still playing baseball?"

"With this body? Slow-pitch sometimes with the geriatric league. But my boy, Frankie Junior, Tori, I got my fingers crossed, but I think he's the real deal."

"How old is he?" I asked, more out of politeness than interest: Frank always thought someone or something was going to be the real deal that made his fortune for him.

"He's fifteen now, made varsity at Saint Eloy's, even though he's only a freshman. He's got a real arm. Maybe he'll be another Boom-Boom."

Meaning, he could be the next person to make it out of the 'hood into some version of the American dream. There were so few of us who escaped South Chicago's gravitational pull that the neighborhood could recite our names.

I'd managed, by dint of my mother's wishes, and my scholarships to the University of Chicago. My cousin Boom-Boom had done it through sports. He'd had seven brilliant seasons with the Blackhawks until he injured his ankle too badly for the surgeons to glue him back in any shape to skate. And then he'd been murdered, shoved off a pier in the Port of Chicago, right under the screw of the *Bertha Krupnik*.

When Boom-Boom and Frank hung out together, Frank hoped he'd be a real deal, too, in baseball. We all did—he was the best shortstop in the city's Catholic League. By the time I started law school, though, Frank was driving a truck for Bagby Haulage. I don't know what happened; I'd lost touch with him by then.

Maybe he could have been a contender. He wasn't the only kid in South Chicago with a spark of promise that flared up and died. They start to spread their wings and then they fall to earth. It's hard to leave the world you know. Even if it's a painful place at times, you grow up learning how to navigate it. The world north of Madison Street looks good on TV, but it has too many hidden traps, places where a homey can make a humiliating mistake.

Perhaps Frankie Junior would have the drive, the mentors and the talent to be another Boom-Boom. All I said was I hoped Frank was right, it would be great. "You stayed in South Chicago?" I added.

"We moved to the East Side. My wife—uh, Bet—uh," he stumbled over the words, his face turning a richer shade of brick.

Frank had left me for Betty Pokorny when we were all in high school. Her father had owned Day & Night Bar & Grill. When the mills were running three shifts, no matter what time you got off or went on, you could get steak and eggs with a boilermaker.

When Betty started smirking at me in the high school hallway, I'd been heartbroken for a few weeks, but my dad told me that Frank wasn't right for me, that I was looking for love in all the wrong places because Gabriella had died a few months earlier. He'd been right: it had been years since I'd thought about either Frank or Betty.

Looking at Frank this morning, in his ill-fitting jacket and uneasy fidgeting, he seemed vulnerable and needy. Let him imagine that hearing about Betty could cause me a pang or two.

"How are Betty's folks?" I asked.

"Her ma passed a few years back, but her dad is still going strong, even without the bar—you know they had to shut that down?"

"Someone told me," I said. Day & Night had followed the mills into extinction, but by then I was so far removed from the neighborhood that I hadn't even felt Schadenfreude, only a vague pity for Frank.

"Her dad, he keeps busy, he's handy with tools, builds stuff, keeps the house from falling over. I guess you don't know we moved in with him when, well, you know."

When they got married, I guessed. Or maybe when Stella went to prison. "What did you do about your place on Buffalo?"

"Ma kept it. My dad's insurance or something let her make the payments while she was in Logan. I looked in on it once a week, made sure nothing was leaking or burning, kept the rats and the gang-bangers from moving in. Ma says she owns it clear and free now."

"She's out?" I blurted.

"Yeah. Two months ago." His heavy shoulders sagged, further stressing the shoulders in the jacket.

Annie Guzzo had been three years younger than me and I was finishing my junior year of college when she died. I counted in my head. I guess it had been twenty-five years.

South Chicago was a neighborhood where violence was routine, ordinary. Stella Guzzo had grown up in a hardscrabble house herself and shouting and hitting were her main modes of functioning. We all knew she hit her daughter, but what turned people's stomachs was that Stella had beaten Annie to death and then walked up to St. Eloy's to play bingo. Not even my aunt Marie, Stella's chief crony, stood up for her.

"I never made those marks on my girl," Stella protested at the trial. "They're lying about me, making me look bad because I was trying to get Annie to see the facts of life. She was getting those big ideas, way above herself. She didn't think she needed to vacuum or do the laundry because she was going to school, but she needed to remember she was part of a family. Everyone has to carry their weight in a family. She's got a brother, he's the one with a future and he needs looking after, I can't do it all on my own, especially not with their father dead. But Annie was fine when I left the house."

Father Gielczowski, the priest at St. Eloy's, had testified for Stella: She was a good woman, a dedicated mother. She didn't spare the rod, but that was what made her a good mother; she didn't tolerate the rudeness a lot of modern women let their children get away with.

Priests usually play well with Chicago juries, but not this time. Stella was built on massive lines, not fat, but big, like the figurehead of a Viking ship. Frank took after her, but Annie was small, like their father. The state's attorney showed pictures of Annie's battered face, and the family photos where she looked like a dark little elf next to her mother's broad-shouldered five-ten.

Instead of manslaughter, the state went for second-degree homicide, and got it. I didn't remember the trial clearly, but I don't think the jury deliberated longer than half a day. Stella drew the full two dimes, with a little extra thrown in to punish her for her belligerent attitude in court.

I never would be a Stella fan, but the thought of her alone in a decrepit South Chicago bungalow was disturbing. "Is she there by herself?" I asked Frank. "It's hard dealing with the outside world when you've been away from it so long. Besides that, South Chicago is a war zone these days, between the Kings, and the Insane Dragons and about five other big gangs."

He fiddled with a chrome paperweight on my desk. "I told Ma it wasn't safe, but where else was she going to go? Betty didn't want her living with us. It didn't seem right, turning my own mother away after all she's been through, but, you know, she's not the easiest person to have around. Ma said she knew when she wasn't wanted. Besides, she insisted on returning to the old place. It's hers, she says, it's what she knows.

"She doesn't care that the neighborhood's shot to heck. Or she cares but all her old pals, they've moved further south, or they're in assisted living. Either way, she doesn't want to be near them. Thinks they'll always be talking about her behind her back."

Frank dropped the paperweight. It bounced onto the floor where it dented one of the boards. We watched it roll under my worktable.

"That isn't why you came up here today, is it, Frank?" I asked. "You're not imagining I'll babysit Stella, I hope."

He picked up a stapler and started opening it and snapping it shut. Staples began falling onto the desktop and floor. I took it from him and set it down, out of his reach.

"What is it, Frank?"

He walked to the door, not trying to leave, just trying to pull words together. He walked around in a circle and came back.

"Tori, don't get mad, but Ma thinks—Ma says—she thinks—she says—"

I waited while he fumbled for words.

"Ma is sure she was framed."

"Yeah, that doesn't surprise me."

"You know she was?" His face lightened.

"No, Frank. But I believe she wants to rewrite the story of her life. She always set herself up as the most moral, pious woman in South Chicago, then she does time, can't face the women she used to look down on. Of course she has to change the past so she's the martyr, not the villain."

He pounded his thighs in frustration. "She could have been framed, it could have happened. I never believed she would have hit Annie hard enough to hurt her."

"I am not going to spend time and energy trying to prove your mother's innocence." My mouth set in a tight line.

"Did I ask you to do that? Did I? That isn't what I want." He sucked in a deep breath. "She can't afford a lawyer, a real lawyer, I mean, not a public defender, and—"

"And you thought of me?" I was so angry I jumped to my feet. "I don't know what the gossip about me is in South Chicago, but I did not become Bill Gates when I moved away. And even if I did, why would I help your mother? She always thought Gabriella was some kind of whore, that she cast a spell over your dad and then stole Annie. Stella liked to say I was a bad apple falling close to a rotten tree, or words to that effect."

"I—I know she said all that stuff. I'm not asking you to be her lawyer. But you could ask questions, you're a detective, and people know you, they'd trust you the way they wouldn't trust a cop."

By now his face was so scarlet that I feared he'd have a stroke on the spot.

"Even if I wanted to do this, which I don't, I don't know the neighborhood anymore. I've been away as long as Stella has. Longer."

"You were just back there," he objected. "I heard about it at Sliga's, that you'd been to the high school and everything."

I shouldn't have been surprised. South Chicago and the East Side are like a small town. You sneeze on Ninetieth Street, they whip out a handkerchief on Escanaba Avenue.

Over the weekend, I'd taken Bernadine Fouchard, Boom-Boom's goddaughter, on a tour of my cousin's old haunts. I showed her the place near Dead Stick Pond where he practiced skating in the winter, and where I'd help him hunt for the puck when it went into the nearby marsh grasses. We'd gone to the breakwater in Calumet Harbor where Boom-Boom and I used to dare the freighters by jumping in to swim. I'd taken her to the public high school where I played on the state champion basketball team, picked up tacos at Estella's on Commercial Avenue. We hadn't gone to Sliga's bar, but probably someone at the high school mentioned it over a boiler-maker.

"I went as a tourist, Frank. I can't help your mother."

He came over to me, gripping my arms. "Tori, please. She went to, well, to a lawyer, who told her there wasn't any evidence."

I pulled away. "Of course there isn't. If she'd had any evidence when Annie died, she could have used it at her trial."

"Tori, come on, you know what it's like, you go to court, it's all confusing, she never pled guilty but the lawyer, he was inexperienced, he didn't know how to run the case."

Frank was right: a trial is bewildering for inexperienced defendants. I didn't like Stella, but I could imagine how unbalanced she must have felt. She'd never been to court, not even to fight a traffic ticket. She wouldn't have known the first thing about how evidence is presented, how everything you say on the stand, or before you ever get to trial, is taken apart and put together again in a way you'd never recognize.

"Even so, I am not wasting time and energy on problems Stella brought on herself."

"Can't you let go of that old grudge? Ma's had a hard life. Dad died in the mill, she had to fight the company for his workers' comp, then Annie died—"

"Frank, listen to yourself. She *murdered* Annie. And she had to fight the company for the comp claim because *she* started spreading rumors that your father committed suicide. Don't you remember what Stella did at Gabriella's funeral? She marched in on the middle of the service and dragged Annie out, yelling that Gabriella was a whore. I do not feel sorry for your mother. I will never feel sorry for your mother."

Frank grabbed my hands. "Tori, that's why I thought—hoped—don't you remember, that was the night—Annie was that upset, I never saw her like that, when Ma dragged her home—if someone told me Ma or Annie, one would kill the other, I would have thought Annie for sure, after your ma's funeral. But I—don't you remember?"

My mother's funeral was a blur in my mind. My father and I, uncomfortable in our dress-up clothes. The pallbearers—my uncle Bernie; Bobby Mallory, my dad's closest friend on the force; other cops, all in their dress uniforms; a police chaplain, since my unreligious mother hadn't known a rabbi. Gabriella had been a wisp by the time she died; her coffin couldn't have taken six big men to lift it.

Mr. Fortieri, my mother's vocal coach, fought back tears, twisting a silk handkerchief over and over, but Eileen Mallory wept openly. I could feel the tightness again in my throat—I had vowed I wouldn't cry, not in front of my aunt Marie. Annie Guzzo's sobs had angered me. What right had she to cry for Gabriella?

And then Stella roared in, beside herself. Mouth flecked white with spit, or was that a detail I was adding? At home that night I'd sat alone in the dark in my attic room, staring at the street, unable to move, leaving my dad to deal with his drunk sister Elena and the stream of neighbors, of cops, of my mother's piano and voice students. And then—

Frank had appeared at the top of the steep flight of stairs, come to say how sorry he was, for my loss, for his mother's behavior. In the dark, sick with loss, tired of the adult world on the ground floor, I'd found a comfort in his embrace. Our teenage fumblings with clothes and bodies, neither of us knowing what we were doing, somehow that got me through the first hard weeks of Gabriella's death.

I squeezed Frank's fingers and gently removed my hands. "I remember. You were very kind."

"So will you do this, Tori? Will you go back to South Chicago and ask some questions? See if there's something that didn't come out at the trial?"

Past the naked, unbearable pleading in his face, I could see him as he'd been at seventeen, athletically slender, red-gold curls covering his forehead. I'd brushed them out of his eyes and seen the lump and bruise on his forehead. *I got it sliding into second,* he'd said quickly, scarlet with shame, pushing my hand away.

My mouth twisted. "One free hour, Frank. I'll ask questions for sixty minutes. After that—you'll have to pay like any other client."

2

HOME BASE

Over dinner that night with Jake, I found it almost impossible to explain why I'd agreed to go back to South Chicago.

"This woman—what's her name? Medea?—she doesn't even merit a phone call," Jake protested. "You know she was guilty, you know she's venomous, why go near her?"

"It's not about her, so much," I said.

"What—this guy, Frank—you want to recapture the dreams of your youth?"

"Jake!" I said. "Don't start carrying on like a low-rent Othello, where you run around the stage in the third act shooting yourself because jealousy got the better of you in the second."

He made a face at me. "I hate guns. I'll stab myself with a bow in the last scene, way more melodramatic, and heartbreaking because it will be a historic bow that makes an ominous appearance in Act One. But you did date him."

"When I was sixteen and he was a good-looking ballplayer."

"Is he still good-looking?"

"In a way."

"The way being?"

I paused, enjoying the way Jake's lips twitched. He spends his days around twentysomething violinists with long straight hair and serious dedication. I try not to be jealous but I liked seeing I could inspire a twinge in him.

"Oh, if you like a big feather pillow to sink into on cold winter mornings."

Jake shadowboxed me. "Then why bother? From the sound, you don't owe him or Medea anything. And it's not like you have any real ties to South Chicago anymore."

"You didn't grow up in a neighborhood. You got together with other kids when your moms organized playdates. Besides, you were a boy wonder on tour from the time you were eleven. But South Chicago, those people, we lived on top of each other like puppies in a pet store, they're who I am. When they call on me, it's like some—"

I broke off, struggling to put my complicated feelings into words. "It's way more melodramatic than you being jealous of a guy I dated for six weeks thirty years ago. It's more like one of these horror movies, where some chip was planted in my blood, and when the master monster presses a switch, I'm sucked into the vortex willy-nilly."

Jake pulled me to him across my plate of pasta. "Not going to happen. I will knot my bass strings together and attach them to your waist so I can haul you out."

We heard my front door slam; a moment later, Bernadine Fouchard clomped into the room. She was small and it always amazed me how loud her footsteps were. She bent over to kiss me, said the dinner smelled "divine," and went into the kitchen to fix herself a plate.

Bernadine—really, just Bernie—looked like her father, the same smile—a lightning flash that lit her whole face—the same soft brown eyes, the same reckless self-confidence. She'd been named for my cousin, Boom-Boom, Pierre Fouchard's closest friend on the Blackhawks. Boom-Boom's birth name had been Bernard, but only his mother ever called him that.

Pierre had phoned me a month earlier to say that Bernie was planning to visit Chicago. "She's such a skater, Victoria, such a natural on the ice. If the NHL wasn't a bunch of sexist you-know-whats, she would be playing on a farm team right now! Boom-Boom would be so proud. One of these expensive universities, Northwestern, they are inviting her to play for them, all expenses paid for an education if she will show them good form, which she will—that goes without saying."

And then the request—Bernie was being recruited by many schools, but because Pierre and Boom-Boom had played for the Blackhawks, well, it stood to reason that Chicago would be her first choice, *naturellement*, only before she committed herself she would like to see the city, visit the school, all these things, and this was his busy season—he himself was a scout for the Canadiens, and Arlette, poor Arlette broke her leg skiing, so would it be possible—

I'd interrupted to say of course, I'd be delighted to put her up, show her the sights. Her school year was essentially over; she'd go home for graduation, but her parents had gotten the Quebec high school to agree to let her turn in her final papers early. She'd be spending an intense summer in hockey training camp, and they wanted her to have a few months of freedom. Syracuse and Ithaca were apparently willing to wait-list her if she decided against Northwestern after spending a few weeks here.

I'd picked her up at O'Hare a week ago. I'd been afraid that a seventeen-year-old would be a worry or a burden, but as Pierre had said, Bernie had her head screwed on right. She enjoyed exploring the city, she helped me run the dogs, she delighted Mr. Contreras, my downstairs neighbor, who's been bereft since my cousin Petra joined the Peace Corps in El Salvador. The only major change in my life was that the nights I slept with Jake Thibaut were spent exclusively in his apartment.

Five days into her stay, Bernie hooked up with a team in a girls' peewee hockey league, as a volunteer coach. She loved teaching the girls and began toying with the idea of spending the rest of the spring in the city if she could find a job.

She approached the world around her with the confidence bordering on recklessness that reminded me of my cousin, or perhaps myself when I was a teenager, when I didn't feel the anguish of people whose lives had come uncoupled from their dreams.

Despite the pity I'd felt for Frank, I still made him sign my standard client contract. Even though I was giving him a free hour and a reduced fee structure, he tried to fight it.

"Boom-Boom would be ashamed of you, charging someone you grew up with."

"Boom-Boom would have high-sticked you and laughed about it if he knew you wanted to stiff me."

Frank grumbled some more, but finally signed both copies. He had a hard time figuring out how to leave the office, but I solved that problem by telling him I had a client meeting. "You came in between a couple of conference calls, Frank, but I have to get back to work."

"Yeah." He tortured his copy of the contract, folding it into ever tinier squares. "Yeah, me too. They dock me for time away from the route. Yeah, I'd better get back to it."

I smiled sadly, for him, for me, and put up a hand to touch the tight dark curls around his bald spot. It wasn't until the end of the afternoon, when I had time to look up Stella's trial, that I got angry with myself for giving in to the emotional soup Frank had stirred up in me.

Illinois v. S. Guzzo had been a minor proceeding. No appeal had been filed, which meant that only a minimum of information was available in the archive—the indictment, the names of the jurors and the sentence. Unless Stella's attorney had ordered, and kept, transcripts, there wouldn't be a record of her testimony.

I knew there wouldn't be any police files I could look at, not after all this time, but I double-checked with the Fourth District, which serves South Chicago. Conrad Rawlings, the watch commander, wasn't in, but the desk sergeant who took my call was willing to answer my questions: *A twenty-five-year-old murder? Was I joking? Those papers had gone to the warehouse a long time ago.*

The next morning, I got up while Bernie was still sacked out on the pullout bed in the living room. That, actually, was the one negative about her staying with me. She was a teenager, she slept late, and she did it in my public space. If she stayed for the next two months, I'd have to find her someplace else to live.

I packed the dogs into my car and drove south, before I had a chance to think about it. Getting to South Chicago and back would take most of an hour. I hated to give Stella anything, but I'd eat the time and expense of the drive.

It was one of those early spring days in Chicago that turns the city into the most beautiful place in the world: sunlight glinting on little waves on Lake Michigan, the sky the soft clear blue that makes you imagine you could take up painting. I sang *"Vittoria, Vittoria, mio core"* as I passed Grant Park and moved on to the South Side. True, it's a love song, but the melody and the beat are martial, and I, too, would be victorious. Victoria, vanquisher of villains.

At Seventy-fourth Street, I turned off and went to Rainbow Beach so the dogs could have a workout. Rainbow had been the nearest beach to my home when I was growing up and we often came up here in the summer, my parents and I and some of their friends, for a Sunday picnic, or Boom-Boom and I on our bikes. It used to be packed with people, but today the dogs and I had it to ourselves.

Only a couple of women, one African-American with a short 'fro, the other a gray-haired white woman, were out, deep in conversation at the far end of the bike path. A mixed-race duo would have been assaulted in my childhood. Not all change is bad.

Stopping had been a mistake. Throwing tennis balls for the dogs gave me time to think about Stella, to anticipate my conversation. She'd done the full sentence, unusual for an older woman. She must have been an angry and uncooperative prisoner, and I couldn't imagine her personality would have changed much now she was out.

I leashed up the dogs and returned them to the car, still dragging my feet. I waited through three lights before turning south again, then drove so slowly that people were honking and shouting abuse out their windows as they roared around me.

"Yeah, right," I muttered. "You're mad, but no matter what you say, it won't be a patch on what lies ahead."

3

SLUGGER

The landmarks had changed since my childhood, the giant USX Southworks plowed under to make an extension for Highway 41. What hadn't changed was the pollution. The air used to be stained yellow by sulfur from the mills. Now it was black, dust blowing from the pet coke mountains along the Calumet River. I started sneezing as soon as I hit Ninetieth Street. Pet coke, sounds like a bottle of the Real Thing that follows you down the street. Really, it's the residue of superheated coal that gets reused as industrial fuel. They don't allow it to be stored out in the open across the river in Indiana, but everything is easier in Illinois. Down here, the city didn't look like the most beautiful place on earth.

I turned onto Commercial Avenue, the retail heart of the neighborhood. When I was a child, the street was always crowded. It used to be filled with shops, anchored by Goldblatt's, one of Chicago's great department stores. The grand Beaux Arts building, where everyone shopped for everything from socks to refrigerators, was still there, but most of the windows in its three stories were boarded over. The ground floor had been divided into small shabby storefronts.

The Navral Building, where our doctor and dentist had had their offices, was gone as well, replaced by weeds and broken asphalt. Discount beauty stores, wig shops filled with luridly colored hair, jostled with bars and carry-out joints. In between were too many boarded-over buildings, and a handful of general stores that looked like garage sales—unmatched kitchen chairs and racks of dusty clothes filled the sidewalks outside the doors, next to carts holding boxes of DVDs and shoes. A little boy was playing with the heel to a black stiletto. He'd almost ripped it free when his mother, who'd been inspecting shirts, smacked him.

His howls were drowned by the surround sound from the car next to me, a bass so loud the car was rocking on its axles. At least it inspired me to start moving faster, across the tracks to Buffalo, where the Guzzos lived. Like Commercial Avenue, Buffalo was a mix of run-down buildings and empty lots—the city was bulldozing vacant houses in an effort to cut back on drug centers. The open green spaces gave the neighborhood a curious semirural feel.

One thing about the sorry streets of South Chicago—besides sinkholes, drunks, addicts and garbage—they hold easy parking options. No pay machines and you had your choice of spaces. I pulled up directly in front of Stella's bungalow.

It was almost eleven now, and the few people in the area with jobs were long gone. Boys flashing gang signs and showing off their tattoos were gathering on the corners. They watched me go up the walk to Stella's front door, but no one tried to stop me.

Stella's bungalow and the Jokich place next to it were twins, down to the peeling paint on the wooden window frames. Age and poor maintenance had caused them to lean into each other, like an elderly couple clinging together to stay upright.

The house sported a heavy steel door with a peephole. I rang the bell. The chime echoed inside. Nothing happened. After the second ring, I was ready to walk away when I heard a heavy step coming to the door. After another moment, where Stella stared at me through the peephole, a series of locks tumbled back.

She opened the door a crack. "Who are you and what do you want?"

"V. I. Warshawski. Answers."

She stared at me, frowning as she tried to connect me to my adolescent face. "The whore's daughter."

"Good to see you, too, Stella," I said. So Frank hadn't had the guts to tell her I was coming.

I was going to keep my temper if I had to swallow my tongue to do so. Or at least I wasn't going to blow up in front of her; I figured nothing would bring her a greater sense of perverse pleasure.

"You might want to lock up while we talk. Lot of Communists out there." I pushed past her into the house.

"What are you talking about?" She peered down the walk. "Those are just the Mexicans that started littering this neighborhood while I was away. Breed like flies, the lot of them."

"Gosh, I remember what they used to say about the Irish." Stella had been a Garretty before her marriage. "Weren't you one of nine?"

"Eight," she snapped. "And we all worked our fingers to the bone. Me, especially, keeping house for my father and my brothers after Ma passed. Not like these wetbacks, wouldn't know a job if it jumped out of the beer bottle and waved a paycheck under their noses."

"It was a little easier to find work when the mills were running," I said. "No one's ever replaced those eighteen thousand jobs."

She glowered at me, but decided I was too big for her to throw out. She shut the door with a bang and turned one of three dead bolts. "That's not my fault. If they wanted to work—"

"I know. They could sell appliances at Goldblatt's or work for one of the doctors in the Navral Building."

"Neither of those even exists anymore, Miss Smartmouth."

"Yeah, kind of my point, Stella."

The entryway was so small that we were touching each other. I went into the living room. I moved automatically, not because I'd spent a lot of time there—even when Frank and I were dating, we always met someplace else—but because the layout was identical to my childhood home.

The house wasn't as run-down inside as out, which was probably true for much of the neighborhood. Keep yourself looking too poor to rob. The floors were clean, the flat-screen TV was new, and so were the two armchairs that faced it.

"What do you want?" Stella rasped.

She'd kept her height even after all the years of bad diet and poor exercise. Her hair had gone that iron shade of gray that makes the face beneath it look hard—or harder, in her case—but her eyes were still a bright blue, like the sky over the lake as I'd driven south, and her arm muscles remained firm. She must have been attractive when she was young, in an athletic kind of way. In a different era she might have become a sports star herself.

"Frank asked me to talk to you."

"That's a flat-out lie."

"He came up to my office yesterday. He says—"

"Oh, so we have an *office* now, do we, Miss Hoity-Toity. Frank drives a truck, but you have an office. Frank would have an office, too, if you hadn't destroyed his chances."

"Me? Please. You bullied Frank into breaking up with me thirty years ago. Don't tell me that made him so depressed he stopped trying to make a success out of life."

"No one ever got depressed when they got the Warshawskis out of their lives, but your family, they lived to bring mine down. Your whore of a mother broke up my marriage—"

"I thought Mr. Guzzo was still married to you when he died," I objected. "Had he divorced you? Is that why USX tried to deny the comp claim?"

She swung an arm back, a reflexive urge to hit me. I took her wrist, not hard, just firm.

"Beating people up is what got you into trouble to begin with. You're not going to hit me, Stella, so calm down."

"Don't you tell me what to do or not to do. I didn't take shit from guards and wardens and bitches of drug dealers all those years to come home and take it from a Warshawski."

She had a point. I perched on the arm of one of the easy chairs. "Let's leave Gabriella and Mateo out of the discussion. They've both been dead a lot of years and can't defend themselves. Tell me what I did to ruin Frank's chances."

"Not just you, your whole family." Her lips were tight, but I didn't like the way her eyes looked, too much white showing around the irises. "You Warshawskis always had to be number one, and when it looked like Frank had the same chance that Bernard got, you ruined it."

"What?" I was genuinely baffled. "My uncle never had any special chances; he worked the docks his whole life. If Frank had wanted a job there instead of—"

"Shut up, numbskull," Stella spat at me. "*Young* Bernard. You couldn't stand—"

"Oh, you mean Boom-Boom. Frank didn't play hockey, but if he had, Boom-Boom would have welcomed him like a brother."

"Of course Frank didn't play hockey."

Stella's exasperation was turning her skin a mottled red. She probably looked like this the night she killed Annie. I kept my weight forward, so that I could jump out of her way if her rage got the better of her—she might be close to eighty now but she still looked strong.

"Baseball. He was going to have his chance, they promised it, they promised he'd be at Wrigley Field where the top brass could see him, but it fell apart. That's because you Warshawskis didn't want it to happen. You've tormented us for as long as I've lived here. Your mother seduced my husband. Your cousin didn't want Frank to have the same success as he got, your *father*"—she gave the word a horrible sarcastic inflection—"could have helped me, but he couldn't be bothered to lift a finger. Little Annie was a saint or something to him and he figured he'd get his own back."

"No, Stella. You're making this up. There is no evidence, there's no conspiracy, there's only you, hating my mother and wanting to blame her for your troubles."

She lunged at me so suddenly that I fell off the armchair to get out of her way. She tried to kick me but hit the chair instead. I scuttled backward on my butt and got to my feet as she lunged again.

I shoved the armchair into her path. "No, Stella, I told you no hitting. Frank said you want an exoneration. Are you going to tell the lawyer that Boom-Boom blocked Frank's chances to play baseball and this made you so angry you killed Annie?"

"I didn't kill my girl," she panted. "It was an intruder. When I left the house to go to the bingo, Annie was alive. Everyone thought she was so sweet, they should have heard what she was saying. If she died with those words in her mouth she's been burning in hell for it."

Even across the armchair I could smell her sweat: bath soap and talcum mixed with the rankness of the hatred coursing through her.

"Why didn't you bring that up at the trial?"

"I told that useless baby they gave me as a lawyer. I told him it was an intruder, but he didn't know enough about the law to use it. Or maybe Boom-Boom bought him off. He had plenty of money, all those endorsements, all those girls going flat on their backs for him. Maybe Annie did, too. I told her she was going to turn out just like your mother, and she had the gall to say that was her prayer! No wonder I hit her! Anyone would have, but I didn't kill her. That was someone else, maybe your cousin, that's why your father buried the evidence. Your cousin came to the house and murdered Annie while I was at church, praying for her soul!"

I edged around the chair and headed from the room. "If this is what you believe, you need a psychiatrist, not an exoneration lawyer. Don't ever repeat any of this in public, or I will sue you faster than you can spit."

She jumped across the room and socked me. I ducked in time to take the blow on my shoulder, not my throat, and ran to the door. I had the dead bolt undone and was outside a nanosecond before she caught up to me.

She stood in the doorway, screaming, "People have been playing games with me my whole life, making fun, but I don't take that shit anymore. You watch out, Missy, you watch your step."

The punks on the curb stared, mouths agape. No wonder Stella was safe in the middle of Insane Dragon territory.

4

OUT AT THE PLATE

I was shaking when I got back to my car. I should have listened to Jake and stayed far away from here. The dogs jumped up, whining and nuzzling me, responding to my distress, but what I wanted was my mother. She'd lived across the alley from Stella all those years, but the ugly words never seemed to bring her down. She worried about me and my father, but not what an unhappy, unhinged woman might be saying or thinking.

I saw the curtains twitch in the Guzzo front room. No point in letting Stella think she'd upset me.

My route north took me past St. Eloy's, the church where Stella and my aunt Marie and hundreds of steelworkers used to worship— Eloy was the patron of metalworkers. On an impulse, I pulled over to the curb and got out.

I'd gone to funerals here as a child. The foul air we all breathed, the smoking all the men and most of the women did, and the unforgiving heavy machinery created a lot of orphans.

It was a plate rolling machine that had killed Annie and Frank Guzzo's father. Mateo Guzzo's foot slipped, or a gear on the machine slipped, or Mateo couldn't take another hour of life under Stella's rule, local gossip provided a number of versions of his death. When the company heard the stories, they went with the suicide version so they wouldn't have to pay workers' comp to his widow. The union fought, some kind of compromise was reached, but as Stella had remembered the story, it was my family that tried to block her comp payment.

The old priest, Father Gielczowski, had ruled his parish with an iron fist. He'd set up one of the infamous block clubs, an effort started by a priest named Lawlor to keep Chicago's South Side parishes all-white. Gielczowski and my mother had had some memorable clashes, particularly because he wanted me baptized. Gabriella, who'd grown up in a country where Jews could be declared unfit parents for failing to baptize their children, had been scathing in her responses:

"A god who cares more about a little water on the head than my daughter's character is not a deity I want her to spend eternity with."

On my way up the walk to the office door, I stopped in front of the statue of St. Eloy. Steelworkers had created it out of scrap, so that it looked like a daring avant-garde piece of sculpture. I took a picture to show my lease-mate, who mauls big pieces of metal into giant abstractions of her own.

"You don't have a good track record down here, you know, Eloy," I said to the statue. "Mateo Guzzo is dead, along with his daughter, and so are the steel mills. Even your church building is falling to bits. What do you have to say about that?"

The metal eyes stared at me, unblinking. Like everyone else around me, the saint knew secrets I couldn't fathom.

It was a heavy brick Victorian complex, church, rectory, school, convent. I knew the school was still active—Frank had told me his kid was playing baseball for the high school team, and anyway, I could hear children's voices drifting faintly from the playgrounds on the far side of the building.

As I walked up to St. Eloy's side door, I wondered what I'd say to Father Gielczowski, but of course he was long gone. The man in the church office was younger, darker, more muscular.

Unlike Gielczowski, who always roamed the neighborhood in a cassock, this man was on a ladder in jeans and a T-shirt, spackling a hole in the ceiling. He didn't interrupt his work to look at me, just grunted that he'd be finished in a few minutes, to have a seat.

The hole in the ceiling wasn't the only damage in the room, but it was the worst, exposing part of the lath near the windows, and spidering down from there in a series of large cracks. I figured the Spackle would hold for a month, or until the next big storm sent water into the building. The room should be gutted, probably the whole building, and fresh plumbing and wiring put in before anyone tried repairs, but I didn't imagine the archdiocese put South Chicago parishes high on its budget list.

Father Gielczowski's picture was on the wall facing the windows, along with the other priests who'd served the parish. Their names, German, Polish, Serbian, Italian, reflected the waves of immigrants who'd come to the South Side to work the mills. The current incumbent was Umberto Cardenal. I imagined addressing him if he was made head of the archdiocese: Cardinal Cardenal.

The desk, which was as battle-scarred as the walls, sat near the windows where Father Cardenal was working. I moved the visitor's chair across the room, since chunks of plaster were dropping almost faster than the priest could fill in the hole.

When he finally climbed down, a gray sheen covered his face, glued on by his sweat, and the tone in which he asked what I wanted was barely civil.

"I don't mind waiting if you want to wash up," I offered. "I can even put the ladder away if you tell me where it goes."

The lines around his mouth relaxed. "I look that bad, do I?" He opened a closet door and studied his face in a small mirror hanging inside. "Yes, this face would do for the Day of the Dead, but perhaps not for church business. The ladder goes in the utility storage room next to the parish meeting hall."

I went with him to the hallway, but he headed toward the rectory, waving a vague arm to his left. I opened doors but didn't see a meeting hall or a utility closet. At one point I found myself in the side aisle of the church, where a young woman was clutching the arm of a short squat man. He looked so much like Danny DeVito, down to the wings of wild hair flying away from his bald head, that I couldn't help staring.

"Uncle Jerry, please! We just can't do it anymore."

He shoved her roughly away. "You should have thought of that when—" He caught sight of me. "Who are you and what do you want?" Even his husky voice sounded like DeVito's.

"Utility closet, the one where this ladder belongs."

"In case you didn't notice, this is the church, not a closet." He turned back to the woman. "Get out of here before you get me in trouble."

"Are you okay?" I asked the niece.

"She's fine. She's leaving because she's on her lunch hour and she can't afford to get fired."

The niece wiped her eyes with her sleeve and started down the aisle to the front entrance.

I followed her. "Do you need help?"

She turned to look at her uncle, shook her head at me and kept going. I put the ladder down and went after her, but she pushed me away.

"Don't bother me. I can't afford—it was a mistake—I just thought—never mind."

I pulled out a card. "If you change your mind, give me a call. If he's hurting you, I can get you to a safe place."

She shook her head again, but at least she pocketed the card. When I turned back up the aisle for the ladder, Uncle Jerry had disappeared through one of the many side doors that littered the building. He'd left behind his old voltmeter, the pre-digital kind. In a spirit of malice, I carried it with me. When I finally stumbled on the utility room, I put the meter on a shelf behind the ladder. Let him spend an hour or two hunting for it.

When I got back to the church office, Cardenal was at his desk, wearing a clean T-shirt, his face scrubbed shiny. He was working at his computer, but he stopped when I carried the visitor's chair to its original spot.

"What is it you need so badly that you are willing to lug around building equipment?" he asked.

I couldn't help smiling. "Help with one of your parishioners."

"And you are not one of them. I recognize most people who come to Mass more than twice a year, but you I don't remember seeing."

"You wouldn't: I moved away from this neighborhood a long time ago." I explained who I was.

"Frank Guzzo asked me to make some inquiries on his mother's behalf," I added. "She's always been volatile, and now she seems even more so, but—you know she was in prison for a good long stretch, right? For the murder of her daughter?"

"The gossip has been here, ever since Mrs. Guzzo showed up at Mass two months ago," Cardenal admitted.

"I just spent half an hour with her, and I am worn out and confused. She says she's looking for an exoneration, but it sounded as though what she really wants is to pin her daughter's murder on my family."

Cardenal raised an eyebrow. "Does your family have a vendetta against her?"

I smiled sadly. "Stella used to spread the word around the neighborhood that my mother was seducing her husband. And then, when Mateo Guzzo sent Annie to my mother for piano lessons, Stella became furious with envy, thinking my mother was undermining her with her own child. I was startled when I saw her just now to find out she still is obsessed with the idea. Only she's added my cousin Boom-Boom to the mix—Boom-Boom Warshawski; he's dead now, but he used to play with the Blackhawks. Stella ranted at me that Boom-Boom had destroyed Frank's chance to have a baseball career, that he seduced Annie, then killed her."

Cardenal thought it over. "I don't know your family or hers, so I can't evaluate who is right or wrong or if there even is a right or a wrong. What is it you think I can help you with?"

I hesitated. "Being in prison is hard, and Stella was in for a long time. I don't know if she really thinks there's some missing evidence that might exonerate her, or if she spent her time in Logan twisting events to make them my family's fault. Do you have any idea what is actually going on with her?"

Cardenal pulled at the flesh under his chin. "I've been here two years and some of the old Eastern European women still don't trust me: Can a Mexican really administer the Sacrament? Some even take a bus all the way to Saint Florian's to hear the Mass in Polish. Mrs. Guzzo, she at least comes to Mass here, but she hasn't wanted to confide in me. Not that I could repeat a confidential statement, of course," he added hastily.

"Of course," I agreed. "What about a nonconfidential statement? I'm wondering what she said when she arrived at the bingo game the night she killed her daughter. Or why Father Gielczowski thought he should testify for her at her trial. Do you know if he's still in the Chicago area?"

Cardenal shook his head. "He has advanced dementia, from what I've heard. The Polish ladies visit him sometimes and come back sad because he doesn't know them."

Gielczowski with dementia. What a horrible punishment, even for someone as hurtful as he had been. "Would he have written something down? Notes for his testimony at her trial, something like that?"

"If he made notes for trial testimony they'd be in his private journals, not here." He held up a hand as I started to ask. "No, I don't know if he even kept a personal diary, or who has it if he did. Parish records are about money and meetings."

"Can I look at the meetings the night that Annie Guzzo died?"

Cardenal made a face. "I wish you'd asked me when I still was covered with plaster dust, but yes, we can find them, I guess."

The records were in yet another chilly room with a cracked ceiling and dirty windows. Cardenal left me alone with the cartons. They weren't stacked in any particular order, and the parish had celebrated its 125th anniversary five years back. Twenty-seven of the forty-two years Gielczowski had been the priest had been among the most active in St. Eloy's history. I read about baptisms and weddings until my eyes glazed over. The only thing that was remotely relevant was the report of the bingo game for the Wednesday night Annie died: 192 people had taken part, the top prize of $250 had gone to Lyudmila Wojcek, and the income net of prizes and refreshments had been $318.50.

I put the registers back where I'd found them, and brushed as much of the dust from my shirt and jeans as I could. Father Cardenal wasn't in his office when I went to say good-bye, so I left a short thank-you note. I added a twenty, with a message to put it into the building fund.

5

WHIFFING THE CURVE

Back in my office, back in my present life, I put on Mozart's *Requiem*, with Emma Kirkby singing the soprano line—almost with Gabriella's purity. The music suited my bleak, elegiac mood.

I had given Frank his free hour and then some, but I couldn't quite let the matter go. He wouldn't have come to me if he hadn't been feeling desperate, or at least worried, by what was going on with his mother.

I wrote down everything I could remember, both from his conversation and from hers. The choir had finished their plea for eternal light before I finished comparing what Frank and Stella had each said. I studied the chart I'd made before calling Frank's cell.

I could hear traffic noise in the background when he answered. Don't talk while driving, I thought of admonishing him, but really, I wanted to get the conversation out of the way as fast as possible.

"Frank, I went to see your mother this morning, and I don't know who is more confused, her, me or you."

"You went to see her?" he repeated, indignant. "Why did you do that? I thought you were going to investigate Annie's death."

"I had to start someplace, and she's the person with the most intimate knowledge of your sister's death. You can't have thought I wouldn't go to her."

"Why didn't you start with the cops?"

"I did: those files went into cold storage a long time ago." Clients are always thinking they have a better action plan than the investigator they hired—even clients who tried to comfort you when their mothers had disrupted your own mother's funeral.

"Ma let you in? How did she—what did she say?"

"A lot of stuff: the same old, same old about my mother and your dad, and then newer stuff about Boom-Boom and Annie, and then stuff I never knew about you. Your tryout with the Cubs."

"She talked about that?"

"Yes. When did that happen?"

I heard honking and braking in the background. Frank swore at some other driver and hung up. When I reached him again, traffic sounds had been replaced by Muzak and people shouting out orders.

"I had to get off the road. Taking my break, which means I've got fifteen minutes."

"Tell me about the Cubs," I said.

"It was a long time ago. Old dead news."

"Tell me anyway."

"It was the fall before Annie died." He sounded tired, as if dredging up the story took more energy than he had, but he plowed ahead. "I was already driving for Bagby, but I played in a league, the real deal, not sixteen-inch, and we got this call, our team did, saying the Cubs were having an open tryout day and some of our guys had been picked to play a couple of innings. Their scouts would be there, and so on."

"Pretty exciting. Who set it up?"

"I don't know. Someone at Saint Eloy's, I think was what the guys said, someone who knew someone in the Cubs organization. You know how that goes."

I knew how that went. You always need someone who knows someone. Even Boom-Boom might not be in the Hockey Hall of Fame if the Tenth Ward committeeman hadn't known someone who dated a woman who knew a man in the Blackhawks organization.

"What was it like?"

"Sitting in the dugout at Wrigley Field? Running across that grass? When I get to heaven, it better be exactly like that."

I couldn't help laughing. "I hope it is, Frank, but what I really wondered was what the tryout was like."

"I'm driving a truck, aren't I?" he said roughly. "Not admiring my statue in Cooperstown."

"What happened?"

The sigh came across the phone like the hiss of air leaving a balloon. "You lose those muscles. I mean, I was strong, I was driving a truck, all that stuff. But my baseball muscles, my eye, my timing, all those were gone.

"Boom-Boom, he coached me. Not the baseball, he couldn't play baseball for shit, but he was a professional athlete, he knew what it took to get in shape. Bagby gave me a leave. Not Vince, who's in charge now, but his old man. Hell, they were rooting for us, five of us going for the tryout worked there, and Boom-Boom and me, we worked out together every morning. If he was in town—the hockey preseason had started, but I worked out on my own, two hours every morning. I followed his training diet, everything."

I hadn't known about this. Guy things that Boom-Boom didn't think were worth sharing.

"So I was in great shape. I could run a hundred yards in fifteen seconds."

"Impressive," I agreed.

"I should have tried out with the Bears," he said bitterly. "They could have used a guy with fast legs and a truck driver's muscles."

I waited: this was a painful memory. Any words from me might shut him up completely. When he spoke again, it was quickly, in a mumble that I could barely understand.

"I couldn't hit major league pitching."

I still didn't speak. Who can hit major league pitching? Even the best pros only do it once every three tries, but that wouldn't be a consolation to the guy driving a truck instead of playing in the show.

"Ma—Ma blamed Boom-Boom. I shouldn't have said anything to her, but, you know, I had to talk to her about something, so I told her when we heard we were going to get the chance to try out. She was excited, never seen her like that, she kept saying she'd been waiting for this, waiting for me to get my big chance, prove to the world that Guzzos counted as much as—as Warshawskis. And then, of course, I had to tell her how it came out."

I looked at the dialogue boxes I'd created of Stella's invective. "She said Boom-Boom made you fail."

"That's not fair, she shouldn't say that kind of thing, but at the time I was hurt, you know, the way you are when things don't pan out."

I sat up straight. "What did you tell her about Boom-Boom?"

"Oh, Tori, you know what it was like when Boom-Boom showed up anywhere, at least anywhere that people cared about sports. He sat in the dugout, he was cheering me on. Only everyone in the place went nuts when they realized Boom-Boom Warshawski was there. He was signing autographs, even the Cubs brass wanted them."

Anger and grief—he was still feeling them. His one chance at the big time and Boom-Boom had stood in his sunlight.

"I'm sorry," I said inadequately.

"Yeah, not as sorry as me." He gave a bark of laughter. "I probably couldn't have hit the curve if Boom-Boom had gone to Edmonton—he skipped a game against Wayne Gretzky to come to Wrigley with me! But it wouldn't have felt so—so bad. Boom-Boom watching me whiff, it was worse than when old Gielczowski used to make me lower my pants. And Ma took it like that. To her, it was more proof that the Warshawskis had it in for us. Even later, when I'd visit her in prison, she'd go on about it."

"I hope you didn't believe her, Frank," I said. "No one in my family wished anyone in your family ill. My mother loved Annie, your dad was a wonderful man, and you know, there were a couple of months where I was in love with you."

"Just as well we split when we did," he jeered. "Ma would have put arsenic in your wedding champagne."

It was a gallant effort at humor and I laughed obligingly. "She may manage yet. She gave me a good belt in the shoulder, and if she gets hold of poison or a gun I'm definitely toast."

"She hit you? I thought you were tougher than that."

"Not tough enough, not quick enough." I took a breath. "Did you know she's saying Boom-Boom killed Annie when you asked me to investigate?"

There was a long pause. I could hear people ordering sandwiches and muffins, room for cream in that thing, hon.

"She's saying all kinds of wild things," he finally said. "Not just that, other crazy stuff. I don't know what she wants to say or do to get her name cleared, but if she goes completely off the skids, Frankie, Frank Junior—my boy, you know—I want him to have the chance I never had."

"And you think Stella could derail him? No, Frank. She's old, she's still got a temper"—I rubbed the place on my shoulder where her punch had landed—"but she doesn't have power, except the power you let her have in your life."

"You of all people, I'd think you'd know that when she gets a head of steam she can do anything."

"Yes, and that's what's telling me there's nothing for me to find out about your sister's death. Your mother is angrier than ever after all those years inside, and she's looking for targets, not evidence."

Frank tried to get me to say I'd get the police to dig his sister's file out of the warehouse, but his arguments lacked punch. The sadness in his voice made me brusque: I didn't like the feeling that I had to pity him. I told him to send me the St. Eloy's schedule so I could watch his kid play when the scouts were there and hung up.

I started to write down the conversation, but it was hard. If it hadn't been me talking to him, he probably would have cursed my cousin. Maybe he would have gotten a piece of a ball if Boom-Boom hadn't been there, who knows? The star taking all the attention, that probably made Frank try too hard, tense up at the wrong moment.

"Oh, Boom-Boom," I said out loud. "You meant well, you were doing a good deed. I bet the Hawks fined you for skipping the Oilers game, too. No one got anything good out of that tryout."

The throwaway line about Gielczowski making Frank lower his pants, that was sickening, the whole story was sad and painful and sick. I'd never heard allegations about Gielczowski. Maybe he'd been caning boys, beating immorality out of them. When I think of immorality I think of the payday loans and hidden bank fees, the failure to pay a living wage, the preference for crappy schools in poor neighborhoods. I don't think about sex.

My morning with Stella, and now this—I felt dirty, so dirty that I went into the shower room behind my lease-mate's studio. Her steelwork means she needs a place to clean up at the end of a long day. She'd put in a shower with those multi-head scrubbers, and I stood under them for a good ten minutes, wishing the needles of water could get inside my head and clean it out. Even scrubbed and in a clean T-shirt, I still felt rumpled.

6

FORCE PLAY

It was the second week of the regular season, that brief window when Cubs fans forget the eleven-month winter of their discontent and imagine that the glories of New York or St. Louis will become ours. The team was away, playing in Cincinnati, but the front offices would be well staffed.

The ballpark is walking distance from my apartment. I parked at home so I could change into presentable clothes, including my Lario boots, which always make me feel important. Bernie arrived as I was coming back down the front walk.

"You look tough, Vic, where are you going?"

"Wrigley Field—want to come with me?"

"Oh, baseball. *Merci, non, trop ennuyant.* Since you won't be home, I can take a proper bath." We'd had a bit of a tussle over whether an hour in the bathroom was really essential for proper hygiene. "And, no worries, I will take my hair out of the tub when I'm done." Another discussion.

Even when the team is away, even when the baseball season is over, the doors at Clark and Addison are open for guided tours. I paid twenty-five dollars to join a group. While they were admiring the spot where Harry Caray used to lead fans in "Take Me Out to the Ball Game," I slipped away, until I found a door labeled Media Relations.

A woman was on the phone, a bright smile on her face as she answered questions about rumors of an injury to Enrique Velasquez's left knee. When she hung up, she flashed another smile in my direction.

"I'm V. I. Warshawski. I was looking for Will Drechen." I'd looked up the front office staff before leaving my apartment; Drechen was assistant director of media relations.

The smile turned into regret; Will wasn't in, but she was Natalie Clements, his assistant. Could she help?

"I'm on a wild-goose chase. I'm writing a biography of Boom-Boom Warshawski."

"I'm new to the organization," Natalie said apologetically. "I don't know all the old players' names yet."

I shook my head. "Boom-Boom played for the Blackhawks, tied Gretzky for most goals in 1990. And right about that time, he spent an afternoon here at Wrigley, during one of the amateur tryouts. I know it's a long shot, but I'd love to find someone who was at the tryouts that year. If there was a photo, that would be a plus, but mostly I want background and color on how the day went. He could be a bit of a hot dog—I'm wondering if he tried to hit a ball or field or anything."

Natalie held up a finger while she answered her phone; two more calls came in and I wandered to the window to look out. Frank was right: that perfect grass under a spring sky, you did think heaven might look like this.

Natalie finished her calls and apologized again. She took down a detailed message for Mr. Drechen, who was in a meeting, and noticed my last name. Yes, I was related—I pulled out my iPad and showed her the photo of Boom-Boom and me with the Stanley Cup the day it was his turn to have it. He and I had rented a convertible and driven the length of the city, me at the wheel and Boom-Boom sitting on the trunk, holding the Cup.

"Gosh, wish I'd been the press officer that day," Natalie said. "Great photo op. Anytime your cousin wants to bring the Cup to Wrigley Field—"

He was dead, I said, but added that the Blackhawks were always game for publicity opportunities. Maybe when I'd finished the project we could work something out.

I wondered if I'd ever hear back from the Cubs, wondered, too, what had made me go up there. Maybe I wanted reassurance that Boom-Boom hadn't jinxed Frank's tryout.

Bernie was still in the bath when I got home. It was only midafternoon—still time to do some actual paying work. I drove to my office, where I put my Guzzo notes into a hanging file before turning to the fires my regular clients needed help extinguishing. That night, Jake took me dancing at Hot Rococo, where friends of his were playing. Maybe he couldn't sucker punch a punk in an alleyway, but no one else had ever made me feel lighter than air on a dance floor.

Jake was having his own problems—congressional failure to act on a federal budget had set cuts for everything from roads to military equipment. Arts budgets had been slashed to the bone. Below the bone—funding had already been chopped many times over. His High Plainsong group might have to dissolve: they'd laid off their administrator and were scrambling for free rehearsal space.

When his friends' gig at Hot Rococo ended, we all went out for pizza. The musicians grumbled, then imagined the opera they could write about starving artists.

"It would be like *La Bohème*, except Congress would be watching

Mimi and Rodolfo and laughing their heads off," the drummer explained. "As Mimi dies of malnutrition in the last act, a chorus of Congress members sings the spirited finale, 'She got what she deserved for not being born rich.'"

We all laughed, but there was a bitter undercurrent to it. They worked hard, they took multiple gigs, but the music that lay at the core of their beings kept getting shoved to the sidelines.

Over the next week, the Guzzos disappeared nicely into the tar pits where they belonged. And then came the afternoon I was preparing sea bass alla veneziana for Max, Lotty and Jake. Bernie was going out with a couple of young women she'd met through her peewee hockey coaching, Mr. Contreras had a regular poker date with his retired machinist buddies.

I whipped the egg whites and coated the fish and was laying them in their salt bed when my phone barked at me, the signal that a preferred contact had sent me a text.

I peered at the screen. *The Boom-Boom story is going out on our six o'clock local news. Any comment? M.R.*

Murray Ryerson. Murray had been a great investigative journalist until Global Entertainment bought the *Herald-Star*, slashed the number of reporters by two-thirds, and left him doing odd jobs on their cable news network.

I washed my hands and called him. "What Boom-Boom story?"

"Ah, V.I., you're restoring my faith. Can she have been sitting on this all these years and not shared it with her closest comrade in the fight for truth and justice? No, I thought, but then I remembered the time you left me at a party to cover a homicide and didn't bother to call. I remembered when you were outing the Xerxes Chemical CEO for malicious misconduct and didn't call, and I thought, the Girl Detective is two-timing you again, Ryerson, but I'll give her the benefit—"

"Murray, do you have a point, or has TV made you think everyone around you is a captive audience?"

"I was just trying to lighten your mood," he complained. "Did Boom-Boom kill Annie Guzzo and let her mother spend twenty-five years in the Big House for said murder?"

"What?" Fury was rising in me. I struggled to keep it at bay, to make sense of what Murray was saying. "Is this some creepy made-for-TV movie that Global is confusing with reality?"

"You really didn't know?" Murray said. "It's about to be all over the airwaves. And the Internet."

"Global is putting that out, with no digging, no verification?"

"Of course they're not," Murray said. "They're asking me to do some fact-checking. Which is why I've called you for a comment. In the meantime, though, people have been tweeting about it all day. It went viral this afternoon, so Global has to look as though we're ahead of the story. Boom-Boom may have been dead a lot of years, but his name is still news in this town. What can you tell me?"

"That your involvement in this cesspool means you will never get another break from me again. Ever." I hung up.

Max and Lotty arrived as I was bent over my laptop, following Global's Twitter feed. I hugged them both, mechanically, explaining what was happening. Jake wasn't home yet; he'd sent a text that his rehearsal was running late.

I left the fish lying in their salt bed to turn on the TV for Global's breaking news. Boom-Boom was the top story. They led with him at the Blues net, stick up after scoring a game-winning goal, and moved from there to Annie Guzzo's murder. They'd dug up her high school yearbook photo. She wasn't smiling, but she conveyed an eager intensity: she'd been a girl with a sense of mission.

The camera switched back to Beth Blacksin at the news desk. "Speaking through her lawyer, Ms. Guzzo says she came on a diary that her daughter kept in the months before her death. In it, Anne Guzzo supposedly reported that Bernard 'Boom-Boom' Warshawski was increasingly jealous of her wishes to leave Chicago and have an independent life. Channel Thirteen has not been able to see the actual diary, but Ms. Guzzo's lawyer gave us a typescript of the relevant page."

Blacksin held up a piece of paper, meaningless, since we weren't seeing the actual diary. "Stella Guzzo is making a case that Boom-Boom Warshawski murdered Anne in a fit of jealous rage and framed her for the murder, with the assistance of Warshawski's uncle, police officer Tony Warshawski. Ms. Guzzo says that the Warshawski family has feuded with her ever since her husband, the late Mateo Guzzo, spurned sexual advances from Officer Warshawski's wife, Gabriella."

They flashed my father's picture on the screen in his dress uniform, my mother at his side. Blacksin further identified Tony as father of Chicago private eye V. I. Warshawski.

A rage so huge it blinded me filled my head. I was at the safe in my bedroom closet, getting the gun out, checking the clip, without knowing how I got there.

"Victoria. No!" Lotty appeared behind me.

"She's attacked my mother for the last time." The hoarse voice wasn't mine.

Lotty slapped me. "You will not act like this, Victoria!"

I gasped, glared at her, but put the gun down. I'd been clenching the clip so tightly it had sliced my palm. Blood welled around the cut.

"Vic, have you seen—they are telling horrible lies about Uncle Boom-Boom."

It was Bernie, pushing her way past Lotty to get to me. "I was out with the girls from the hockey club and they had a television on. This is terrible. I called my papa, and he says he can get a leave of absence from the Canadiens, we'll do what— Ah, you've got a gun. This is good, Papa told me you wouldn't take it lying down!"

"She is not going to shoot anyone," Lotty said, her face set in hard lines.

"But—Dr. Lotty—have you heard what they're saying? That Uncle Boom-Boom murdered some girl all those years ago because of reasons so ridiculous no one could believe them?"

"Yes, I'm almost beside myself with fury," I said. "But that clouds the mind, and—and I think I need to sit down."

Lotty put an arm around me, leading me from the bedroom into the living room, into the big armchair. She brought a damp cloth from the kitchen, bathed the blood from my palm, but held on to my hand when she was done.

"Victoria, you love your cousin, you love your parents, these lies against them are hard to stomach, but believe me, when you have lost everyone, the people left to you are more precious. I can't lose you and that's what will happen if you give way to that kind of fury. I— please, my dear one, don't let me see that in your face again."

"Right." I tried to smile, but my face felt as though it were made out of putty, not able to form a shape. "My mother would hate it, too."

Bernie hovered a little way from us, frowning. "But you must stop those lies!"

"Yep, I agree. But I'm not up to figuring out how to do it tonight. We'll make a plan in the morning."

"What's up? What's wrong with you, V.I.?" Jake had come in, holding a bottle of Orvieto. I'd forgotten asking him to pick up wine to go with the fish.

"Only a brief brainstorm. I'm over it." I'd succumbed to the rage of Stella, the rage that led her to bludgeon her daughter to death. The rage that filled her head day after day. No wonder she hadn't bought time off for good behavior.

Max gave Jake a short précis of the news.

Jake nodded. "She is Medea, isn't she? You think it's a myth, and then you meet it in real life. Euripides knew something about human nature."

"Medea gets off scot-free at the end," I said, "she rides off in Apollo's chariot. I guess that's what Stella's trying to do."

"In Cherubini's version, she's burned up in the temple with the children she murdered," Jake said. "I like that one better."

"Fine," Bernie said. "Turn it into a game, don't do anything to help. I thought you loved Uncle Boom-Boom."

I forced myself out of the chair. "Bernie, racing around town firing my gun wouldn't solve any problems, just get me killed or arrested. I wouldn't even know whom to shoot."

"That terrible old woman, that Medea!"

"No, darling. She may be demented or delusional, which isn't a reason to shoot her. Or someone else may be manipulating her for reasons none of us can even begin to guess at. We don't know if this diary is real or if someone planted it in her house to stir up Stella's passions."

Bernie glared, her lower lip thrust out. "What will you do?"

"Try to get a few facts. But not until morning, when my head is clearer. Come help me set the table while I try to cook this branzino the way I had it in Venice."

7

CROWD NOISE

While we ate, my landline kept ringing. Max answered. Every television station in North America wanted to talk to me about Boom-Boom. Max told callers it was a mistake that would be absurd if it wasn't so vile and that all questions should be directed to my own attorney. It shouldn't have surprised me that Max had Freeman Carter's name and number in his Rolodex—he's the kind of person who knows everyone and puts people together.

When dinner was over, I called Freeman myself, on my cell, to let him know what was going on. "I don't suppose I can sue Stella, or whoever made up this story."

"Didn't you go to law school, Vic?" he said. "This is stomach-turning, but you know as well as I that the dead can't bring a cause of action for defamation. Nor can their angry relatives. It will be a two-day wonder. The only thing reacting to it will accomplish will be to keep the story alive longer."

I snarled at him, but I knew he was right. When he'd hung up, I went into the walk-in closet next to the living room. I have a trunk full of memorabilia there, and after carefully laying aside my mother's velvet and gauze concert gown, I dug through the papers, looking for a condolence letter Annie Guzzo had sent Tony and me when Gabriella died.

When I came on it, I called Freeman again. "I have a sample of Annie's handwriting. If you can get Stella's lawyer—"

Freeman cut me off. "Stella's lawyer just called me: he's persuaded a judge to sign an emergency restraining order against you."

I was almost too astonished to be angry. Almost. "On what spurious grounds did that happen?"

"She says you came to her house and hit her."

"Damn it, Freeman, she aimed a punch right at my throat. If she'd connected, I'd be dead. As it is, I have a bruise on my shoulder that went pretty deep."

"Vic, I don't doubt you—but who's a judge going to believe? An eighty-year-old grandmother, or an athletic younger detective? Just make sure you do not go within fifty feet of her until we can settle this in court."

The muscles in my neck were so taut Jake could have strummed on them, but I forced myself to keep my voice level. "Who is her lawyer? Is it the same person who represented her in her murder trial?"

Freeman deliberated. "If I don't tell you, you can find it out easily enough: Anatole Szakacs. Don't go calling him: you talk to him through your own lawyer, namely me."

"Did he happen to say why none of this was brought up at her trial? Why she didn't try an appeal?"

"I don't know if Szakacs defended her twenty-five years ago. And anyway, it doesn't matter, Vic. It's not your story, it's not your problem. Don't let them make it that."

I told Freeman about talking to Stella the week before. "She didn't say anything about a diary then. It makes me think—"

"Don't," Freeman ordered me. "Don't even pretend to think. Stay away from her. For pity's sake, for Lotty's sake, if not your own, do not go near that woman. Got it?"

"I understand, I do, but this is nuts. Boom-Boom never dated Annie, not that I ever saw or heard, and even if he had, he wasn't the jealous, threatening type."

"As far as you know, and you don't know what he did when he was out of your sight. Even if he was in love with Ms. Guzzo and wanted to marry her, you don't respond to this," Freeman reiterated.

"Has anyone seen this so-called diary? They didn't show it on the news, you know—just flashed a copy of a typescript. I will put a sample of Annie Guzzo's handwriting in a safe for now. If we ever get a chance to look at the actual document, I can get a forensic expert to—"

"It doesn't matter," Freeman said. "If Stella wants to pursue an exoneration claim, that's between her and the state. If she wants to say that Boom-Boom was a Chihuahua dressed up in ice skates, and that your father doctored his team photo—let her. Ignore her, ignore her, ignore her. Can you do that?"

"I suppose," I grumbled.

"I want the words spelled out, Warshawski. I know you."

"I promise I will not talk to her, go to her house or pay attention to her slanders about my cousin or my parents."

"Or about you," Freeman ordered.

"Oh, I don't care what she says about me," I assured him. Which was mostly true.

Before Lotty and Max left, Lotty made me lock my gun back into my safe. "I wish you would get rid of it, Victoria," she fretted. "You know I don't like these weapons. I've taken bullets out of too many children to want people to carry them wantonly."

I kissed her. "Lotty, I promise I am not going to use it wantonly. I will leave it locked away and will take it out only to go target shooting. Or if my life is in real peril, as opposed to psychically threatened."

She didn't like it. Max nodded at her, and she gave a reluctant assent, but her footsteps dragged as she followed him to the front door.

My phone continued to ring as calls started coming in from Asian outlets. I changed my message to refer callers to Freeman's office and turned the voice mail to outgoing message only, then went with Jake to spend the night in his place.

"I wish we could get attention like that for High Plainsong," Jake said. "Maybe if I murdered someone we'd find a new revenue stream."

"Don't tempt me, *caro*: I could send you out with a gun and an address," I said.

We made love, but Jake got up again to work on a tricky passage in a piece the group had commissioned. When Jake is nervous or depressed, he plays for hours. When I'm nervous or depressed, I want to shoot people. I fell asleep with his bass making deep soothing noises from the living room.

In my dreams, my mother and Stella were singing Cherubini's *Medea* together, not on an opera stage, but on the hockey rink at the old Stadium. Boom-Boom was sitting next to me in the front row. Annie appeared from nowhere, in the manner of dreams, and my cousin and I watched, paralyzed, while Stella stabbed her. When Gabriella tried to pull her away, Annie's arm came off. The crowd roared its approval; hockey fans love blood. Stella and my aunt Marie pointed accusatory fingers at Gabriella, while in front of them Annie bled to death.

I woke with my heart racing, sweat drenching my T-shirt. By the time I'd calmed down, I was thoroughly awake. Jake was sleeping soundly next to me. It was five-fifteen; dawn was coming. I might as well get back to my own place and face the day.

While I waited for the espresso machine to heat, I turned on my laptop to look at the messages from my answering service. Forty-seven media queries had come in overnight, including four from Murray. I sent my service an e-mail, saying to tell everyone I had no comment and that I would not be returning press calls.

When I checked my e-mail, I found hundreds of messages. Seven from Murray, ranging from belligerent to begging *(Come on, Warshawski, you know the rules of the game, don't pull this kind of stunt on me . . . Please, Vic, we've been friends for so many years, don't shoot the messenger).* He was right, but I wasn't feeling very forgiving yet.

I recognized some names from local news shows, but many of the addresses included country codes: Serbia, Russia, Kazakhstan— Boom-Boom would be pleased to know his fame lived on in the hockey world.

Pierre Fouchard had also left an e-mail. *I see you've turned your phone over to the lawyers, but what is this filth they are spreading about Boom-Boom? I talked to Bernadine, but she can tell me nothing. Call me, Victoria: I can be in Chicago in two hours. Those of us who played with Boom-Boom know this is the worst of lies, so tell me what you need. Muscle? Love? Money? All at your disposal.*

I reached him at the Canadiens front office.

"Victoria! These *crapules*, what are they trying to accomplish?"

"I don't know. The mother did major prison time for the crime, so I can't understand why she's trying to accuse Boom-Boom now. Did Boom-Boom talk about the murder when it happened?"

"This I am trying to remember since last night, when I am first seeing the news. He was very shocked, of course, because she was a girl from his childhood, and I am thinking there was a brother, is that right, that they were friends. I am not remembering much, but,

Victoria, if he had said to me, Pierre, I have murdered this girl, that I would not have forgotten."

"Likely not," I agreed dryly. "The mother, Stella, is claiming she found a diary that her daughter kept, and that Annie was writing about how jealous Boom-Boom was, and how she was afraid of him."

Pierre laughed. "That is impossible to picture. If you are imagining Boom-Boom as Bluebeard, no, you know him better than that. Yes, if you were against him in a game, then you should defend yourself against attacks from all sides, but Boom-Boom and women—there were so many, and they all had a good time with him, no one ever walked away from Boom-Boom weeping because he had frightened her, surely you don't need me to tell you that. As for a girl and a diary, how can I know about that? But if she wrote it, it came out of her own imaginations. This mother, this *salope*, she has maybe made her daughter to be afraid of every man in the world."

That was a shrewd insight, plausible, given Stella's obsession with sex, but not something I had any way to prove. I led the conversation around to Bernie, how well she was doing, how much I enjoyed her company.

"Yes, she's loving Chicago," Pierre agreed. "When she comes back to us next month, you must come with her. A week in the Laurentians, that will put all this *tracasserie* out of your mind."

When we hung up, I felt better than I had since Murray's text came in yesterday afternoon. I took an espresso out to the back porch. I had promised Freeman not to go near Stella or her house or her current lawyer. But what about her old lawyer, the useless baby who didn't bring up Boom-Boom's relationship with Annie at Stella's trial?

When I'd looked up Stella's trial last week, they hadn't given the baby's name. For that I would have to go to the County building, to the more complete records that had been kept on microform.

I was heading to the bathroom to shower and change when my doorbell rang. Bernie was sleeping deeply. I walked behind the couch to peer out at the street. I swore under my breath: three TV vans were double-parked on Racine. The early birds waiting for their prey: vultures are birds, too.

I shook Bernie awake, no easy task. When I'd finally roused her, I explained we were under siege. "If you go out, use the back door. Otherwise the wolves from cable-land are going to jump you, okay?"

Her eyes lit up: at last, a chance to take action against Boom-Boom's enemies. "This will be fun."

"No, Bernie. It won't be. They'll make mincemeat out of you. Please believe I know what I'm talking about, or if you won't believe me, please at least promise me that you will stay away from them. Okay?"

She gave a reluctant agreement, but she still tried to rehash last night's argument: we needed to act, not bury ourselves in libraries, doing research.

"Bernie, if I discover that someone planted that diary, I'm not going to tell you, unless I can trust you not to run headfirst into trouble."

"Okay, okay, I'll do it your way for two days. If you don't find out anything and start acting on it—"

"You will return to Canada so that you don't get arrested and deported." It took an effort not to shout at her. For the first time I began to see how hard it had been on my mother when Boom-Boom and I went roaring off without a thought of the consequences. "What would you do if I showed up at one of your games and started telling you how to play?"

"You don't know enough about hockey to tell me anything."

"Exactly. And you don't know enough about the law, and evidence, and how to uncover secrets to tell me what to do."

Her small vivid face bunched up into a gargoyle grimace, but she finally gave a reluctant nod, a reluctant promise to do as I'd asked.

I ran down the back stairs. Mr. Contreras's kitchen light was on. I owed it to him to explain what was going on, even though conversations with him are never short. He'd seen the story, of course, and was appropriately indignant.

"Bernie is up in arms, and thinks we ought to be out shooting or at least whacking people. I don't want her going to South Chicago. It's gang territory and she has no street smarts, only ice smarts. Can you waylay her, get her involved with the dogs, the garden, keep her from doing something that will get her hurt?"

"I never been able to keep you from getting hurt, doll," the old man said, truculent, "no matter what I say or do. Talking to my tomatoes gets me better results."

I felt my cheeks flame, but meekly said he was right. "But she's seventeen, she's been left in my care."

"And what are you going to get up to?" he demanded.

"Exactly what I said to Bernie, and what I promised both Lotty and my lawyer. Looking for information, nothing physical, I promise."

I kissed his cheek, told the dogs they could swim when I got home tonight, and jogged down the alley so I could come to my car from behind. One of the reporters had been enterprising enough to find the Mustang. He was facing my apartment and I startled him when I unlocked the car and jumped in. He tried to hold on to the door, but I was maneuvering out of the parking space and he had to let go.

I might have been a worm slithering away from the early birds, but my reward was the morning rush hour. Lake Shore Drive at this hour is pretty much a parking lot. It may be the most beautiful parking lot in the world, with the waves on nearby Lake Michigan dancing and preening in the sunlight, but it was still slow and tedious going.

I was early enough to find street parking three blocks from the

County building and took the stairs up to the records room, where I paid twenty dollars for a chance to look at the microform. It didn't include the trial transcript—those are expensive. Only the lawyers involved in a trial order up copies, so if Stella's lawyer hadn't done so, there was no transcript available. I did find a list of the exhibits used at the trial, and the names of both the state's attorney and the defense counsel. Stella had been represented by a Joel Previn.

8

CALLING TIME

Previn is one of those names you think is common, maybe because of André and Dory, but there aren't very many of them. I'd only ever heard of one in Chicago: Ira.

Ira Previn's about ninety now and at least according to local lore, still goes into court once or twice a month. He'd been a legend as a labor and civil rights lawyer in my childhood, when he battled the Daley Machine from his storefront practice on the South Side. He'd taken on the Steelworkers over racial discrimination, gone after the fast-food industry for wage discrimination, supported equal pay for women and African-American janitors at City Hall. The fact that he'd lost many of his battles didn't make him any less heroic, at least not to me.

I looked up Joel. Sure enough, he was Ira's son. He was about my age, had attended Swarthmore College, then Kent Marshall School of Law. Never married. Lived in an apartment in the Jackson Park Highlands in the same building as Ira, worked out of Ira's office.

They must be a tight-knit family. Joel would have handled Stella's defense when he was new to the bar; surely he'd remember one of his first cases.

Traffic had eased by the time I finished at the County building: I made the run from Buckingham Fountain to Seventy-first Street in twelve minutes. The route led past the South Shore Cultural Center. It's run now by the park district, which can barely afford to maintain the main building, but when I was growing up, it was an exclusive country club with guards at the gates and horses stabled near the private beach. In those days, Jews were banned from membership along with African-Americans, even though the club sat smack in the middle of what used to be a vibrant Jewish community.

The South Shore Club could handle living cheek by jowl with Jews, but the arrival of African-Americans had been too much for everyone: white Chicagoans looking in fear at black neighbors had fled to the suburbs like a pack of jackals smelling a lion. The Catholics mostly bolted westward while Jews ran north. Only Ira stayed on.

Previn's office was on Jeffery, in a building like the one with the fancy shops of my childhood: little stores on the street level, two floors of apartments overhead. I didn't see the entrance at first and passed two bars, "Flo's Clothes, All Dresses $10 or Under," and five storefronts for rent before I found it tucked between a fried fish outlet and a wig shop.

It looked as though Previn maintained his own cleaning crew: the bottles and fast-food detritus on the sidewalk stopped where his office started. The sign on the window, Previn & Previn, Attorneys at Law, had been painted recently; a phone number and a website were both listed underneath.

The Previns weren't blind to the risks of the area: white circles indicating an alarm system were mounted on the windows. They had installed a security camera in the doorway. Its red eye took me in when I rang the bell. After a long moment, a buzzer sounded, an old-fashioned noise like a school fire bell. I pulled the door open.

An African-American woman who seemed eighty or ninety herself was alone in the small room. Under the low-hanging fluorescent lamps, her face showed a network of lines, like the cracked patina of an ancient oriental vase. She wore a severely tailored suit, which might have come from France. Certainly not from Flo's. The pearls in her ears looked real.

"What can we do for you here?" Her voice quavered slightly with age, but the assessing look she gave me, taking in everything from my faded jeans to my expensive boots, was shrewd.

"My name is V. I. Warshawski. I'm a private investigator and I was hoping to speak to Mr. Joel Previn about a woman he represented some years ago."

"Is he expecting you? He had an early meeting outside the office."

I looked at my watch. Nine-thirty. I said I could wait half an hour.

"He doesn't—I don't know what time he might get here. Tell me what you want; I'm familiar with most of the cases the office handles."

"Stella Guzzo. She—"

"Oh, yes." The woman's face took on an expression I couldn't interpret, sadness, maybe, or wariness. "She murdered her daughter. I remember it well."

"Hnnh. Stella Guzzo. What kind of business are you doing with her?"

I turned, startled. Ira Previn had come into the room through a door behind me. Age had shrunk him. His missing inches had settled around his midriff, which looked like the mound in the middle of the boa constrictor that ate the elephant. His face and hands were covered with dark age spots, but his voice was still deep and authoritative.

I repeated my name.

"Hnnh. Warshawski. You connected to the hockey player?"

"His cousin," I said. "His goalie when he was ten and couldn't get on a rink. His executor when he died."

"Eunice, did you already look at her ID?"

I took out my wallet and showed them my PI and driver's licenses. Ira looked at them, grunted again and moved to a desk on the far side of the room. His gait was uneven: it was hard for him to move his right leg, but he frowned at Eunice when she reached for a cane propped against her desk. When he was seated in the old-fashioned swivel chair, he took his time getting settled—patting his forehead with a handkerchief, refolding the cloth and putting it back in his breast pocket, lining up a couple of pencils next to a legal pad. These were his courtroom strategies, buying him time, annoying opposing counsel, but they'd probably become second nature now.

"Saw your cousin play a few times, back in the old Stadium, when your eardrums could burst from the sound. So you were his goalie. And now you think you need to block shots aimed at him after death."

I couldn't help smiling at the metaphor. "Something like that, sir."

"And what are you planning on doing?"

"That depends on what kind of information I can get about Stella Guzzo's trial. I'm thinking she invented the story about my cousin when she was doing time, but if I could see the transcript, there might be something to suggest she'd already thought about it when she was arrested."

Doing time, what a strange expression. You and time behind bars, you're suspended in time, or passing time. Time is doing things to you, not you to it.

Eunice and Ira exchanged looks. They were a team with a lot of years of shorthand between them. Eunice said, "If you're thinking of suing Joel for malpractice, the statute of limitations—"

"No, ma'am!" It hadn't occurred to me, but of course, that was one reason a stranger might be nosing around the case. "I'm trying to figure out why Stella Guzzo is making this preposterous claim. She's saying Annie—her daughter—kept a diary that she only stumbled on now, long after the murder. I find it hard to believe it's genuine, but I wondered if she said anything to Mr. Joel Previn at the time. About Annie and my cousin, or Annie and a diary, or another possible suspect."

"Did your cousin in fact date her?"

"Not as far as I know."

"Either Stella Guzzo has evidence, or she has an animus," Previn pronounced. "Which is it?"

I shrugged. "It could be both, but it's definitely an animus. Annie adored my mother. Most people did, but to Annie, Gabriella represented, oh, sanity, I guess. And a window to a larger world. Stella Guzzo decided that my mother was deliberately undermining her authority as a parent. She responded with some vile statements, so I can't say I've ever been a fan."

What Stella had said was that Gabriella used the secret sexual arts of Jewish women to seduce her husband, Mateo. We got chapter and verse on this from my aunt Marie, Boom-Boom's mother, who was one of Stella's cronies. Marie loved conflict, and she was at perpetual loggerheads with my mother. Gabriella, Italian, Jewish, a singer, was way too exotic for the sulfurous air of South Chicago. Marie was happy to report Stella's insults to us when she and Uncle Bernard came over for Sunday dinner.

"Mateo never would have thought about music for the girl if the Jewish whore hadn't gone to work on him. Me, I've worn the same dress to Mass for six years running, but the Jew bats those big eyes and he shells out money we don't have so the girl can pretend to study music. He doesn't think about me, his own wife, let alone Frankie, who's the one

with the future in this house. Frankie could play in the big leagues, that's what Mr. Scanlon told us. No, it's what the whore wants; Mateo takes bread from my mouth so she can buy those fancy Italian shoes."

"My mama doesn't buy fancy shoes," I started to say at one meal, but Gabriella hushed me in Italian.

"Carissima, your aunt is a pipe carrying water in two directions. Don't pour into it at this end; it will only bring satisfaction to Signora Guzzo if she thinks her spiteful words bother us."

What really enraged Stella Guzzo wasn't the waste of money on something as frivolous as music, but the way Annie began quoting my mother on every conceivable subject.

"Mrs. Warshawski says the sky is bigger than what we see in South Chicago and we girls should go where we can see the stars at night. Mrs. Warshawski tells Victoria if she gets a bad grade from laziness that's more of a sin than saying a lie, because being lazy is acting a lie. Mrs. Warshawski says smoking hurts the heart but dishonesty kills it, she says—" until Stella smacked her and said if she heard Gabriella Warshawski's name one more time, she wasn't going to be responsible for what happened next.

"We all knew Ms. Guzzo's temper," I said to Ira and Eunice. "The fact that you remember her, remember the case after all this time, makes me wonder if something special went on at the trial."

Ira and Eunice looked at each other again: Should we trust her?

Ira made an impatient gesture, but he said, "We didn't want Joel to take the case. We didn't think he had enough experience, certainly not for criminal law. It was hard on him, it took a toll."

"Why did you let him do it, then, instead of handling it yourself?" I asked.

Eunice shook her head. "Joel wasn't working here—we thought he should have wider experience, and if he'd been here, he'd have always been in Ira's shadow. Joel started with Mandel & McClelland, doing general law. The girl, Anne Guzzo, worked as a file clerk there part-time. Making money to help pay for college, if I remember correctly. When she was killed, Mr. Mandel felt responsible, felt they should do something."

"And that something included providing her mother with a defense attorney?" I was puzzled, not to say incredulous, but I tried to keep my tone one of polite inquiry.

"It's a tight-knit neighborhood, or it was. You should know that, having grown up there."

"Yes, but—"

"Mr. McClelland went to the same church as the Guzzo family," Eunice said. "He thought, at least I believe he thought, that the murder, including the mother's defense, was the community's business. Ms. Guzzo couldn't afford an attorney, and he probably believed that even someone as inexperienced as Joel would be better for her than an overworked, underprepared public defender."

There was a scrabbling at the lock as she was speaking. Joel Previn came in before she finished.

"And of course, we all know how wrong he was," Joel said. "Why are we rehashing my earliest failure? There are so many others, more recent, that would be worth recounting."

9

MINOR LEAGUE

Joel Previn was taller than his father, but he had the same heavy cheeks. On Ira they were sagging, like kangaroo pouches, but Joel's were still upright, pushing his eyes up so that he almost had to squint. The likeness between father and son was remarkable, but so was the resemblance to his mother: Joel had Eunice's high round forehead, her short flat nose, her biscuit-colored skin. What belonged to Joel alone was the unhealthy beading of sweat across his face. His appointment outside the office had been with a bottle.

I walked over to him, holding out my hand and introducing myself. He ignored the hand. I felt foolish, as one does.

"Did you know Stella Guzzo had been released from prison?" I asked.

Joel looked from Eunice to Ira, not the silent signals his parents shared, but as if he were seeking guidance. If they'd sent him to another law firm to keep him out from under Ira's shadow, the strategy hadn't worked well.

"I knew, yes," he said. "Her parole officer told me, in case Stella wanted any legal advice."

"Did she?"

"Not from me. Why would she? I'm the guy who couldn't keep her out of prison in the first place." He had his father's baritone, too, but in him the undertone held a whine.

"So would you be surprised to learn she's thinking about trying to get exonerated?"

"Am I on the stand here? Do I know, am I surprised, do I care? No, no and no."

"I know it was a long time ago, Mr. Previn, but I'm wondering what she said during the trial to help with her defense."

"She was impossible," Joel cried. "I wasn't the right attorney for her. Like my mother said, I was too inexperienced, not even for the crime so much as for working with someone like her. Annie, her daughter, she was nothing like that. When Mr. McClelland and Mr. Mandel asked me to handle the defense, I didn't want to: Annie was so special, she kept the whole office bright, and I didn't want to work for anyone who'd killed her, but I never in a million years imagined how different her mother would be from her."

"I grew up with Annie," I said. "I know she wanted to get away from South Chicago, get away from all the fighting that went on in her home. And I know Stella used to beat her children, but back when you were prepping her for the trial, did she ever suggest that someone else killed Annie?"

"She said it must have been an intruder, but she also told me she'd hit Annie that night. She claimed it was self-defense. Would you have believed that? She said Annie came at her with a knife, which I couldn't credit. Little Annie attacking someone with a knife? And Stella was twice her size. I did my best, but Stella already told everyone she'd had to hit Annie, to protect herself. But she also said that

Annie was still alive when she left for her bingo game, so someone else must have come to the house while she was at Saint Eloy's."

"Was there any sign of forced entry?"

"It was so long ago," Joel said. "I don't remember all the police evidence. Dad would, of course, if it had been his case. And if he hadn't been tied up with some big federal suit, he'd have been in court and made sure I asked all the right questions. Or leapt up and asked them himself."

"Joel, please," Eunice said. "Please don't bring all that up now. We know it was an impossible situation, one which we should have tried to stop—"

"What difference does it make now? Mr. Mandel, Dad—the two of them tutted about it at shul. Mr. Mandel and Mr. McClelland both said— Oh, never mind what they both said. In the end, we all agreed I'd be happier elsewhere. Mr. Mandel sent me to a downtown firm as an associate, but after a few years we all once more agreed I'd be happier elsewhere. Ira feels the same way, but there's no other else-where for me these days."

Ira held up a hand, not trying to stop his son, trying to ward off the pain of the words.

"Did you keep a transcript of the trial?" I asked.

"No. When I left Mandel & McClelland, they kept all my files." He looked at Eunice. "Someone wants to rent 206. I came back to get a lease."

"Someone you met at the Pot of Gold? Can I talk to them first?" Her eyes were pleading with him not to have a tantrum, but he went to a filing cabinet, pulled out a couple of forms and slammed out of the office, saying he was tired of being treated like a mental incompetent.

I followed him quickly—the pain in his mother's face was hard to take. Joel was disappearing into a tavern half a block up the street.

The Pot of Gold was a small room, with a narrow bar running its length, a couple of minute tables squeezed against the wall, the requisite TV hung in the middle where people could sort of see it. It was tuned this morning to a rerun of an old Notre Dame football game.

Joel was sliding onto a stool when I walked in. Three other people were in the room, a heavy woman tending the bar and two men, seated on adjacent stools near the back. They were older. Every now and then one of them would say something, the other would respond, then they'd relapse into silence.

Joel looked up when I sat next to him, but his expression wasn't welcoming. "You can tell my mother that the rental prospect took off before I could show him the lease. She doesn't need to guard the assets any longer."

"I'm not interested in that. I'm curious about how Stella behaved at the trial."

"It was a long time ago. I don't remember." He signaled to the heavyset woman, who came over with a bottle of vodka. She looked at me questioningly, but I shook my head.

"She's like one of those unstable chemical reactions they teach you about in school. You have to keep her behind a bulletproof shield so you don't get acid in your eyes when she explodes," I said. "At least, that's the way she seemed when I was a kid. When I saw her last week, she slugged me. Even though she's eighty, she would have killed me if she'd connected just right. I could believe she murdered Annie in a fit of rage. Did you ever think of pleading insanity?"

"*I* did, but the priest and Mr. McClelland jumped on me like I was a cockroach on the bathroom floor. But, Christ, she was so fucking out of control that Judge Grigsby kept cautioning me. It wasn't the worst thing that happened to me, just one of the bad ones. He said if I couldn't control my client's behavior in court, he'd have to fine me."

"You can't tell a judge your client is uncontrollable," I agreed. "How did you handle it?"

"I talked it over with Mr. Mandel and Mr. McClelland, and Mr. McClelland got the priest at Saint Eloy's to talk to her. Old man, mean guy, but Stella thought he walked on water. I guess that did the trick."

"Why did you agree to represent her?"

"You had to be there. The partners decided. Probably because they knew it was a losing case and they wanted the biggest loser in the practice to have it on his record, not one of the go-getters."

"Who were the go-getters?" I asked, more to move him away from his bout of self-flagellation than because I cared.

"Connor Hurlihey was there."

"Spike Hurlihey?" I said, my eyes widening.

"Yeah. He was one of the East Side boys, he was a pet of old Mr. McClelland. He rode up, I rode down."

Connor "Spike" Hurlihey. Speaker of the Illinois House. Maybe the most powerful man in the Land of Lincoln, although of course in the pit where Illinois vipers writhe and hiss, it's kind of hard to tell the top snake. I knew his district was south, but I'd always assumed it was the south suburbs, Flossmoor or Olympia Fields. I didn't realize he'd grown up across the Calumet River from me.

"You and Hurlihey get along?"

Joel gulped down his drink and held up his glass to the bartender. "Hurlihey was three years older than me. When I was in fifth grade and he was in eighth, he used to give me wedgies in the hallway. The teachers looked the other way, the other kids laughed because he was a popular bully, and I was a mixed-race kid in a neighborhood with a low tolerance for difference. I begged my parents to send me to a different school and they finally did for ninth grade, but neither of us forgot the other.

"When I joined Mandel & McClelland, he started saying things to Annie: he knew I admired her, and he was pretending to draw her attention to that, but really he was using it as a way to make fun of me."

It's depressing how often school bullies become successful CEOs or politicians. "Annie was an ardent soul. I can understand why you responded to her."

"Ardent. That describes her. She was ambitious, she wanted to leave South Chicago, but she was sweet. She was the smartest girl in her school, probably the smartest person in the firm, but she never complained if one of the lawyers dumped a stack of photocopying on her at the end of the day. She'd stand at the Xerox machine with her history book propped up on the shelf, reading while she fed documents in. In those days I thought I was ambitious, too."

"Did you believe Stella when she said Annie had attacked her?"

He fidgeted with his glass. "I went over there one night, on the spur of the moment, I wanted to see if Annie would go to a show with me. She and her mother were shouting at each other, they didn't even hear the doorbell."

"It was a family that fought and shouted a lot," I said. "When Stella's brothers would come over with their wives and kids, my dad couldn't even hear the game on the radio and there was an alley between us. When old Mrs. Jokich—Stella's neighbor—was dying, the family had to call the cops to shut up the braying at the Guzzo place."

Stella was sure it was my dad who'd called the district station, and nothing could convince her otherwise. That was probably why she was squawking now that Tony had suppressed evidence during her trial—she could carry a grudge until the grudge took on a life of its own and carried on without her.

I put my card on the bar next to Joel. "Even if you're fifty, you can make other choices, change directions. Your parents don't own you."

"Spare me the pep talk. I've had plenty and they make my head hurt."

"Maybe, but I'm betting it's all that vodka before lunch."

I walked back to my car, which had a sporty orange envelope under the windshield wiper. My second in a week, and I couldn't expense Frank, not without crossing the line Freeman had warned me against.

I hadn't noticed the pay-to-park sign. The cash-strapped city was handing out sixty-five-dollar fines even on the city's more derelict streets. I guess it meant someone had a job in this dismal economy, but somehow that thought didn't cheer me.

I couldn't understand why Mandel & McClelland had agreed to assign someone from the firm to represent Annie's killer, and why that someone had been Joel, young, green, obviously with a crush on the victim. They should have left Stella to the public defender. I'd been one, I'd worked hard. Like all Cook County PD's, my caseload had been too big, but I still gave each client careful attention—by working the long hours that made my husband scowl and complain during the fourteen months of our marriage.

It occurred to me that if Stella had drawn a PD, it might have been me being cautioned by Judge Grigsby. I laughed, picturing Stella's horror if I'd been assigned to her defense.

The other side of the question was the client side—why had Stella let Joel represent her? She didn't suffer ordinary people gladly; she'd have eviscerated an inexperienced young man. Or maybe the shock of Annie's death and her own arrest had silenced her.

None of the story made any sense. Maybe Mandel or McClelland was still alive and could recall what had gone through their heads at the time.

I remembered Mr. Mandel. When I was in middle school, he used to give our graduation speeches. Every year we heard the same rambling reminiscence about his arriving as a poor immigrant and making his way through law school while working the swing shift for Wisconsin Steel. Only in America. My mother sat next to me, making sure I at least looked at the stage, even if I wasn't paying attention to the words.

I pulled out my iPad and looked up Mandel & McClelland. Their office had been in the Navral Building, which wasn't standing any longer. There'd been an obituary for Mr. Mandel some seven years back. He was survived by one daughter, four grandchildren and three great-grandchildren. If any of them were lawyers, they did it someplace else—the firm of Mandel & McClelland had also vanished, although I didn't see any stories about McClelland's retirement or death. Where would the client files be if both building and practice were gone?

I made a face at myself and went back to Ira Previn's office. Eunice and Ira were huddled over a document when she buzzed me in, but they put it down and looked at me expectantly. When I asked if Mandel had sold the practice they seemed disappointed—they must have watched me follow Joel to the Pot of Gold and hoped I would perform a miracle of some kind.

"I don't know why you want to dig around in this, Ms. Warshawski," Ira rumbled at me. "The Guzzo woman can't harm your cousin, she can't prove anything. And I don't think she can harm Joel, either."

"But you know who bought the firm?"

Eunice said, "Please, if you're determined to get involved in this, promise me you won't drag Joel in with you. He— Stella Guzzo's trial destroyed him."

I looked at her helplessly. "If something about Stella and the trial destroyed him, he's already involved. I can only promise not to drag him in unless there's a truly compelling reason for it."

Eunice looked at Ira. He nodded slowly, his pouchy cheeks quivering with the movement.

"Very well, but—"

"Neesie, she can learn another way. Just tell her."

"Nina Quarles." The words were almost unintelligible, Eunice's lips were so tightly compressed.

10

BALK

Nina Quarles, Attorney, had her office on Commercial Avenue, just a couple of miles from Ira's. The building was a converted three-flat at the corner of Eighty-ninth Street, and looked like one of the few on the street to be fully occupied. The top story was home to the South Side Youth Empowerment Foundation: *Say, Yes!* while the ground level held the insurance office of Rory Scanlon, Auto, Homeowners, Life, Health, Pension. Sandwiched between was the office of Nina Quarles, Attorney, boasting three lawyers and a bail bondsman.

When you're a child, all adults seem both old and fixed in time, so I didn't know if Rory Scanlon was still alive, or if the torch had been passed. Either way, the business was clearly a success. Looking through the street windows, I saw that the computers were new, the desks in good shape. Five people were talking into their headsets, smiling the way you do so the person at the other end feels your energy and wants to buy from you.

My parents bought their insurance through the Patrolmen's Union, so I'd never been to Scanlon's office, but he was such a lively presence in the neighborhood that everyone knew him. He'd been a fixer, the kind of guy you went to if you were going to be evicted or had your gas turned off. He turned out for community events, underwrote the Little League team that Frank Guzzo used to play on. When Boom-Boom made his home-ice debut with the Hawks, Scanlon got the CTA to send buses to ferry the neighborhood from Ninetieth and Commercial to the old Stadium.

My dad had driven up in his own car. One of the few times he took police privilege, he brought me and my uncle Bernie through the streets with his lights flashing, parking right next to the main entrance. He hadn't gone to the party Scanlon sponsored at Rafters afterward.

"Too old for drunken crowds, Tori. And don't you need to be studying?"

I'd been surprised—his usual concern about my work was that I kept at it too hard. He was worried, too, about leaving me on my own, which he also never did—at least not out loud.

"Boom-Boom's signed on for a rough life, but I don't want that for you, and you know your mama didn't want it, either."

My mama wouldn't have wanted a lot of the things I choose to do. Maybe if she'd lived, I wouldn't keep tempting fate by skating so close to the edge. Perhaps my recklessness was what destroyed my brief marriage. Or perhaps it was because Richard Yarborough had been a money-obsessed bore.

I went into Scanlon's building, and looked up a flight of steep stairs. A sign in Spanish and English said there was an elevator behind the stairs. A security camera, the tiny modern kind that is almost invisible to the thief in a hurry, had been installed high on the stairwell wall. Another was set in the lintel above Nina

Quarles's door. It glowed red when I approached, presumably taking my picture. I must have looked honest and sincere: the lock clicked open before I rang the bell.

The walls of the original apartment had been removed to create a long room that stretched from the windows overlooking Commercial Avenue to the alley behind. It wasn't divided into cubicles, but the desks were far enough apart that people could have private conversations if they kept their voices down. Two doors stood open along the north wall, showing private offices beyond in what probably used to be bedrooms. A third door at the back provided the staff with a toilet.

As in Scanlon's office, the staff here were hard at it on the phones. Most of them were middle-aged and solidly built, a few wrinkles, hair turning gray—not the lean, workout-obsessed youth that might repel people like the elderly couple conferring in the near corner with a man in a rumpled suit.

I looked around but didn't see any sign of Nina Quarles. I was on my way to the offices, to see if that's where she was, when a woman came up behind me and asked what I needed. She was about my age, tall, angular, wearing a shapeless cardigan over beige slacks and spiked heels, which put her about three inches over my head.

"V. I. Warshawski," I said, putting out a hand.

The angular woman's eyes widened. "Warshawski? There was something about Boom-Boom Warshawski on the news this morning."

"Yes, I'm his cousin."

She said the usual things: she'd grown up on the East Side, she adored Boom-Boom, his death had been a terrible tragedy. In the middle of the outpouring I was able to get her name, Thelma Kalvin.

"What can we do for you?" Kalvin asked.

"I don't know if you paid attention to the whole story, but my cousin was in the news today because someone is trying to link him to Annie Guzzo's death."

Thelma shook her head. "If the name is supposed to mean something to me, it doesn't. I'm sorry we can't help you."

"Stella Guzzo was convicted of killing her daughter Annie a number of years ago," I said. "Nina Quarles bought this practice from Mandel & McClelland, the firm that handled Stella's defense. If Ms. Quarles kept files of old Mandel cases, I'd like to read Stella's trial transcript."

Thelma shook her head. "Nina doesn't actually practice here. Our lawyers mostly work on job or property issues—a lot of this community got slammed in the mortgage crisis. And we have a criminal defender. But there isn't room to store old case files here—they're in a facility down in Indiana. Anyway, I doubt Nina would let you look at confidential files."

"It's not a confidential document," I said, trying to keep frustration out of my voice. "Just a rare one. I want to see if Stella Guzzo made any effort to blame my cousin for her daughter's death during her trial. I also would love to know why Mandel & McClelland took on the defense—Annie Guzzo worked for them. Why would they defend her killer, even if the killer was her mother?"

Thelma began saying that Mr. Zapateca would be available at two. I was startled, then realized she was talking to her device; she wore one of those clips that look like a beetle is trying to burrow into your ear.

When she finished she said there was nothing she could do to help, she hadn't been part of Mandel & McClelland—another interruption for the beetle, this time about Ludo's bail hearing—no one remembered that far back, and no, I couldn't talk to Nina Quarles— "Sorry, not you, Mrs. Bialo, talking to someone in the office, please hold for one minute"—because Nina was in Paris.

The beetle had her full attention at this point. I stifled the impulse to yank it out of her ear and stalked out of the office, unreasonably annoyed. What had I really expected, after all?

The elderly couple who'd been with the guy in the rumpled suit were leaving as well. I held the door for them and put my ill temper to one side to offer an arm down the stairs—although the woman held herself erect, the man was bent over and walked with a slow shuffle.

"There is an elevator," I suggested when they insisted they were fine on their own.

"It's out of order, but they say climbing stairs is good for the heart," the woman said brightly.

"We can't afford to get dependent on anyone, young lady," the man said. "Especially since we have to pay the lawyer bill now on top of everything else. Sounds as though you got the lady at the front desk kind of upset."

"Hard to know why," I said. "I was just asking a few questions. You buy your insurance here?"

"Oh, yes. The lawyer sends you down to the agency, and they give you a special rate if you're a customer with the lawyer. And then, if you need a lawyer, the insurance man sends you up here. That's why we were here, we were hoping to cash in our life insurance now that we need extra help. But the fine print, that's what always does you in, isn't it." He pronounced the word as IN-surance.

I walked down in front of them, slowly, in case the couple changed their minds about wanting help. They were murmuring softly to each other. When we got to the front entryway, they stopped beside the inner door to Scanlon Insurance.

"We heard you asking about Stella Guzzo," the woman said.

"Do you know her?" I tried to sound casual.

"No." The woman looked up the stairs, to see if anyone was watching. I noticed the camera eye in the entryway ceiling, and ushered the couple outside.

"It was the girl," the husband said. "Annie. She was a clerk in the office, a bright little thing. We still remember her being killed. Gangs. You're always reading about children killed by gang violence, but when your own mother murders you—awful, awful!"

The woman squeezed her husband's hand. "Don't get so worked up, Harold: it all happened a long time ago. But Sol Mandel took it to heart, her working for him and so on. We were surprised that he gave the job of defending the mother to Ira Previn's son."

"It surprised me, too," I said. "Do you know why he did it?"

"Sol had some explanation," Harold said. "He felt responsible because the girl had planned on running away to college without telling her mother and he told her to stand up to her mother, be an adult. It didn't seem like much of a reason, but that's what he said."

"How do you know so much about it?" I asked.

"Oh, we all belonged to the same temple, back when Har HaShem was down here," the woman said. "Poor Joel."

"What do you mean, 'poor Joel'?" Harold snorted. "It's poor Ira."

"Poor Joel," the woman repeated. "He could never live up to Ira's reputation. He shouldn't have gone into the law, but he so wanted Ira to pay attention to him, to admire him. Ira never could see it. All his emotional life, it was focused on the courts, and what wasn't there, he felt he owed to Eunice. He knew how much talk there was, he felt he needed to protect her."

"Even at the temple," Harold said mournfully. "It's an embarrassment to know how mean-spirited your own kind can be."

"Yes, it caused quite a stir back when they married," the woman sighed, "her not being a Jew, plus her being a Negro. African-American, we should say now. Oh, Harold! Look at the time, I'm running on, and we have to see about the payments before we go home."

I handed her a card, asking her to call if anything else occurred to her. "And would you give me your phone number? I'm a detective, I'm inquisitive by nature and I might have more questions."

Her husband objected sharply: the world was full of scam artists, she shouldn't tell me their names. She patted his arm sympathetically but spelled it for me, slowly, Harold and Melba Minsky. They lived in Olympia Fields now, but they'd kept their legal affairs with Mandel for so long they didn't feel like shifting when he died, even after Mr. McClelland sold the practice to Nina Quarles.

"Not that it's much of a practice here in South Chicago anymore. If it's a big case, they send it to the people who bought Sol Mandel's downtown office, of course, but they can take care of the little things we need help with, not that they helped us much today."

"They must have big cases, if Nina Quarles has to be in Paris to handle them," I said.

Melba laughed, the sound like a rustling of paper. "I doubt that Nina has ever been in court, dear, unless she was trying to get out of a traffic ticket. She goes to Paris to buy clothes. But Thelma Kalvin is a first-rate office manager and the gentleman who looks after us knows his business. We don't mind."

She waited until Harold, clucking at her impatiently, pushed open the door to Scanlon's office. "One person you might talk to is Rabbi Zukos's son. The rabbi, may his name be a blessing, died after the congregation moved to Highland Park, but his son Rafael was in the same bar mitzvah class as Joel Previn. Good luck, dear."

11

FLEEING THE LIONS

It was past two. I'd been too agitated by the television invasion to eat breakfast this morning and I was suddenly ravenous. I was standing in the street to see what restaurants were nearby when a car honked right behind me. I jumped and scrambled back to the curb. A late-model silver SUV pulled into the spot where I'd been standing.

Two men climbed out, laughing about someone named Robbie. The driver said, "You go on in, Wally, I'll follow you in a sec."

He came over to me, a white-haired man wearing a red-checked shirt, a leather bomber jacket slung over one shoulder.

"Is your life insurance paid up, young lady?"

He laughed at my startled expression. "If you stand in the middle of a busy street, better make sure your family is taken care of. What can we do for you?"

"Are you Mr. Scanlon?" I asked.

"Guilty as charged. And you are?"

"V. I. Warshawski."

He'd been laughing, his cheeks pushing his eyes into twinkling slits, as if he were practicing for a role as Santa. At my name the twinkling vanished and I could see his eyes, blue and cold.

"I knew the hockey player," Scanlon said. "Who's back in the news these days."

"Yes, indeed he is. I remember the night you chartered buses to take the neighborhood up to watch his debut at the Stadium. Or was that your father?"

He laughed, delighted that I remembered, but the laugh didn't thaw his eyes. "That was me, a very young me. In those days I loved throwing big parties, getting people together, watching them have a good time. I still love a good party but can't take the hours anymore. Warshawski wasn't married. Let's see—you're a sister?"

"Cousin," I said.

I could almost see zeros and ones shifting in his face as he calculated who I was, where I fit into his files.

"Your father was the cop, right? They said he couldn't be bribed, right? One of the pillars of justice in an unjust world."

"I'm glad people knew that about him," I said formally: Scanlon's voice had held an undercurrent that sounded close to scorn.

"And you went off to school someplace, left the neighborhood."

"Guilty as charged," I echoed him.

"So what brings you back to South Chicago?"

"Stella Guzzo." I waited a beat, to let him fill in the blanks.

"Right, it was on the news, she claims Warshawski terrified her daughter. And so you've hotfooted it down here to clear his name. It's what I love about this neighborhood, families in it stick together. What did you think we could do for you here?"

"Not you, Nina Quarles's office. They took over Mandel & McClelland's business." I knew he knew that. "I was hoping they might have a trial transcript."

"Oh? And did they?"

"No one seems to have one. Poor Annie—her death wasn't considered important enough for anyone to record all the details."

"She was a bright kid. Too bad it had to end that way."

"Had to end that way? That makes it sound as if her mother was preordained to kill her."

"Oh, these South Side Irish families, with their outsized voices and quarrels squeezed into tiny houses, they're tinderboxes. I know them well—I grew up in one of those families."

Scanlon started to open the door but stopped when I asked how he knew Annie Guzzo.

He shrugged impatiently. "How we all know each other. She was a bright kid in my lawyer's office—Sol Mandel used to handle my family's business. Nina does now. Keep it all in the neighborhood, that's what I tell people."

"Did Mr. Mandel ever tell you why he pressured Joel Previn into defending Stella? It seems so strange, defending the killer of his young clerk."

"We all hoped something would put some spine in Joel. He had chances most people down here never come close to, but he was a whiner and a crybaby. Sol wanted to see if he could buck up, act like a man, and sad to say, it didn't happen. Good talking to you, Warshawski the cousin, but stay out of the street—people drive like lunatics."

He laughed again, clapped my shoulder and went into his office. I stared after him thoughtfully, wondering what that conversation had been about. And the meeting itself—it had seemed like a chance encounter, but it was odd that he'd stopped to talk to me. Was it possible that Thelma Kalvin had sent him a message—detective in the office asking about Stella Guzzo? Or had the Guzzo business gotten me so off-balance that I was seeing conspiracies under every streetlamp?

One thing I was sure about: I was still hungry. I found a taco stand up the street with some bar stools set up on the sidewalk for customers. After hours of slogging around the South Side, my anger about the slander against Boom-Boom was waning, but everything about Stella's story was so odd I couldn't leave it alone.

Maybe Scanlon's theory as to why Mandel had asked Joel Previn to defend Stella was correct: tough love. Make the boy grow a spine or balls or whatever. It was possible—there'd definitely been a culture of bullying in the Mandel & McClelland office, with Spike Hurlihey, now the House Speaker, leading the pack. Would the partners have participated in the bullying to such a degree that they'd taken on Stella's defense just to humiliate Joel?

What had Stella said, when I called on her last week? Something about Annie rotting in hell if she'd died with her last words to her mother on her lips. Maybe Sol Mandel had also seen something malicious in Annie that made him silently sympathize with Stella.

I tried to picture it, but that image wouldn't come into focus. The Annie I'd known was hardworking, but not malicious. I'd been jealous of her sometimes when I was young because of the way she attached herself to my mother—I wanted Gabriella's love all to myself and when Annie practiced her music harder than I ever did, I felt she was showing off. I had a couple of embarrassing memories of my own malicious acts, but not of Annie's. Even so, it wouldn't surprise me to know she'd fought with Stella. When you grow up in a violent household, you tend to lash back.

If Annie had kept a diary, I wanted to see it. "Sorry, Freeman," I muttered, "I know you told me to keep away from the Guzzos, but I'm calling Frank."

He wasn't ecstatic at hearing from me, so I spoke with extra heartiness to make up for it.

"Frank! Your mom's all over the news, so is Boom-Boom, and I'm even getting a shout-out. This is so cool—is this why you came to me? To help me with publicity?"

"I'm driving. What do you want?"

"Annie's diary. It's so amazing that it showed up like this out of the blue. Where was it all these years?"

"How should I know? I only know Ma said she found it while she was cleaning out the dresser in Annie's bedroom. No one did that after Annie died, and all those old clothes, they'd been sitting in there for twenty-five years."

"You and Betty never went in there?"

He didn't say anything. Betty hadn't seemed like the kind of person to sit idly by while someone else's possessions were waiting for a home, and Frank's long silence confirmed it.

"So after Stella went to prison, Betty went through Annie's things, took what she wanted and left the rest," I said, ignoring the indignant sputter from the other end of the phone. "Did she remember seeing this alleged diary?"

"Come on, Tori, it's been a long time ago. Betty doesn't remember one way or the other."

"Of course not." I made my tone soothing. "But you—when you looked at the diary they flashed on TV, did you recognize the handwriting? Did your heart turn over in your chest as you saw Annie's last words on the page? Did you curse Boom-Boom for terrifying your baby sister?"

Again he was quiet, so I nudged him. "Your mother did show it to you, didn't she, Frank?"

He cut the connection without saying anything. I studied my tostada. Either Frank hadn't seen the diary, or he had seen it and knew it wasn't Annie's. This wasn't evidence, nothing I could take to court, but it worked for me.

While I sat there, Melba and Harold came out of Scanlon's. I watched their slow progress down the street toward the train station, Melba clutching her handbag tightly to her side, Harold bent over his cane.

Rafael Zukos, the rabbi's son. Melba had told me to talk to him.

I finished the tostada, noticing to my annoyance that the wheat-colored jacket I'd put on for my visit to Ira Previn's office now sported a glob of green.

I patted it off with a napkin dipped in fizzy water, which left a damp patch and pilling on the lapel. Nuts.

I wiped off my fingers and looked up Rafael Zukos on my iPad. There wasn't much about him, except that he collected Japanese art, specializing in work from the middle Edo period. An article in the *Herald-Star* described an eighteenth-century painting of a geisha crossing a street that Zukos had presented to the Japanese consul.

The article also mentioned Zukos's father, Rabbi Larry Zukos, who'd led Temple Har HaShem for forty years, first on the South Side and then for eight years when they moved to Highland Park. Rafael apparently had not been called to the spiritual life, at least not to the conventionally religious life. He didn't have a listed number, but a subscription search engine gave me an address in Rogers Park on Chicago's northeast edge. There was no sign that he worked for a living. Maybe I could just drop in.

As I followed the twists of the northbound road, I'd been trying to decide what story might get Zukos to let me in. The truth was simplest. I found a parking space on Sheridan Road and left my jacket in the car. Nothing makes you look less professional than food on your clothes.

When I got to the tiny street—a mere half-block leading to Lake Michigan—I saw that Zukos had gutted the building, replacing most of the brick in the upper two stories with glass. The third floor was recessed, with glass panels leading to a wide balcony, where Zukos could stand and stare at the lake.

The building was secluded, good for privacy, good, too, for thieves, but all the right security devices were in place: cameras, laser gates, manual locks to override the electronic ones. Very sensible if Zukos's Japanese art collection was valuable.

"Yes? What do you want?"

A man was calling down from the balcony. I squinted at him but couldn't make out his face against the sun.

"I'm V. I. Warshawski. Are you Rafael Zukos? Melba Minsky suggested I talk to you."

"Rafe!" the man called, turning away.

A few minutes went by. I practiced my scales: I was terribly breathy still, but getting firmer through the diaphragm.

A man appeared around the corner of the building. He was short, stocky, balding, wearing a kind of Japanese jacket over khaki pants.

"I'm Rafe Zukos. Ken didn't get your name."

"V. I. Warshawski. Melba Minsky suggested I talk to you."

"Melba," he repeated softly. "I haven't heard from her in years, didn't know she was still alive. Harold?"

"Frail but mobile," I said. "I don't really know them—we met this morning in South Chicago."

"So they stayed south when the rest of us fled to a new reservation. They were braver than their rabbi."

"Your father was a coward, you think?" I asked.

"Jews stayed in Minsk and Slonim during pogroms, but a black family buying a house next door? You'd think a whole regiment of Cossacks was sweeping through the neighborhood. Rabbi Zukos wasn't very brave, but then, neither was I. Why did Melba send you to me?"

I gave him my story, the truth. Not the whole truth, not Frank's and my history, but Annie's murder, my cousin, trying to find out what happened at the criminal courts all those years ago.

"Melba thought you might know why Mr. Mandel assigned the case to Joel," I finished. "She thought Joel might have talked to you about the trial."

Rafe stepped back a few paces. "She did? She was wrong. I don't know what either of you hoped to gain by her sending you here."

Ken, the man who'd called down to me from the balcony. Joel. Rafe's belief he'd been a coward. These old stories, these old dramas, they wore me out. I sat on a boulder and spoke tonelessly.

"You and Joel were lovers, or at least the people at your dad's synagogue thought you were. You didn't come out directly to your father, so you think you were a coward."

"How do you know?" Rafe said fiercely.

"It's what I do for a living, Mr. Zukos, put fragments of stories together into a narrative that makes sense. I'm not always right, but I need a narrative to work with. Lies, secrets and silence. Everyone's clutching them to their chests as if there were some value in being tightly bound and fearful."

"Don't preach to me. You don't know what it was like growing up down there. The hypocrisy, the fear, not knowing who was part of what clique, who might beat you up after school because you were Jewish, or black, or a nerd who liked Japanese art."

I looked up. "I grew up near Ninetieth and Commercial, Mr. Zukos. You can't tell me much I don't know about being a child down there. My middle name is Iphigenia. Kids used to dance around me shrieking 'Iffy Genius' at me because my mother had college ambitions for me."

"It's not like being beaten up because the other boys think you're a pansy or a sissy," he said, his voice low, shaking with passion.

"Maybe not. I'm afraid my reaction was to do as much damage as possible as fast as possible to anyone mocking me, instead of following my mother's advice, which was to hold my head high and pretend it wasn't happening. And she had her share of violent bullying in Mussolini's Italy, so believe me, everyone has a hard story buried in them. Right now, today, I don't care about your private life, what you did with Joel, or didn't do. You seem to have made a good life for yourself." I waved an arm at his building. "Joel's a sad case; he lives inside a bottle, not a private art gallery."

"Joel." Zukos's lips tightened in a bitter line. "Joel didn't know who he was or what he wanted. Maybe he turned to me because he was unsure and was testing the water, although I thought he was trying to shock his father and mother: he had to be the role model for African-Americans, so that the people in the congregation who muttered against Eunice wouldn't have any grounds for saying they'd been right all along, black people were rude or dirty or criminals. He had to be a model Jew in the black world so the goyim couldn't say Jews were cheats or obsessed with money."

"Heavy load."

"I never knew what Joel wanted and he couldn't figure it out, either. I don't know what Joel looks like today, but back then he was pudgy, flabby. He was bright but the kids today would call him a geek. Girls didn't respond to him. The only reason I did—all those years ago—I needed someone. And I hated being the rabbi's model son; I could relate to Joel hating having to live up to Ira Previn's halo."

"He couldn't do what you did," I said. "Break away from the South Side, I mean—he went to Mandel & McClelland out of law school and he's still down there, working for his father. But why did he get stuck with Stella Guzzo's defense?"

A wind was starting to rise off the lake. Rafe pulled his silk jacket across his bare chest. "Joel thought Sol made him defend Stella as a punishment for being queer, although I thought it was because Joel had a crush on Annie and Sol wanted her to himself."

That startled me so much I lost my balance on the boulder and slid onto the sidewalk. "Annie was having sex with Sol Mandel?"

Zukos hunched a shoulder. "I don't know. Joel thought she was. Or he thought Mandel was a predator trying to seduce her."

"I thought your family had moved to the North Shore years before Annie was murdered. He talked to you during the trial?" I picked myself up from the sidewalk and dusted the seat of my jeans.

"Joel and I stayed in touch. For a while. Force of habit." Rafe was speaking slowly, as if the words were being squeezed from his diaphragm. "We were in the same bar mitzvah class, our parents sent us out of the neighborhood to the U of C lab school, we went off to Swarthmore together. I was doing an MFA in curatorship at the Art Institute when Joel was in law school. We'd meet for dinner and he'd whine how much he hated the law."

The wind was getting stronger. Clouds blew in, like a conjuror's trick: in an instant, the sky, which had been cornflower blue over Ira Previn's office, turned gray.

"Rafe!" Ken was leaning over the side of the balcony again. "Are you coming in or do you want me to bring down a pullover?"

Rafe looked at the sky, at me shivering—the wind was coming straight in across the water. "Come in and see the art," he offered unexpectedly.

12

BRUSH WORK

I followed him around the lake side of the building to the entrance, which opened into a living area that seemed part museum, a gold kimono dominating it from one wall, a scroll of geese taking flight on another, and in between stands holding lacquer or pottery.

The furniture was severely modern, which seemed to suit the art. I recognized an Eames chair, and supposed that the sofa, thin tan leather with chrome tube arms and legs, was also designer work. How had a rabbi's son come by the money for this?

As if he'd read my thoughts, Rafe said, "Ken's an artist—you'll see his work upstairs. I was a curator and a collector and a wannabe—it was hard to admit that my only talent lay in admiring it in others. Anyway, I was working at the Field Museum, they were doing a special exhibit on the history of calligraphy as art, and two of Ken's pieces were included. And then I had an incredible piece of luck: I recognized a *raku* pottery cup at a garage sale. Seventeenth-century work, very rare," he explained, seeing my blank expression. "I bought it for a dollar and sold it for—let's just say enough to buy this building and start collecting and selling."

I made the noises we always make when we know nothing about the subject someone else is passionately discussing. Rafe led me up a broad wood staircase, pointing out lacquer in niches along the wall. The top of the stairs opened onto Ken's studio, where Ken, in jeans and a sweatshirt, was closing the big glass doors to the balcony. Rafe went to help him and then introduced us—Kenji Aroyawa.

Rafe went to an alcove and fussed with a charcoal heater to make tea, leaving Kenji and me watching the lake through the glass window: it was starting to boil up, waves rocking back and forth, spume beginning to form.

"When it's like this, it's like Hokusai's print of *The Wave*—you've seen it? The great wave that looks as though it could swallow the world?"

"Do you try to paint the water?" I asked. "I don't know how an artist captures the motion."

"Like this." Ken turned to an easel set back from the front. He dipped a brush in a pot of ink and after a few short strokes, the water came to life on his sheet of paper.

My enchantment with seeing him work took my mind briefly from the question I'd been chewing on since Rafe's comment about Mandel and Annie.

"You like it?" Ken said.

"I'm completely blown away," I said. "I won't pretend I can make an intelligent response, though—it's the first time I've seen this kind of painting."

Ken laughed and clapped his hands.

"You brought me a new disciple, Rafe," he called. "Now sit down—what do we call you? Vic? I think Rafe has finished smelling up the place. Powdered green tea—I hate it, maybe from too many obligatory events as a child—my father was in Japan's diplomatic service—but green tea is part of Rafe's attempt to remind me I'm Japanese, or maybe to turn Japanese himself."

He gave another loud laugh, then said he assumed I wasn't with the Jehovah's Witnesses, since Rafe had spent so much time with me.

"She works with another kind of witness," Rafe said. "You know, law, courts."

Ken cocked his head at Rafe. "Is someone suing you? Do you need to put all the art in my name?"

Rafe gave a perfunctory smile. "She's a detective. She cares about a very old case where I was a witness to the torment of one of the lawyers."

"Joel?" Ken asked.

Rafe turned his teacup round and round without looking at either of us. "I believe the dead past should bury the dead, but Vic wants to dig it up. I thought someone from my father's old temple had sent her here to paw through old gossip about Joel and me, but she's after different gossip. What exactly are you hoping to learn?"

"It's that old trial," I said. "But now—I can hardly say what I do want. If you've seen the news reports, you know that Stella Guzzo is saying she found a diary her daughter kept, implicating my cousin in her murder."

"Rafe doesn't watch the news; he thinks it's vulgar," said Ken, "but I do, I know what you're talking about. Your cousin was the hockey star?"

Ken's English was accentless and idiomatic. Perhaps the result of his childhood in Japanese consulates.

"Right." I took a sip of the tea and decided I wasn't crazy about it, either. "Stella Guzzo has a long history with my family and I let her rattle me. I don't know why she's trying to prove her innocence now, instead of twenty-five years ago when she was in court, and I got obsessed with finding a copy of the trial transcript, to see if she or Joel had tried to suggest my cousin could have come to the house and—and assaulted Annie while Stella was out playing bingo."

"Someone must have a record of the trial," Rafe said impatiently.

I explained that most trials didn't have complete transcripts unless someone paid for them. "I hoped Joel's old firm had kept one, but they don't exist anymore. You talked to him while the trial was going on. Do you remember what he said—besides whining, I mean."

Rafe grimaced at my repetition of his word. "It was a long time ago and I wasn't paying attention. I kept asking Joel why he'd gone into law when he didn't like it, but he didn't have a métier of his own and it was too easy to do what Ira and Eunice wanted."

He steepled his hands, put his chin on his fingertips. "He was scared. Not of what his parents thought or wanted. Someone had frightened him. I didn't want to know about it at the time, because I thought— He and I had sex together when we were teenagers, sixteen, seventeen. It didn't last, but I thought someone was threatening to expose him, and that it could land on me. It's hard to remember now, but twenty-five years ago, public outing could kill a career. Mine, I mean. That's why I stopped listening to him. I told you I was a coward."

"No," I said, "when you're struggling to survive, no one gets to label you a coward, not even you yourself in your private thoughts."

Ken clapped my shoulder. "I like this Jehovah's Witness."

I smiled absently but spoke to Rafe. "You were afraid of exposure, so if Joel said anything that showed he feared something else, you didn't register it at the time. Think back now. What did he say, why did you realize he was afraid?"

Rafe thought for a long moment, but shook his head. "Sorry. I can't remember nuances or words from back then. Just the feeling."

"And the possibility that Annie was sleeping with Mr. Mandel?

Stella says Annie told her terrible things and that's why she beat her to death. It—I—" I shook my head, trying to clear it.

"Annie was one of my mother's pupils, she was ambitious, but young and inexperienced. Maybe Joel was right, maybe Mandel was preying on her—it's a commonplace, older man in a position of power, vulnerable young woman. But what if it was the other way around? What if Stella was right about this one thing?"

"That justifies her killing her own child?" Ken was scornful.

"Of course not," I said impatiently. "Nothing justifies that, not even Stella's claim that Annie attacked her. I can't explain it—it's twisted up in my childhood, my memories of my mother, my cousin—"

I broke off, unable to put it into words, and even a bit embarrassed at blurting it out in front of these two strangers.

"I want to see the diary Stella claims she found," I finally said. "It seems too pat that it showed up right after I went to see her. If she knew about it during the trial, why didn't Joel use it in her defense?"

"Yes, Vic, but what if Annie wrote about Joel in it?" Ken suggested shrewdly. "He wouldn't want his bosses or the judge and so on to read it."

"You're right. He enters it into evidence and it's a public record, everyone in Chicago gets to know that he—what? Is harassing Annie? That she's making fun of him? If it painted him in any kind of un-flattering light, he was so morbidly sensitive he couldn't bear the humiliation of it being made public. Maybe that's what he was afraid of—does that ring a bell with you, Rafe?"

Zukos flung up his hands, annoyed. "You mean, did anything he said back then make me think he knew about a diary? I can't possibly remember. But was he so sensitive he wouldn't use a document that betrayed his private feelings? Yes, I can believe that."

So if Stella had found the diary before the trial, Joel might have persuaded her to keep it quiet on the grounds that laundering Guzzo family business in public would harm her. It made a certain sense.

"Also, I can't picture the way my cousin is being painted in this lurid picture. He was reckless and attractive and a lot of women went for him, but I can't see him threatening a woman the way Stella's claiming is in Annie's diary."

"You think it's a fraud?" Ken asked.

"Yes, even though your argument makes good sense. However, I don't understand one thing about the trial, about Mandel & McClelland involving Joel, about Stella doing her time and now trying to get exonerated. Maybe Rafe's right: I've been like Ahab chasing a great white whale of paper, and it's time to let it go."

When I got up to leave, Ken went back to his easel. He added a few more strokes, which made it look as though a leaflet was in the waves, the pages blowing so that you could imagine they formed the wide-open mouth of a whale.

I laughed, but I knew that in the morning I would be going back to Jeffery Avenue to talk to Joel Previn again. Early, before he fell into the Pot of Gold.

13

BUY ME SOME PEANUTS

As it turned out, Joel was able to get quite a long lead on his vodka the next day. After leaving Rafe and Ken, I drove to my office, where I learned that the media obsession with Boom-Boom's alleged involvement with Annie Guzzo hadn't abated. A car was parked in my space in the lot by my building, meaning I had to pay to use a meter on the street. When I walked over to confront the driver, he jumped out with a handheld mike and a video cam. Another crew emerged from the coffee bar across the street.

The guy in my parking space shoved his mike into my nose. "Les Fioro with Global, Vic. How do you feel about these accusations?"

I backed away. "Sorry, what accusations?"

Another mike appeared—the people from the coffee bar were piggybacking onto Les's interview.

"Your cousin, wasn't he?" the second mike said.

"My cousin? What cousin?"

"Haven't you seen the news? Stella Guzzo is claiming your cousin killed her daughter," Les said.

I shook my head. "My cousin has been dead for a good decade now. I doubt he's come back as a zombie to murder anyone."

Les was getting exasperated. "This happened before he died."

"Ah, that would explain it," I said.

"So how do you feel about it?" the second mike demanded.

"I still don't know what you're talking about."

I went to the front door to type in the code, but Les wasn't so easily put off. He came up behind me, telling me about Annie's murder, and Stella's claims. I dropped my briefcase and when I stood up with it, knocked the mike out of his hands.

"I'm sorry," I said, smiling. "I didn't realize you were standing so close to me. I hope it still works."

The second mike retreated to the street: I was too unstable to waste more time with. I retyped the code and went inside while Les was chasing the mike, which had rolled to the curb.

I stood with the door open a few inches. "Mr. Fioro, my first phone call is going to be to a towing service: you are in a space that is clearly marked as reserved for tenants. Unless you want to pay towing fees, move your car."

Once in my office, I scrubbed the avocado off my jacket as best I could, but the lapel of the wheat-colored linen now had a green cast to it. It can always get worse, I reminded myself, so don't curse what's already gone wrong. At least the tostada had been light and crisp, the vegetables fresh, the beans homemade.

I opened my file on Stella and tried to type in what I'd learned today. Not much of anything. I couldn't see a trial transcript, no one knew if she'd been going to blame Boom-Boom in court when he was still alive and could sue for slander, no one knew why Sol Mandel made the hapless Joel defend her.

I'd told young Bernadine that I was going to get information but so far, the score was Stella ten, V.I. nothing. Or maybe one: I did have one new fact: Mr. Mandel's first name had been Sol. And I knew, or at least was pretty sure of, another: that the diary hadn't been in the Guzzo house twenty-five years ago.

I wanted to see it myself, so badly I began imagining ways to break into Stella's and look at it. Really poor idea, V.I., let it go.

I still wanted to shoot Stella, but it was time to move on. However, when I logged onto my server, the media inquiries were sprinkled with fretful messages from clients. Had my cousin been involved in murder? Was I covering it up? That seemed to be the common theme, although some had an avid curiosity covered by a thin veneer of concern, what could they do to help, and what had Boom-Boom done, really? I could trust them.

I put on a big grin and started returning calls—yes, I'm an upbeat, problem-solving professional and your affairs are safe in my hands. No murderers anywhere.

When I'd taken care of the most urgent calls, I went into Lexis-Nexis for some background on Nina Quarles, current owner of the Mandel & McClelland firm. Quarles had apparently seen the firm as an investment opportunity, despite the violent neighborhood and the nearly nonexistent income of the client base. The firm mostly handled wills and real estate matters for people like Melba and Harold Minsky, petitioned for orders of protection against people like me. No, just joking—mostly against violent domestic partners. They also handled criminal defense for people with enough money for a private lawyer.

I couldn't believe that kind of business generated enough income to support a woman like Nina Quarles in her travel and shopping habits, but when I looked up her personal profile, I saw she had other resources. She'd grown up on the East Side, only child of Felicia

Burzle and Norman Quarles, a guy who'd had a successful business manufacturing brakes for freight cars.

Both her parents were dead and her trust fund would keep her in Givenchy and Armani for another two or three hundred years, even if she bought a new outfit every day. This didn't explain why she'd bought the firm, but maybe McClelland had put her trust together and she'd felt sentimental about it. I shrugged and shut down my system.

I was turning out the lights when a call came in from Natalie Clements in the Cubs media department. Her young voice was vibrating with cheer. "Ms. Warshawski? I'm sorry it took me so long to get back to you, but we do have a few photographs of Boom-Boom Warshawski at Wrigley Field. Mr. Drechen says you can come up to see them when it's convenient for you, as long as it isn't a game day."

I'd forgotten about going to the Cubs in an effort to double-check Frank's story about the tryouts. Now I wondered if it was really worth it, but the publicity crew at Wrigley seemed to be the only people willing to help me. It would be churlish to say I'd lost interest: I told her I'd stop by first thing in the morning.

Bernie was still asleep when I left the next day. She'd announced when she came home last night that she'd found a job at a Bucktown coffee bar. I hoped she hadn't been hired for the early shift.

No one bothered me when I cautiously looked out my front door. The media vultures, who'd still been hovering last night outside my building, had finally gotten bored.

When I got to Wrigley Field, crews were hard at work getting ready for an upcoming home stand. They were doing everything from bringing in supplies to testing the PA system. Food vendors were lined up along Clark, unloading through the big doors. Behind them was a fleet of beer trucks. I'm not much of a beer drinker at the best of times; the sight of so much of it, so early in the morning, made me queasy.

Bagby Haulage, the outfit Frank Guzzo drove for, had a truck there, too, parked along Addison. I'd thought they were local to the far South Side, but they clearly were bigger than I'd imagined if they had a contract with someone who served the Cubs. It would be a cruel punishment for Frank, if he had to ferry peanuts or Cracker Jacks to the ballpark where he'd hoped to play. I craned my neck to see who was in the cab, but the truck was empty.

Natalie Clements had left a pass for me with the security staff at the main gate. As I hiked up the ramps to the floor with the press offices, I passed the crews moving their loads of food and souvenirs into the storage caves behind the vending booths.

The belly of Wrigley wasn't pretty. Work lamps were hooked under low-sloping ceilings. There were small cracks in the concrete, and the massive cables that fed the stadium's power were attached to the outside of the weight-bearing columns, snaking along floors and walls— it would have cost too much to break into the concrete and install them out of sight.

Before going into Natalie Clements's office, I went to the doorway leading to the stands. A team was hosing down the seats, collecting trash they'd missed after the last home game. The grounds crew would have been out already at first light, but they were finicking around the pitcher's mound, getting the slope the way tomorrow's starter liked it.

The grass was greener than it had been a week ago. The thick vines along the outfield wall were starting to turn green. I was facing the bleachers, where Boom-Boom and I used to climb the back wall and scramble into the seats—after sneaking onto the L by shinnying up the girders. We didn't have any pocket money, but I guess that's no excuse for a life of crime. I was still committing cons and crimes, I suppose, since I was letting Natalie Clements think I was writing my cousin's biography.

I followed the ramps to the section where the press offices lay. They were cubbyholes, really, since every cubic inch in a ballpark needs to generate revenue. Natalie Clements introduced me to her boss, Will Drechen, who told me he hadn't thought at first that they'd kept any of the pictures from that particular day.

"I happened to mention your project to my old boss when I went to see him last night. He's been retired a long time, but he was a big fan of your cousin," Drechen added. "He'd found these when he was going through old files."

Drechen had the photos laid out on a tabletop. One showed Boom-Boom on the field, clowning around with Mitch Williams, who'd been a wild man on the mound, equally terrifying to fans and opponents. Boom-Boom's face was alive with the excitement I'd seen a thousand times, whenever he was doing something high-risk. It was such a vivid photo I thought if I turned around my cousin might be standing behind me.

Natalie said, "Mr. Villard, he's the gentleman who had the photos, he used to handle community relations, he said when Boom-Boom couldn't come close to hitting Mitch Williams, Boom-Boom said it was because he was used to being in the penalty box for having his stick up that high."

"Sounds like him," I agreed.

I busied myself with the rest of the array to hide an unexpected spasm of grief. Seeing Boom-Boom's face so filled with vitality, hearing my cousin's words, the loss suddenly felt recent, not a decade old.

The pictures included three shots from inside the dugout. Frank was seated halfway down the bench, his face just visible behind Andre Dawson: the great right-fielder was leaning over to talk to my cousin, who was sitting at the end farthest from the field. Poor Frank. No wonder he felt bitter. No wonder he'd whiffed the curve.

I said, "It must have been hard on the guys who came to try out to have Boom-Boom in the spotlight there. Do you know if any of them actually got picked up by the franchise?"

Drechen bent over a group photo. All the men were in the uniforms of the amateur teams they played for. I could see the "Ba" from Bagby on the front of Frank's warm-up jacket. Frank's head was up, shoulders back, but his expression was fierce—a man holding back tears. The picture must have been taken after the guys had their chance.

Drechen said, "This guy back here"—he tapped the face of a man in the second row—"he played a season for us in Nashville, but he couldn't adjust to the pros. We sent him to a development squad the next year, but he quit before the season was over. The rest of them, sadly, no. Open tryouts are like that. Every now and then you find that diamond in the rough, but we chiefly hold them because it's good community relations. Fans give their heart and soul to this franchise and we want it to be a welcoming place for them."

"Ever get any women at your open tryouts?" I asked.

"Every now and then," Drechen said. "You want a shot?"

"If my cousin couldn't hit major league pitching when he was at his peak, no way do I have a fantasy about doing it myself. Although a chance to stand on that turf—let me know the next time you're holding them."

Drechen laughed, said he understood I was writing a biography of Boom-Boom; they'd be glad to get me permission to use the pictures.

"The one of Boom-Boom with Mitch Williams, I'd like a copy of that for myself if it's possible. The rest, I'll let you know when I get that far."

I left, offering a shower of thanks, before Drechen or Natalie could ask me for the name of a publisher or a publication date. On my way out, I stopped to study the pictures along the walls. Great moments in Cubs history covered everything from the time they brought elephants onto the field to Wrigley's "League of Their Own" team in the 1940s.

I slowly followed the ramp back down to the ground, sidling past a forklift hoisting a crew up to do something with an overhead pipe, almost getting run over by a motorized cart hauling beer kegs. When I got outside, it was a relief to be in the open air, away from the dank pipes and the smell of beer.

I was at the corner of Clark and Addison when I heard my name called; it was Natalie Clements from the press office, breathless from running down the stairs.

She held out a folder to me. "I was hoping I'd catch you—I made a print of your cousin for you. And Will wanted to give you a pass to next week's game against New York."

She darted back inside on my thanks, running in high heels without tripping, which ought to be an Olympic event. I walked along, bent over my cousin's face, and ran into someone.

"Sorry!" I looked up, smiling my apologies.

The man I'd bumped scowled and growled at me in a thick Slavic accent. "Watch where you put your feet."

It wasn't his hard-lined, cold-eyed face that wiped the smile from my mouth, but his companion: a short wide man who bore an amazing resemblance to Danny DeVito.

"Uncle Jerry," I exclaimed.

"Who told you my name?" Uncle Jerry glanced involuntarily at the hard-faced man.

"No one. That's what the woman you were with called you when I saw you in the church."

"I wasn't in church." He looked again at the other man, whose eyes seemed even colder.

I don't like to see people in fear, even rude angry men. "I must be confusing you with someone else," I agreed.

"What church Jerry was in?" the hard-faced man asked. His syntax was Slavic but his accent was gravel in any language.

"I said I mistook him for someone else," I said. "Let's all just get on with our day, okay?"

"What woman he was talking to?"

"I don't know," I said. "I don't know you, I don't know him, I don't need this interrogation for the simple misdemeanor of not looking where I was going."

"You know his name is Jerry. Where are you meeting him?"

"Tell you what," I suggested. "You give me your name and tell me why you want to know, and I'll answer the question."

"When I ask question, I expect answer, no smart broads making funny. Got that?"

He bent over me, breathing garlic down my shirt. Beads of sweat stood out on Uncle Jerry's forehead and my own throat felt tight, as if I were being strangled. I started to cross Clark, but the man grabbed my shoulder in a steel grip. I kicked hard against his exposed shin and twisted away, running into Clark Street.

Cars honked and swerved around me. Mr. Gravel-voice was trying to get at me but the street was lively with cabs; one stopped when I pounded on the door.

"Drive around the ballpark," I said. "I want to see which way those two creeps are going."

"He going to shoot me?" the cabbie asked, watching Gravel stick a hand inside his jacket.

"He's going to realize he's in the middle of a busy street with a thousand cops around him."

The cabbie accelerated and turned left across the northbound traffic. As we turned, I saw a cop blowing a furious whistle at Gravel, forcing him back to the sidewalk. Hands on his hips, Gravel swiveled to keep an eye on the cab I was in.

I lost sight of him when we turned up Sheffield. The cabbie made the next left onto Waveland. I stopped him at the corner, handed him a ten for the three-dollar fare, stopped a cab from a different company and got him to drive me back down to the corner I'd just left. We were in time to see Gravel and Uncle Jerry climb into the Bagby truck. I took pictures as best I could from the moving taxi, but photos couldn't begin to convey the menace in Gravel's face or the fear in Uncle Jerry's.

14

EJECTED

Joel was actually at his desk when I got to Ira's office, typing on an old-model Dell. One thing about habitual heavy drinkers, they can stay upright and even function when the rest of us would be comatose. Ira wasn't there, but Eunice was talking with an African-American woman around her own age. They were going through a thick stack of documents, checking them against an old calendar.

Eunice had buzzed me in, but her face was stiff with disapproval. Joel wasn't ecstatic at seeing me, either.

"Are you here to nag some more about Stella? I told you yesterday that I know I fucked up her defense. There's nothing else to say."

He spoke loudly, belligerently, and Eunice froze in the middle of her own conversation.

"Joel, please take Ms. Warshawski into the office. Mrs. Eldridge's affairs are complicated and we need quiet to focus on them."

Joel muttered under his breath that he wasn't a baby, he was tired of being bossed around, but he got to his feet and clumped his way to a small room at the back, not bothering to see if I was following.

"Well?" He stood just inside the door, arms folded across his chest, the edges of his full cheeks stained red.

"I talked to Melba Minsky yesterday and she sent me to Rafael Zukos."

The red spread across his face. "Melba Minsky, she always was a goddam buttinsky. Minsky Buttinsky. She tell you the boy wonder's amazing success stories, or did she fill your head with smutty gossip?"

"Neither." Joel was blocking the visitor's chair. I went around and sat behind the desk, facing him as his father must often have done. "All she said was that you and Rafe were in the same bar mitzvah class. Rafe told me—other things."

Joel looked behind him at his mother, who couldn't help turning around to send him an anguished glance. He closed the door and plopped heavily onto the visitor's chair.

"Did you come here to threaten to tell Eunice and Ira those things?"

I shook my head. "Mr. Previn, your private business is no concern of mine, your parents or any other soul on the planet. Not unless your private business involved concealing evidence in Stella's murder trial."

A glaze of sweat covered his face, as if glass had been poured over it. The vodka, the fear, they were hammering his heart; he would be dead before Ira if he didn't change soon.

When he didn't speak, I said, "This diary of Annie Guzzo's— when did you first learn about it?"

"On the news two nights ago." His voice was thick—another sign of fear, or of lying? On the TV shows, the FBI or the con artist always can tell by body language, or the way the eyes are moving, when someone is lying, but it actually isn't that simple.

"Stella didn't bring it up when you were prepping her for her trial?"

"What are you getting at?"

"This diary. Is it real?"

"How should I know?" he said sullenly. "You think she's smart enough to invent a diary? She never seemed that bright to me, the way she carried on in court no matter how many times I or Mr. Mandel or the judge told her it made her look out of control."

"She's angry and volatile, but not stupid. You were in love with Annie Guzzo."

"That's a goddam lie! Who told you that? Minsky Buttinsky?"

"I learned it from you. From the way you talked about her yesterday. What no one can understand is why you agreed to defend her killer. I know you were pushed into it by Sol Mandel, but he must have had quite a substantial club to hold over your head. Rafe told me he knew you were afraid, but he didn't know of what—he assumed you were afraid someone was going to reveal that you and he had a few boyhood liaisons. But it wasn't that, was it?"

He glared at me, the same look he gave his mother: angry, impotent.

"You'd seen the diary, and Annie had made fun of you. You were terrified that Stella would—"

"That's not true! I never saw a diary, Annie never made fun of me, she knew I admired her, she knew I wasn't out to hurt her. Not like some of the others."

"Who in the office was hurting her?" I asked. "Mr. Mandel?"

"Oh, Mandel!" Joel made a dismissive gesture. "She knew he was an old goat wanting to act like he was still a young stud, she let him kiss her, he gave her money to help with her college fund, it was a game to her."

"She blackmail him?"

"Annie wasn't a criminal," Joel cried. "Don't make it sound dirty when it wasn't."

"Of course she wasn't a criminal. She was a young woman with a big dream and no resources. She was getting help where she could find it. How much money did he give her?"

"I don't know. I saw him one night when I was working late, she was in his office and I saw him kissing her, and then I went to the john and he was slipping something into the photocopier. I looked on my way back—it was a hundred dollars, and then Annie came out to copy something a minute later, and she stuffed the money into her purse. I never said anything to her, but I could see it was like a game to her."

That meant that if anyone had been afraid of a possible diary becoming public knowledge, it should have been Mandel, not Joel. But Joel had been afraid during the trial, at least according to Rafe.

I thought back to yesterday's conversation. "Spike Hurlihey? Is he the person you were afraid of during the trial? What did he know about you that you wanted kept a secret?"

"Nothing," Joel said thickly. "Nothing, because there was nothing to know."

"Were you afraid he was going to talk about you and Rafe?"

"Spike didn't know about me and Rafe because we were at University High and he was down at Saint Eloy's. I represented Stella because Mandel and Mr. McClelland told me to."

"Didn't that make you wonder?"

Joel's sullen expression deepened. "I figured Mandel felt ashamed of giving Annie money. I thought he was afraid Stella would start asking questions, or bring up Annie's—Annie's behavior. Stella cared more about sex than anything, she couldn't stop being angry about the way Annie attracted men. I couldn't get her to shut up about it, it was why she was so hard to defend."

"Everything you're saying explains why Mandel might have been nervous during Stella's trial. Not why you were, or why you agreed to take the case."

"Everything you're saying explains why you and Melba Minsky hit it off. You don't have any grounds for asking me questions and I do not have to answer them."

The words were brave but the tone was querulous, not confident. He looked around involuntarily, not at his mother but as if he feared an eavesdropper.

"Of course you don't. But whatever happened to you at the Mandel & McClelland offices has been haunting you for a long time. If you told me about it, it's possible that I could make it go away. Assuming you aren't hiding a crime."

His cheeks turned red again and he stumbled to his feet. "Whatever you think you're implying, you are way out of line. Get out. Get away from Ira's desk and go mind your own fucking business."

I got away from Ira's desk. Eunice was wrapping up her appointment with Mrs. Eldridge as I passed back through the main room. She gestured at me to wait. She helped the client into her coat, escorted her to the door, assured her that they were always happy to help, she knew Mrs. Eldridge was carrying a load too heavy for one woman and that's what she and Ira were there for, to share the load.

She wasn't nearly as gracious when she came back to me. "I don't approve of Joel's language, but I do share his sentiment. Annie Guzzo died a long time ago. So did your cousin. Let them all rest in peace, let Stella Guzzo alone. She can't do you any harm. There's no reason for you to keep coming around here."

"You're probably right," I agreed. "But do you know what Joel was so afraid of that he agreed to represent Stella?"

"Leave now, Ms. Warshawski."

She stared at me implacably until I left.

15

INTO THE GAP

Who had held Joel's feet to a fire that scared him worse than Stella? I hoped it wasn't Spike Hurlihey—the Illinois Speaker had a phalanx of protectors around him thicker than any wall I could penetrate.

I bet that Eunice knew, or at least guessed. The way she dismissed me—Joel might be a worry and a disappointment, but he was still her tiger cub, she was still protecting him. I also bet that I could bring down Spike Hurlihey before I persuaded Eunice to confide in me.

Joel came out of the office while I was brooding over his unknown sins. He didn't see me, but beetled straight to the Pot of Gold. My stomach turned: I had browbeaten him and he was turning to his tried-and-true consolation, the Grey Goose.

I thought of the scroll hanging in Rafe Zukos's living room, the geese in flight. Rafe, the boy wonder, Joel had bitterly called him. Rafe had moved far away from his unhappy South Side adolescence, the geese in flight, but Joel had been pulled earthward by some unhappy mix of family history, personal issues. Maybe Stella Guzzo's trial, as well.

Joel was sure Spike hadn't known about his and Rafe's sexual fumblings, but bullies have a way of sniffing out secrets, or at least their targets' weaknesses. As Rafe had reminded me yesterday, twenty-five years ago, even a whiff that a lawyer was gay could have derailed a career. Spike could have taunted Joel with the possibility—but twenty-five years ago, Spike was still a pretty young lawyer himself. He wasn't in charge of the office, Mandel and McClelland were, so no matter how much tormenting Spike did, he wasn't the person who decided what cases the firm took or who the partners assigned them to. How had it happened? That was what no one could tell me.

I was like someone trying to get over a video game addiction: just one more hand and I'll give it up for good. One more conversation and I would let the Guzzos pickle in their own brine. I'd spoken to Stella's current priest, to her trial lawyer, to the manager at the firm that had taken over Mandel's practice. And I'd spoken to her son. I hadn't talked to Betty, the woman Frank left me for when we were back in high school. I hadn't seen the restraining order yet, but I didn't think it included Stella's daughter-in-law.

My route to the East Side, where Frank and Betty lived with her father, took me past the west side of St. Eloy's, the side where the school and the playing fields stood. Boys were playing baseball. I stopped to look. These were high school teams, St. Eloy in silver, the visitors from St. Jerome in scarlet.

The bleachers were full of kids and parents from the two schools. It was the parents who were engaged by the action on the field; the kids were mostly listening to their devices rather than watching the action. Father Cardenal was in the front row, clapping enthusiastically.

St. Jerome's was batting in the top of the third. The first batter reached on a routine single, the second hit a sacrifice fly to right field, but when the third kid hit a line drive headed to left field, the St. Eloy's shortstop leapt into the gap, lay almost horizontal in midair to make the catch, and turned to double up the kid on second.

As St. Eloy's trotted off the field, his teammates pounded the shortstop's back, knocking his cap off. I didn't need to see the crown of red-gold hair to know this was Frank's son. It wasn't just the grin, like his father's at the same age, but those fluid moves.

Frank had covered the gap like that at sixteen. My stomach twisted. No wonder he was bitter, and wistful, seeking vindication through his son. It might happen, too, if young Frank got the right coaching, if he caught the eye of the right scouts, if he didn't injure himself, if he continued to mature—if all the imponderables of luck and talent came together in him, Frank was right, his son had a ticket out of South Chicago, to college for sure, maybe even to the show.

The priest got up from his seat to fist-bump the kids, then started climbing the stands. I picked up the sweet-acrid smell of weed a second after he had, and saw the users bunched together on the top row. I watched the comedy play out, the desperate extinguishing of roaches, the taking of names, the promises of detention. Cardenal stayed up on the top of the stands, rummaging in the boys' backpacks, while St. Eloy's took the field. As he looked around he caught sight of me.

"*Hola*, Detective, come on up and sit down."

He was messing with his dopers by calling me a detective, but I threaded my way up through the rows of students and parents.

"What should I do with these children smoking on my school yard?" the priest asked, jovially grabbing one of them by his shirt collar. "Set up a trace on their bank accounts, find out who they're buying from and selling to?"

"You're confusing me with the FBI, padre. I can't do magic tricks with people's money."

"Ah, but you could follow them, right?" He slapped their shoulders. "Keep an eye behind you, this is one crafty detective. We never know whether she's going to be on the North Side or the South Side, so you have to look in both directions."

I didn't say anything: I didn't want to be part of his intimidation scheme. He let the boys sweat for a beat or two, then said, "So, Detective, come with me, tell me about your North Side investigations."

I followed him back to the ground, looking at the action on the field while he stopped to talk to parents and children. I was hoping young Frankie would come to the plate while I was there, but St. Eloy's already had an out and Frankie was still in the dugout.

When Cardenal finished glad-handing, he took me a short way away from the stands. "What is it you really want down here, Detective?"

I looked at him steadily. "Some slice of the truth, padre."

"But which slice? And what do you plan to do with it?"

"Certainly not intimidate a bunch of high school kids. If they are drug-dealing gangbangers, they belong to the cops. If they're bored, undermotivated kids with no future, you can do more for them than I can."

"Oh—those boys up there. Yes, they're a worrying problem all right. If they're bored and undermotivated then they will inevitably become gangbangers. That's why I don't expel them for smoking dope in the ballpark—I don't want to move them faster into gangland than they're already going. I don't expect you to take them on. I'm more interested in why you are looking at people in my church and then up at Wrigley Field."

I stared. "Who— Oh. Uncle Jerry? He complained to you?"

"'Uncle Jerry'?" Cardenal repeated. "He didn't tell me you were a relative."

"I don't know his real name," I said. "The first time I saw him, he was expostulating with a young woman; she called him 'Uncle Jerry.' I bumped into him this morning, quite literally. It was only five or six hours ago, but it's fascinating that he came running to you. What did he say?"

"He says you taunted him about being in church."

"Taunted?" I gaped. "I reminded him that we'd seen each other at Saint Eloy's. I couldn't find the utility closet when I was trying to stow your ladder; I lugged it all over the place and ended up in the church, where Jerry was arguing with a young woman. This morning, Jerry claimed he'd never been in church. He seemed terrified of the guy he was with, so when he denied all knowledge of Saint Eloy's, I let it go."

I pulled out my phone and opened the photo I'd taken of Jerry and Gravel. "This Uncle Jerry?"

Cardenal peered over the screen. "Yes, that's Jerry. The other guy I don't know. Who is he?"

I shook my head. "No idea. Who is Jerry?"

Cardenal paused before answering, as if trying to decide whether I wanted him to violate the confessional. "Jerry Fugher. He sometimes works on the electrics for us. He's a kind of handyman, I guess. I don't think he has a regular job, although his work for us is always good enough. Not creative, but functional, if you know what I mean. Maybe Bagby hires him to take care of wiring on the trucks."

"What was he doing at Wrigley?"

"I didn't ask," Cardenal said, his tone reproving. "When I told him you were a detective, he became quite angry, wanting to know who hired you to stalk him. So you can see why I want to know your real business. Did you come to this church last week looking for him?"

"I didn't think paranoia was an infectious condition, but you seem to have caught it from him. I have no interest in Jerry Fugher. My business down here is just that: *my* business. My cousin, remember? Stella Guzzo slandered him all over Chicago. Which brings me to a question for you: Did she give you this infamous diary for safekeeping?"

"If she did, that would not be any business of yours."

"Have you seen this diary?" I said, impatient. "I'd like to know if it looks convincingly like a twenty-five-year-old document."

"What does that mean?"

"A forensic expert would have to test the age of the paper, but there are a few simple things. Like, if it's in a 'Princess Fiona' book, it's definitely a forgery."

A teacher came over to claim Cardenal's attention: a fight had broken out behind the stands between a couple of boys from St. Eloy's and a group from St. Jerome's. I stopped at the home plate fence for a last look at the field. St. Eloy's was still batting with one on and two out. Frankie was on deck. The batter ahead of him dribbled a ball back toward the mound, which should have been a routine out, but this was high school; the pitcher bobbled the throw and both runners were safe.

Frankie stepped up to the plate and the St. Eloy students and parents came to life, shrieking, stomping, yelling encouragement. The loudest cheers came from a heavy woman in the front row wearing a St. Eloy's cap and warm-up jacket.

She screamed at me to get out of the way. "Do you own this ballpark? No one can see over your fat head."

I backed away to the side of the stands. Frankie took strike one and a collective groan rose from the spectators.

The woman kept yelling. "Keep steady, Frankie, make him throw your pitch, he doesn't have an arm, he has an old sock sewn to his shoulder."

The women on either side of her were laughing and encouraging her. "You tell him, Betty! Frankie, listen to your ma, get us a hit!"

Betty Pokorny? I gaped at her. She'd put on thirty or forty pounds since high school, but it was her face that had changed. When I'd known her, she'd had soft round cheeks framed by light brown curls. Somewhere along the way she'd started bleaching her hair until now it hung in pale ropes to her shoulders. She had deep grooves along her mouth and in her forehead. Too much worry, too many cigarettes, maybe a few too many beers, too.

Frankie popped up while I was staring at her. One of her neighbors nudged her and pointed at me.

"What are you looking at?" she called. "You think your boy can outhit my boy?"

I shook my head, held up my hands, universal sign of peace, I don't want any trouble, but the two women next to her were egging her on. Don't let a St. Jerome's mother dis your boy, and so on.

Betty started to her feet, fists clenched.

I went over to her. "Betty: it's V. I. Warshawski. I stopped to watch Frankie—he's an amazing—"

She slapped me before I could finish the sentence. "You?" she screeched. "I *knew* it, knew you'd never forgive me for stealing Big Frank from you. You've been up there on the North Side all these years, plotting—"

"No!" I roared.

She stopped shouting, but stood clenching and unclenching her fingers. Her two friends eyed her uneasily. They liked a shouting match but not a fight.

Other parents began yelling at us to shut up: "We didn't come to watch two old broads fight." "We're here to watch our boys." "Shut up!" "Get out of the way."

I took Betty's arm and hustled her away from the stands, to the back where Father Cardenal was dealing with the remnants of the fight he'd been summoned to break up.

16

BRUSH BACK

"You never did forgive me for stealing Frank," Betty repeated, but uncertainly, as if she didn't really believe it.

"You two broke my heart," I agreed, "but it mended. I only stopped here today to see your son play. Frank told me he thought he might go all the way and—"

"So you have been sneaking around with Frank behind my back!"

It was the tiredness in her face that kept me from losing my temper, the heavy lines that I'd seen on the faces of my classmates' mothers when I was growing up. She wouldn't have wanted my pity, but poverty is an unrelenting taskmaster.

"Didn't Frank tell you? He hired me to try to help Stella with her exoneration claim. Which only led to her slandering Boom-Boom, and then slapping me with a restraining order. We have been having fun without you, I suppose."

"He hired you without talking to me? And me, trying to pay the bills and raise the kids on what he brings home from Bagby? Where's that money supposed to come from? Stella's right—you and your mother, you live to ruin our lives."

"I hadn't thought about you in years, Betty, not until Frank came to me two weeks ago. Sounds as though you and Stella are pretty close, though. I'm surprised—I didn't think you wanted her moving in with you when she came home from prison."

"I'm looking after enough people with my dad, the kids, Frank, I don't need Stella. But that doesn't mean I don't respect her for standing up for her beliefs."

"What beliefs?" I asked. "She has some moral code I don't know about?"

"No, you wouldn't," Betty said scornfully. "You're the one who encouraged Annie to go on the Pill, to sleep around, all that stuff. If she hadn't hung out around you and your mother, she never would have carried on the way she did."

"Carried on how?"

"She was like you: she'd go after anything in pants. Maybe Stella reacted too hard, but if either of my girls goes on the Pill and I learn about it, I'll be just as mad as Stella was."

"You'll kill your kids? It's an interesting riff on safe sex. You think Stella was right to murder Annie?"

Betty reddened. "You're twisting my words! Of course not. I'm just saying Annie wasn't the little saint you and your mother thought."

Out of the corner of my eye I could see Father Cardenal looking at us. I was afraid he might interrupt, but the mother of one of the kids he'd been dealing with started shouting at him and he turned back to the other fight.

"How did you know Annie was on the Pill? Did she tell you?"

"Goddam right she did. Frank and me, we were married, Lucy was two and I was pregnant with Kelly—Frank Junior, he was my third before the two youngest girls. Anyway, Annie came over to watch Lucy for me while I went to the store. You never were pregnant, were you? That's how you kept your figure, but babies take a toll, so I mentioned my sore back. And little Miss Priss says, 'You ever hear of birth control?' showing off her packet. Like this."

Betty picked up a twig and dangled it between her thumb and forefinger. "I wanted to smack her, she was so smug and smirky. 'Don't you know it's a mortal sin to take those pills?' I said. I tried to grab them from her but she laughed, stuck them in her purse.

" 'I'm going to Philadelphia to college,' she says. 'No one's going to tie me down with a baby and a husband. Mortal sins and coal dust, they're both about as useful as Daddy's pension.' Mateo Guzzo's pension disappeared along with everyone else's when the steel company went bankrupt," Betty added.

"Did Annie say who she was sleeping with?" I held my breath, hoping Betty would say Joel or Sol Mandel or even Spike Hurlihey.

"I asked who the lucky boy was and she got this look on her face, you know, like she's *Cosmo*'s sex adviser. 'No boys for me. They're too young, they don't know how to treat women.' That's how I knew it was Boom-Boom, because he was the only older man she was close to."

I opened and shut my mouth without speaking. Annie had been close to my dad, and to Sol Mandel, and maybe to the other partner at the law firm, but I didn't want to add to the muck Betty was carrying in her head.

Betty was still ranting. "Of course I told Frank about it and we agreed Stella should know. I mean, Annie wasn't even going to be eighteen for another month!"

The field and stands seemed to shimmer behind me. Frank, coming to me, not telling me about that conversation? What a total fuckup, him, Stella, the whole situation.

"You told Stella. Is that why she had her final big blowup with Annie? Is that why Annie had to die?"

Betty's chin jutted out in a major-league scowl. "You can't say things like that! It's not my fault if Stella went off the deep end. I thought she had a right to know, a right as a mother. She went through Annie's dresser. Besides the pills, she found an envelope with two thousand dollars in it!"

"I hope neither of you is imagining Boom-Boom paid Annie to sleep with him. He was pushing women away with his hockey stick in hotel lobbies all over North America."

Betty bunched up her lips. "Stella took the money. When Mr. Guzzo's pension disappeared it was hard for her to keep up the mortgage payments, and for Annie just to sit on that cash! Me and Frank had to live with my folks, trying to save something extra for a house, which you don't do when you've got a baby and another one coming. Annie thought she was so much better than us, going off to some East Coast college. Just like you she was, sleeping with anyone and everyone, flaunting her education."

I couldn't tell which the real grievance was—sex or education. Maybe both. "Did Annie reveal where the money came from?"

"Stella demanded, she had a right to know, and Annie said Mr. Mandel gave it to her, a present to help with college. And Stella asked what special favors Mr. Mandel asked for to help send Annie away. Annie slapped her, can you believe that? Hitting her own mother? So Stella had to fight back. It went on and on, night after night, the fighting, the shouting—the Jokiches even called the police—until the night, well, the night Annie died."

"Don't you see? If it was Mandel who gave Annie the money, then *he* was the older man in her life, not Boom-Boom."

"She was so promiscuous, who knows how many people she took her pants off for," Betty spat.

Her rage and her obsession with Annie's sex life seemed to swirl around like a cloud of gnats, annoying but impossible for me to come to grips with.

"Who told you Annie slapped Stella?" I asked instead.

"Stella, of course. Annie would never admit she did one wrong thing in her life. And then of course the night she died she actually came at Stella with a kitchen knife."

"Or so Stella claimed," I said dryly. "If Stella went through Annie's things hunting for her pills, why didn't she find the diary when she found the two thousand dollars? Did you see the diary when you were searching Annie's clothes after the trial?"

"What do you mean, searching?" Betty's face quivered.

I meant she probably hoped there was another envelope full of cash. "Looking for mementos," I suggested hastily. "Even if you had your differences, she was your husband's sister, you must have wanted a keepsake."

Betty still looked suspicious, but she said, "I wasn't looking for the diary, for anything special, I mean, just what clothes could go off to the church rummage sale. She must have spent half her paycheck at Victoria's Secret. Only a girl like Annie would own underclothes like those. I threw out the pills—I didn't think Stella needed to stumble on those again when she got home—but I didn't take the drawers apart, why would I?"

"So you didn't see the diary," I prodded.

"Stella told me when she found it last week, it was on its spine, wedged against the back of the drawer. You had to take the whole drawer out to see it, and I didn't do that when I was clearing things out."

"Did Stella show you the diary?" I asked.

"She's given it to someone to keep safe, so you can't get your dirty Warshawski fingers on it. She knows you want it."

I inspected my Warshawski fingers. They didn't look that dirty.

"Father Cardenal?" I asked.

"Never mind who she gave it to, it's none of your business."

"Why did you leave the house standing empty all that time that Stella was away?" I asked. "Frank could have sold it, used the money to buy Stella an apartment when she got out."

"We didn't expect her to be gone so long, you know, the lawyers, Mr. Scanlon, they all told us a good woman like Stella, never in trouble with the law—Mass every Sunday, First Friday devotions almost every year—they told us she'd be home within three years."

"Mr. Mandel told you?" I asked.

"That's what everyone said." Betty scowled.

"Who in particular said she'd be out in three years?" I repeated.

"It was just the talk, Father Gielczowski, Mr. Scanlon, everyone who knew her, they all knew she didn't mean to kill Annie, it was an accident, she shouldn't have been in prison so long, that's all I meant. They all said the judge would reduce the sentence, but then he didn't."

"What did Scanlon have to do with Stella's trial?" I asked.

"Mr. Scanlon pays attention to everyone in this neighborhood. He's in church every Sunday, pays for the prizes at the bingo. When Ferrite Workers S&L wanted to foreclose on Daddy, who do you think made them refinance us instead? If Frankie keeps his grades up, Mr. Scanlon's going to get him into a good baseball camp this summer, one where the real scouts come and see the boys play."

"Sounds like Santa Claus," I said dryly, wondering what Scanlon got out of it. Frank's offhand revelations about Father Gielczowski made me think about the horror stories that had come out of Penn State University. How many sports programs, sports camps existed as a cover for grown men to abuse boys?

I should have kept the thought to myself, but I made the mistake of asking Betty if she'd had the talk with Frankie Junior, the one where you remind your children that they don't have to let people touch them, no matter how many promises they give about baseball careers.

"How dare you?" Betty's eyes glittered dangerously. "Are you going to start making up smut about Mr. Scanlon so you can screw up Frankie's chances? If you hurt him the way Boom-Boom did Big Frank, I swear on my mother's grave that you will be sorry you ever were born."

Father Cardenal had been hovering uneasily in the background. "Problem here, ladies?"

"Ms. Guzzo and I went to high school together," I said. "We were catching up."

"Remember what I said, Ms. Know-it-all. Remember what happened to Annie, she thought she was better than the rest of us, too."

Betty turned to walk away, but I caught her arm and turned her around. "Betty, that sounds like a cross between a death threat and a confession. Did *you* kill Annie? Is that why Stella is looking for exoneration now? She wore the jacket to protect Frank and her grandchildren, but—"

Betty drew back her arm to slug me, but I ducked at the last second. Her momentum toppled her.

Father Cardenal helped her to her feet, dusted off her St. Eloy's warm-up jacket. "Let's get you back to the stands, Betty. Frankie's playing a beautiful game. Don't spoil his day by getting involved in a fight."

He put an arm around her and propelled her toward the stands. I left: I didn't care if I ever saw young Frankie play. I was walking back to my car when Cardenal jogged up behind me.

"That was a very serious accusation you made to her. I don't blame her for being angry."

"She tried to punch me. After making a most sinister comment about her sister-in-law's death. I am not the aggressor here."

Cardenal said, "You're right, but only in a way. I'm trying to protect my flock and you're getting everyone perturbed in a way I've never seen them."

"Look, padre: I came here reluctantly after Frank Guzzo fed me a line about his mother. I have no idea what he hoped I would do, but I'm quite sure it isn't what he asked me to do. The fact that people are getting *perturbed* by my presence has to do with the volcano of secrets they're afraid will erupt if they get off the crater that's opening below them, not with my climbing up the mountainside. I have no idea who Jerry Fugher is or why he's so rattled at the thought of a detective on his trail, but I'm getting a nasty feeling about the secrets the Guzzo family is hiding."

I could hear the crowd noise swell in the background. Someone had scored, but I couldn't tell if it was St. Eloy's or the visitors.

"The Guzzos have suffered a great deal. Maybe they're protecting themselves from more pain," Cardenal suggested.

"I don't know about you, but my life hasn't been a crystal stair, either. That doesn't give me license to punch people or make death threats. And do you honestly believe—without flapping your wings in flights of rhetoric—if Betty Guzzo killed Annie and her mother-in-law took the rap, do you think that's a secret they all should protect?"

"You're speculating," he protested. "That's why you make people unhappy. You make up stories about them that you have no way of proving."

"It's the way I work as a detective: I make up stories to see which ones cover the most facts. These are the facts I'm looking at—Frank Guzzo afraid of what his mother will uncover, Stella scrambling to blame my cousin for the murder as soon as I start asking questions,

Stella and Betty both obsessed by Annie's sex life. If Stella spent twenty-five years in the joint to protect her son's marriage, she sure wouldn't welcome my uncovering that crater. So she quickly invented a diary that casts blame on a high-profile third party. I like it as a story, or at least a hypothesis."

I continued to my car. Cardenal followed me, expostulating. I ignored him and in another moment, a crowd of children raced over to surround him.

"Father, you should have seen it, Frank stole home, he won the game, we beat them."

The excited cries echoed up the street as I drove away.

17

KEEP ON TRUCKIN'

I drove over to Buffalo Avenue and stared broodingly at the Guzzo house. Some kids, those bored, undermotivated boys with no future, were eyeing me, perhaps trying to decide if a strange white woman in an old Mustang was an undercover cop, or a worthwhile target. I grinned at them ferociously: undercover cop, they seemed to agree, and moved several doors away, swaggering, so I'd know I hadn't frightened them.

My rage from two nights ago started to rise in me again, but if I forced my way into Stella's house, all I'd get out of it would be jail time. And maybe the loss of my detective license.

I took those deep breaths they're always recommending as protection against stress. There's almost always a second way if you calm down and think. I was about to put the car into gear when Frank phoned me. Sometimes the second way comes to you.

"What the hell are you up to, Warshawski?"

"Frank, just the man I was hoping to talk to. I stopped to watch your son: he looks impressive."

"Don't try smearing butter on me. Betty told me you want to jinx Frankie's shot at baseball camp."

"Why is everyone in your family always on the brink of hysteria?" I demanded. "I think it's fantastic that Frankie has a chance at a first-class camp where college scouts can see him."

"Crap. Betty says you threatened to start a smear campaign against Rory Scanlon just to screw us."

The blinds twitched in Stella's front window. She was watching the street, I guess, but she must have recognized my car because she pushed two slats apart and stared for twenty or thirty seconds. I drove a few doors away, outside the fifty yard perimeter of the restraining order.

"No, Frank. I asked if Betty and you were sure that Scanlon wasn't another Jerry Sandusky."

"Based on what, Warshawski? What makes you think a good, decent guy like Scanlon—"

"Nothing," I said. "But nobody thought a committed priest like Father Gielczowski—"

"Who told you about him?" Frank said fiercely.

"You did. You let it slip last week. It's made me think, that's all. But if I'm letting my imagination run away with me—if he doesn't have boys sleep over at his house, or take them on those special one-on-one camping trips—"

I let my voice trail off.

Frank breathed heavily into the phone. "He only does things with the boys to help them use sports to stay out of gangs. Sometimes if a kid is troubled, he takes him off on his own. Is that a crime?"

"Depends on what he's doing on those solo trips. Sexual abuse is a high price to pay for a shot at a sports career."

"Damn you, Warshawski, get your mind out of the gutter. Why is it always about sex with you?"

"With me?" I sputtered. "Your mother and your wife both are obsessed with Annie's sex life. Betty seemed to think that murdering Annie was the right way to handle her being sexually active."

"That's not true, that's not what Betty said."

"Betty said your mother took the moral high ground by beating Annie for using the Pill. She also said that you and she felt honor-bound to tell your mother that Annie was sleeping with Boom-Boom, for which you had zero evidence. Or did Boom-Boom sidle up to you at Rafters and confide all over a boilermaker?"

Frank didn't speak for a beat, trying to collect his thoughts. "It wasn't like that. We just thought—it was how Annie said it—but anyway, it turned out we were right. Annie wrote it in her diary that she was afraid of Boom-Boom."

"Ah, yes, that diary. One of those wonderful mythical books one is always hearing about but never seeing."

"My mother found Annie's diary. She did not make that up."

The kids who'd moved up the street were drifting back toward me. "Frank, from the day you showed up at my office I've been trying to figure out what you really wanted from me. Your story about needing me to help your mother with her exoneration claim was so bogus I'm embarrassed I responded to you. But now, I'm thinking you used me as a smokescreen to protect your wife."

"From what?"

"From the secrets that will spill out if a group like the Innocence Project takes on Stella's exoneration. If there's something there to show that Betty played a role in Annie's death—"

Frank swore at me and cut the connection.

I stared blankly at the street. Until Betty blurted out that Annie got what was coming to her, I'd never doubted for one second that

Stella was her killer, but what if Betty had played a role, too? Stella had admitted that she beat her daughter the night Annie died, but maybe she sincerely believed she hadn't killed her. Maybe she really did believe someone had come to the house and finished Annie off while she was playing bingo.

If Stella had thought Boom-Boom was involved in Annie's death twenty-five years ago, she would have trumpeted the claim at the top of her lungs back then. And I doubted she would have protected her daughter-in-law. The milk of motherly love didn't exactly course through Stella Guzzo's veins, but maybe she would have taken the full rap if she thought it would help Frank.

More likely, Stella was guilty as charged but had thought she'd weasel out of the worst consequence of her acts. Betty said Stella had been promised a shorter sentence. Had someone offered to dig up evidence of another assailant, and dropped the ball? Or had the obligingly helpful Rory Scanlon paid a bribe for Stella that hadn't worked, or she'd pissed off Scanlon and he hadn't paid the bribe?

If Rory Scanlon had been involved in paying for Stella's defense, or trying to get her sentence reduced, what would induce him to talk to me? Nothing I could think of off the top of my head. I couldn't get access to the mythical diary. But if money had changed hands . . .

I took out my tablet to see whether the trial judge had been pulled into the FBI's old undercover operation in Chicago and Cook County's courts, famous forever to us locals as Operation Greylord. However, showing the iPad was like waving a raw T-bone at a Rottweiler—the drifting kids swarmed around the car. I flashed my smile of death and gunned the car into reverse. The kids jumped out of the way. I made a U and roared up Buffalo. In my rearview mirror I saw one of them pull out a gun, but mercifully, he didn't fire it—gangbangers are notoriously lousy shots. I didn't want a crossfire victim on my conscience.

I'd gone a couple of blocks when I realized there was one person I still hadn't spoken to down here and that was the current owner of Bagby Haulage. What had Frank called him? Vince. I pulled over and took out my iPad again. Bagby & Family Haulage had their headquarters on 103rd Street, in the bleak landscape around the old CID landfill. I followed one of Bagby's panel trucks down a deeply rutted track to the yard, where a dozen or so trucks were parked. Bagby headquarters consisted of a large hangar for mechanical work and a permanent trailer that housed the offices.

I parked as close to the office entrance as possible, but still had to cross several mud wallows. At least I'd worn sensible shoes to my meeting at Wrigley Field this morning.

The trailer door opened onto a single room. It was utilitarian space: a wall of filing cabinets, four metal desks, a barred area with a safe and a desk inside—presumably for payday. Two men about my own age were lounging over one of the desks, chatting in a desultory way. A young woman with a cascade of Botticelli curls hastily switched screens on her computer when I came in and busied herself with a stack of papers. She relaxed when she saw it was me—not whatever authority figure she'd been fearing.

"You lost?" one of the men asked.

"Not if this is Bagby Haulage. I had a question for Vince Bagby."

"He's not here, but this is Delphina Bagby. Don't let all the hair fool you—she can handle an eighteen-wheeler if you need a load hauled this afternoon."

Delphina blushed but sat up straight and offered to help.

"I'm V. I. Warshawski. I met Jerry Fugher outside Wrigley Field this morning."

"He must have had a delivery up there," she said, just as one of the men said, "Fugher, we don't have a Fugher on our books."

Delphina's blush deepened. "I'm sorry, I guess I didn't hear you right."

I pretended not to notice the slip. "Maybe I'm confused. He was getting into a Bagby truck up there." I pulled out my phone and showed her the photo I'd taken.

Delphina looked at the screen, then at the two men. The man who'd said they didn't have a Fugher on their books picked up my phone.

"That's one of our trucks all right. What did you say the guy's name was? Jerry? He looks like Danny DeVito."

"Since you know the DeVito clone is Jerry, what about the guy who's with him?" I asked.

The two men froze for a millisecond, before the spokesman gave an easy smile. "Lucky guess. I don't know either guy, but the tall one doesn't look like anyone I'd want to mess with. Toby, you'd better check into this, see if one of our guys let someone borrow a truck."

The second man grunted. "Forward the photo to Delphina here and I'll check around. License plate shows up clearly, should be easy to sort out. Whoever did this better have a savings account—Vince doesn't stand for this kind of nonsense. He'll fire the driver who let a truck out of his possession. You don't get a second chance if you lend out a truck."

It wasn't until Delphina and I had taken care of the photo that it occurred to Toby to ask why I'd traipsed all the way down here after this man Jerry whoever he was.

"Since he doesn't work here, I don't need to trouble you," I said vaguely.

"No trouble," the first man said. "Vince will find him, or Toby will—Toby's our dispatcher—so we can pass on a message—besides 'Don't borrow Bagby trucks,' of course."

I smiled. "It's not that important. He seemed frightened by the other guy and I hoped to see him when he could talk more easily, that's all. Sorry to bother you."

I stopped at Delphina's desk on my way out. "Your computer screen is reflected on your lampshade. If you don't want your dad to catch you playing solitaire, move your lamp back."

The two men looked at each other. "You're a sharp observer. What'd you say your name was? Sherlock Holmes?"

"V. I. Warshawski. Same line of work, though."

Again a fractional pause, as if an electric current were briefly switched off, before the spokesman said, "Meaning you're a detective?"

"Yep," I agreed.

The two men laughed easily and told me to look after myself, the yard was full of spikes and wires that were hard on a passenger car. They were a jolly lot at Bagby, laughing and chatting with the boss's daughter and random private eyes. Maybe I'd imagined that moment of suspicion.

I bounced and jolted my poor old car back to 103rd Street. If I'd been a TV character I'd have planted a bug in the room, and then my trusty electronic devices would have broadcast the conversation between Toby, Delphina and the other guy. I'd have learned Mr. Gravel's name, and what was going on with Uncle Jerry that was so secret they had to pretend they'd never heard of him. I, alas, didn't have that kind of equipment.

I reminded myself that I didn't have a need to know what was going on with Uncle Jerry. I'd only become curious because he'd run complaining to his priest about me. He was doing something so illegal or so dangerous, or so both, that a PI on his perimeter had terrified him. I would love to know if it was PI's in general, or me specifically that had him rattled.

18

BALLPARK CHATTER

I stopped at the Pot of Gold on my way north, hoping to ask Joel whether he had known that someone promised Stella an early release. Joel wasn't there. Good bartenders don't give up their most loyal customers' whereabouts; the man working the counter tonight stared at me blankly and disclaimed all knowledge of Joel Previn.

The owner of my own regular bar, the Golden Glow in the South Loop, guards my privacy with the same care, a thought that made me get off Lake Shore Drive at Balbo and head to the financial district. I didn't want to be like Joel Previn, turning to alcohol whenever the going got tough, but I was definitely in the mood for whisky.

At six-thirty, only a clutch of hard-core drinkers was still at Sal Barthele's famous horseshoe bar. Sal's head was visible in the middle of the group—she's five-eleven in her stockinged feet, and is the only woman I know who not only likes to put on four-inch heels, but can actually walk in them without falling over. She saw me come in— another trait good bartenders share, eyes always covering the room, making sure the regulars feel welcome, and that troublemakers are eased out before they reach the boiling point.

I chatted with Erica, Sal's head bartender, for the five minutes it took Sal to leave her traders and keep them all feeling special. We talked about ships and shoes and sealing wax while I sipped a Johnnie Walker. Sal sailed back and forth among her regulars, but kept returning to me at the open end of the great mahogany bar. By the time Erica poured me a second drink, the bar was almost empty.

"There's sex all over this story," Sal said when I told her how I'd been spending my week. "Joel and the man he briefly slept with, Joel and the crush he had on the murdered woman, the old law partner and the money he gave her. And then that mother! It sounds as though all she's thought about for sixty years is sex. I know that kind of woman—sex is so vile that she can't get enough of talking about it. There was a woman like her in my building growing up—not that she murdered her daughter, but whenever you saw her, her eyes and lips were glistening with whatever deviance she was going to reveal. You're going to get very dirty if you climb any further into that mud pit."

I nodded gloomily. "It sounds as though Stella beat Annie to death for bragging about being on the Pill. But something Betty said to me today seems very odd."

"Everything about Miss Betty sounds odd to me, but what in particular?" Sal nodded at Erica, and then at the corner. A couple who'd been holding hands under one of her Tiffany lamps had been trying to get a bill for thirty seconds—take it up to forty-five and they'd think they were having a bad night out.

"It sounds as though someone cut a deal with Stella, some kind of deal. Betty said no one thought she'd do all that time. She said, 'They told us she'd be out in three years.' When I pushed her to tell me who, she uttered what sounded very much like a death threat."

"You seriously think this Betty murdered her husband's sister?" Sal raised one beautifully sculpted eyebrow. "She sounds more like a whiner than a doer."

"Yeah, it was probably just babble. I'm thinking more along the lines of bribery gone wrong. The first Greylord indictments were coming in when Stella was being tried. Maybe she or Frank made a down payment but the judge got cold feet."

It used to be that a big enough bribe in Cook County could get almost anyone off any hook, including murder, but Operation Greylord netted about fifty judges, another fifty attorneys, deputies and assorted small fry. I knew of one guy who'd appealed a murder conviction, arguing that he'd paid the judge twenty thousand to have it overturned and the judge hadn't delivered. The justices on the Seventh Circuit had a good long belly laugh over that.

"If she has enough money to bribe a Cook County judge, why is she still in South Chicago?" Sal asked.

"There's that," I agreed. "The money is a big question mark in the middle of this. Stella kept up payments on the house while she was in Logan. Frank told me she used his dad's insurance to cover the mortgage—Mateo Guzzo's pension disappeared when the mill went bankrupt. Mandel or McClelland, or Rory Scanlon, are the folks who would have known how to bribe a judge."

"Maybe Annie had more than two thousand in her bra drawer," Sal suggested. Her mind was on the room: the pre-theater crowd was starting to build, people who can't get through the first act without a double something. "I don't really see what it has to do with you, girlfriend."

She swept off, her long feather earrings bobbing in rhythm with her stride. I put the rest of my second drink back on the bar—I'd breathalyze myself if I had any more whisky, as tired as I was.

Jake said something similar when I got home, not about the

whisky, but the investigation: even if Betty had murdered Annie and blackmailed or bullied Stella into taking the rap, why was it my business? We were on my back porch with a bottle of Torgiano, watching Mr. Contreras and the dogs down in the garden.

"But this is good news," Bernie objected. She'd come home from her first day of work so filled with caffeine that I'd sent her out for a run with the dogs. When she brought them back forty minutes later, she still had energy to burn. "I thought you were doing nothing, but I see you are working hard. Now this man, this Uncle Jerry, he is so scared of you he goes running to his priest."

After another minute of energetic speculating on what Stella would do next and how we could retaliate, Bernie ran down the back stairs to rejoin Mr. Contreras and the dogs.

"You scare me, too, V.I.," Jake grumbled. "If I thought running to a priest would do me any good I'd be on my way to church right now. I wish you'd give up on these Guzzos. You're not getting paid, and when these people get into your dreams, I'm the one who gets punched."

"I'll put Mitch into bed between us," I offered. "He's tough enough to wrassle with me."

Mitch seemed to know I was talking about him—he lifted his great black head and grinned up the stairs at me.

"Do that, Warshawski, and you will be startled by how fast I can wrap a bass string around your neck."

"Those strings set you back six hundred dollars," I said. "You sure you can afford to strangle me?"

"Yep, you're right, best use my hands."

We put the matter behind us and went out to catch a show with a friend of his who played oboe. One thing led to another and we ended up dancing at Hot Rococo until after midnight.

The Guzzos got into my sleep, not enough that I started punching

Jake, but enough that I woke around six the next morning. When I realized I wasn't going back to sleep I stared enviously at Jake. He was beautiful in sleep, his black hair falling over his forehead, his long fingers curled around the corner of his pillow. I stroked his shoulder and his muscles rippled, but he didn't wake up.

I gave it up and went next door into my own place, where Bernie, of course, was heavily asleep in the living room. She also didn't stir, not even when I rummaged noisily in my bag for my laptop.

While my espresso machine heated, I looked up Stella's trial again. The street kids had interrupted me yesterday and I'd forgotten to go back to look for the judge's name. It had been a guy named Elgin Grigsby, not one I'd ever encountered, but there are some five hundred judges in Cook County.

Grigsby had survived the Greylord scandal and had taken an honorable retirement from the bench four years ago. He was "of counsel" at the downtown firm where he'd started his career before joining the bench. Grigsby wintered in Arizona, but had returned to his Chicago condo a few weeks ago. I did a double take when I saw the address: the judge was living in the Pulteney building on Wabash where I used to have my office.

When I rented at the Pulteney, the elevator worked about half the time, the wiring was so old that you needed special battery interfaces to run a computer, and I could have retired if I'd been able to charge union scale for repairing the women's toilet.

After the owners forced out me and the other hardy renters—by cutting off utilities while still holding on to our rent money—they'd gutted the place and turned it into high-end condos.

It was Saturday, not a day for business cold calls. I put work behind me for the weekend, but Monday morning, I took the L to the Loop. Maybe because of the iron girders down the middle of the block, this stretch of Wabash still looked tawdry. Arnie's Steak Joynt was still flashing its neon on one corner, and the bar that used to make me think I was catching some bad disease was still in business across the street from it.

This made the rehabbed lobby of the Pulteney all the more striking when I went inside. I'd always wondered what lay under the decades of grime that crusted the mosaic floor. Pharaohs, elongated cats, boats on the Nile. The Pulteney apparently went up in the 1920s, at the height of the Egyptian craze that followed the discovery of King Tut's tomb.

In addition to legal odd jobs, Judge Grigsby worked as a docent for the Chicago Architecture Foundation; his shift started at ten, his wife had told me when I'd called earlier. He could give me forty-five minutes before strolling over to Michigan Avenue to start his tour.

The doorman, in white gloves so as not to smudge the Art Deco figurines when he held the brass elevator doors open for me, phoned upstairs to confirm the appointment. White gloves, polished brass, even an indie coffee bar in the lobby, while management had sucked up my rent money for fifteen years without bringing the electrics up to code. I rode to the seventeenth floor, trying not to let sour grapes make me sour-faced.

I had done as much research on Grigsby as I could without talking to anyone. I didn't want him to know I was asking questions, since even a retired judge in Cook County has a lot of people owing him favors. Grigsby had been elected—over and over—with a "Qualified" rating from the Illinois Bar Association. Sort of like being a reliable C or B student. He and his wife, Marjorie, had been married forty-seven years next month; they had five children and seven grandchildren. Besides his judge's pension, he had a nice little portfolio that brought in almost four hundred thousand a year, letting him maintain condos in Scottsdale and Chicago.

I'd found photos of Grigsby online at all sorts of regular Democratic Party functions. He'd been at fund-raisers with Illinois House Speaker Spike Hurlihey, with ward committeemen, the head of Streets & San—crucial for getting out the vote, even in these supposedly post-patronage years—and various senators, representatives, corporate leaders. Even Darraugh Graham, my own most important client, had been in one shot. I was pretty sure Darraugh voted Republican, but in Cook County, anyone trying to do business shows up at Democratic political functions.

Grigsby's apartment was in the southeast corner of the building. The judge, in an open-necked shirt and soft sports jacket, had the door open and called to me to come to the front room. He was looking out across the Art Institute at the fringe of trees along Lake Michigan. The south view showed the L tracks that used to run past my office window—I'd been on the fourth floor, where I could look into commuters' faces as the trains rattled by.

"Ms. Warshawski? A good Chicago name. I never get tired of watching the city from up here. I grew up in Back of the Yards and Gage Park and I never imagined back then that I would be living among the chardonnay drinkers downtown. How about you?"

"South Chicago," I obliged. "And I still don't live among the chardonnay drinkers."

We picked our way through each other's career highlights—me, *University of Chicago Law Review*, clerking for a judge in the Seventh Circuit, my time with the criminal public defender ("Step down for a *Law Review* student, wasn't it?" the judge commented). Him, DePaul University law, assistant state's attorney, partner at a big downtown firm, followed by thirty-three years on the bench. Prosecutors move up, defenders move down, law of the jungle.

I told Grigsby about the decade I'd spent in this building, and my envy of the space as it looked now. He threw back his head, laughing, as if delighted that he had something I couldn't afford. It didn't surprise me: growing up behind the old stockyards, you competed for every beam of sunlight that filtered through the haze of blood and smoke.

He was drinking coffee but didn't offer me any. Power play, assertion of status, obliviousness, maybe all three.

"Judge, I know you're busy, and this is a long shot, but an old South Chicago murder has been rattling cages lately. The case was tried in your court."

He nodded over the rim of the cup. "Stella Guzzo. I looked her up when I saw the news—Boom-Boom War— Oh. Your family? Cousin? That explains why you're nosing around the story."

I eyed him thoughtfully. "I wonder who told you I was 'nosing around'?"

"It's not a secret. You've been talking to some of the lawyers that I've known for decades."

"I haven't been talking to Nina Quarles, because she's in France. Sol Mandel is dead, his partner's retired. Ira Previn come to you?"

"He didn't come to me, but we eat breakfast at the same restaurant when he has an early court date. He's worried you digging up old dirt might hurt his son."

I watched the Dan Ryan L chug down Wabash, the Ravenswood passing it in the opposite direction. The double glazing shut out street noise; it was like watching toy trains in a paperweight.

"No questions of mine could give Joel more pain than he's already feeling. People who knew him back then tell me that he was afraid, not of what would happen at the trial, but what would happen to him if he refused to defend Stella Guzzo. How did that play out in your courtroom?"

"Who told you Joel was afraid?" Grigsby asked.

"I've talked to a lot of people this week, Judge; it seems to be the consensus."

"Ira never said anything about that." Grigsby's voice took on an edge.

"He may not have realized it. He worried more about the mistakes Joel was making in the trial. How bad did Joel look?"

"You're asking me to remember details from a case more than two decades old." Grigsby's voice was sharp—objection sustained.

"That was your reputation on the bench." I smiled winningly, using the soothing tone that had worked for me when I was a PD. Judges then hadn't liked women attorneys who challenged their rulings. It had been an ongoing effort to curb my pit-dog instincts, but it often paid off. "When I was with the PD they used to call you 'Wolf Trap Grigsby' because facts stuck in your mind like a wolf in a trap."

Grigsby looked startled, as well he might, since I'd made that up on the spot, but he preened a bit, asked if I'd ever appeared in front of him. Since he seemed well oiled, I repeated my question about Joel's performance at Stella's trial.

"She was a difficult client, unsympathetic. I knew dozens like her from growing up at Forty-seventh and Ashland—rock-hard women who had to fight for every piece of bread their children ate. My own mother, God rest her soul, was one of them. But Joel couldn't make Guzzo look good to the jury, and he couldn't control her in court. I had to reprimand him more than once. If he was afraid, it was of her—she's probably haunted his nightmares ever since."

"Why did Ira let Joel take that case? By all accounts Joel was in love, or at least infatuated with Annie Guzzo. For that matter, why did Mandel & McClelland want him to defend her killer? Mandel thought so highly of her he was funding her college education."

Grigsby stiffened. "Funding her college education? What do you mean?"

"Hearsay, Judge, sorry. Her mother found thousands of dollars in

Annie's lingerie drawer—it was one of the things they fought about. Supposedly fought about. Annie told her mother that Sol Mandel gave her the money to help her get to college. Allegedly."

"I hope you're not suggesting any impropriety. Sol Mandel was a fine lawyer. We golfed together at Harborside many times. Many times."

"No one has suggested anything out of line there, Judge. My mother gave Annie Guzzo piano lessons, and Sol Mandel probably saw the same qualities in her my mother did—ambitious, hardworking, wanting a chance to live a life away from South Chicago. The neighborhood gets a bad rap, like Back of the Yards used to, but there are plenty of decent people who want to help kids. Rory Scanlon, for instance. He made important connections for my cousin when Boom-Boom was starting out, and from what I hear, he's still doing it for kids today."

"Scanlon is still active?" The question was casual, but Grigsby eyed me closely, again using his coffee cup as cover.

"He's apparently still working with kids and sports."

"You're an investigator, right?" Grigsby added. "Is someone paying you to poke around in this old case?"

Definitely a C student, if it had taken him this long to think up that question. I smiled again. "It's such an odd case that people keep raising questions about it. During the trial, did Joel ever try to suggest Stella had been framed?"

"Every criminal defendant claims they've been framed. If you were with the County Criminal Defender's office, you know that."

I laughed, hoping he would think I was on his side. "Five million people in Cook County, but only three stories: 'I wasn't there,' 'I was set up,' 'It was a Vice Lord.' But Stella is pointing a finger straight at Boom-Boom. I'm sure you'd remember if she suggested that at the trial. He was big news at the time."

"She was convicted of a very heinous crime," Grigsby said in his sternest courtroom voice. "She did her time. My best advice to you is to leave the trial alone. No good can come of scratching those old sores after all these years."

"I don't disagree, Judge, but, as I said, people keep coming to me with odd questions. Just yesterday, someone told me that Stella had been told she'd get an early release, despite the length of the sentence. Who would have made a promise like that?"

"Are you daring—daring!—to suggest I fixed a trial?" His face started to swell with fury.

I looked at him curiously. "I assumed the state's attorney would make an offer like that, not the judge."

"Who told you such a thing about a trial in my courtroom?" he demanded.

"Someone in the neighborhood," I said vaguely. "As I said, I grew up there, I know a lot of people, a lot of them have been talking."

19

MY LAST DUCHESS

Before Grigsby said anything else, the swinging door to the back of the apartment opened and a woman came in. Marjorie Grigsby was short and plump, her gray hair a thick bubble around her head. Her daytime makeup was carefully applied, but her smile was warm and genuine.

"Elgin, you need to get over to the Architecture Foundation."

She turned the same warm smile onto me. "I'm sorry to interrupt you, dear, but Elgin was a judge for so many years he stopped wearing a watch: his clerk always got him where he needed to be and now I do it."

The judge preened some more—apparently he thought this was a tribute to his status, not a criticism. Marjorie straightened his lapels, took his coffee cup, told him to enjoy himself.

"Although he always does," she added to me. "Presiding over an architecture tour, Elgin has the same chance to lay down the law as he did at Twenty-sixth and California, except he gets to rule on the whole city."

It was hard to tell from her voice if she was mocking him or praising him. She stood on tiptoe to kiss his cheek and held the outer door open for us.

The judge and I stood in a strained silence until the elevator arrived. The engraved brass doors slid open, a whisper of noise, not the clanging they used to make. The pulleys didn't groan on the way down, either. The judge stood in front, right next to the doors, pretending I wasn't there. We stopped on the ninth floor to let in a woman with two Harlequin Great Danes. She was dressed for running, her phone in an arm sleeve, the music from the earphones tinnily audible.

"You're supposed to take those down in the service elevator, young woman," Grigsby said sternly.

She paid no attention to the judge, but patted her dogs' shoulders until they sat. Grigsby yanked out her earbuds and shouted that she needed to use the service elevator. The dogs began to curl their lips, not a good sign.

"My dogs don't like it when people cross into my personal space," the woman said. "We don't use the service elevator because we don't like the alley. Get used to us."

I moved between the dogs and Grigsby, forcing him to the far corner of the car. The dogs continued to stare at him until we reached the lobby. Grigsby flung the woman's earbuds to the floor and marched over to the doorman. He was pointing at the woman and the dogs, gesticulating, while she sailed out the front door, a dog on either side.

I slipped into the coffee bar, watching the doorman soothe Grigsby. When they're in their courtrooms, judges have great power over the people in front of them. They can fine insolent parties or lawyers, lock them up for contempt, rule against them. Grigsby obviously had come to expect so much deference to his rulings that he thought it carried over into daily life. But would he have been as angry about the dogs if I hadn't rattled his cage first?

The indie bar had a shiny Simonelli machine and advertised organic small-batch beans that were probably hand massaged, but the baristas were sloppy and the espresso had a sour edge. Too short an extraction time. I was going to demand a repour when I saw Marjorie Grigsby in the lobby, wearing a lilac-colored trench coat against the edge in the April air. She chatted briefly with the doorman, giving him the same smile she'd turned on her husband and on me.

I put the cortado back on the counter and followed Ms. Grigsby, catching up with her in front of the Art Institute. I wondered if she volunteered there while her husband pontificated on architecture for tourists, but she was holding out her arm for a cab.

She put her hand down when she saw me. "Were you looking for me, dear?"

"Just catching a cab back to my office, ma'am," I said.

"Is your office north? You can ride with me as far as Division."

When a cab pulled up, I helped her into the backseat.

"I heard Elgin shouting at you, dear. Why?"

When I didn't say anything, she patted my hand. "My husband has a sensitive skin, but I don't. Does this have something to do with the hockey player named Warshawski who was in the news last week?"

"Right you are, ma'am." I gave her an abbreviated version of the Guzzo soap opera. "I learned on Friday that someone told Stella Guzzo she wouldn't have to serve her full sentence, that she'd be out in three years. I wondered if it was your husband who'd made that promise."

I braced myself for an outburst, but she merely said, "I see, dear:

you wanted to know if someone paid Elgin to overturn the sentence. I don't think my husband has shoeboxes filled with cash in the Cayman Islands—of course, I'd know if he were keeping them in the apartment."

"I'm sure you would, ma'am."

A legendary Illinois secretary of state, who lived in a fleabag in Springfield, left a closet filled with cash-stuffed shoeboxes when he died. Whenever someone needed to buy a favor, he supposedly rubbed his hands and exclaimed, "I can smell the meat a-cooking."

"It's not easy to be an elected official in Illinois," Ms. Grigsby sighed. "You have to go to everyone's fund-raisers in the hopes that they go to yours. Your staff is tied up selling tickets to the Speaker's events, or the governor's, or whoever is in power at the time, when they ought to be researching case law for you. It got so my friends wouldn't answer the phone if I called during primary season." She gave a merry laugh.

The drive from the Art Institute to LaSalle and Division doesn't take long. We had already crossed the river and were waiting to turn left onto Ontario. I frantically tried to think of something to say besides, "Did the judge have an unusually large portfolio when he retired?"

The thought of large portfolios reminded me that I'd seen a photo of Grigsby with my most important client: Darraugh Graham had a large enough portfolio to own whole chunks of the Caymans if his tastes had run in that direction. "I understand that the judge knows Darraugh Graham. If you have any questions about me, Mr. Graham knows me well."

"Does he, dear?" she said thoughtfully. "I don't know if I would mention that to Elgin. He never felt that Mr. Graham responded appropriately to him. Of course, that may be because Elgin has a chip on his shoulder about elbowing his way out of Back of the Yards.

He felt Darraugh Graham was looking down on him, although I always thought Mr. Graham was most painfully shy."

I murmured agreement. Darraugh's wintry manner didn't exactly hide a heart of gold, but he'd definitely been a poor little rich boy.

The taxi pulled up in front of a women's health clinic. Ms. Grigsby laughed again when she saw the surprise in my face.

"I volunteer here. You younger women think you have a corner on these issues, but believe me, I've been in these trenches since you were in kindergarten. I had to give it up when Elgin was on the bench; it wouldn't do for a judge's wife to be seen on one side of this issue or another, so I was happy for many reasons when he decided to step down."

She handed the driver a twenty and told him to take me where I was going. He took me to my office—I'd driven down there with the dogs, since I hadn't had a chance to run them this morning, and Bernie looked as though she was going to sleep until a second before her shift started.

The dogs were whining and pacing in my office. I drove them over to Lake Michigan. The water was bone-numbingly cold, at least for me—the past winter had been brutal, even by Chicago standards. In the middle of March we still had temperatures below freezing. Now, in April, no one trusted sunny days to stay warm. No country for old detectives.

I didn't let the dogs go very far out, in case they got into trouble, but they were happy to swim and run. I was the one who got chilled, standing in the sand while the wind picked up speed again.

"What do you think, guys?" I asked the dogs on our way back to the parking lot. "Was Marjorie trying to tell me something that was too subtle for me to follow?"

Mitch lunged for a squirrel, but Peppy furrowed her golden brow, seeming to give the question serious thought.

"You think she was trying in a delicate way to suggest that Grigsby did favors for people who supported his election campaigns? And maybe Stella or Frank promised him something but couldn't deliver, so there was no quid, since there'd been no quo?"

Peppy gave a sharp bark.

"You're right: it's a good guess, but it doesn't explain where Stella got the money to keep up her mortgage payments. You know, it might be time to follow that money trail. After we do a little work to earn some money ourselves."

Betty had mentioned Ferrite Workers S&L on Friday. It had been the bank of choice for most families in my neighborhood and I was betting they'd held the mortgage on the Guzzo house, too.

Of course, Ferrite didn't exist anymore. Like a lot of neighborhood S&Ls, it had died in the savings and loan debacle of the 1980s, but Fort Dearborn Trust had taken over those accounts. And left the Ferrite name on the door in the hopes of keeping what was left of the steelworking customer base.

After three hours of steady work on my paying customers' concerns, I took the dogs for a walk down Milwaukee to the nearest branch of Fort Dearborn, where I opened an account. On the way back we stopped for falafel, which I took to the office to eat while setting up Internet banking for my new account.

Security questions: mother's date of birth, street where I grew up, my first-grade teacher. All questions I could answer if I was looking at Frank Guzzo's account, but not his mother's. How creepy did I want to be on my quest? I called the Streeter brothers, who help fill in the blanks for me when my workload gets out of hand.

"Hey, V.I." It was Kimball Streeter, the brother I almost never saw, who answered the phone. "I see you got your face in the news again."

I gritted my teeth for another conversation about my cousin and Annie's murder.

"No, not that. They say you're writing the story of his life. About time someone did that, but I didn't know you could write."

"I didn't, either," I agreed feebly. "I'm not sure I can make it happen."

While we spoke, I looked up my name in the daily news. Natalie Clements, the woman in the Cubs media office, had been so enthusiastic about my project that she'd put out a press release, including the photo of Boom-Boom on the mound with Mitch Williams.

Local Detective Takes on a New Case: Investigating a Sports Legend's Life, was how the *Herald-Star* pitched it. They quoted Mr. Villard, the retired media relations man who'd dug up the photos, on what a great sports town Chicago was, and how he knew the Cubs would be delighted to cooperate with me and the Blackhawks on writing Boom-Boom's life story.

The *Star* had dug up their own old story of the day of the open tryouts. Boom-Boom had apparently led both the press and the official Cubs photographer on a merry chase around the ballpark, trying to get into all the parts of the stadium that were normally closed to the public.

Warshawski loved to play pranks, on the press and on his teammates, but the Cubs asked us not to publish the photos at the time—they didn't want kids or other fans to get ideas about how to get into closed-off sections of Wrigley. The paper got rid of a lot of print archives in the transition to new media. Those tryout shots were never digitized, so we can't show you what he was up to, but the book itself should help fans remember what Boom-Boom Warshawski did for this city besides his practical jokes: three Stanley Cups, and endless goodwill with local charities.

My cheeks turned hot: with this kind of publicity, I would have to write the book.

I realized I'd been carrying on some kind of conversation with Kimball Streeter, but not paying attention to the words. I had to drag my mind back to the reason I'd called: I wanted to hack into Stella Guzzo's bank account—but I didn't tell Kimball that.

Kimball agreed to be a researcher for the Hibernian Genealogical Society and to try to get answers to the questions I e-mailed him.

He called back forty minutes later to report that Stella had hung up on him, but that Betty had been very chatty. She didn't know her mother-in-law's first-grade teacher, but she knew Stella's mother's date of birth: March 29, when the family had to go to Grace O'Rourke Garretty's grave and pray the rosary.

"Betty was peevish because now that Stella is out of prison, they had to go to Resurrection Cemetery again this year, when there was still snow on the ground, and kneel there doing the decades. Oh, and Stella grew up on Oglesby."

No sooner had Kimball Streeter hung up than Murray called. He was fuming that I'd started a book project without consulting him.

"Warshawski, the only thing you know how to write is a case report. You're clueless about narrative, story arc, building suspense. You got a ghost writer?"

"Don't start by insulting me, or I'll make you read my senior thesis, which won top honors in the Social Sciences Division the year I graduated."

"Sorry, sorry," Murray said hastily. "I know you're mad at me, Warshawski, but honestly, it's hard to learn about something like this in my own paper when everyone knows how tight you and I are."

I sighed. "Murray, if I tell you something off the record, you had better keep it off the record, or I will post candid pictures of you on your Facebook page."

He promised, but when I told him, he was enthusiastic. "Let me do it, V.I.—it's the perfect refutation for the diary story, and anyway, the city still loves him."

"Maybe, Murray, maybe. Let me get out from under the Guzzos first."

When I hung up, my eye caught the engraving of the Uffizi on the wall to my right. It had been my mother's. I could feel the sternness of her disapproval as I dialed Fort Dearborn's Internet help line.

I was afraid scam artists had helped themselves to my mother-in-law's debit card, I said. She was eighty-eight and so rattled that she couldn't remember her account number; could they help me? No, I didn't have her Social Security number, but I could verify her current address on Buffalo, the street she grew up on and her mother's date of birth.

Three clicks later and I was looking at Stella's bank account. I couldn't get statements from twenty-five years ago, which might have shown whether or not she had enough cash to bribe Judge Grigsby, but I could go back two years. The house must have been owned free and clear some time before that, because every month showed automatic debits to the utility companies, and twice a year the property tax of $546.50 had been paid, along with the home-owners insurance.

Once a quarter, enough money had come in to cover those bills via wire transfer from an account at Global American Bank. The transfers had stopped the quarter before Stella's release. Once she'd been released, she started collecting Social Security survivor benefits, slightly more than what her benefactor had been putting into the account.

I printed out the screen, but didn't know how to dig any deeper than that, not without a professional hacker, a bigger budget and even fewer scruples than I'd already demonstrated.

"But we've learned something," I said to the dogs. "We know that someone was paying Stella's bills. She didn't have any money—Mateo Guzzo's pension disappeared in the big meltdown of the steel industry and none of those Garretty brothers had two nickels to rub together. Who paid her bills?"

Mitch flattened his ears. "She threatened someone, is your theory? Could be. Or did a big favor for someone. They stopped paying when she got out. Is that why she decided to look for exoneration? Because her invisible angel stopped pouring gold coins on her?"

As I shut down my computer, Freeman called. "Vic, I don't know what you think you're doing, but you cannot go near the Guzzo family, or Stella's house, or her grandchildren."

"Freeman, I stopped to watch the kids play baseball. That's a crime?"

"It is if you attack one of the mothers."

"This is beyond outrageous. She tried to slug me."

"It doesn't matter. *Stay away from that family if you want me to continue to represent you.*"

He hung up, sending me home in a thoroughly unpleasant mood.

20

DOG DAYS

The dogs woke me, barking in the upper landing. I bolted out of bed, pulling on jeans and a T-shirt. Jake mumbled something, turned over.

When I cracked open his front door, I saw Mr. Contreras struggling to hold Mitch, who was lunging at a couple of uniformed cops outside my own apartment. Peppy stood sentinel, barking short urgent warnings. One of the cops had his gun drawn, and maybe he would have used it, except that Rochelle, who lives in the unit underneath mine, was also in the upper hall.

"Go ahead and shoot them!" she was screaming. "They're a menace. It's only fucking seven in the morning and they've woken the whole building."

"Watch your language," Mr. Contreras panted, trying to hold the bucking Mitch.

The police were shouting warnings, the Soong baby started crying on the floor below and the two men who lived across from Mr. Contreras on the ground floor were yelling up the stairwell to make the damned dogs be quiet.

I took the sash from Mr. Contreras's magenta dressing gown and used it as a leash to tie Mitch to a baluster. Once Mitch was sitting, Peppy stopped barking, although the hair at the back of her head stood up and she kept growling in the back of her throat.

"Want to tell me what's going on?" I asked the cops.

"Are you Victoria Iphigenia Warshawski?" He pronounced it "Ipp-jin," but close enough.

On the other side of the door I heard Bernie call my name, her voice pitched high with fear. "Are you out there, Vic? Someone's trying to break in! I called nine-one-one."

"Yeah, I'm out here, honey. Good job. I'll hold the fort until the police get here."

"We are the police," one of the uniforms said.

"My houseguest couldn't possibly know that." I peered at his badge. "Officer Burstyn. She assumed you were housebreakers. You can explain it to your friends when they get here."

"Lieutenant Rawlings wants to talk to you."

"Now I feel really special," I said, "but he has my phone number, no need to send an armed escort all the way across the city to find me."

"Are you arresting her?" Rochelle demanded.

"We don't have a warrant," the second man said. "But—"

"She's dangerous," Rochelle said. "I want her out of this building. Those dogs aren't safe, and—"

"You need to talk to your local district, miss," Officer Burstyn said. "If the dogs are running wild, or biting—"

"They never bit anyone," Mr. Contreras said, indignant. "This gal has her undies in a bundle over the dogs, but I hear your music playing at all hours, young lady, and if you want to bring the cops here, well, what are those boys doing when they're leaving your place at three in the morning? Bet these cops could find all kinds of drugs if I asked them to take a look."

Rochelle's face flamed fuchsia. "You dirty old man, how dare you—"

Mr. Soong appeared, barefoot, in jeans and a T-shirt. "Please. Please, everyone, be quiet, so the baby can become quiet again. The stairwell is not the place for an argument."

"Right you are, Mr. Soong," I said. "Officer, I can take the dogs inside and reassure my houseguest, but only if you promise not to follow me into my home."

"Our orders were—"

"Yep, I know. I'll come with you to talk to Conrad, but I need time to put on more clothes, calm a teenager and get these dogs where no one can bite them."

This last phrase pushed Rochelle into another stream of invective: the police could see that I treated her fears as a joke, the dogs should be shot or impounded.

The cops, who'd lost control of the situation as soon as Mr. Contreras appeared with Mitch and Peppy, had started to order me to come right now, with the clothes I had on, but Rochelle made them decide to give me the benefit of the doubt. To show he wasn't soft on PI's or dogs, Burstyn phoned the Fourth District for instructions. Conrad, or some henchperson, agreed I could be trusted to get dressed and not to emerge firing a weapon.

"Bernie, you decent?" I called through the door. "I'm bringing your uncle Sal in."

I didn't exactly trust the cops to keep their promise, so I stood in the doorway with Mitch and Peppy until Mr. Contreras was inside, then backed in, shutting the door as soon as Peppy's long plume of a tail had cleared the opening.

The local district's response team was ringing the downstairs bell as I slid the dead bolts home. I buzzed them into the building, but left them for Officer Burstyn and his pal to sort out.

Bernie was sitting on the sofa bed, her legs tucked under her, her dark eyes black with fear. "What's going on, Vic?"

"No idea, honey. The cops are from South Chicago, though. Turn on the news, see if there's anything about Stella Guzzo."

Mr. Contreras put an arm around Bernie and gave her a reassuring slap on the shoulder. "Don't you worry about nothing, young Bernie. The dogs and me, we'll walk down to your job with you and we'll come get you when the day is over. No one can hurt you with Mitch and me looking after you, okay?"

Bernie nodded, smiling tremulously, and scooted over to make room for him on the end of the bed. While the two of them flipped through channels looking for local news, I went to the back to get ready. I took my time, heating up my espresso machine, taking a shower, dressing for comfort in case I had a long day in cop-land in front of me. I made a cheese sandwich with cucumbers and spinach, something I could eat in the back of the squad car without worrying about spills or stains.

Jake came in through the back door in the middle of my routine.

"You're up," I said.

"They're probably up and about in Milwaukee with that racket." He put an arm around me and drank my espresso. "You in trouble?"

"The police don't have a warrant, so I don't think so. Someone I talked to yesterday must have complained—I won't know until I get to South Chicago if it was Judge Grigsby or Betty Guzzo."

"I think we got something, doll," Mr. Contreras called. "That Ryerson guy is on."

Jake came with me into the living room in time to see Murray in front of a mountain of coal dust at the Port of Chicago.

"Are the pet coke mountains in South Chicago toxic? That question has been hotly debated lately between the residents of the city's southeast side, who claim that breathing the dust particles is a health hazard, and the state's Pollution Control Board, which says there's no proof. However, this mountain of pet coke was definitely a hazard to the health of a man whose body was found here early this morning by tugboat pilot Gino Smerdlow."

The cops were pounding on my door again, demanding that I get going.

"Police have not yet released the identity of the dead man, but we were able to catch up with Gino Smerdlow near the Guisar slip at the Port of Chicago."

Murray's interview of the tugboat pilot was uninteresting and predictable: Murray looking nautical in the wheelhouse, wind whipping a navy scarf around his red hair, getting the grisly details from Smerdlow. Early morning on the Cal, returning from towing the *Lucella Wieser* out onto the open water, spotting the arm sticking out of the coal mountain.

"We see float fish here from time to time," Smerdlow said, "but a body in the coal? I couldn't believe it," and so on.

Jake, Bernie, Mr. Contreras and the dogs all came to the door to see me off, which made me feel as if I were on my way to the guillotine. Mr. Contreras told the police that he had their badge numbers if anything went wrong. Even so, Burstyn and his pal, a man named Dubcek, didn't treat me roughly—no grabbing of the arms or snatching away my briefcase.

When I asked them how they'd handled the officers from the Town Hall District who'd responded to Bernie's SOS, Dubcek grunted. "We didn't have to tell them anything. That woman downstairs from you, she stepped up all hot and bothered, demanding they do something about your dogs, so they thought she had called in the complaint. You better be careful there, miss. Make sure they have licenses, don't let them run through the halls like they did this morning. It's dangerous, especially with little children living in the building."

They were less forthcoming about why I was being dragged to the South Side, even after I said the dead body in the Guisar company's pet coke mountain had been on the morning news: the lieutenant would explain why he wanted to see me.

The back of a squad car is an uncomfortable place to sit, especially if you're taller than about five-three. Your knees are up against a grille and the seat feels like cement blocks. The smell isn't too appetizing, either—too many bodies covered in who knows what effluvia have been there before you. I lost interest in my sandwich.

Instead, I looked up news on my phone. Everyone was very excited about the body in the coke, but no one had a name.

I hated making nice with Murray, but I finally texted him.

You looked at home on the tugboat. Career change imminent?
-VIW

The Queen is speaking to the commoner? You must want
something. -MRyerson

Love and recognition, as we all do. Wondering if you knew the vic.
-VIW

They had him covered and carted before the 5th Estate arrived. If
you can ID him and don't tell me, our relationship really is over.
-MRyerson

I debated for a minute—I was still feeling pretty stiff toward
Murray—but finally texted that I'd been summoned to the Fourth
District and was looking for a heads-up. That excited Murray into a
frenzy of texting, the upshot of which was he'd take me to dinner at
Trefoil if I got him a name ahead of the pack.

LOL, I wrote back, and turned to client e-mails.

When we finally reached the station—a long trek on the Dan
Ryan at rush hour—my escort left me in the public area while they
checked in with Conrad.

The building was new since I'd moved away, but the sergeant behind the desk was old, with deep grooves in his cheeks, his slate-gray
hair overdue for a trim. He was telling me where I could sit in the
hoarse baritone of a drinking smoker, but I was squinting at his
badge.

"Sid?" I said. "Sid Gerber?"

"Yeah. Who are you when you're at home?"

"I'm V.I.—Vic Warshawski. Tony's daughter."

He stared at me, then smiled, pushing the grooves in his face
toward his ears. "You're never. You're never Tony's girl. How about
that?"

A young officer filling out a form at the end of the counter turned
to look at me, decided whoever Tony was, his girl held no interest,
and went back to his clipboard. A woman waiting on the visitors'
bench loudly demanded when she was going to get to talk to someone about the police *totally illegally* impounding her car.

"Ma'am, your car was holding eight kilos of uncut cocaine. As
soon as—"

"Put there by some street scum who you ain't even *trying* to find, while you got my son locked up."

"That could be, ma'am, but the car is still evidence." He turned sideways, his back to her. "Vic, how long's it been?"

"How'd you end up down here, Sid?" I asked. "I thought you knew better than to put yourself in the crosshairs."

"Nobody asks me to go out on the street anymore and I got me a weekend place down near Schererville." He winked, meaning, I suppose, that he was actually living down in Indiana—a no-no for someone on Chicago's payroll.

Sid had been one of my dad's last partners, after Tony had been redeemed from cop hell: my dad had been sent to West Englewood for reasons he'd never talked about.

Near the end of my dad's active duty life, his former protégé Bobby Mallory started becoming a power in the department. Bobby plucked Tony from Sixty-third and Throop and sent him to one of the soft districts, out near O'Hare, where he'd met Sid. Sid was one of those guys who was born knowing how to avoid hard work, but Tony let it ride in a way he wouldn't have earlier. He said Sid was a born storyteller, and a good story got you through a dull shift better than station coffee. When Tony had to go on disability, Sid was one of his most faithful visitors.

Sid gossiped with me now about the good old days, while the phone rang, the woman on the bench ranted, and officers checked in and out. I asked what he knew about the body in the pet coke mountain.

"Looks ugly." He lowered his voice. "They think he was still alive when he was put in."

"Who was it? They didn't have an ID on the news yet."

Sid gave an elaborate shrug. "My grandkids will see it on Facebook before I know."

His cell phone rang; Conrad was ready for me. I was to make a right turn, ID myself to a woman at the entrance to the holding cells, and she'd take me to the looey.

As I went into the back, a patrolman was pleading with Sid to book his captive and the woman with the impounded car had come up to the counter to scream in Sid's face.

21

THE UMPIRE
STRIKES BACK

My escort took me around a partition where a minute office had been carved out for the watch commander. Most of the space was taken up with a dry-erase board that held the week's duty roster. The watch commander's desk was wedged against the facing wall. There were a couple of chairs in front of it, both of them covered with reports.

Conrad Rawlings had his cell phone to his ear with his left hand and was hunting and pecking on his computer keyboard with the right. When he saw me, he gestured toward one of the chairs with his typing hand.

"Put those on the floor. I'll be with you in a sec."

By the time I'd shifted everything, he'd finished his conversation.

"You wobble on the line, Warshawski. I'm wondering if you've crossed it."

"What line are we talking about, Lieutenant?"

When Conrad is feeling mellow toward me, he calls me "Ms. W."

He was not feeling mellow. I took my sandwich out of my briefcase and started eating, which made him even less mellow.

"Put that away. This isn't a restaurant."

"Your guys woke me, not to mention my entire building, at seven this morning. I need to eat. You implied I crossed a line. What are you talking about?" I wondered if word had drifted to him of my poking into Stella Guzzo's bank account.

"You don't think you're bound by the same rules of law the rest of the country runs on. You think you can make up the rules to suit your own needs. I've seen you do it time and again."

I put down my sandwich. "Are we recording this conversation, Lieutenant? Because that is slander, and it is actionable."

Conrad glowered at his desktop. He'd gotten off on the wrong foot and knew it.

"Come over here: I want to show you some pictures."

I went around to his side of the desk. He turned and typed a few lines on his computer and brought up a slideshow of the pet coke mountain at the Guisar slip. It wasn't really a mountain, but a lopsided pile of coal dust perhaps five hundred feet long. It came to an off-center peak about fifty feet high and sloped from there to a plateau around fifteen feet from the ground.

The first frame was shot from some distance back, giving a panorama of the mountain, with bulldozers around the far end and men in hard hats gawking up at the higher peak. Conrad flipped through the slides, stopping every few frames to take phone calls. We got closer to the mountain, watched a team in hazmat suits standing in the bucket of a cherry picker on the deck of a police boat. The boat pulled up alongside the coke mountain and swung the bucket over so the guys in the hazmat suits could start excavating.

Conrad had brought me here because he knew I was connected to his dead body. He kept glancing up at me, his expression hostile, to see how I was reacting. It took conscious work to keep breathing naturally, those diaphragm breaths I was relearning as I practiced my singing with Jake.

The crew carried the body to the ground and laid it on the concrete lip of the dock. A scene-of-the-crime expert used a fine brush to clean the face.

I was expecting Frank Guzzo. Instead, it was Uncle Jerry. My first foolish thought was that in death his soot-blackened, flaccid face didn't look much like Danny DeVito.

"You know him." Conrad made a statement, not a question.

"I know his name," I said. "I don't—didn't—know him."

"Okay. His name, what's his name?"

"Jerry Fugher. Or so I was told—we were never introduced."

"Then how come you know his name?"

I went back to my chair and finished my sandwich.

"I asked you a question," Conrad snapped.

"I'm in a police station without a witness or legal representation," I said. "I don't answer questions that have bombs and barbs tucked into them."

"It's a simple question." Conrad spread his arms wide. "The only reason you'd expect bombs or barbs is because you know they're there."

I brushed the crumbs from my jeans and got to my feet. "You can get your guys to drive me home."

"We're not done."

"We're not starting," I said. "You hauled me down here on no excuse whatsoever to ask me questions about a dead man. All I know about him is his name, and I'm not even sure it's his real name or how to spell it. You have no further need to talk to me because I know nothing else."

"I can get a warrant to hold you as a material witness."

"In that case, I'm calling my lawyer." I pulled my cell phone out of my jeans pocket and touched Freeman Carter's speed-dial button.

I got his secretary and gave her my location and situation while Conrad was telling me to calm down, we didn't need lawyers muddying the waters.

"If I don't call back in half an hour, you should assume I've been charged and don't have access to a phone," I said to Freeman's secretary.

When I'd hung up, I added to Conrad, "We like to take potshots at lawyers in America. They muddy the waters, you say. I say they're all that stands between an ordinary citizen and a forced confession. My least favorite line on cop shows is when they sneer at suspects for 'lawyering up.' The sneer is a protective cover over their annoyance at not being able to ride roughshod over the person in custody."

"You're not in custody," Conrad said, "although at the moment I'd like to see you there. Tell me how you know the dead man."

"Back to square one, Lieutenant. I didn't know—"

"All right. But you know his name, which we didn't. The police appreciate your helping them move this inquiry forward. Could you please tell this sleep-deprived public servant how you came to know the dead man's name?"

We were friends now, I guess. "I saw him twice in the last two weeks, both times by accident. The first was in Saint Eloy's church, when I was talking to the priest, and the second time was outside Wrigley Field last Friday."

"You were never introduced, you said. How did you learn his name?"

"In the church he was in the middle of a heated conversation with a young woman who called him 'Uncle Jerry.'" I looked broodingly at Conrad, trying to decide if it was a mistake to be forthcoming.

"I have a friend down here whose high school kid has been described as a baseball phenom in the making. I stopped at Saint Eloy's the other day to watch the kid play. The priest—Father Cardenal—came over to me and told me Uncle Jerry had asked for my name. The priest had given it to him. I thought it was only fair to get the guy's name in turn. Cardenal didn't like it but he coughed it up."

"Why were you in church to begin with?" Conrad asked. "I mean, when you saw the dead guy arguing with a woman?"

"This is why it's a mistake to say anything to a cop," I said. "You always assume that you have license to ask any question you want. You don't. I helped you as a citizen doing my duty. End of chapter."

"You're not a Christian," Conrad said. "Why would you go to church?"

I took out my phone and started scrolling through my mail.

"If you're trying to ride me, you're doing a great job," Conrad said. "I got yanked out of bed at five to look at Uncle Jerry. I need help, I need sleep, I don't need lip."

I finished typing an e-mail and looked at the time. "In five minutes, if I don't call Freeman Carter, they're going to put wheels in motion to find me, get me bail, all those things."

"You're not being charged, or held," Conrad said, his lips a thin tight line. "Now will you please tell me why you were in church?"

"I was there on family business. Tell me how you knew to connect me to Jerry Fugher."

Conrad is like all cops: he hates to share information, but he finally said, "He had your name in his pants pocket. Wadded up in a Kleenex. He'd been stripped of IDs, even the brand names of his clothes, which aren't rare high-fashion items. We figure his killers overlooked the dirty Kleenex, but maybe they wanted to send us to you."

"He had my name? Written down?"

"One of your business cards."

"I never gave him one." I thought it over. "I gave one to his niece. I suppose she could have given it to Fugher."

"What's your theory on who killed him, or why?"

"I have no theory because I know nothing about him. Also, I only just learned he's dead. I'm guessing that whoever killed him had access to the Guisar slip. Fugher was at the top of the mountain. He'd have to have been driven up in a bulldozer, or maybe someone came from the water side with a cherry picker. He wasn't a lightweight and anyway, I'm guessing you don't climb up a pile of coal dust very easily."

"Yeah, Sherlock, we figured that out."

"Father Cardenal said he did odd jobs in the neighborhood," I offered. "Fugher did freelance work on the church's electrics; maybe he mis-wired the Guisar brothers' Palm Springs mansion and they buried him in coke as a warning to other electricians."

My phone rang: Freeman's secretary, checking on me. "I think the lieutenant has decided I'm not a person of interest in the murder of Jerry Fugher, but if that changes I'll text you."

Conrad glared at me, but didn't pick up the bait. "What about the woman in the church, the one Fugher was arguing with the first time you saw him?"

I shook my head. "No idea. I didn't get a good look at her because the lighting in there was poor, but I'm guessing she was around thirty. White woman, maybe five-six, her hair might have been dark blond. You could ask Cardenal."

"We'll both ask Cardenal."

"You know I have a life, a job, things that don't revolve around you and your needs."

Conrad grinned, showing his gold incisor. "You've been down on my turf lately, Warshawski. I don't believe in the Easter bunny and I don't believe you'd travel all the way from Cubs country just to look at a high school kid play baseball. You're up to something down here, and that means you get to come with me so I can watch you and the good father interact."

22

THE TOO-REAL
THING

Conrad dropped me at the commuter train station when we'd finished talking to Father Cardenal. I was furious: he'd had his men
bring me the length of the city, but he refused to drive me back, even
though the commute on public transport would take close to two
hours. But Conrad, who waxes hot and cold with me, or maybe cold
and lukewarm, felt I'd been obstructing his investigation. Leaving
me to find my way home was punitive in a petty way. Police don't get
paid much, but power is a job benefit most of the rest of us don't
have.

If he hadn't been so abrasive, I might not have left the station—or
if there'd been a train due soon, but they only run once an hour this
time of day and I'd just missed one.

The station wasn't all that far from the Guisar slip. As soon as Conrad's car turned south, I climbed down from the platform and walked
along Ninety-third Street toward the docks. It was hard to keep my
sense of direction on the roads that twisted around the Calumet

River. My phone's map app was also baffled. There are a lot of ware-houses, scrap metal yards, loading docks, abandoned steel plants and so on along the river and I made a couple of time-wasting detours.

The confusing trail was kind of a metaphor for my conversations this morning, first with Conrad, then with Father Cardenal.

We'd talked to the priest under the crumbling ceiling to his office. The patch I'd watched him install two weeks ago was still in place, but another hole had appeared over the photo of Father Gielczowski.

Cardenal had expressed shock at Jerry Fugher's death, and had asked if I was involved in it. Of course, that made Conrad jump on me like Mitch on a shinbone, so the conversation, which had not been cordial from the outset, deteriorated further.

When I'd finally persuaded the two men that accusing me of all the crimes in South Chicago wasn't a recipe for my cooperation, Conrad remembered the woman I'd seen talking to Fugher, or as he put it, that I "claimed" I'd seen talking to Fugher.

I gave Cardenal the same description I'd given Conrad.

"She could be anyone," the priest said, looking at me suspiciously.

"She could be any white woman with dark blond shoulder-length hair, about thirty years old," I said. "She called him 'Uncle Jerry.' Who was his family?"

"He wasn't an employee, so he didn't fill out the forms that people on the payroll do. We paid cash; I don't even have a home address for him," Cardenal said.

In South Chicago, this didn't sound as strange as it might on the Gold Coast: this was a neighborhood where people bartered services or got paid under the table. "How much work did he do for you?"

"It wasn't like that, I mean not like he'd come every Monday," Cardenal said. "I kept a punch list that I'd give him when he came around. He knew how to handle wiring in an old building, but he only showed up when he needed money."

"The day I saw him, two weeks ago, had he been working in the church?"

Cardenal threw up his hands. "I can't remember after all this time. He might have been."

He rummaged through the papers on his desk and picked up a sheet. "The light on the lectern, they reported that three weeks ago and it's still flickering, the circuit breaker on the organ, that keeps blowing. We can't afford a new panel, so Jerry would reroute wires for us, but he didn't do either of these projects."

"So the day I saw him here, he likely chose the church as a meeting place," I said. "Or the woman chose it. You don't have any 'Fughers' on your parish rolls or teaching at the school?"

Cardenal shook his head. "It's an unusual name; I'd remember it."

"You say Fugher came around when he needed money," Conrad said. "Drugs? Booze?"

"Not that I ever noticed," the priest said, "but maybe he had other habits, like gambling, or didn't know how to manage money. Or maybe he was supporting a family, like this woman Ms. Warshawski says she saw, although he didn't seem like a family man. You could check with the shops on Ninety-first Street; he told me he did some odd jobs for them. Talk to Mr. Bagby, since Ms. Warshawski saw him in a Bagby truck."

"You *what*?" Conrad's voice was a whip-crack. "You saw him with Bagby and didn't think it was worth mentioning?"

"Is this a big deal? Is Bagby connected?" Trucking is a good Mob cover—you can go anywhere and carry anything, including dead bodies to coal dust mountains.

"As far as I know, Bagby is a model citizen. Unlike you," Conrad said.

I'd pulled out my iPhone to show him the picture I'd taken of Fugher and the gravel-faced man, but that needless bit of sarcasm made me keep it to myself. Probably a mistake, since if anyone had hitman written all over their scarred and pitted faces, it was the gravel guy.

"You could still ask him whether Fugher did any work for them. Although the dispatcher told me he didn't recognize him."

Conrad became even more incensed. "You *went* to Bagby?"

"I have yet to meet Vince Bagby, but I did stop at the yard to ask about Fugher. I couldn't figure out why he was so nervous around me, but the dispatcher claimed not to know him."

"And you say you were only on my turf on family business?" Conrad demanded. "This is crossing a line, even for you."

"Excuse me, Lieutenant, but at what point did we morph into Russia or Iran, where a citizen has to get police permission to walk into a business and ask questions? The dispatcher might have lied to me; you could probably charm him into telling you the truth, flashing your badge and your gun and maybe a bullwhip."

"Vince Bagby has been very generous to our youth scholarship fund," Father Cardenal interjected. "Please don't say anything that would make him think we don't appreciate what he does."

"What about Rory Scanlon?" I asked. "I know he's offered to help young Frank Guzzo go to baseball camp. Does he support your youth programs?"

"Mr. Scanlon also does a lot for us. Betty Guzzo talked to me after you left. She's frightened of you. She thinks you came to the game the other day to ruin Frankie's chances with Scanlon," Cardenal said.

"The whole Guzzo family seems to have been sniffing glue or something that rots the brain," I said. "All I want is for Stella to stop slandering Boom-Boom. I hope Frankie gets his big chance, but he's only fifteen; you don't know what he'll be like at nineteen."

"Is that a threat?" Cardenal asked.

"You mean you're taking Betty's rantings seriously? Of course it's not a threat. When my cousin was fifteen, there were other kids his age who looked as good as him. They worked just as hard as he did or maybe even harder, but they were as good as they were ever going to be when they were fifteen. I don't know what Scanlon's quid pro quo is, unless community goodwill helps turn out the vote in the Tenth Ward, but if he gets young Frank into a quality baseball camp, that will be a big help in the kid's development."

"Why can't community goodwill come because someone cares about the community?" Conrad demanded. "Why does it always have to be something ulterior with you?"

"Conrad. Dear, kind, naive Lieutenant Rawlings: this is Chicago, Scanlon's a fixture in the Democratic machine, Tenth Ward committeeman for starters—"

"Scanlon's a *fixture* down here," Conrad interrupted. "Gives to our widows and orphans funds, takes part in our programs against gang violence. The quid he wants personally is a piece of the insurance action. We let him sell life insurance to any of our cops who want more coverage than the union offers. It's a fair deal in exchange for all he does for the community."

"Frank Guzzo told me he takes boys off on solo trips if they need special counseling. Do you ever see any change in them when they come back?" I asked.

Conrad and Cardenal both blew up at that suggestion, which left me uneasy, not reassured. It sounded as though they were hearing the same warning bells I had, only they didn't want to acknowledge them because they needed Scanlon's support. When I said as much, it only made them angrier. Conrad and I left soon after that, with Conrad giving me a biting lecture on outside agitators coming into a community and getting everyone hot and bothered.

"I remember that language directed at civil rights workers," I said.

"No one's confusing you with Ella Baker, so don't get a swelled head. What are you really doing down here? Don't ask me to believe crap about your family. You don't have relatives here anymore."

"Where families are concerned, it doesn't matter if they're alive or dead, you're always carrying them with you. Frank Guzzo brought me down here to talk to his mother. Who responded by digging up this alleged diary. You followed the story, I assume."

"I called up the old case files on Anne Guzzo's murder after I saw your cousin's name in the papers. The crime scene photos were eye-popping. Stella must have gone completely off the rails. I don't know what you think you're doing digging through it after all this time."

I made a face. "Me either, but after watching the kaleidoscope spin for a while, I'm beginning to think Frank was trying to divert my attention. Something about him or his wife or even his mother is going to come to light because of Stella's determination to get an exoneration. He's afraid I'll get wind of it, so he was trying to pre-empt me."

"What was going to come to light?" Conrad asked.

"I don't know. Betty, Frank's wife, said something odd when I was down here on Friday to watch her kid play—it almost sounded as though she was admitting she played a role in Annie Guzzo's death."

"I've got enough active gang murders down here to keep me busy until I retire and even then I won't have made a dent. I can't care much about an old woman who's done her dime. I talked to a guy I know at Logan, and Stella Guzzo was one of the wilder inmates. She's not a noble soul. Highly unlikely she covered for a daughter-in-law. Unless you think they were lovers?"

I stared at him, astounded. "With your imagination, you should be writing lurid romances, Conrad."

"You tried to smear Rory Scanlon with a pedophile rap just now, and you're offended? You can dish it out, but you sure can't take it."

He put the car in gear and drove four blocks to the Metra Electric train station. "End of the ride for you, Warshawski. I'm sorry Stella Guzzo is trying to offload her guilt onto your cousin, but why don't you let that dog sleep in the dirt with her own fleas instead of dragging a priest and a good community figure into the mess?"

"Oh, to hell with you, Conrad. I'm not dragging anyone anywhere. You're the one who dragged me down here without a car, so you can drive me to the Loop."

"You can find your way, Warshawski, you're a big girl."

I tried not to keep replaying the conversation as I slogged along—anger is a terrible way to make decisions. On the other hand, anger kept me moving around the mud holes and broken bottles at a good clip.

At one point I remembered Murray. I was still annoyed with him over Boom-Boom, but we have been colleagues of a sort over the years and it's better to have a friend than an enemy in the media. While I was texting him Fugher's name, I stumbled over a piece of rebar and grazed my forearms in the gravel. I put my phone in my hip pocket—definitely not the place to walk distracted.

I started coughing and sneezing before I actually saw the pet coke mound. When I turned at the next bend, I found myself at the locked gates leading to the Guisar slip. A guard station was at the entrance but the guard wouldn't talk to me, just waved a hand at me to go away.

I backed away from his sight lines and followed the fence where it skirted the river and the train tracks. Signs along the fence warned that the area was under high security, but not all the slips had guardhouses. I found a set of gates with just enough leeway in the chains that I could wriggle through. I now had rust stains on my red knit shirt, but there is no gain without some pain, at least not in my life.

The potholes were filled with water from last night's rain. The surface was that purple-greeny color you get when your transmission fluid leaks all over the street. As I squelched through the oily mud, I cursed my impulsiveness. I could have watched this on Murray's cable show. I also could be downtown by now—the next train to the Loop had taken off while I was being waved away from the Guisar slip's gate.

I came at the coke mound from the back. A police van for the forensic techs was parked on the lip and a crew in hazmat suits seemed to be taking the top of the mountain apart. I moved around to the water side of the mountain. I wasn't sure what I was hoping to find, since the techs were going over the area, but I was trying to imagine how Fugher's body got to where it had ended up.

I peered over the edge of the dock. Besides the usual waterfront garbage—bottles and cans, remains of McDonald's and Popeye's, tampons and Pampers—pieces of drywall, two-by-fours, a car fender, Styrofoam cups, swirled around. The Cubs would be in the World Series before anyone sorted through this muck for clues about Fugher's death.

I edged my way along the narrow strip between the coke mound and the water, pulling my knit top up to cover my nose and mouth. Even so, the dust made my eyes water. I was sneezing violently when a hand grabbed me roughly by the shoulder.

"Who the hell are you and how did you get out here? You some goddam reporter?" A man in a hard hat and orange safety vest, his skin like tanned leather from life in the great outdoors, had appeared behind me.

"Nope. I'm a goddam detective. You with the police?"

"I'm with Guisar and I'm tired of strangers on my slip. I want to see your badge."

I pulled out the laminated copy of my license. "I'm private."

"Then you sure as hell have no business out here. How'd you get past the front gate without a pass or a hard hat?"

"Just lucky, I guess."

He frog-marched me around to the front of the mound, where his crew were sitting on overturned barrels or leaning against their earthmoving machines, watching the forensic teams at work.

A silver Jeep Patriot pulled up, splashing mud on my jeans. The driver, a guy around fifty with a marine haircut, lowered his window.

"Jarvis, what the hell you doing sticking dead bodies out here on the dock? You let a game of hide-and-seek get out of hand?"

He was grinning widely and the Guisar man smiled in turn, but perfunctorily. "Bagby—you saw the news?—it was—"

"Awful. I know," Bagby cut him off. "Shouldn't make a joke out of it. Did you find out who the dead man was?"

"The cops just learned. Guy named Jerry Fugher. They say he did odd jobs around the neighborhood, but what he was doing here on the docks, no one knows."

"Who's the talent?" Bagby asked, jerking his head at me.

"I'm trying to find out. The lady got in here without a pass. I don't know how she got past Kipple at the main gate, but I'll have a talk—"

"You look like you walked up the tracks," Bagby said to me, taking in my mud-spattered clothes. "Whatever you want must be pretty important. What can we do for you, Ms.— Uh?"

"Warshawski," I said.

"The hockey player?" Bagby asked.

"I'm retired. These days I'm an investigator."

Bagby looked startled, then threw back his head and guffawed. "I earned that. You're related to Boom-Boom Warshawski?"

"Cousin." I smiled: two can play nice. "I'm the person who ID'd Jerry Fugher for the police. I understand he worked for you?"

Bagby shook his head. "If you told the cops that, they knew before I did. Never heard of the guy."

I pulled out my cell phone and showed him the picture of Fugher getting into one of his trucks with Gravel.

Bagby took the phone from me and frowned over the picture. "The shot's too blurry to make out their faces that well, but the short fat guy looks a hell of a lot like Danny DeVito. I recognize the truck, though, damn it. Some SOB is going to be collecting unemployment before the day is over, letting a stranger drive one of our trucks. Huge legal exposure to that. Forward that photo to me, okay? I can read the plate; that'll tell me who was supposed to be driving that morning."

"I gave the photo to your daughter on Friday. I'm surprised she hasn't shown it to you."

He shook his head, mock sadness. "Delphina! If the guy had looked like Johnny Depp instead of Danny DeVito, she'd have tracked him down by now instead of letting it go completely out of her head."

I smiled, mock understanding. "She must have your dispatcher wrapped around her finger for him to forget, as well."

He gave me another appraising look, but dropped the subject, saying he'd give me a ride out to the road. "Save you schlepping all the way back on foot."

"I'll stay out here, see what the cops turn up."

"She can't stay here," the Guisar man said to Bagby. "She doesn't have a pass or a hard hat, she's not with the city. Drive her out."

Drive me out. It sounded as though I was a demon possessing a pig.

"Yeah, sorry about that, Ms. Warshawski, but Jarvis is right. No pass, no hard hat, no visit."

I gave in with as much grace as I could muster, stopping at the squad cars to see if I knew anyone on duty. No luck. Jarvis, who'd followed me, lecturing me on how I was trespassing, started sneezing mid-sentence. I kept my top pulled over my nose.

Bagby honked. "Warshawski! Train's leaving the station."

I climbed into his front seat and looked mournfully at my clothes. My running shoes were caked with mud, my socks were soaked through, and my almost-new jeans had a long tear up one leg—I must have caught it on a piece of wire when I was sliding through the fence.

"This guy Fugher must be something special if you wrecked your wardrobe to look at his burial plot. How'd you know him? He part of one of your private investigations?" Bagby asked.

"And that would be your business because . . . ?"

Bagby grinned, but he kept his eyes on the road, swerving around the biggest potholes. "Just making conversation. Although if he was driving one of my trucks, I guess I'd better find out what he was up to. Every now and then a cargo does go missing."

"You know Frank Guzzo?" I asked.

"Is this a trick question? Of course I know Guzzo. He's been with the company forever. Don't tell me you thought he'd be on Guisar's dock back there."

"Just making conversation," I said primly. "When Frank tried out for the Cubs, Bagby's gave him time off to get in shape."

"That was my old man, may he rest in peace. Heart attack seven years ago." We were at the outer gate, which swung open for the Patriot. Bagby stuck his head out the window to hallo at the guard.

"Kipple, this lady got lost out here, found her way to the Guisar slip. Ask Security to check the fences, make sure you don't have any holes. You don't want anyone else wandering in here after dark and dying in the coal dust."

"You know he died in the pet coke?" I asked. "I didn't think the ME had even started an autopsy."

"Figure of speech," Bagby said sharply. "Are you always this literal-minded?"

"Usually. People say what they actually mean more often than not. Lieutenant Rawlings at the Fourth District—you know him, right?—only told me a couple of hours ago that they thought Fugher was alive when he went into the coke."

Bagby grinned again, his mask of good nature back in place. "In that case, I'll check with Rawlings. You know how to get home from here?"

I thought about making a smart remark, something Chandler-like or Bunyanesque, like "I am home here," or "Here I have no earthly home," but I only said, "Oh, yeah," and started the long trek back.

23

THE PLAY'S
THE THING

Yet another train had gone when I got back to the station. I was hungry and thirsty and cranky and sneezy. I also was sweaty and grimy, I realized, looking at myself in the dimly lit station bathroom.

After a day of hard slogging, on foot as well as with Conrad, the priest and the guys on the dock, I sought refuge in comfort food, a BLT with fries. While I ate, I looked up Fugher in a subscription database.

He hadn't left much of a trail, which wasn't surprising for a guy in the cash economy. He'd grown up on the East Side, son of Wilma and Norman Fugher, both now dead. He'd attended St. Francis de Sales High School, then done a degree in business at one of the local community colleges.

As far as I could tell, he'd never married and didn't seem to be supporting children. He also didn't seem to have any siblings, so he must have been a courtesy uncle to the woman with honey-colored hair. Which meant tracking her down would be difficult. Not that I had any real reason to look for her, except to validate my story with Conrad.

It wasn't clear where Fugher had picked up enough electrical know-how to fix St. Eloy's wiring. He didn't seem to have been filing taxes, so it wasn't possible to follow his work history.

Fugher's last listed address was in Lansing, a small town sandwiched between Chicago's southeast edge and the Indiana border. My map app showed his home as a garage behind a bungalow. A visit there would have to wait until I had a car. Which would never happen if I didn't get back to the train station in time for the 12:21 train downtown. I wiped the mayonnaise from my iPad screen and scurried back to the station.

From the Loop, after three guys wouldn't let me in their cars, I found a cabbie who was willing to drive me home. The cabbie had a news station turned on: police were not confirming the identity of the man who'd died in the coke until they'd located any relatives, so they weren't confirming Global Entertainment's report that his name had been Jerry Fugher. I smiled to myself: Murray hadn't been able to sit on the ID. Good that Conrad was getting goosed.

Jake had left for a day of teaching, but I let Mr. Contreras know I'd returned without handcuffs and only minimal bruising. Bernie was presumably pulling shots for yuppies right now, which meant I had the luxury of a long bath.

My clothes were so crusted with mud and coke dust that I stripped on the landing and left everything there. I wasn't sure the running shoes or jeans could be salvaged, they were so soaked with industrial oils, but I might be able to get the knit pullover clean.

I had to run water in the tub three times before I got all the pet coke out of my hair and pores. For the next day, every time I sneezed or coughed I left a gray residue on the Kleenex. Thank goodness the Pollution Control Board had assured us there was no known individual health risk to coal dust. Like black lung or epithelial cancer.

My plan had been to go to my office, get caught up on client reports, and map out a strategy for talking to Rory Scanlon, but I had gotten as far as putting on clean underwear when I couldn't keep moving one minute longer. All those sleep experts tell you not to nap during the day, that your sleep urge will become so strong that you will get eight hours the next night, no problem. Those sleep experts, of course, aren't wakened early by the police or tormented by thoughts of the Guzzos. I was out to the world within a second of lying down.

Jerry Fugher was covering the Stadium ice with soot. Boom-Boom skated in from the side and knocked him down. The buzzer sounded, the game was over, but Boom-Boom was rolling Fugher in the soot, and the buzzer kept sounding and I stuck an arm out to shut off the alarm, but it was my phone.

"Vic? Are you in there alone?" It was Bernie.

I pulled myself blearily upright. "Where are you? You okay?"

"Yes, yes, I'm fine, but there is a person here to talk to you. Can we come in?"

"No. Who is it?"

Bernie opened my bedroom door, still talking to me on her phone. "I don't know who it is, some lady who wants to talk to you. When I saw all your clothes out front, I thought maybe you and Jake—"

"Right. Now get out and let me get dressed."

When I'd pulled on jeans and a sweatshirt, Bernie was waiting outside my bedroom door, anxious about my visitor. I was in that groggy state you get from heavy sleep in the middle of the day. I shook my head at her and went into the kitchen to make an espresso. While the machine heated, I ran cold water from the kitchen tap over my head.

Bernie followed me in. "What if she is another policeman? Or a killer? You should come see her now."

"Don't let strangers into the building, Bernie, in case they are police or killers. What did she say that made you let her in?"

Bernie shifted uncomfortably. "When I was unlocking the front door, coming back from work, she appeared next to me. She asked for you, asked if I knew you, and when I said, yes, of course, because I am living with you, she followed me."

I let out a moan. "Bernie—after I get rid of her, we'll have a little class on how to respond when people accost you. For now, go down the back stairs to your uncle Sal, in case she's an ax murderer."

When I'd scooted her out the kitchen door, I pulled two double shots. The first I drank in one breath, the second I carried with me—I could fling it in my visitor's face if she turned violent.

Far from threatening violence, she was hovering in the hallway, looking nervously around as if fearing an ambush herself. Her honey-colored hair was swept back from her face as it had been when I saw, or claimed I saw her at St. Eloy's two weeks earlier.

"You—you're a detective, right?" she said.

"I am. And you are Jerry Fugher's niece?"

"I—are we alone? Who was that girl?"

"The young woman you talked into letting you into the apartment lives here, she has a right to be here, so forget about her and focus on who you are and what you want." I moved past her into the front room and sat cross-legged in my armchair, rubbing my calves, sore from this morning's hike.

She perched on the edge of the piano bench. "How did you know he was my uncle?"

"I don't, actually. I heard you call him that in church, the day I gave you my card. But Jerry Fugher didn't have any siblings, so tell me who you are, and why you're here."

"He did have siblings."

I was having trouble following her, even with the aid of espresso. "Have the police talked to you?"

"No! They don't know about me, they can't know about me."

Murray would buy me dinner at Filigree for a month if he knew I had Fugher's niece with me.

"Okay. Let's go back to your uncle. Why did he keep his siblings a secret?"

"He didn't do it on purpose, he never knew about us. My mother, she was his sister, but their mom, my grandma, she gave him away to this other family when he was born, so they adopted him. Then when my brother and I were sixteen, she was dying, our mother, I mean, and she told us about him, so we looked him up. He wasn't very friendly, he wouldn't even come to Mom's funeral, but we didn't have any other family, so we tried to stay in touch, sort of."

She was winding a tissue around her fingers.

"And your name is?"

"You have to promise not to tell anyone, anyone at all, not the police or reporters or anyone!"

I looked at her curiously. "If you've committed a crime, I'm not going to hide you from the police."

"I haven't committed any crimes, but look what happened to Uncle Jerry!"

"I won't tell anyone your name, but I can't go on with this conversation until you reveal it."

She looked around again. "Viola. Viola Mesaline. Where did you see Uncle Jerry? Is he really dead?"

"He's in the morgue but the police showed me photos taken of him in the coal dust at the Guisar dock. If you want to see his body, or claim him for burial, you'll have to talk to the police, let them know you're his next of kin."

Viola sprang from the piano bench. "I can't! I—please! You mustn't tell them about me."

"Ms. Mesaline, please. If you want to talk to me, sit down, talk to me, but if you can't trust me, then leave." I finished my second coffee, wishing it was doing a better job of clearing my wits.

Viola sat again, about an inch of her body touching the bench. She'd made up her mind to talk to me when she decided to look me up, but the story was slow in starting. She stopped frequently to demand my silence while she listened to footsteps on the stairs.

She'd come about her brother, her twin brother, Sebastian.

"Mom, she was an LPN, a practical nurse, but she was always taking these night school classes to improve herself. She was taking a Shakespeare class when she got pregnant with us, so she named us like that, after Shakespeare. Of course, no one in our school knew about Shakespeare, or they would have made fun of us for being stuck-up, but even so I got called 'violin,' or even 'violence,' all the time."

She edged farther onto the bench. "Mom always wanted us to go to college, and I started at DePaul, but Sebastian, he made good grades and he got himself a scholarship to IIT to study engineering."

"What kind? Electrical?" I wondered if that was where Uncle Jerry picked up his wiring skills.

"Electrical? Why would you think that? He's in construction engineering, but he hasn't been able to find a full-time job. He does contract work with Brentback."

Brentback was one of those contractors whose name always pops up on the siding around the city's big construction sites. "Sounds as though your brother has his foot in a good door," I said.

"Yes, I suppose. But he's disappeared, that's the problem, and Uncle Jerry, I'm sure he knows, knew, what happened, but he won't say. Wouldn't say."

I sucked in a breath. "How long has Sebastian been gone?"

"Almost a week now."

"And why did Uncle Jerry know about it?"

"When Sebastian was in school, we didn't have any money." Viola spoke to the floor in a whisper. "He worked in the bursar's office and—and he borrowed money from the accounts to pay his bills."

"Was he expelled?" I asked when she came to a complete halt.

"They found out right away. I guess Sebastian didn't really know what he was doing, so he didn't know how to cover his trail."

"Embezzling is hard to conceal," I agreed, "especially for a beginner."

"It wasn't embezzling," she said reproachfully. "It was *borrowing*. He was going to pay them back, only they found out about it too soon."

"How was he going to pay them back?" I tried to keep the impatience out of my voice. "By borrowing from someone else?"

"No, he thought—he knew someone who'd made a huge amount of money playing online poker and Sebastian got him to show him the system he used. Only he lost, it was like thirty thousand dollars in twenty minutes. I was watching, it was terrifying—he kept thinking he'd start winning. He only stopped because I turned off his computer. We didn't know what to do, so I went to Uncle Jerry."

"Jerry had money?"

"He said he could get the money but we'd have to pay him back and of course we agreed, but we didn't know—it was so expensive! The interest, we could barely keep up, even with us both working. I can't really date anyone, seriously, I mean—if some guy gets interested in me I break it off so I won't have to explain about the money. I can't even take a real vacation: all our money goes to Uncle Jerry!"

I wondered if she had any idea how good a motive for murder she was giving herself, but I didn't suggest it. "How long has this been going on?"

"Seven years now. It's like—the thirty thousand Sebastian lost, plus the twelve thousand he borrowed from the school accounts, we've paid that much three times already but we still keep owing Uncle Jerry."

So Jerry had juice connections. "Your brother got to graduate from IIT?"

"Yes, thank goodness, at least the school let him pay back what he borrowed. He was on probation for his last two years, but they didn't put anything bad on his transcript. Only that's how the money to Uncle Jerry got so huge, because we could only make small payments when Sebastian was still in school and Uncle Jerry said the interest was like really expensive because none of us could get credit from a regular bank. I started working full-time as soon as I saw how much it was. I take classes at night, like my mom, but I've never been able to finish my degree. As soon as Sebastian gets full-time work, I'll quit my job and go back to school, but construction these days, it's hard."

"You're a good sister," I said.

She flushed. "We're all each other has."

"You couldn't persuade your uncle to let you off the hook? If you've already paid him, what? A hundred and twenty grand? That should have been enough."

"That's what Sebastian and I kept telling him. That's what we were arguing about in church the day you saw me there. Sebastian— he's afraid they're going to let him go at the place he's working and we can't keep those payments up. You saw how Uncle Jerry acted. But then a few days later he said he could make it all go away if Sebastian would do him a favor."

"And the favor was what?"

Viola looked at me with large unhappy eyes. "I don't know. Sebastian wouldn't tell me, but I know he didn't want to do it, he and Uncle Jerry fought over it, I heard them, Sebastian saying if he got caught he'd never be able to work as an engineer again, and Uncle Jerry saying did he want to get out from under a rock or not. When they saw I'd come in, they stopped talking. After Uncle Jerry left, I begged Sebastian to tell me, but he said it was better if I didn't know, he caused the problem, he'd solve the problem. And then *he* left, and it was the last time I saw him."

"Do you live together?"

Viola nodded. "It was how we could save a little money, not having to pay rent separately, you know."

"Why are you here?"

Viola twisted the tissue so tightly that it tore, shedding confetti onto her jeans and the floor. "On TV they said you were one of Chicago's best investigators. Not with the police. I thought you could find Sebastian."

"It would be better if you went to the police," I said. "They have the resources—"

"No, no, no! I keep telling you, no police. If I had to tell them what I told you, they'd think Sebastian was a criminal, and they'd arrest him."

"The statute of limitations on his embezzling has expired," I said. "They won't arrest him, unless what he was doing for Jerry was criminal. Are you sure you don't know what your uncle asked him to do?"

"I don't," she wailed, "but, you know, the way Sebastian said I was better off not knowing . . ."

"Who did your uncle work for? Did you meet the people who gave him the money for Sebastian's rescue?"

"He didn't like us to be around him," Viola said. "Like, we knew he lived in Lansing, but we were never supposed to visit him. We'd meet him once a month at Saint Eloy's to pay him; he volunteers there. Volunteered."

I didn't try to tell her Jerry got paid for his church work, but pulled out my cell phone and showed her the picture I'd taken.

Viola didn't recognize the gravel-faced man. "I keep telling you, we hardly ever saw Uncle Jerry. He said he didn't want to talk to me in public, he didn't want people tracking him, but I'm so desperate about Sebastian, I kept trying to phone Uncle Jerry, but he wouldn't answer—I guess he saw my name on the caller ID. And now he's dead, and what if the same people are after Sebastian? I have to find him. Can you do it? If he gets—if someone—I'll never be able to go on without him."

I didn't like this, not one little bit. If Fugher had arranged a juice loan for his nephew, he had ties to some of the scariest people in Chicago. The way he'd been killed meant he for sure had the wrong kind of enemies. As for Sebastian, missing for almost a week after signing on to one of Uncle Jerry's projects, he was almost certainly dead, as well. Remember Nancy Reagan: *Just Say No.*

"I charge one hundred dollars an hour," I heard myself saying instead.

Viola looked at me in astonishment. "I told you, we don't have any money."

"You'll have more money now that your uncle is dead," I said bracingly. "Anyway, either you sign a contract and agree to my fee, or we shake hands forever."

24

SHORT RELIEF

We both froze at what sounded like a cavalry regiment on the stairs—Viola because she was afraid of who might be coming, me because I knew who was coming. Viola scuttled down the hall toward the kitchen. I stayed in my chair. Bernie burst into the apartment, the dogs pushing past her to run over to me. We'd been separated for ten hours and the reunion was noisy and heartfelt. Mr. Contreras, who is ninety, trudged slowly up behind them.

"Doll, we was worrying about you. Bernie said she let some strange lady in and when we didn't hear anything—and then your clothes in the front hall—"

Bernie was seventeen. She imagined disrobing as the result of uncontrolled passion. Mr. Contreras thought it meant I'd been abducted.

"She's a potential client. Viola," I called, "come on back. These are my neighbors."

Viola returned to the living room, looking suspiciously at Mr. Contreras, the dogs, and even at Bernie, who had let her into the apartment in the first place.

"If you want me to work for you, come to my office, not my home, and we'll sign a contract and you can give me an advance against expenses. You have to go now; I'm out of time."

Viola didn't want to leave by the front way, in case the people who'd killed Uncle Jerry had tracked her down here. That made me think she knew Fugher's killers, but she denied it vigorously, starting to cry again. I'd run out of patience with her; I got Bernie to take her down the back stairs and out through the gate in the alley.

"What's she want you to do?" Mr. Contreras asked.

When I told him, he expostulated that I didn't need the Mob on my case.

"No quarrel here," I agreed. "Hopefully, finding her brother won't mean tangling with the Mob."

"You turn it over to Captain Mallory," Mr. Contreras said. "This is police business."

"What's police business?" Jake came in through the open front door. "V.I., have you been mud wrestling, and you didn't get me a ticket?"

"I'm going to make my filthy clothes an art installation," I announced. "People will fill out a survey on what the clothes mean to them and I'll guess their age, sex and sexual fantasies. Like, who thinks mud wrestling first instead of, I don't know—"

"Alligator wrestling," Jake suggested.

"Way sexier," I agreed.

"Can you be ready to leave in twenty minutes? In something not covered with mud or alligator skin?"

One of Jake's students was playing a concert in a small venue off the Loop. Bernie, back from escorting Viola, followed me into my bedroom while I changed into going-out clothes. Living with a teenager means kissing any privacy farewell.

"What have you found out about this Stella woman's attack on Uncle Boom-Boom?"

I was pulling a silver top over my head, which gave me time to organize my thoughts: I didn't want to expose myself to a barrage of Bernie's urgent questions by saying I'd gotten bogged down in all the family relations involved and couldn't make sense of any of them.

"I think the diary is a cover-up for something else," I said, when I'd adjusted the sleeves and draped a scarf across my shoulders. "What I don't understand is why the Guzzos tried to drag me into their drama in the first place."

"So you're going to let them get away with attacking him?"

"I didn't say that, Bernie. The attack is a smokescreen. And I have to ask myself whether it's the best use of time and energy, my two scarcest resources, to figure it out."

"You mean you've given up trying to prove this diary *c'est de la scrape.*" She waved her hands around, trying to think of the English word. "Phony."

"Right now, Stella is the only person who admits to seeing the diary—her son and his wife both say they never had a look at it. The TV stations only had a typed transcript that the lawyer gave them; no one has seen the actual diary. It is pretty hard to hunt for something if it doesn't actually exist."

"Did you ask the priest? I thought you said she gave it to the priest."

"*If* the diary exists, she *might* have given it to him. The first time I talked to him, he said she didn't trust him because he was Mexican, but now he's eyeing me with suspicion—that's the only thing that makes me think it's possible that he has it, or at least he's seen it."

"Then go in and look for it!" Bernie urged. "I know you can, Papa has told me how you are like a cat burglar when you want to be. Or have you gotten old and slow and stodgy?"

"You nailed it. I am old and slow and stodgy."

"So you'll go to work for this woman Viola, who seems like the dreariest person in Chicago, instead of looking after Uncle Boom-Boom?"

So much for avoiding a barrage. "No, *cara*, but I work for a living. I'm not one of those amateur detectives who can live off my bond interest while I dabble in investigations. So don't ride me, okay? What are you up to tonight?"

She muttered that she was going out with some of the kids she'd met at the coffee shop. And yes, she huffed: she had my cell phone if anything went awry, yes, she'd be home by midnight, but would I be here to check?

"No, but your uncle Sal will. And he won't go to bed until you're in; he worries about you. And if he's worried he'll call me and then I'll come after you with long rakes and red bats."

Bernie's vivid face puckered into a grimace, but she wasn't sullen by nature; she let me give her a farewell hug, and promised to re-member her curfew. And to call if she got stuck someplace where she needed a ride home. What made me uneasy were the little mischief lights dancing in her eyes when I said good-bye.

Jake's student's group played a modern repertoire well, finishing with a Ned Rorem requiem that was particularly effective. We had a good meal afterward on Chicago's Restaurant Row, but I was still uneasy about Bernie and cut the evening short to make sure she came home.

"Never figured you for a helicopter aunt, V.I.," Jake said.

"Now you know two new things about me," I said. "Alligator wrestling and helicoptering. Bernie's pushing on me to break into the church. Pierre—her dad—has fed her stories about Boom-Boom's exploits, and some of mine, her whole life. I wouldn't put it past her to think she could show me up by going to Saint Eloy's and doing it herself."

Bernie arrived a few minutes after that, though, and I decided I'd been imagining the mischief in her eyes. Even so, I spent the night in my own place, but she was still asleep in the living room when I got up the next morning.

I ran the dogs, dropped Bernie at her coffee bar and drove down to my own office, where I went resolutely to work. I'd been behaving lately like one of those independently wealthy dilettantes who detected as a hobby. I finished three reports, and made a security study for a bookstore whose inventory was evaporating.

I sent out bills, including one to Frank Guzzo, amounting to $1,567.18 including expenses. I sent it, with a copy of the contract Frank had signed, to my lawyer and asked that it be delivered to Frank Guzzo—I couldn't mail it myself because of the order of protection. I didn't expect to collect, but it wouldn't do for him to imagine I hadn't been keeping track.

It wasn't until I broke for lunch that I had time to read the day's news. The buzz about Boom-Boom's putative bio had vanished, mercifully, but Mr. Villard, who'd supplied the photos I'd seen last week, had a little paragraph—there'd been a break-in at his Evanston mansion last night when he was having dinner with friends in the city.

The rest of the paper was the usual round of mudslides, children murdered in civil wars in Africa and Syria, children murdered in gang wars in Chicago and Detroit. Disease, famine, the whole Apocalypse was there. I put away the news and listened to a concert through my earphones.

Around the middle of the afternoon, Viola Mesaline appeared. I was surprised—I hadn't really expected to see her again. She was shaking and her eyes were red, grief or maybe lack of sleep.

"I'm scared," she announced. "Someone's been in Sebastian's and my apartment."

I took her into the cubicle set aside for clients. It's kind of like a psychiatrist's office—couch, box of tissues, water cooler in the corner, a discreet recording device in case the client later disputes what she or he told me.

"At work today, everyone was talking about Uncle Jerry. I mean, his death was all over the news, and people were talking like it was a horror movie, not someone's life. I couldn't take it because I couldn't say, shut up, you're talking about my uncle, you know? So I told my boss I was really sick and needed to go home, and she could tell I looked bad, so she signed me out. And when I got home, someone had been in there. They'd pulled open drawers. It was so scary and—and disgusting. I found one of my bras on the floor, and then Sebastian's room, it was a mess, they'd pulled out all his DVDs and hadn't put them back."

"Did you call the police?"

"And have them all over me about Sebastian and Uncle Jerry? Why do you want to get me in trouble? Why aren't you on my side?"

"I'm not on anybody's side," I said. "I'm trying to understand what happened. Could it have been ordinary burglars—I mean, did they take any of the obvious stuff?"

"Like computers?" She paused. "I'm not sure. Sebastian's laptop wasn't there, but I hadn't looked before. He could have taken it with him when he left."

She got an *A* for that observation—more objectivity than I'd expected from her. "Anything else?"

"The TV is old, so a burglar wouldn't take that anyway. And I don't have a computer, I just have my tablet and my phone and I had those with me."

"If it wasn't burglars, what would they have been looking for?"

"Stuff about Uncle Jerry, don't you see? What Sebastian was doing for him!"

"And you still say you have no idea what that was?"

She shook her head, tears forming on the red-crusted rims of her eyes. "Won't you please start looking for him?"

I went back to my desk and printed out a copy of my standard contract. "Read it before you sign it: it makes a number of financial demands on you, and it is binding in court."

She read it, she argued about the expenses and the advance, she reminded me she didn't have any family or anyone but her brother to fall back on.

"I still think the police are a better option for you than me," I said, taking the contract back from her.

That made her pull out her wallet and give me her bank card. The card went through without a whimper, despite my hope for a message saying "insufficient funds."

25

HIGH AND OUTSIDE

I went early to the Virejas Tower site. This was the project that Sebastian had been working on at the time he disappeared, Viola had told me. I wore my heavy boots and my parka: the construction site was near Navy Pier, just off Lake Shore Drive, and the wind blowing across Lake Michigan would be cold up on the exposed deck.

Even though I got to the main gate before seven, a crew was already on-site. I put on my hard hat and asked the guard at the gate to direct me to the project manager.

Viola had tried to argue me out of going to the job site, out of a free-flowing fear that she couldn't or wouldn't parse for me. My second client in a month who'd persuaded me to go to work based on the flimsiest of incomprehensible stories. I was beginning to wonder if I had "sucker" embroidered on my forehead, or maybe in my brain.

Viola had tapped into one of my wells of grief, but I hadn't realized it until talking about her last night with Jake. She'd mentioned casually that her mother died when she and Sebastian were sixteen.

"Not to play Dr. Freud with you, V.I.," Jake drawled, "but isn't that how old you were when Gabriella died?"

"Just call me 'Dora,'" I'd agreed ruefully.

At least in Viola's case, Sebastian was actually missing and someone really had been searching their apartment—I'd gone there yesterday after Viola signed my contract.

She and Sebastian lived in a frugal way on the poorer fringe of Ukrainian Village on Chicago's West Side, the edge where rehabbed buildings bleed into Vice Lord territory. Despite the cracks in the stairwell walls, and the sour smell in the hallway, the twins kept the apartment clean and neat—or had done before their intruder trashed the place.

Both beds had been pulled apart, the closets ransacked, but when Viola started picking up clothes, there wasn't an underlying layer of junk the way there would have been in my apartment.

The intruders had come in through the kitchen door, with a crowbar, not a slick set of picklocks. While Viola was calling the twenty-four-hour board-up service I contract with, I canvassed the neighbors. A woman on the floor below thought she'd seen a stranger going up the back stairs, but her baby had been fussing and she hadn't really paid attention.

White, black, male, female, she couldn't say, although she was pretty sure it was a man. Wearing? Jeans, maybe a gray hoodie, so she didn't see the hair. No one had been home in the other three apartments on Viola's landing.

"What were they looking for?" Viola was sobbing again when I got back.

"That's the question I get to ask you. Did Uncle Jerry leave a will, or give you any documents to look after? He was murdered two days ago; someone may be looking for something they thought you had."

She made a helpless gesture. "We hardly ever saw him, I told you. He didn't really *like* us, he just used us for money. If he even had a will I'm sure we're not in it."

"The Fughers, the people who adopted him, where is their house?"

"They died a long time ago," Viola said. "They lived somewhere on the South Side, I mean, Uncle Jerry, he grew up at 103rd and Avenue O, and they didn't have any other family. That's why we thought Uncle Jerry would be glad when we got in touch with him. Only he wasn't."

The drawers from the cardboard filing cabinet where the twins kept their bills and receipts had also been dumped onto the floor. Buried in the middle of them was the loan document Sebastian had signed. The money came through Sleep-EZ, one of the payday loan companies. I'd seen their ads on TV: *Debts keeping you awake? Come to Sleep-EZ. We'll get you the money you need and you can sleep-ez at night again.*

The only difference between Mob-run juice loans and the payday business was that payday loans are legal. Interest tops out at 355 percent a year under current laws halfheartedly designed to curb usury. Eight years back, when Sebastian had signed this paper, there hadn't been an upper limit.

The twins' copy of the loan agreement was barely legible after years of handling. I squinted at it under the light from my flash. Uncle Jerry had cosigned it, since Sebastian had been underage when he got the loan. The twins paid Uncle Jerry directly. Since he presumably had long since paid back Sleep-EZ, he was pocketing a handsome bundle of change. Which reinforced the idea that Viola and Sebastian were the best candidates to have killed him.

"What about your brother's room—was there anything in there they might want, anything that would show what he was doing for your uncle?"

"It could have been on his computer, only that's gone, like I told you already."

It was all unsatisfactory and frustrating, made more so by her resistance to my suggestions for action. "Viola, all this reluctance to talk to the cops points in a bad direction. Are you sure Sebastian didn't kill your uncle?"

That opened the sluice gates completely. How could I say such a thing? She was worried sick, she didn't want to go to the police because they would think like me, but if I wasn't going to look for Sebastian, she'd do it herself.

I wondered if I was exuding some subliminal hormone that made all my clients hysterical. "Then you have to let me know where your brother has been working. If you don't tell me anything, there's no point in your signing an agreement with me."

She capitulated, not happily. Which took me to the Virejas Tower early the next morning.

Presumably the city would supply a road to the building when it was completed, but right now the only access was a gravel track that I found by following the dump trucks rattling along Illinois Street toward the lake. I bumped my long-suffering Mustang behind them and parked outside the gate. The guard inspected my ID, made sure I had a hard hat—my silver number with "V. I. Warshawski Investigations" on it in red—and decided I could talk to the project manager.

Up close, the building's footprint was massive, covering the same amount of ground as the tower formerly known as Sears. As I approached the building, I felt tinier and tinier, an ant approaching Everest. Even the flatbeds looked small as they unloaded girders.

The building was supposed to top Trump Tower when it was finished; so far, they'd poured the deck for the seventeenth floor. The hoist operator took me to the sixteenth, where the concrete was now dry and ready for work. A crew member who'd ridden up with me escorted me across the acreage, past the open holes for the elevator shafts, to the cranes on the far side where the project manager was overseeing delivery of steel for the day's work. He wasn't eager to interrupt his job to talk to a detective, and even less eager when he learned I was private, not with the CPD.

He also wasn't interested in Sebastian Mesaline's disappearance. "We have a dozen construction engineers on a project like this. We expect them to come early and stay late—we need materials double-checked, we need stress points assessed, we need the CE's to isolate flaws the architect or design engineer didn't foresee. This design is every project manager's nightmare, too many curved surfaces, too many unusual materials. So when I have a CE who isn't on time or is phoning it in, I don't trust him. The longer Mesaline stays missing, the happier I'll be. My eleven other guys and gals are picking up the slack nicely, thank you very much."

"Why don't you fire him?" I asked.

"Brentback, the contractor, they put him on the job. I told them he wasn't pulling weight but they said he needed the experience of a big project. I'm supposed to babysit him."

"You didn't bury him in the deck, did you?"

That drew a reluctant laugh from the manager. "Would've if I'd thought of it in time. But a kid that useless probably would have made the concrete bubble. Anything else?"

I got him to take me to the makeshift office on the twelfth floor where five of the other construction engineers were already at work. After comparing notes, they agreed they could pinpoint the last day they'd seen Sebastian at the job site.

"It sticks out partly because he was the first one here," an African-American woman with beaded braids said. "I'm one of the newbies so I'm almost always doing setup and making the sludge Tyler likes to drink."

Tyler was the senior construction engineer on the project, a man in his forties with a square, wind-beaten face. "Aliana treats coffee like an engineering project, not the art form it is. She's always calculating air pressure and humidity and adjusting the measurements, instead of realizing you need hot mud to keep you going on a day like this."

"Herbal tea, Tyler," Aliana said. "I don't want your intestines when I'm your age."

I brought the conversation back to Sebastian's last day on the job.

"Right. So that morning, Sebastian was acting kind of furtive," Aliana said, "like there was something he didn't want me to see, but it didn't look like he was stealing materials or anything."

"What about your computers?" I asked, waving a hand at the array of monitors.

"They're all accounted for," Tyler said.

"Software," I said. "Could he have been putting something onto a thumb drive?"

The engineers looked at each other and shrugged. "Could've been," Tyler said, "but there's nothing unusual on our machines. Even if he wanted to give materials specs to a rival firm, it's not like they're secret formulas."

As to the last time they'd seen him, he'd worked a full day, but with even less than his usual lackluster performance. "I went back over his report with him twice," the senior man said. "He'd made a couple of mistakes that could have been costly. Aliana here, she makes a mistake like that once and she goes back through her entire workload for the day. She's the other rookie Brentback sent over, she's shaping up to be a first-class engineer."

Aliana blushed and fiddled with the buttons on her work jacket.

"I had a heart-to-heart with Sebastian at the end of the day, and he seemed to be listening, but when he didn't show up the next morning, I thought he'd chickened out, decided he couldn't face the heavy artillery again. But they told me at Brentback that he hadn't quit, that they didn't know where he was."

That seemed to be the end of what they knew about Sebastian. The young engineers had felt honor-bound to invite him for drinks after the senior engineer chewed him out, but he'd said he was going to the night game at Wrigley. We all whipped out our cell phones to look up the Cubs schedule. April 8, nine days ago.

"That's right," Tyler said. "We'd poured the deck for the tenth floor and he damned near put a foot in the wet concrete."

The room was filling up as the other engineers arrived. The architects came, with changes to the design. The senior engineer left us, giving Aliana a master key so I could look in Sebastian's locker.

"Take her back to the hoist as soon as she's seen it, then meet me on thirteen. We have a problem with the soffits on the first recess."

The engineers all had lockers where they mostly kept extra socks or earmuffs, Aliana explained, opening Sebastian's. He'd left behind a gym bag with running shoes, shorts and a cup. I riffled through the bag and found wadded-up receipts for food or toiletries.

"Sebastian had to save money," Aliana said, looking over the receipts with me. "He told us his mother left him and his sister with a humongous debt to pay off, so we weren't surprised when he wouldn't go out drinking with us. He didn't really drink, anyway. And he tried to take care of his sister—it's one of the good things about him. He isn't a very good engineer, but he's not a bad person."

Among the receipts was a scrap of paper with "11 P.M., 131" written on it in a black felt-tip. Aliana couldn't say whether it was Sebastian's writing or not.

"We do everything by text, so I never see his handwriting, and anyway, it's just a few numbers."

She also couldn't explain whether the 131 referred to anything in the Virejas job site. A building involved so many numbers, so many calculations, this could refer to almost anything, but not to anything that jumped out at her.

Her phone trilled—the senior engineer, texting her to wrap things up with the detective. She steered me to the hoist gate, then trotted to a rough-poured stairwell in a far corner to climb up to thirteen. A couple of the steelworkers catcalled at her; she laughed and bantered back, her beaded braids dancing under her gold Brentback hard hat.

The worksite had filled while I was talking to the project manager and the engineers. From twelve stories up, I felt as though I was look-ing at a movie set, something like the pyramid-building scene in *The Ten Commandments*. Lots of miniature figures crawled across the landscape hauling steel, mixing concrete, loading dump trucks.

While I was staring, the hoist passed me going up, carrying three men along with the operator. They all turned to look at me, the lone figure in the foreground. I'd seen one of them before, walking down Clark next to a frightened Jerry Fugher. I hoped my hard hat put my face in enough shadow that he wouldn't recognize me.

When the hoist came back down to collect me, I asked the opera-tor who he'd been taking up just now. "More engineers?"

"Nah, they're with the cement contractor. You guys ought to join a dating service," he said. "They wanted to know about you, too."

"'Engineers Measure Up,' that'd be a good dating site for geeks," I said, but my stomach tightened: the gravel-faced man had recognized me.

"Nah, if you want to meet them, you need to go to 'Cementing Relations.'"

I laughed obligingly. "Who's pouring for you? Ozinga?"

"This crew is with Sturlese. Brentback usually subcontracts with them on their big jobs. What dating site do you detectives use?"

"I don't know. 'Caught Flatfooted' doesn't sound attractive, does it?"

We stopped at the sixth floor to pick up another couple of guys and the conversation switched to the weather and the White Sox.

"The Mesaline kid was a Cubs fan," I said. "Any of you see him at Wrigley Field?"

"Yeah, he would be a Cubs fan," the hoist operator said. "He didn't have the balls for this kind of work."

When we got to the bottom, before he let the next upward-bound group onboard, I pulled out my cell phone and showed him the blurry shot I'd taken of Jerry Fugher at Wrigley Field. "You ever see this guy with your Sturlese Cement crew?"

"What, with Danny DeVito? Don't tell me Nabiyev is making movies in his spare time—a dead carp on the sand has more emotion than he does."

Nabiyev. At least I had the gravel guy's name now. "Maybe deep down Nabiyev is a boiling pot of feeling and the hitman façade is just that—a cover to keep us from seeing his profound emotions."

"Hitman façade? It wouldn't surprise me if he was a hit man all the way to the bone. If you can't detect that, better find a new line of work."

26

ROACH MOTEL

All the way back across the job site to the gate, I felt as though I had a bull's-eye painted on the back of my hard hat. It wasn't until I'd gotten the Mustang safely up the gravel track to Illinois Street that I breathed normally.

Instead of going to my office, I drove the thirty miles down to Lansing, to the address I'd gotten for Jerry Fugher. As the map app had suggested, it was, in fact, a garage behind a single-story frame house. I parked around the corner and walked up the alley to the garage. I had my picklocks out, but the door opened easily—someone had been ahead of me with a crowbar.

Jerry Fugher hadn't been a warm and cozy guy, and a garage, even one where someone has added insulation, a stove, a toilet and a skylight, is still a garage and not a warm and cozy place to live. This one was made particularly repellent by the level of chaos. Whoever had pried open the door had emptied drawers, the little refrigerator under the countertop and even the garbage can.

I tried to poke through the papers and garbage, using a barbecue fork that I found on the bed. Cockroaches flicked their whiskers at me contemptuously as I upended a sardine tin. When I backed away, more roaches crawled out from under the papers and sauntered to cover under the kitchenette counter. The backs of my legs tingled: I'm not afraid of bugs, exactly, but cockroaches always seem as oily and arrogant as rats.

If seven maids with seven mops swept the place for half a year they might find something of value, but I couldn't hunt when I couldn't even guess what I was looking for. Among the papers I turned over were wadded-up printouts from online bets on horses. In the pages I looked at, Uncle Jerry had won twenty-seven hundred dollars but lost over twelve thousand. No wonder he was putting the screws to his niece and nephew over the loan he'd set up for them.

I probably could track the betting losses to dates when he showed up at St. Eloy's to exchange electrical work for cash, but the gambling seemed irrelevant. It might explain Fugher's behavior, but it didn't seem to be a reason for taking his place apart.

Footsteps in the alley made me stiffen and back up to the room's only exit. A gray-haired man in jeans and a Bears jacket loomed in the doorway.

"What the fuck? Did you do this?"

"Nope. You the owner?"

He nodded toward the frame house. "Yeah, I rent to Fugher. Who are you? What are you doing here?"

"You know Fugher is dead, right? I'm a detective. I'm investigating, but this is too much for one person. When did this happen?"

"I don't know. My tenants pay me on time, I leave them alone."

"Then why are you here now?" I asked.

"Lady who lives back of me, she called to say she saw you go in here. We don't have much crime here in Lansing, but I never heard of Fugher bringing any females home with him before."

"Who did he bring home—besides every cockroach in Chicago, I mean?" I pulled out my phone and showed him my shot of Fugher and Nabiyev. "This guy? He one of the regular visitors?"

The man looked at the screen. "Never saw him before. You with the Lansing police?"

"I'm from Chicago," I said. "Fugher died in Chicago. If Nabiyev comes around, call the Chicago PD Fourth District. That's where the investigation is based."

"Nothing here for the police to care about." He stomped across the yard into the back entrance to his house. I followed him, wanting to ask him how long he'd rented to Fugher, and how he knew Fugher. He refused to open the door, crying at me, "Go away! I don't need to talk to Chicago cops, I live in Lansing, I don't know anything."

On my way back to my car I stopped at the faucet on the outside of his house and ran water over my running shoes: I didn't want to trail cockroach eggs into my own car or home.

When I got back to my office, I opened a case file for the Mesaline twins. There wasn't much to enter, but I'd learned three things this morning: Sebastian Mesaline wasn't a hardworking employee. He was a Cubs fan. I'd also learned Nabiyev's name, and that he had a job at Sturlese Cement. Four things.

I spread out the wadded-up papers I'd taken from Sebastian's gym bag at the Virejas site. Aliana, the young engineer who'd opened the locker for me, was right: Sebastian was careful with money. The receipts were for sandwiches, pizza slices, candy bars, all from grocery stores or drugstores, where prepared food is cheaper. He'd bought a CTA pass, a monthly gym pass. I entered the name of the gym into his file—it might be worth checking to see if he'd left anything behind in a locker there.

And then there was the paper that didn't relate to any purchases, the paper with "11 P.M., 131" scrawled on the back. The front was a receipt for toothpaste; he'd bought it April 6, two days before he was last seen. He'd written down where he was supposed to meet someone, that was my best guess.

A room number in a hotel, maybe. Or a location in the Virejas building that didn't mean anything to Aliana. Sebastian had come in early his last day, he'd been doing something at the computers—he could have been checking the specs for where to find 131. A junction box, an equipment unloading site. They'd poured the tenth floor the day Sebastian disappeared, the project manager had told me. Maybe Sebastian really was buried there.

I'd told Uncle Jerry's landlord to call the Fourth District if Nabiyev came around. I should call them myself to tell them I'd seen him with Uncle Jerry outside Wrigley Field. I didn't know his first name, I realized.

He didn't exist in any of my databases, which was usually true of high-profile celebrities, but true, too, of people trying to avoid any profile at all. Such as hitmen.

The chatty hoist operator had made it clear that everyone at the Virejas site knew I was a detective. It doesn't take a detective to find me: Viola Mesaline had tracked me down at home two days ago, and my office is advertised online. I didn't like a putative hitman knowing more about me than I did about him.

I took a burn phone out of my electronics drawer and dialed Sturlese Cement. Spoke from the back of my mouth, where the tone gets garbled and rougher, and said I was looking for Nebisch.

"For who?" the receptionist asked.

"Guy didn't tell me his first name. Nebisch, he called himself. Supposed to meet me at the Virejas job site."

"Nabiyev, do you mean? It's Boris. I'll page him for you. What's your name?"

"Fugher," I said, hanging up. I taped Nabiyev's name to the back of the phone so I'd remember to use a different one if I tried to call Sturlese Cement again.

Cement, like trucking, is a good Mob front. You moved all over the metro area, and if you were in fact a hitman, you had a ready-made place to bury the body. On *NCIS* or *White Collar*, I'd forcefully persuade a reluctant judge to issue a search warrant and then persuade my equally reluctant boss to give me access to a portable X-ray machine, and then I'd find Sebastian's body and make an arrest—after a near-death escape from Nabiyev, whom I'd overpower despite his bigger size and more massive gun power. I wished I were a TV detective.

This being real life, I tore off a big sheet of newsprint and started writing down the names of people I'd been talking to this past week. I made up two columns, one for people connected to the Guzzo inquiry, the other to the Mesaline investigation.

Judge Grigsby. Rafe Zukos, the rabbi's son. Joel and Ira and Eunice Previn. Mandel & McClelland, now gone, but they'd handled Stella Guzzo's defense. Rory Scanlon, who was going to get young Frankie into an elite baseball program. Trucker Vince Bagby, his daughter Delphina. Betty and Stella and Frank Guzzo.

I made a separate list for the Mesaline twins. Uncle Jerry, Boris Nabiyev, Father Cardenal.

I pinned the newsprint to the wall next to my desk. It was interesting that both sets of people had a link to St. Eloy's. Perhaps Father Cardenal was masterminding a crime ring to raise money for building repairs.

Assumption: whoever killed Jerry Fugher (Boris Nabiyev?) had broken into Sebastian and Viola's apartment. Unless, of course, it was Sebastian who had killed Jerry. I knew I was only buying trouble with the cops down the road by not going to Conrad now.

I slapped the desktop in frustration. I had to find a way to work more effectively. It was as if I were trying to move through tar pits, my feet leaden, my brain petrified. I went across the street to my expensive coffee bar—maybe a cortado would unglue my brain.

While I drank it, I called Viola. "I went to your uncle's apartment. Someone had tossed it, probably the same people who ransacked your place yesterday. What could they have been looking for?"

"I don't know, how could I know? Did someone follow you there? How do you know they aren't listening in on your calls?"

"Right," I said. "Moving on, your brother had written 'eleven P.M., one thirty-one' on a scrap of paper that he left in his gym bag at work. Any thoughts on where one thirty-one is? The other engineers didn't think it referred to anything at the job site."

Viola couldn't help with that, either. We hung up in mutual frustration.

As I was putting my papers and iPad back into my briefcase, I glanced out the window: Bernie Fouchard was across the street, ringing the bell to my building. Tessa was working today; before I could get outside, Bernie had gone inside.

I crossed Milwaukee Avenue at a trot and found Bernie in Tessa's studio, demanding to know where I was.

"Bernie! Aren't you supposed to be at work?"

She flung up her hands. "I quit that job. They wanted me there at six in the morning to start heating up boilers, which is an insane hour to be out of bed."

Tessa was wiping her face and arms with a heavy towel: sculpting is physically taxing work. "Can you two take the conversation across the hall? I need to get into the shower."

I stopped to look at the work in progress. Granite this time, not steel. Shoulders emerging from an unformed base. "Rising or sinking?" I asked Tessa.

"Depends on your perspective," Tessa said. "The client is a firm that works on climate change strategies—they wanted something that could be either hope or despair."

It reminded me uncomfortably of my tar pits. I took Bernie across the hall to my office.

"I suppose quitting looks better on your résumé than getting fired. What will you do now? Go back to Quebec?"

"The coach for the peewee hockey team where I volunteer, she works for a program that does sports with girls in schools. She thinks maybe I can get a job with them, at least until my summer training camp starts in July."

"That would be great, if your parents agree—I thought you were only coming for a few weeks to check out the city."

Bernie gave an impish grin. "Oh, Northwestern's camp is near the city; I'm sure I'll sign with them—I *love* the coach there, I love being where Uncle Boom-Boom and my papa played, so maybe I'll only go back to Quebec for my high school graduation."

"If your parents agree, and if we can find a place for you to stay on the Northwestern campus," I said firmly. "You can't live with me long-term."

Bernie caught sight of the newsprint full of names I'd created earlier. "These are all the people you are working on now?" She frowned. "I see this *ostie de folle*, this Madame Guzzo, is on your wall, but who are these others, these Nabiyevs and Mesalines? What do they have to do with Uncle Boom-Boom?"

"They're part of a different case."

"Ah, so you are not abandoning Uncle Boom-Boom. This Viola,

she maybe will show you how to silence the Medea woman." Bernie nodded sagely.

"Maybe," I agreed. "There's someone I need to talk to again. Come down to the South Side with me—maybe you'll think of something that hasn't occurred to me."

27

DEAD BALL

Joel was alone in the Previn law office when we got there, an unexpected bonus. He was hunched over a computer with a super-size soft drink nearby. He buzzed us in, but his greeting was surly.

"Ira's in court and Eunice is at the hairdresser if you were expecting to talk to them."

"Nope. You're the man I was looking for."

"What do you want? Who's the girl? Is she supposed to make me think of Annie and confess crimes I never committed?"

Bernie as Annie Guzzo's double? Except for being small and dark, they didn't look much alike. However, if Joel was obsessed with Annie, every small dark young woman might make him think he was seeing her.

"This is Bernadine Fouchard; Joel Previn. Joel is a lawyer, Bernadine is a hockey player. She's my godchild: I inherited her from my cousin when he died."

"Oh, hockey." If I'd introduced her as a toilet cleaner he couldn't have been more contemptuous. "Of course. That cousin of yours played."

"He had his moments," I said. "What uncommitted crimes will Bernadine make you confess?"

His skin turned a muddy color. "None. It was a figure of speech. I assume you know what those are."

Bernie was frowning at me, wanting me to fight, but I said, "I talked to Betty Guzzo the other day—Annie's sister-in-law."

"I know who she is. She hated Annie."

"How do you know that?"

"Annie liked to talk to me. I was the only person in that office who thought there was more to life than sports and getting drunk."

"What did Annie tell you about Betty?"

"She couldn't wait to leave Chicago, leave all the small-minded people like her sister-in-law behind. Betty and Stella didn't get along, but they both liked to beat up on Annie. Annie came in one afternoon after school with a big bruise on her face and on her shoulder. Some women, they try to cover up bruises with makeup or scarves or whatever, but Annie wanted the whole world to know what her family was doing to her."

"And she said Betty had done this?" I asked.

"First Betty, then Stella. She'd tried to talk to her sister-in-law about contraception, that she didn't need to keep having one baby after another, and Betty punched her in the mouth, then called up Stella and told her, so when Annie got home she got a double whammy from her mother. Next they got that priest to preach a special sermon on the hellfires waiting for girls who used contraception, and unmarried girls who had sex. Annie walked out in the middle of the sermon and when Stella got back from church, she hit her again."

"And this Annie didn't fight back? She didn't kill them?" Bernie interjected, trembling with anger.

"Her mother was eight inches taller and a hundred pounds heavier," Joel said. "If you'd ever been beaten up by bullies, you'd understand how hard it is to fight back."

"You go for the ankles," Bernie said fiercely. "Me, I know this because I am small, too, smaller than girls who play half as well as I do. If Annie didn't know that, then it was not Uncle Boom-Boom who was sleeping with her: he would have taught her."

I couldn't help smiling, but Joel had hunched himself deeper over his computer, his biscuit-colored skin an ugly shade of umber, as if Bernie was criticizing him for not standing up to the bullies in grammar school.

"Your logic is impeccable, babe," I said to Bernie, "but I'm not sure a jury would buy it. Not unless you could make sure they were all Blackhawks fans."

"But Uncle Boom-Boom isn't on trial! It's that *salope*, the *ostie de folle*, who should be on trial for lying about him."

"Maybe," I said. "Let's go back to the trial that actually took place. I can't find a transcript so I don't know what you said in Stella's defense. But what did she say to *you*, to her lawyer?"

"Just what I said in court," Joel said. "Stop harassing me! I can't turn the past into something that you or anyone else wants it to be."

I ignored that. "Until I talked to Betty, I was completely convinced of Stella's guilt. I thought it was her delusions about her own probity that made her think she could get a post-sentencing exoneration. But the other day, when I stopped to watch her son play baseball, when Betty threatened me, she made me think for the first time that Stella might not have been guilty, or at least, not the only guilty party. Stella beat Annie, but maybe Betty finished the job while Stella was at bingo."

"This is game playing," Joel said, sullen. "If you'd been there at the time, you'd know Stella was off the rails. She didn't care about anyone else enough to protect them. She never even talked about Betty."

"Stella wouldn't protect Betty, but she might protect Frank," I said. "It's barely possible she wore the jacket for his sake, to keep his children's mother out of prison. Now, Stella's done her time, Betty won't have more kids, and the ones she does have are almost grown. As soon as Frankie gets his shot at baseball camp, Stella can name names. I'm betting she will."

"Wore the jacket?" Bernie said. "Whose jacket?"

"Mob talk, sweetie. Means she confessed to a crime she didn't commit."

"No one would do that!" Bernie was scornful.

"You're wrong: people do it all the time, usually because they feel confused and helpless when they're interrogated."

"Stella never confessed," Joel protested.

"And she didn't say one word that implied she had a theory about who actually did kill Annie?"

"I don't remember!" Joel shouted. "It was twenty-five years ago."

He took a long swallow from the soda cup. It isn't really true that vodka is odorless, it just doesn't smell as noticeably as scotch or rum.

"Betty went through Annie's things while Stella was in prison, looking for a secret stash. Stella had already taken two thousand dollars from Annie and Betty hoped there'd be more. She also took Annie's lingerie, even though she thought it was the kind of underwear that sends you to hell."

I could picture the greed on Betty's face, the justification: she was a whore, I'm righteous, I should have these pretty things. They wouldn't have fit—even twenty-five years ago, Betty wasn't the elfin creature her sister-in-law had been. I had a skin-crawling fantasy of her hiding them, taking them out to play with, and started speaking to cover my discomfort.

"If there'd been a diary in Annie's bra drawer, Betty would have seen it. No, the diary and the implication of Boom-Boom only appeared when Stella started talking about exoneration."

Joel put the cup down halfway to his mouth. "You're saying someone planted a made-up diary to shut Stella up?"

"No one can shut Stella up; you told me not even Judge Grigsby's warnings kept her from outbursts in court. No, someone wanted to divert attention from Stella's exoneration claim."

"This Betty?" Bernie asked.

"Betty isn't imaginative enough to make up a diary. Someone else is pulling those strings behind the scenes." I eyed Joel thoughtfully: he was smart, even if he was drunk, smart enough to seem more belligerent than he was. "You're sure Stella hasn't been consulting you?"

"I keep telling you, her opinion of me was lower than, I don't know, Ira's and Sol Mandel's put together. She wouldn't come to me for a glass of water if she was dying in the desert." The metaphor made him tilt his head back and drain the cup.

"Mr. Mandel went along with the bullying in his office, I gather— the way Spike Hurlihey taunted you, for instance. What about Mr. McClelland? No one ever mentions him."

"McClelland? He wined and dined politicians and got them to throw a few alewives our way. He and Mandel figured out how to get rich in a poor neighborhood, but they needed bigger clients, downtown clients, the kind that can pull strings for you. McClelland worked that angle."

"The Loop office." I remembered Thelma Kalvin, the manager at Nina Quarles's law office, mentioning it. "The downtown connections; they were something that Nina Quarles bought from

Mandel & McClelland when she took over the South Chicago practice?"

Joel hunched a shoulder. "I suppose. I stopped paying attention to their business a long time ago. Anyway, McClelland wasn't in the office very often, but when he was, he laughed and clapped along with the rest of the audience over how Hurlihey and his clique talked to me. Only Annie . . ."

"Only Annie didn't laugh?"

"I helped her with her college applications," Joel muttered. "She needed to stand out, going up against all those prep school graduates. I helped her write her essays, then I helped her write a song. Her piano playing, she was technically good, but she didn't have the—the passion to stand out in a crowd, so we thought if she could be a composer . . ." His voice trailed away again.

My brows went up: Joel did have an interest beyond sports and drinking. "Do you still write music?" I asked.

His round cheeks bunched up so high his eyes disappeared. "I fail at everything I touch. My music was derivative, Ira knew enough to tell me that."

I couldn't think of any suitable response and even Bernie looked daunted. Joel took the plastic cover off his cup and dug out a handful of ice, which he crunched noisily.

"What about Rory Scanlon?" I finally asked. "The firm is in his building now and there's a sort of revolving door between the insurance and the legal part of the operations. Was that true in your time, too?"

"Come on, you know the South Side, everyone's got a finger in everyone's business," Joel said. "McClelland and Scanlon both worshipped at Saint Eloy's. Sol Mandel and my parents belonged to Temple Har HaShem. They pray together, then they get out of the pews and do business with each other."

"Ira does business with Scanlon and with Nina Quarles?" I asked.

"Quarles doesn't practice, she just spends the profits. But why shouldn't we buy our insurance from Scanlon? He's loyal to the neighborhood, after all, and so is Ira. Scanlon sends Ira some legal business now and then."

"Most of the people I talk to think Mr. Mandel got you to represent Stella to taunt you. Is that how you felt?"

Next to me, Bernie was quivering with impatience, wanting to leap in with advice about going for the ankles or whacking people under the chin. I put a restraining hand on her arm.

Joel took another handful of ice out of the cup. His eyes flickered to the door—this was painful, he wanted to get away from me to the Pot of Gold. I felt as though I were on Spike Hurlihey's side, bullying him, and I didn't like it.

"What about Mandel himself? Nothing anyone is saying makes it possible for me to understand why he would take on Stella's defense. Annie was his pet, she was the office pet, for that matter—"

"Not everyone felt that way," Joel said. "She teased Spike and he didn't like it."

"Teased him how?"

"Spike passed the bar, but that's because his dad was the Tenth Ward committeeman, he was tight with the mayor's family, they pulled a few strings in Springfield after Spike failed the first two times. Word processing was just starting when I worked there, and guys like Spike or Mandel couldn't type—they'd dictate their mail, so Annie picked up legal ideas from typing everyone's letters and briefs and so on. She'd give Spike back his letters with paragraphs circled in red and write next to them, 'I don't think this is what the statute says. Want me to change it before you send it out?'"

My eyes widened. Hurlihey's temper was the stuff of legends down in the legislature. Annie must have been brave, or foolhardy, or convinced that Mandel would protect her. Maybe all three.

"You think Hurlihey pushed Mandel to defend Stella because Annie got under his skin?"

Joel reddened but didn't say anything.

"Did you have a theory at the time?"

"It wasn't my job to have theories. It isn't my job to have them now. It's my job to finish this motion before Ira gets back and shakes his head like a mournful cow over how I can't get the least thing done in his absence!"

"Right. We'll get out of your way." I got to my feet. "Is there anyone who worked in that office, I mean besides Spike Hurlihey, who's still around?"

"Besides Thelma, you mean?"

"Thelma Kalvin?" I echoed, incredulous.

"She was the full-time secretary. She was another one who didn't like Annie because Annie muscled her out of the way of working personally for Mr. Mandel. Annie got twice as much done in the three hours a day she put in after school as Thelma did all week long, so of course the partners started giving Annie their dictation. Thelma ended up working for me and Spike and the other associates, and her nose was so out of joint she wouldn't type for me because she knew I was close to Annie."

"I talked to Thelma after I left here last week, and she claimed she didn't remember ever hearing about the Guzzos," I snapped.

"Don't shout at me," Joel said. "I don't know why she'd lie, except no one in that office ever told the truth. It was the perfect place for Spike to start his illustrious career. He bullies everyone in Springfield, but he got his start right here on the South Side."

I was heading to the door when another question occurred to me.

"What about Boris Nabiyev? Was he a client when you worked at Mandel?"

Joel snarled that he'd never heard the name. "I have to work if you don't." He turned back to his computer, his wide back a wall of silence.

28

BLOOD SPORT

When we reached the street, Bernie made a face. "He's a creep. Did you see his hands? Big soft paws, no muscles in them. Can you imagine him touching you? He was in love with that murdered girl, wasn't he? Do I really look like her? Is that why you brought me down here, to see what it would make him do?"

"No, *cara*. I brought you because I didn't want you roaming around the city with nothing to do. And yes, he was in love with Annie Guzzo, or infatuated, anyway. Which is why you made him think of her. Have you ever been in love, or had someone you were close to die?"

"Not really. There was a boy last year, but really, it was over before it began."

"What, you went for his ankles?"

She started a hot protest, then realized I was teasing her. "It was infatuation. I thought he was in love with me but really, it was my answers on the maths exams. Why?"

"You see the beloved object everywhere," I said. "The man I married—there was a time when my heart turned over every time I thought I saw him on the street. Even more, though, there are still days when I think my mother has passed me and I turn—and it's a stranger and for a second I'm in raw mourning once again."

Bernie shifted uncomfortably. "Anyway, this Joel, he was lying. And you let him."

"What should I have done?"

"Made him tell the truth."

"I don't have any way to do that, at least not yet."

"Threaten him, tell him you'll follow him day and night until he shows you the diary."

"I don't think he has the diary."

"Because he said so? But all he did was lie!"

A Lincoln Town Car pulled up in front of the building. The driver held the back door open and a walking stick emerged, was planted in the road, followed by brown wool trousers that ended in orthotic shoes. Another moment, and the top of Ira's head appeared over the car. The driver followed him around the car to the sidewalk, but didn't try to take his arm. Ira straightened his lapels, adjusted his bow tie and nodded to the driver.

"See you Monday morning, Mr. Previn," the driver said.

When Ira spotted me, his heavy cheeks contracted, turning his eyes into puffy slits. "What are you doing here, young woman? I thought Judge Grigsby told you there was nothing in that old case."

I guess to a ninety-year-old man fifty looks young. "That's what everyone says, but I'm like the cat in that old song: no matter how many times the ship goes down or the rocket blows up, I keep coming back."

"This is beginning to look like harassment. I can have an order of protection issued."

"Of course you can. You can join Stella Guzzo behind a barrier, trembling at my footsteps."

Ira scowled.

"It's this pesky business about why Sol Mandel undertook Stella's defense, and why he insisted Joel do the heavy lifting," I said. "Rory Scanlon said it was to put some backbone into your son. There was a lot of bullying in that office, and it's not—"

"Joel couldn't take the heat. He never could take the heat. His mother and I believe in public schools, but we ended up sending him to a private school because he didn't know how to stand up to boys who taunted him.

"You don't give in to them, I told him this time and again. If I'd been that sensitive I'd have crumpled the first time I went up against the Machine. A few schoolyard insults, they were nothing compared to the threats and hang-up calls I've gotten my whole life."

His cheeks puffed out and in like the bellows of an old pedal organ. "His mother and I, we wanted him to be proud of the life we were making. We marched in Selma, we marched in Marquette Park, and instead of being thrilled at making history, all he wanted to do was 'fit in.' As if a boy like him could ever fit in!"

I felt my mouth twist in disdain and tried to straighten it. It was hard to listen to one of my own heroes talk so contemptuously about his only child.

"I can't see how forcing him to defend Stella would have given him a deep and abiding respect for principles of social justice. Why not get him involved in some of your own work—weren't you acting on behalf of Guatemalan asylum seekers back then?"

Ira leaned heavily on his cane. "Mandel & McClelland didn't do that kind of law, and Eunice and I agreed that Joel would wither if we tried bringing him into our firm. In the end, we had to, of course, because he couldn't make it anywhere else. I can't retire, not the way men who live to my age usually do, because—"

"Because you'd miss the applause you get for showing up in court and tying witnesses into knots."

I hadn't seen Joel come out of the office. Ira said, "How dare you, sir? That's—"

Joel cut him off again. He'd apparently overheard most of our conversation, because he added to me, "If you really want to know how I ended up defending Stella, Mandel and McClelland liked to pit their associates against each other. Genteel blood sport, no physical blows exchanged. We'd meet in the conference room, go around the table, everyone got thirty seconds to pitch how they saw the case. Then we'd all leap on the pitch and tear it to shreds, trying to score points with the partners. I got good at shredding, but not as good as Spike. Mr. McClelland liked Spike, he took him to the downtown office where he started making the connections that carried Spike to Springfield. And so Mr. McClelland would feed Spike the good cases before we ever got to the conference room."

"That's the voice of envy and insecurity speaking," Ira puffed. "You imagine because you couldn't—"

"I don't have a good imagination, as you've kindly told me many times. A big case came into the office, the kind of thing we hardly ever had a crack at, a class-action case involving the women at the local Buy-Smart warehouse. I stayed late to work on my pitch." Joel's lip curled into a sneer. "I didn't talk to you about it—I thought if I could make the winning pitch without your help it would prove to you that I wasn't a loser and a whiner and a crybaby and a drunk and whatever other epithets you like to use about me."

An elderly woman came up the street, using a cane herself. She stopped to greet Ira, reminded him they had an appointment.

"Let Ms. Murchison into the office, Joel," Ira rasped, "and let's not hear more of this nonsense."

"Ms. Murchison, go inside and make yourself comfortable. Ira will be in soon."

Joel spoke to the older woman with unexpected gentleness, took her arm while he unlocked the door. Once she was inside, he stood with his back against the door, facing his father, who was stumping up the walk toward him. Bernie was silent, her vivid face turning from father to son, her brow puckered with trouble at their argument. I put a comforting arm around her.

"This isn't nonsense," Joel said. "This is something you haven't wanted to hear all these years, but you can hear it now. Your friend Sol, he wasn't a nice man, and neither was his partner. You can say all you want about South Chicago being a hard place, and lawyers needing to be tough to stand up to the grime and corruption, but those two *enjoyed* seeing associates like me humiliated. They wouldn't get their hands dirty themselves, but they liked having someone like Spike on board to make it a fun game for them!"

"That's—that's such a perverted version of the lives of two good men," Ira puffed. "You couldn't handle the job and so someone else had to be in the wrong, never you! You've been like that since a child. I golfed with Sol Mandel a hundred times, we were on the board of Har HaShem together—"

"I know. He was a saint and I have a dibbuk in me," Joel said. "You said you don't believe McClelland fed Spike, but I'm telling you, I witnessed it. Pay attention. Stand up straight and listen."

That seemed to be a repetition of words he'd heard from his father more than once; Ira turned red, but subsided.

"The night I stayed late putting together an argument for the Buy-Smart women, Spike was working late, too. Every now and then he'd make some crude crack about how even if I got the case, I'd be a fool in the courtroom—fall over my feet because I was too fat to see them, or get a mistrial for making a pass at the judge—like you, Spike and Mandel and the others assumed I was queer and they loved to rub it in. By and by, McClelland came in. He went to his office and Spike, giving me this shit-eating grin, went in with him. McClelland's office shared a wall with the women's toilet, but Annie and Thelma, they were the only two women on staff and neither of them was in, so I went in and heard their whole conversation through the grate."

"Sneaking into the women's toilet, no, not even that was beneath you," Ira said.

"I heard McClelland feed Spike his presentation," Joel shouted. "I heard that, and then I got to be part of the process of watching Spike win the chance to take the case to trial. Which he lost, even with McClelland in the second chair, and then I realized, after he ran for office and became our state rep, that Spike *wanted* to lose the case. Buy-Smart gave him campaign contributions. The whole thing was a fucking racket.

"And that's what happened with Stella. We all had to make our case, and I didn't want to take part. Was I a crybaby? A queer crybaby, not big enough to play in the big leagues? Didn't I know about *Gideon v. Wainwright*? Stella might be an unpleasant defendant, but she deserved counsel. This was how lawyers proved themselves, but if I wanted to sit in a corner and masturbate over Annie instead of pulling my weight in the firm—apparently I could be queer and in love with Annie at the same time! And so on it went and so of course, whiny crybaby that I am, I caved under the pressure. Not like you:

you would have stood up to Spike and Mandel and McClelland like you did to Richie Daley and the Machine when they came after you. Just like you did to George Wallace in Selma. But not me. And now, by God, I am going to have a drink, and fuck you, Ira Previn. Fuck you and fuck all those like you."

29

IT AIN'T BEANBAG

"That was terrible," Bernie said when we were back in the car.

"Yes, I'm sorry you heard all that. It's the bad part about my job—trying to find out what happened tears scabs off wounds and you see people at their rawest."

"But who was right? Joel *is* a crybaby, like his father says. Maybe he was wrong about the people he used to work for?"

"I don't think so. For one thing, I don't know Spike Hurlihey personally, but I know how he operates, running the House of Representatives in Illinois. He does bully people and pressure people, and force them to give him money if they want to do business in the state."

"What was this machine that the father stood up to?"

I tried to give Bernie a one-paragraph primer on Illinois politics and power. "Politics is a way dirtier game than hockey."

"Hockey isn't dirty!"

"Enforcers?" I quizzed her. "Trying to whack people in the ankles to get them out of your way?"

"Oh, that—it's what you have to do if you want to win."

"Maybe you'll become a U.S. citizen after you finish with Northwestern: you'd be perfect in a state legislature. Congress, for that matter. Money changes hands, and sometimes there's physical violence, too. Like the first Mayor Daley—he had goons who went around breaking windows on people's cars or houses if they put up posters for candidates running against him. Death threats—I'm sure Ira wasn't exaggerating when he said he got those. But the biggest thing is having to give a lot of money to politicians if you want to do business, or have laws passed in your favor. It's a terrible system. And it sounds as though Spike Hurlihey got his training in a nice nest of vipers."

"Hockey is definitely not so dirty as that. And it's easier to understand. Does anything the crybaby said make you know if he was lying about Uncle Boom-Boom and the diary?"

"He made me know about someone else who was lying, or at least holding back on the truth. I want to talk to her while I'm still south, but I can drop you at the Metra station to catch a train back to the Loop."

Bernie elected to ride over to Ninetieth and Commercial with me, to Rory Scanlon's building, where Thelma Kalvin held the fort for the Paris-shopping Nina Quarles.

It was nearly the end of the business day when we pulled up in front of Scanlon's building and Thelma Kalvin was not happy to see us.

"We're about to close the office. If you make an appointment for later in the month we will find a way to fit you in."

"We won't take much of your time," I said, perching on the edge of her desk. "This young woman is a connection of my cousin Boom-Boom, by the way, and she's concerned about the slander against him."

"I told you before that I admired his playing but that I don't know anything about the accusations brought against him by that woman who murdered her daughter."

"That's an interesting phrase, isn't it? 'That woman who murdered her daughter.' You don't remember the meeting in which the partners decided that Joel Previn would represent Stella Guzzo? You worked here then, Annie Guzzo put your nose out of joint. I'd think her and her mother's names would have stuck in your head even after all this time."

I spoke loudly enough for people at the other desks to hear. Except for two people on the phone, everyone stopped what they were doing to watch, including a young couple consulting a man at a desk near the windows. The couple, who'd been arguing softly with each other when I came in, stopped their bickering to watch me.

"It was painful, so painful that I suppressed the names," Thelma said. "If you'd ever worked with—"

"Lame," I said, looking at Bernie. "Would you agree, a pretty lame excuse?"

Bernie was startled, but she picked up the cue and nodded. "For Uncle Boom-Boom I expect a good lie, a creative one that is interesting to hear."

"So you chose not to talk to me about Stella and Annie or Spike Hurlihey or how the partners liked to pit the associates against each other. Is that a practice that Nina Quarles has continued? Oh, right. She doesn't really work here, just spends the profits. Which must be considerable to send her on shopping sprees to Europe. Who were the other associates in the firm at the time?"

Thelma's look would have stripped the blades from a pair of ice skates. "Get out of this office now, or I'll call the police and have you removed."

"Judge Grigsby, he couldn't have been here," I mused, "he would have recused himself from trying the case. At least, I think he would have. It's Illinois, you never know."

Thelma looked at the staff and the two clients, all unabashedly eavesdropping: it didn't look like a group of people eager to back her up. "I keep telling you to leave because we're shutting down for the day. This isn't a safe place for people to be after dark; I can't keep the office open for you when you don't have an appointment."

"That's okay," I said. "I'll be glad to drive you home so we can finish the conversation in safety."

The young couple laughed, but the staff stared owlishly, waiting to see how the story would unfold. Thelma bit the tip of her index finger: she wasn't the boss, just the office manager—she might run the place for Nina Quarles, but she couldn't order the lawyers around.

When Thelma didn't make a move, I asked, "Why does everyone from you to Ira Previn to Judge Grigsby still care about Stella Guzzo? Why did the firm care about her in the first place?"

"Everyone has a right to counsel," Thelma said.

"Now, that is interesting," I said to Bernie. "Do you remember what Joel said when he was describing what the partners said when they were pressuring him to take on Stella's defense?"

Bernie blushed. "It was something nasty about him and Annie."

"That, but also they said, didn't he remember *Gideon v. Wainwright*?"

"But I don't know what that is," Bernie protested.

"It was a famous lawsuit, where the Supreme Court ruled everyone has a right to counsel, even those too poor to pay for a lawyer themselves. What's interesting is that *Gideon* became the party line here at Mandel & McClelland. Everyone repeated the phrase so many times: we are representing Stella Guzzo, who murdered our young clerk, because we are such noble lawyers, we believe in *Gideon*."

I continued to speak exclusively to Bernie, as if Thelma and the rest of the group weren't in the room. "We don't know why the partners wanted to represent Stella, but Thelma has proved that they coached the people who worked for the firm all to give the same story. It makes me wonder if someone in the firm knew more about Annie's death than they ever let on. Thelma, for instance. She's the office manager now, but back then she was a clerk-secretary, and Annie Guzzo muscled her out of the way. Annie was better, faster, maybe even cuter—that shouldn't count, but apparently it did with one of the senior partners—"

"She wasn't better or faster, she just knew how to flirt with old Mr. Mandel!" Thelma interrupted, spots of color burning her cheeks.

"You didn't like her, Joel said."

"Joel—he was pathetic. He was in love with Annie, he would have done anything for her. She made fun of him behind his back but he was such a stupid guy he never caught on."

"It sounds as though the person Joel killed would have been Stella, if he'd do anything for Annie. But maybe you or Spike or Judge Grigsby told Joel that Annie made fun of him and that unhinged him to the point he beat her to death."

"Her mother beat her," Thelma said. "Stella admitted it, right in court."

"Maybe Annie was still alive when Stella left the house. Maybe you stopped by and got into such a ferocious fight with Annie that you ended by finishing her off. After all, you were furious that she'd cheated you out of a prime job, personal secretary to the managing partner."

I was sounding like Hercule Poirot in a particularly ludicrous movie scene, but Thelma was so angry that she forgot she had an audience. "Stella Guzzo murdered her daughter, but I didn't shed a single tear. Annie Guzzo almost ruined this office, this practice. She was like a little cat, purring around Mr. Mandel, until he lost all sense of decency. Giving her presents, giving her money, she was going to be a star, he'd tell me, she was going off to some fancy eastern college where she'd go on to be a dazzling light in the law, another Sandra Day O'Connor.

"Annie'd come here after high school and go into his office. He'd lock the door and after a while she'd come out, purring and adjusting her bra straps. And the way Joel Previn looked at her! It was like working in a porn shop to come in here some days."

"Was she any good at her job?"

"She could type," Thelma said contemptuously. "Like that's a skill no one else could muster. I suppose because she played the piano she was faster than some of us."

"None of this explains what really lay behind the partners' decision to represent Stella," I said. "Those were the days before massive budget cuts took the stuffing out of Legal Aid; Stella could have had a decent public defender, probably one who did a better job than Joel. If *Annie* had killed *Stella*, I can see how Mandel and the others would have rallied around, but why defend Stella? Mandel and McClelland must have felt culpable in some way."

"They thought she wouldn't get a fair trial," Thelma said.

"Get off your high horse," I said. "Tell me the truth. What was going on that made them protect Annie's murderer?"

"She wasn't a saint," Thelma shouted. "Can't you understand that? She made Spike Hurlihey and some of the others look bad with the partners because she was always correcting their briefs. She made me look bad because she could type faster than me, because she'd let Mr. Mandel—touch her. She wasn't smarter, she didn't file any better or keep on top of phone calls, she just had those little fingers that moved fast. The only people who thought she was wonderful were Joel and Mr. Mandel. The rest of us were counting the days until she left town for college."

"It still doesn't answer the question. I can see that *you* would have sympathized with Stella, though—did you persuade the partners that Stella needed help?"

"They wouldn't have listened to a word I had to say. Maybe Spike did, I don't know. He was close to Mr. McClelland. What difference does it make after all this time, anyway?"

"Anatole Szakacs is helping Stella with her exoneration claim. He's not cheap; he must think there's some doubt about Stella's guilt."

"But she *was* guilty. She admitted to beating Annie. The medical examiner explained how someone can have a head injury and look perfectly fine, then start bleeding into the brain and die. We all knew Stella was guilty. I don't know why Anatole is working for her now."

I got off the edge of her desk, which had been cutting into my butt in an unpleasant way. "Do you know why Stella decided to point a finger at Boom-Boom?"

"It was in Annie's diary," Thelma said.

"But it's a lie, it's not true," Bernie burst out.

"Then Annie wrote lies in her diary. Why wouldn't she? She lied to everyone around her, why not to herself?" Thelma shrugged, her anger dying into contempt, and started locking her desk drawers.

"Did Annie date Boom-Boom while she was working here?"

"If Boom-Boom Warshawski had come into this office twenty-five years ago, everyone would have been talking about it. If Annie ever dated him, she kept it a secret, which she might have done if she thought it would stop the flow of money from Mr. Mandel into her hot little hands."

Thelma walked over to the desk where the young couple were sitting. I heard her apologize to them for letting an unruly client disrupt their meeting. She even promised not to bill them for their visit this afternoon. She wasn't a bad person, just someone trying to stay afloat in a shark tank.

30

GAMER GATE

"Now what are you going to do about this Stella?" Bernie demanded when we were back outside.

"Not much I can do."

"She told lies about Uncle Boom-Boom that reporters published all over the world—you said so to Joel this afternoon. And this woman upstairs, she agreed Boom-Boom never dated Annie."

"No, babe: she said if Annie had dated Boom-Boom, she did it very secretively."

"You let this Thelma talk you out of doing anything. You believe her reasons, but they are lame, like you said upstairs. You're making excuses for not *doing*, and excuses are lame."

When I was seventeen, everything was equally clear to me: who was right, who was wrong, no shading between the two. I patted Bernie sympathetically on the shoulder, which made her jerk angrily away. She climbed into the Mustang, slamming the door as hard as she could.

I got into the driver's seat, but took a moment to check my texts and e-mails before turning on the car. While I was scrolling through the messages, the young couple came out of the building and got into a Saturn whose muffler needed replacing. Their lawyer trudged up the street toward the Metra stop. A few of the other staff members emerged, but Thelma was still inside, perhaps making sure everything was locked up and tidy at the end of the day.

A few kids came out of the building, too, and a handful of others went in, some holding baseball gloves. The youth program on the third floor was apparently having some kind of after-school event today.

In the welter of client and personal messages was one from Murray Ryerson:

ME completed autopsy on Fugher. He'd been badly beaten but death due to suffocation: he was alive when he went into the pet coke.

It wasn't a surprise, but it was still a shock. Uncle Jerry hadn't been one of Nature's darlings, but such a horrific end shouldn't come to anyone.

"What is it?" Bernie asked anxiously.

I was starting to answer when a silver Jeep Patriot pulled up in front of us. Vince Bagby hopped out and went into the Scanlon building—not into the insurance office, which was still full of activity, despite the unsafe neighborhood and the end of business hours, but through the door that led to the law offices. Thelma still hadn't come out, so maybe she'd summoned Vince.

"Bernie, it's true I'm a coward, but I want to see what that guy is up to, and I want you to stay in the car with the doors locked. If anyone tries to bother you, lean on the horn. I'll hear you and come running."

"Who is he?"

"His name is Vince Bagby and he owns a trucking company. He may be as pure and wholesome as the flowers in spring, but I saw the man who died in the coke mountain get into one of Bagby's trucks. He was with someone whose face turned my hair white. Lock the doors."

I was halfway up the first flight of stairs when I heard footsteps behind me: Bernie had followed me inside.

"I don't want to wait in the car," she said. "It feels too—too open."

"Bernie, I've already exposed you to more unpleasantness this afternoon than I should have. Please—"

She shook her head, her lower lip out—half-stubborn, half-fearful. I told Bernie she could come on one condition. "If I tell you to run, you run. Understood?"

She nodded and clutched my arm.

At the second-floor landing I signaled to Bernie to hang back while I ducked and sidled to avoid the security camera. I listened at the law office door but didn't hear any voices. On the other hand, the kids on the third floor were laughing and horsing around enough for the noise to come down the stairwell.

I sidled back to the landing and took Bernie up to the third floor. The door to *Say, Yes!* wasn't locked; we walked in on a kind of party in progress. A refreshment table along one wall held soft drinks and chips, but the center of action, if you could call it that, was the facing wall, where a long counter held some dozen computers and Xboxes.

A crowd of kids, mostly boys, was breathing over the shoulders of those lucky enough to have a seat. Each machine had a large timer over it; when one dinged, the user had to give way to someone who was waiting. An older teen in a lime-green *Say, Yes!* T broke up arguments over those who failed to quit when their time was up, or those who'd jumped the queue. Looking around, I saw five other older boys, the monitors, I supposed, all in green T's.

The walls were covered with poster-sized photos. Some were of the kids in *Say, Yes!* shirts at different outings, others were of the neighborhood from the time I knew it, when the mills were running and Commercial Avenue was filled with shops and shoppers.

In the back of the room, a video of a baseball game was being shown. Vince Bagby was standing there, next to Father Cardenal. As my eyes adjusted to the light and the sound, I saw Thelma Kalvin tucked into a corner with Rory Scanlon. Curiouser and curiouser.

We threaded our way through the melee toward the baseball video. Bernie attracted a predictable number of catcalls and thinly veiled invitations to fuck. She curled her lip, flexing her wrists around an imaginary hockey stick. This kind of attention wasn't newer to her than any other teenage girl in the Americas, but she didn't have to like it—which earned further catcalls and a few cries of "stuck-up bitch."

The obscene outbursts caught Cardenal's attention. He stiffened when he saw me, tapped Bagby's arm.

"The detective." Bagby waved at me and pointed at Bernie. "Come on over. You got a kid who can play baseball?"

"She probably can, just won't," I said. "She's a demon on ice, though. Hockey."

"Rory's showing the kids the baseball camp he can help get them into if their grades and skills are good enough. Right, Rory?" Vince looked around for Scanlon, saw him with Thelma and turned back to me. "I was going to say, Keep an eye on young Guzzo, but I hear you've already been looking him over."

"If he keeps playing the way he did when I saw him cover the in-field gap, he's going to make all of us proud," I said. "He's not here this afternoon?"

"Young Frankie is already sold on the idea," Vince said. "This is for the stragglers who think gang life might be more fun than sweat and blood or whatever the quote is. You wouldn't be trying to wreck the kid's chances, would you?"

"Betty been talking to you? Or Big Frank? I want his boy to suc-ceed as much as everyone else down here. Is that what Fugher and Nabiyev were doing up at Wrigley Field? Trying to persuade the Cubs head office to give Frankie a tryout?"

Vince thought that was so hilarious that his laugh drew Scanlon's and Thelma's attention. When Thelma saw me, she turned an un-wholesome shade of puce. I had a feeling she had run upstairs to talk to Scanlon about Bernie and me.

"You know Vic, here?" Bagby called to them. "And—who's the hockey player?"

"Boom-Boom's niece."

Scanlon looked surprised. "I thought Warshawski was an only child."

"You're doing my family proud, Mr. Scanlon, remembering the details of my cousin's life when you see so many young people."

"Boom-Boom's life got a lot of publicity recently," Scanlon said. "Brought it all back to mind, but of course he was exceptional enough that we all remember him. Niece have a name?"

I didn't want this crowd to have Bernie's identity, but before I could speak, Bernie had already identified herself.

"Pierre Fouchard's daughter?" Scanlon asked. "No wonder Bagby knew you for a hockey player. When can we see you play?"

"When the college season starts, I will be here, playing for North-western," Bernie said proudly.

"Pity I only work with middle and high school students or I'd persuade you to play baseball," Scanlon said. "Girl like you would keep the boys on their toes."

Next to me, Bernie tensed, not liking Scanlon's tone but not sure how to respond. I pulled her closer to me, team of two, you're not alone with the creeps, my sister.

"Did you ever figure out what Jerry Fugher and Boris were doing in one of your trucks?" I asked Bagby.

"We fired the driver who let them con him into using it," Bagby said, his easy grin appearing and disappearing. "Our dispatcher had some concerns about him, anyway, going off-route. You have to monitor every truck every hour of the day—too easy for guys to turn themselves into couriers for drugs or crap."

"I'd like a word with the driver," I said.

"No can do," he said. "Private company business."

"I've been hired to sort out Fugher's death," I said.

"Cops don't do a good enough job for you?" Scanlon asked.

"You know how it is in South Chicago," I said. "With all the new gangs moving down here in the Cabrini-Green reshuffle, the cops are stretched thin staying on top of street violence. They'll work Fugher's death, for sure, but an extra pair of eyes can only help."

"Who hired you?" Bagby asked. "I never heard Fugher had any family."

"You're a quick study," I said. "When I met you at the Guisar slip two days ago, you didn't know who he was. Now you know him well enough never to have heard about his family."

The schoolboy grin disappeared again, replaced by something cold, even hostile. Bernie tensed further and Father Cardenal stepped forward, ready to come between us if we started to swing at each other.

"We're okay, padre," Vince said. "I don't like being a butt, but who does? Warshawski, you've been tearing up the South Side the last two weeks because Guzzo's ma took a potshot at your cousin. Bagby Haulage isn't just my business, it's my name—way more personal than a rumor about a cousin. When two guys steal one of my trucks, of course I found out everything there was to know about them."

"So you know where to find Nabiyev," I said.

"I do. How about you?" Bagby's cocky grin was back in place.

"Yep," I said. "Saw him this morning."

Credits were rolling on the baseball camp video. Scanlon nodded at one of the older boys, who turned up the lights in the back of the room. When Scanlon asked for questions, a couple of shy hands went up.

"Where'd you see him?" Bagby asked me in an undervoice.

"Same place he saw me," I said. "Ask him and I'm sure he'll tell you, although I'd probably drop a plate of raw meat in front of him first, so as to keep him occupied."

Bagby thought that was so funny that his laugh drew attention away not just from Scanlon, but even, briefly, the video games. "You're all right, Warshawski," he said, slapping my shoulder. "You're all right."

On our way out of the room, I stopped to look at the old photos of South Chicago. There was one that dated to 1883, when the Ninety-third Street Illinois Central station first opened, and a few from the early twentieth century, showing men going into the Wisconsin or U.S. Steel Works when those were new. Gripping lunch boxes, faces black with coal dust, skies thick with sulfur. My mother and I used to wash the windows every week but we never kept ahead of the dirt falling from the sky.

Bernie's face was tight with worry. She wouldn't admit that the afternoon had scared her in any way, but she clung to my arm in an uncharacteristic way.

I ushered her through the crowd of kids still waiting for time on the computers. When we got to the street, I froze: the Mustang's tires had been slashed. The car was sitting on the rims.

"Someone down here doesn't like me very much," I said to Bernie. "We'll take the train home and worry about the car in the morning. You leave anything valuable inside? Then let's go."

We were three blocks from the Metra station, the same one where I'd ridden back from the Guisar slip the other morning. There should be a train in ten or fifteen minutes.

The April sky was starting to darken. I picked up the pace on an empty stretch where storefronts had been bulldozed, pushing Bernie in front of me. That's where they jumped us.

I kicked back, hard, hit the shin, felt the hands slacken and jerked away. Bernie was on the ground, a hulk of a kid on top of her. I jumped on his head, cracked it against the sidewalk, kicked his kidneys. Two punks grabbed me but Bernie wriggled free.

"Run. Get to the train!"

Passersby were scattering. No one wanted to be part of a gang fight.

Bernie took off down the street and I kicked, punched, shouted, took a heavy blow to the stomach, ducked one to the head. I was gasping for air, kicking, lunging. I was nearly spent. Keep fighting until there's no fight left.

A spotlight swept the street, found us.

"Stop what you're doing. Hands in the air." A police loudspeaker.

The blows stopped. The two punks hesitated and then took off across the open ground. I leaned over, hands on my knees, gulping in air. My nose was bleeding and my left eye was swelling shut.

The patrol unit came over, guns out. Bernie Fouchard ran past them and flung herself against me.

31

ROAD TEST

"Vic, Vic, you're okay."

I stood, wincing as my wounds hit me, folded her against me. "I'm okay, better now you're safe."

"I was so scared, I was afraid they would kill you and find me and kill me. But I ran in the street and found a police car. You're not okay, you're bleeding into my hair, I can feel it."

I kept her close to me, bleeding nose or not. One of the officers started talking to his lapel mike, the other shone a flash across the vacant lot, then at the punk whose head I'd jumped on.

"What happened here?" The officer knelt, fingers on the creep's neck, feeling for a pulse.

"Three punks jumped us. This one had my goddaughter on the ground. I managed to break free long enough to get him off her. Is he dead?"

"Nope. Pity. He's an Insane Dragon, you can tell by the tattoos."

Under his floodlight I saw the dragons circling the creep's arms. He even had a dragon head on his neck, the tongue licking toward an ear.

"You need a doctor, but we need a statement, too," the cop added.

Three more squad cars pulled up, half-blocking Commercial, their strobes pulsing like so many giant fireflies. Three officers picked their way through the rubble in the vacant lot. One of them stood in the road, directing traffic around the squad cars. Now that the police were here, passersby were starting to gather, to murmur versions of the fight to each other.

Two officers kept an eye on the growing crowd: there might be any number of Insane Dragons eager to take action against someone who'd brought down one of their own.

An SUV pulled up behind the squad car and Vince Bagby came over to the sidewalk. "Christ, Warshawski. You get involved in World War Three?"

"Sorry, sir, this is a crime— Oh, Vince—it's you. Hey, man. You know her?"

"Boom-Boom Warshawski's cousin, Knute. She was just at our *Say, Yes!* meeting with this young lady. That your Mustang that got slashed out front, Warshawski? That sucks. You should've come back and gotten me to give you gals a lift. This street isn't safe after dark, you should know that."

Vince's arrival moved the police machinery a bit faster. Within a couple of minutes, Bernie and I were in the back of a squad car, heading to the Fourth District. The responding unit wanted to take us straight to a hospital, but I knew what that would mean: a long night in an ER far from home. I promised we would get to a doctor as soon as we were back north.

Neither Conrad nor my dad's old crony, Sid, was on duty this evening, which meant we gave our statements without a lot of extraneous name-calling or chitchat. A sergeant brought me an ice pack for my eye and nose, and reiterated the responding unit's urgent recommendation that I get medical attention. There are legal reasons for that aside from humanitarian ones: if either Bernie or I had serious injuries from the attack, it upped the charges against the Insane Dragon and his buddies. It also made the state's case stronger in court.

Bagby hung around the station until we were done, telling Knute he would drive us home. I didn't like it; I would like to have had a cast-iron assurance neither he nor Scanlon—or Thelma or Cardenal—had played a role in slashing my tires as a prelude to assault. However, Knute accepted the offer gladly. Spring nights in South Chicago, they could ill afford sending a squad car twenty miles across town to deliver us.

During the drive, Bagby tried to make conversation, but I was phoning: Lotty, to let her know we were coming to her hospital's emergency room; Mr. Contreras, who was predictably distressed; Jake, ditto, although less volubly, and finally, hardest call, Bernie's parents.

"We're going to pack you up and send you back to Quebec tomorrow," I said to Bernie as I typed in the Fouchards' number.

"No! I'm not going."

"*Cara*, I endangered your life tonight— Arlette? Hi. It's V. I. Warshawski in Chicago . . . Not so good. I took Bernie with me to Boom-Boom's and my old neighborhood, which is serious gang turf. We were attacked and we were lucky—"

Bernie leaned over from the backseat and grabbed the phone from me. "*Maman? C'est moi.*" The conversation went on in French, which I don't speak.

"Out of curiosity, what were you doing at *Say, Yes!*?" Bagby asked.

"Admiring Scanlon's organizational ability," I said. "Energetic guy. Runs the insurance agency, keeps tabs on the kids, helps out Nina Quarles's law clients while she's scavenging rags in Paris."

"You may be beat up, but you keep your sense of humor. I admire that," Vince said. "Rory's a good guy. Never married, gives everything to the community."

We were on the Ryan, all sixteen lanes moving at headlong speed. Bagby was a good driver; all those years wrestling trucks into submission, he could talk and maneuver around knots of cars without losing track of either.

I leaned back against the headrest, holding the ice pack the cops had given me against my face. Lotty had been brusque on the phone, but she agreed to get me priority seating at the hospital. *You're safe? The child is safe? I'll try to be thankful for that.*

"Who'll take over the agency when Scanlon retires?" I asked Bagby.

"Can't imagine Scanlon quitting," Bagby said. "As to who will take over the business, hard to know. I think he keeps hoping one of the kids he's grooming in *Say, Yes!* will have the right combination of skills."

"And your daughter Delphina will take over Bagby Haulage?"

"She's got to stop thinking about boys and start thinking about business. Or maybe she'll think about a boy who wants to go into trucking. How about you? You have a kid to take over your agency when you retire?"

"Nope. But maybe young Bernie will when she gets tired of hockey—she's tough enough."

"You have a husband who's going to be shocked by your broken nose?"

"Are you asking whether I'm married, or whether my husband is shockable?" I said.

Vince laughed again. "Married?"

"No longer."

Bernie handed me back the phone. She'd finished her conversation with her mother, but Arlette wanted to talk to me.

"Bernadine wants to stay in Chicago. Me, I say no. Pierre will fly to Chicago as soon as possible: he is scouting in Florida right now. But please, please do not let her go near these gang neighborhoods. I know she is imagining that she is—oh, what is the word, I don't speak enough English anymore—where you imagine someone else's spirit is living in you—"

"Channeling?" I suggested.

"Yes, yes. She thinks she is channeling Boom-Boom, but I cannot have her living the life you and Boom-Boom did. *Comprends?*"

"Yes, I agree, which is why I don't want her to stay on."

Bernie announced loudly from the backseat that she was fine, she had *ras-le-bol* with the discussion. Arlette and I finally bade each other an uneasy good-bye, neither of us happy with me or the situation.

We'd reached the Montrose exit. Beth Israel is on Wilson, a bit farther north and four miles to the east. Bagby reached the hospital without asking me for directions or consulting a GPS. When I complimented him, he gave his easy grin and said he'd been driving the city since he was sixteen.

"I'm better than a London taxi driver, Warshawski. Bet you can't name a road in the six counties that I can't find."

He pulled into the emergency room entrance at Beth Israel and helped us out of the Patriot. Mr. Contreras was on the lookout and surged forward, exclaiming and scolding at the same time.

"The doc called over, doll, they got an advanced practice nurse standing by and everything else, give them your insurance card and you'll get to the head of the line, where you belong, anyway. What'd those SOBs do to your eye?"

"Right hook, I think," I said. "Thank God they didn't have knucks or razors."

"And you, peanut?" Mr. Contreras held Bernie at arm's length. "Scrapes on your face, nothing broken."

"Vic saved me, Uncle Sal, I don't know what she did, this huge guy was on top of me but she got him off and—and—" She burst into tears, all the fear and helplessness of the last few hours pouring out in body-shaking sobs.

Jake had been waiting on the sideline for Mr. Contreras to get over his first burst of relief. While the old man comforted Bernie, he pulled me close to him. The pressure of his shoulder against my face made my swollen eye throb, but I clung to him.

"The first time I met you, you had me hustle you out of the building in my bass case. I thought that was the end of your adventures, not chapter 237 in the *1001 Close Shaves of Warshawskazade*," he murmured into my hair.

He led me to the counter, keeping an arm around me while I handed in my insurance cards, reminded the intake clerk that I was supposed to see someone ASAP. Lotty had paved the way smoothly: Bernie and I were taken into the examining area, shunted off for X-rays, given eye exams, salves for the raw skin, tetanus shots, a little cocaine up the nose for me to stop the bleeding.

Bernie had some deep bruising from where the Insane Dragon had been pounding on her, but he hadn't been on top of her long enough for other more horrible damage. We'd both been exceptionally lucky.

Bernie was finished before me. I stayed to go over my police report with the cop on duty at Beth Israel, but Mr. Contreras took Bernie home.

I didn't want her spending the night on my living room couch. I have good security, steel-plated doors and infrared motion detectors, but if I had become a target, I didn't want Bernie near me.

As the old man got ready to leave with Bernie, I asked if he could put her up in the room his grandsons use when they visit. He brightened measurably. When Jake and I reached home about an hour later, Mr. Contreras was heating up a pot of soup, pulling out clean sheets and giving Mitch the command to patrol.

"You don't really think some gang member is going to trek all the way up here to finish off the two of you, do you?" Jake asked. "I thought they liked to stay on their home ground."

"I have the jitters right now. Besides, I'm responsible for her safety. I shouldn't have taken her with me to the South Side today at all—I was annoyed that she quit her job for no reason other than she didn't like getting up early. I was punishing her by not letting her roam the city shopping or something, and now I feel like a creep."

"Oh, Victoria Iphigenia, you don't control the Universe. You don't know what might have happened to Bernadine if she'd been roaming the city on her own. Perhaps you saved her from a worse disaster by being present to protect her in the one that befell you."

He stroked my swollen eye. "I agree with the cop down there—it's a pity you didn't kill the guy whose head you jumped on. Bernie was resourceful, too. She didn't panic, she flagged a squad car. The fact that she acted, that will help keep her from lasting trauma, at least that's what the self-help articles I read in airline magazines tell me."

I tried to respond in kind, tried to get out of my self-recriminatory mode, but I wasn't doing well these days, as a detective, or a guardian.

32

CHIN MUSIC

In the morning, I called a towing service to haul the Mustang up to my mechanic. Given the neighborhood where I'd left the car, and the distance, the cost was going to be significant. A further depressant.

Jake offered to drive me to Lotty's clinic so she could inspect me in person. We checked on Bernie on our way out. She was still deeply asleep, with Mitch and Mr. Contreras both keeping an anxious eye on her.

When Jake dropped me at Lotty's, he fretted about leaving me on my own, but he had students waiting for him at Northeastern. I assured him I could get around with public transportation and taxis and that I wouldn't be going far—I don't bounce back from street fights the way I used to.

I dozed in the waiting room until Lotty had time to see me. She studied the reports from the Beth Israel ER on her computer screen, studied my face, agreeing the swelling had gone down, that there was no damage to the cornea or retina, took the cocaine-laced padding out of my nose, assured me that I would live to be scarred another day.

She advised me not to drive for a day or two, or at least to stay off the expressways. "And—I know caution is foreign to your nature, but Victoria—please!"

She didn't say anything else, not the words of anger or fear she sometimes gives after an injury. Somehow that made the encounter more painful.

I walked to Western Avenue from her clinic to pick up a south-bound bus. All my muscles felt stiff and sore; the half-mile walk helped pinpoint every blow I'd absorbed last night. When the bus finally lumbered to the stop nearest my office, all I wanted was to lie down and sleep, but I went into the coffee bar across the street for an espresso. Maybe caffeine could compensate for painkillers and pain.

I took a second coffee to my office, did half an hour of gentle stretches, then spent what was left of the morning at work, cleaning up jobs I could manage online. In the middle of a complicated search for funds that a partner had embezzled from his small business, my phone rang. The caller ID was blocked.

"This Warshawski?"

The voice was hoarse, hard to hear.

"Think about your old man, Warshawski, think how he got treated when they sent him to West Englewood. He made the wrong people angry, and so have you. Stop before they do something worse."

He hung up before I could say anything. My computer records incoming calls. Not legal, I know that, don't lecture me. I played the call back four times but it didn't tell me any more than I'd known when I heard it live.

I fingered my swollen eye. My dad had been transferred abruptly, to one of the city's most dangerous districts, without any explanation I'd ever heard. He was a good and experienced beat cop, able to develop relationships in even the most difficult neighborhood. It wasn't the gangbangers who almost did him in, but his coworkers. During his time in Englewood, he was shot at five times. Each time, the dispatcher claimed Tony had never radioed for backup. He found a dead rat in his locker seven times, piss in his coffee cup many times. Most terrifying, he'd found his photo on the cutouts at the shooting range.

The first shooting occurred the summer after Boom-Boom made his home ice debut. I'd finished my third year at the University of Chicago. That summer, I was working as a secretary in the political science department, commuting from home to save rent money. My dad was on the graveyard shift, and in those pre–cell phone days I spent my nights on the foldout bed in the living room, too worried to go up the stairs to my own bed, never fully asleep, half-waiting for the phone to ring with news of disaster.

Tony never told me what had gone wrong, which power broker he'd pissed off. Someone in South Chicago remembered after all this time. And knew that I'd been attacked last night. So someone had persuaded the Insane Dragons to slash my tires and jump Bernie and me. Or they were taking advantage of the attack to threaten me.

My left eye began to throb. I lay on the cot in my back room with ice on my face, trying to imagine which of my cast of characters could have known my dad, which one of them would have known why he'd been flung to the hyenas.

My cell phone woke me an hour later. I was disoriented, my hair and neck wet from the melted ice. I struggled upright in my dark back room and dug my phone out of my jeans.

It was Bobby Mallory, my dad's old friend. He'd been one of Tony's protégés when he joined the force, but he was a savvy player and he was finishing his career at a command post in the shiny new headquarters building on Michigan Avenue.

"Vicki, what happened last night? My secretary saw your name on an incident report and passed it on to me. Why were you tangling with the Insane Dragons?"

Bobby is the only person on the planet who is allowed to call me Vicki. I gave him a thumbnail sketch of the old Stadium events, with a detour to talk about Bernie—Bobby had been a regular at the old Stadium when Boom-Boom and Pierre Fouchard skated together.

"Bobby, I just had a threatening phone call, telling me to remember what happened to Tony when he made the wrong people angry, warning me that the same thing could happen to me. Tony never would tell me what had happened. Do you know?"

There was a long silence on the other end of the line, then Bobby said heavily, "I can't tell you."

"Can't or won't?" I demanded.

"Don't ride me, Vicki. I was in my first command and your father was protecting me, not wanting me to know things that might make me think I had to act."

I didn't say anything. Bobby was leaving something out; I could hear it in the silences, in the awkward ways he was choosing his words.

"I got him out of Englewood as soon as I could, okay?" he said, close to shouting.

"Okay," I said, very quiet. "I always thought it was the Second Area torture ring that did him in, but my phone call was so specific to South Chicago. Did my dad do something that bent Rory Scanlon out of shape?"

"Scanlon was helping your cousin get his career off the ground. He wouldn't have done that if he'd had a beef with your dad, or vice versa," Bobby said sharply.

"Scanlon does a lot of youth work," I said. "He likes adolescent boys who are involved in sports."

"A man can care about kids without there being anything dirty involved," Bobby growled.

"Tony wouldn't have stood for it," I said. "It's the only thing I can think of—Scanlon's the one person I've been talking to who knew Tony from the neighborhood—you know Tony never served at the South Chicago district, but of course people in the neighborhood came to him, used him as a kind of unofficial ombudsman with the Department."

"I called to see if you were all right, not to hear you digging up filth about a guy who has stayed in a neighborhood that most people with a choice ran away from. Including you."

"Yeah, I'm the original turncoat. Everyone is reminding me of it. What about Elgin Grigsby?"

"Judge Grigsby?" Bobby sputtered. "Why not the governor? Why not the president? Why limit your accusations to local figures?"

My nose started to bleed again. I tilted my head back, advice from Lotty, and walked to the hallway refrigerator I share with Tessa for more ice.

"Or Ira Previn," I said. "The priest at the local parish, he was cordial the first time I saw him, but now he's eyeing me as if I were, I don't know, Martina Luther. The guy who was found in the pet coke three days ago did odd jobs at the church, and he hung out with someone named Boris Nabiyev, who looks—"

"Vicki! What the *hell* are you doing in that rat burrow? How do you know Fugher hung out with Nabiyev?"

Bobby knew Fugher's name, which was interesting: I hadn't said it, but that meant it was a high-profile case. Or maybe it was the hideous and unusual circumstances of his death.

"I saw them together," I said.

"Does Conrad Rawlings know that?" he demanded.

"I might not have mentioned it to him," I said, annoyed that my voice sounded small.

"I'm hanging up. I'm hanging up so you can call the Fourth District and tell Lieutenant Rawlings. Nabiyev is one of the pieces of garbage the Russians tossed our way when the Iron Curtain rusted away. We've never been able to make anything stick against him, but I can name at least seven murders I am dead sure he committed. All of them as ugly or uglier as putting a man into a heap of coal dust to suffocate to death. You do not go near him. You stay far away from him and leave him to people who wear body armor and have thirteen thousand officers who will come to their aid if they're in trouble."

He hung up. I called Conrad, who started the conversation with a genial question about my health after last night's attack. However, when he heard about Nabiyev, and that I hadn't told him when I saw him earlier in the week, he shouted that if the Insane Dragons hadn't already broken my nose he'd drive up to Humboldt Park and do it for me.

"I don't know why you think you can say the first thing that comes into your head when you talk to me," I said, "but threatening me or anyone with violence is vile. If you ever say anything like that to me again, we will never speak unless we are in court at the same time."

He paused. "I'm sorry, Vic, but—crap! Nabiyev! He's Uzbeki Mob, he's—"

"No excuse for threatening me," I snapped. "I didn't know his name when you and I talked, nor that he was with the Mob—which I only just learned this second from Captain Mallory. Besides which, you were skating a pretty thin line with me, dragging me across town, treating me like a hostile witness, then dropping me twenty miles from home without a car but with a smart-assed comment. I'm tired of this behavior. It's been eight years since you took a bullet that you wouldn't have taken if you'd treated my investigation with respect. Get over it."

He apologized stiffly. "Can you prove that Nabiyev was with Fugher?"

I texted him the photo I'd taken outside Wrigley Field.

"Before you hang up, how are you involved with him, anyway?" Conrad asked.

"I'm not. I'm looking for Fugher's nephew, who's been missing for over a week."

And whose path very easily could have crossed Nabiyev's, since both worked at the same job site.

"What are you talking about? The guy doesn't have any living relatives."

I'd slipped there, forgetting Viola's panicked pleas not to tell the police about Sebastian. "Everyone has some living relative, even if it's a third cousin ten times removed. Speaking of which, the Insane Dragons who jumped Bernadine Fouchard and me last night—have you found the two that ran off?"

"No, and the one you pounded has a broken jaw, so he isn't saying much."

"I'd like to know who hired them."

"The Dragons maim and kill without needing anyone to hire them," Conrad said.

"That's what I thought last night. But about half an hour ago someone called to tell me that if I didn't want the same treatment my dad got, namely my face on shooting range targets, I should stop annoying powerful people."

"Did your caller tie the threat to last night's attack?"

"Not directly, but—"

"What exactly did he say?"

I played the recording for him. Aside from a dry reminder about how illegal that was, Conrad said, "That wasn't Nabiyev—he has a pretty strong accent. You do annoy powerful people, Vic. What are you working besides Guzzo and this alleged nephew of Fugher?"

"The only powerful person I work for is Darraugh Graham, and I'm not doing anything sensitive for him right now. But last night, right before we were assaulted, we were in a meeting with Rory Scanlon, Vince Bagby and the woman who runs the law office where Spike Hurlihey has ties. Father Cardenal was also there."

"If I saw Rory Scanlon breaking into the safe at Saint Eloy's, I still wouldn't believe he was a criminal," Conrad said. "I'd know he had a good reason for it."

"Criminals always have a reason for breaking the law—usually because they think they're better than the people whose lives they're destroying."

"You cut a wide swath yourself, Warshawski, so careful who you sling mud at." He hung up.

33

FLORAL OFFERING

Conrad hung up without remembering to ask about Fugher's nephew. He wouldn't forget, but if he dug up Fugher's adoption, and his birth family, and found Viola, he might also find Sebastian. Which would be a relief. If the police took over the hunt for Sebastian I would for once get out of their way with a good grace.

I looked again at the newsprint lists I'd made yesterday. I needed to figure out which of these players knew something about my dad, which of them might have called to threaten me. And had one of them orchestrated last night's attack?

It was a fact that my car had been disabled, forcing Bernie and me to take to the street. Which meant the personal attack was connected to the vandalism, whether thought up by the Dragons on their own, or egged to it by someone else.

Joel Previn had told me about the head-butting Mandel and Mc-Clelland encouraged their associates to go through when they handed out cases. I'd also witnessed Ira's contempt for his son. Would either father or son have been so angry or threatened by my questions that they'd sic thugs on me?

Joel was passive enough to let someone else do his dirty work, but he'd spilled out his rage and self-loathing to me; I didn't think he'd feel he had to maim or kill me.

But what about his father? Ira, the hero of workers and civil libertarians, it was painful to believe he'd cross that line between civility and ferality. He was so highly regarded, especially on the South Side, that I couldn't believe he'd risk his reputation to hire thugs. On the other hand, there was a connection between him and Rory Scanlon: Judge Grigsby, who'd presided over Stella's murder trial, had huffed to me about his friendship with Ira.

None of them would give me a convincing reason why the partners took on the defense of Annie's killer. Was that the secret Ira, or Grigsby or Scanlon himself, was afraid I'd ferret out?

It seemed far-fetched, but the whole situation was beyond my understanding. The order of protection I'd been served to keep me from Stella, and now, the addition of Betty and Frank and their children's names to the order, was infuriating. I couldn't talk to them, or pound some semblance of the truth out of Frank—maybe just as well, since my pounding muscles were wobbly today.

My mechanic called as I was uselessly churning my mind. Luke Edwards makes Eeyore sound like Doris Day.

"Vic, that Mustang of yours just arrived at my place. Why'd you leave it down south all night? It's missing the hood, the battery, the wheels and the dashboard. Besides all that, the hoses need replacing, and you've got 132,000 miles on it. You ever hear the word 'maintenance'?"

The news made me feel so tired I rested my head on the desk. "You are a ray of sunshine, Luke, no matter what anyone tells you."

"What the hell's that supposed to mean? I'm merely telling you the story of your car. Why don't you get something big and unbreakable, like, I don't know, a decommissioned army tank. Since I've known you, you've totaled a Trans Am, an Omega, a Lynx and now this Mustang. You want me to try to repair it, it's going to cost more than the car is worth. You gotta learn to drive a car in a way that keeps the engine—"

I sat up again. "This car was parked at a curb when all this damage happened. Even if I was Danica Patrick, I couldn't have kept punks from stripping it."

He grumbled that Danica Patrick wouldn't have left her car overnight where vandals could attack it, but agreed to hold the Mustang until my insurance adjuster could get to his garage. I sometimes think Luke's parents named him that because the sound makes you think "lugubrious," but he's a demon mechanic, and charges less than the dealer's shop.

I had hoped the Mustang would make it to 175,000, but maybe the adjuster would disagree with Luke and offer to fork over six or seven thousand for repairs. Or for scrap. I got up and hobbled around my office, working the stiffness out of my joints again. As I circled back to my desk, someone rang the outside door. Tessa wasn't in today; I went to the intercom.

Delivery for V. I. Warshawski, flowers. It was a big package, covered in florist paper. I told the delivery guy to unwrap it so I could see it on my camera feed. Sure enough, it was an elaborate arrangement of spring flowers, not a sawed-off shotgun or an RPG launcher.

I went down the hall, smiling to myself: Jake had been feeling sorry for me. When I tipped the guy and brought the flowers back to my office, I was startled to see that they were from Vince Bagby. Startled and wistful. Jake had other ways of showing his love, but flowers would have made a nice gesture.

> *Don't let last night turn you against the South Side. Most of us are*
> *decent hardworking people. Sorry about your car—we can lend you*
> *a truck if you need wheels.*

I smiled again, but I also taped the card to the newsprint where I'd
written Bagby's name. Under it I'd noted that he'd shown up right
after the cops last night, that he knew Nabiyev and Jerry Fugher but
had pretended not to, that Nabiyev had been driving one of his trucks
up by Wrigley Field. And he already knew my car had been stripped.
A big bunch of peonies and iris did not make these facts go away.

Is he attracted to me, or trying to distract me? I printed under the
card.

34

MIXING IT UP

Sturlese Cement, Paving Illinois and the World, had their offices on the far northwest side of the city, a difficult destination on public transportation. I stopped at Luke's garage, to look at the remains of my poor old Mustang, which was a heartbreaking sight, and to rent one of his loaners. He let me take a Subaru, with his usual animadversions on my driving. In addition to taking the wheels, the dashboard, the hood and the battery from my car, thieves had helped themselves to most of what was in it, except the towels I carry for my dogs. My hard hat was still in the backseat, as well. I put those into the Subaru, with Luke telling me the upholstery better not be covered in dog hair on my return, swallowed a few ibuprofen and headed north and west.

Even without Lotty's adjuration, I would have stuck to side streets: simply moving my head between the side mirrors started the throbbing in my eye again. Spenser never complained about pain, I reminded myself, nor Marlowe, let alone Kate Fansler. Suck it up, Warshawski, don't let those WASPs show up the Pollacks.

For the last few blocks, I followed a train of Sturlese trucks, with their distinctive blue lines weaving around their cement mixers. When we got to the Sturlese yard, the trucks peeled off to the left, where they could take on a fresh load, while I followed signs on the right to the office and visitors' parking.

Trucks dig heavy ruts. Even at five miles an hour, I bounced enough to make my nose start bleeding. I pulled into one of the visitors' spaces and studied myself in the rearview mirror. Blood wasn't gushing down my face, but a large red stain covered my upper lip. Fatigue and pain had turned my olive skin an unhealthy whitish-gray. The blood added a nice touch of color, but it might also distract people from anything I had to say. I blotted it away, combed my hair, fingered the purple around my eye. Ready as I'd ever be.

On my way up the walk to the entrance I passed a silver Dodge SRT8. I squinted through the tinted windows. It had real gauges, not an iPad screen, satisfactory for a muscle car. Maybe if Frank Guzzo paid my outstanding bill I could afford a set of hubcaps.

I sighed and went on into the nondescript building that housed the offices: a working plant doesn't waste money on corporate frills. No one staffed the entrance, but a signboard listed offices by their function, from Information Technology to sales offices for private, industrial or commercial ventures. I found Human Resources, second floor, and climbed a flight of bare metal stairs.

At the HR office, a man in a hard hat was arguing with a woman behind a gunmetal desk: he needed two more hours to round out a full workweek, but she wasn't budging. "Sorry, Arnie, not my call, you know that. You gotta do it through dispatch."

"Mavis, I wouldn't be here if Shep had given me the hours, but it's the difference between coverage and the exchanges, you know that."

"I do know it, which is why I can't fudge your hours: Mr. Sturlese audits those time sheets himself, and I cannot go into the computer—" She caught sight of me and broke off to ask what I needed.

The man in the hard hat moved aside so I could approach the desk.

"I'm looking for Sebastian Mesaline," I said.

"Not on our payroll," Mavis said.

"He was being considered for a job at Sturlese."

"*I* never heard of him. They never asked *me* to put him in the system." Mavis crossed her arms, her mouth set in an uncompromising line: she was queen of her fief and questions about her rule were not welcome.

"Could you look him up? Maybe someone else put him in without consulting you."

I spelled the name. Mavis's nostrils flared—she didn't like being challenged, but I leaned over the desk, trying to look authoritative. Maybe I just looked scary, because she typed in Mesaline, grumbling under her breath.

"Told you!" She turned the monitor so I could see it, triumph in her face. *No results for M-E-S-A-L-I-N-E. Make sure you are spelling the name correctly or start a new search.*

"Who are you?" a voice demanded behind me.

I turned around to see a man about my age with a hard square face, white shirt and tie but no jacket—the uniform of managers or engineers at industrial plants.

"She came in here demanding information about some guy who never worked here," Mavis said.

"Sebastian Mesaline," I said. "Someone told me Sturlese might be offering him a job."

"You his ma, checking up on her boy?" the man said.

"Nope. I'm a private investigator, looking for Mr. Mesaline." I pulled out a card. "And you are?"

While the man frowned over my card, Arnie slipped past him into the corridor.

"You with the auto parts Warshawskis or the hockey?"

"I'm with the private investigating Warshawskis," I said. "Looking for Sebastian Mesaline."

"People must not want to tell you about him, if that's how you got beat up so bad."

I smiled. "The guy on the other end is in intensive care today, so it doesn't hurt as much as you might think. And you are?"

He frowned some more, as if worried that revealing his name might be a sign of weakness. "Brian Sturlese. I manage this facility, and I can promise you that kid doesn't work here."

"Who said he was a kid?" I asked.

Sturlese gave a fake laugh. "Figure of speech."

"What about Boris Nabiyev? He knows Mr. Mesaline because they've worked together on the Virejas Tower. Would Nabiyev have offered Sebastian Mesaline a job without consulting you?"

"Nabby isn't on the payroll," Sturlese said, flashing a warning look at Mavis. "He does freelance projects for us from time to time. Maybe one of my brothers sent him to Virejas Tower, to oversee our part of the pour."

Mavis didn't need any warning glares; at Nabiyev's name she'd become a whirlwind of efficient administrator, typing so fast her fingers blurred on the keyboard, swiveling to consult documents in a filing cabinet and returning to her keyboard without looking up.

"Going back to your idea that Sebastian Mesaline is a young guy, a kid, I'm wondering if Mr. Nabiyev talked about him, if maybe he said something that stuck in your mind even if you don't remember exactly what."

Sturlese debated that point with himself and decided it was okay to answer. "Could be. There was a young civil engineer at the Virejas site who approached him about a job here, but Nabiyev thought he was a lightweight, and now that you mention it, it could have been this boy Sebastian."

I nodded judicially, as if Sturlese had made a credible argument and I believed him. "Sebastian Mesaline has been missing for over a week. Is Mr. Nabiyev here now? I'd like to know the last time he saw Mr. Mesaline."

"He isn't here, but I'll definitely tell him you were asking."

I thanked Sturlese, as if he were doing me a favor, instead of helping me paint a bigger target on my head so that Nabiyev wouldn't have any trouble spotting me when he came after me.

"If that's all, we're running a plant here and everyone needs to get back to work," Sturlese said.

I bade him a polite farewell, but stopped outside the office, back against the wall, to hear what he had to say next. It was a sharp question to Mavis about what else I had said and what she had told me.

"Honest, Mr. Sturlese, she came in all huffy and puffy, wanting to know about Sebastian Mesaline, but I couldn't tell her anything because I don't know anything."

"Has Nabby been around today?" Sturlese asked.

"I—he came in for a cash advance about an hour ago, but I think maybe he took off again?"

Sturlese grunted. I trotted back to the stairwell and managed to get down to the landing before he came out to the hall. Once outside, I slowed down: jogging only made my head feel worse. I trudged to my car, wondering what I'd accomplished—besides waving my arms like a demented matador in the face of a rogue bull. When I'd left Sturlese and was on Harlem Avenue, I pulled over, leaning back in the seat, pinching my nose to stop the bleeding.

The revving of a heavy engine made me look up. The driver of the silver SRT was honking at the inbound chain of cement trucks, and then gunning the engine to dart around them. A Subaru is no match for a muscle car, but I followed it down Harlem Avenue as best I could, helped by the thick traffic and stoplights—although the SRT was essentially ignoring both. I got hung up in traffic at Foster, about a mile south of the plant, and lost him.

This stretch of Harlem is one long mall. I ended up driving more than a mile before I came to an east-west through street. I was craving sleep, driving with the windows open, hoping the cold air would keep me alert, when it started to rain. I knew what Luke would have to say if I let the Subaru's upholstery get damp so I rolled up the windows and tried singing in an effort to stay awake.

It was only a fluke that made me look to my left as I passed the Firestone outlet near Wilson. The SRT was pulling up in front of an "all you can eat" Thai buffet in a nearby strip mall.

I forgot my wounds and drove to the next mall, where I parked in the middle of a cluster of cars. One of the many items I'd lost in my Mustang's dismemberment was a set of Bushnell night-vision binoculars. And an umbrella. Fortunately I was outside a gigantic drugstore. Even more fortunately, they had umbrellas up front, by the cash registers, so that I didn't have to go into the neon wilderness beyond. I picked up a Kane County Cougars baseball cap to hide my black eye and red nose and plodded through the parking lot, shivering. The umbrella wasn't much protection against the driving rain; my pant-legs were soaked by the time I reached the Thai restaurant.

The SRT was still there. I looked through the restaurant windows. Like every place in mall-land, it was enormous, with the buffet stretching beyond my sight range.

I went inside for a quick look. The place was filling up with shift workers picking up cheap, filling food on their way home. Brightly painted statuettes of deities and demons were hanging from the ceiling. I suppose it was an attempt to make the place look less cavernous, but the plastic figures looked as beaten down as the clientele. The food, colored as luridly as the figurines, took away my appetite. I pretended to study it, and finally glimpsed Sturlese at a table toward the back. He was twisting a drink around, looking expectantly toward the entrance.

I ducked my head to my chest, and shuffled to the exit. Keeping my head low, I mumbled to the bored hostess that I'd forgotten my wallet and went back into the cold. I kept the bill of the Cougars cap pulled over my forehead and the umbrella at an angle to shield my face.

After half an hour, in which I got thoroughly wet and cold, an Infiniti SUV pulled up next to the SRT. The paint was a gunmetal gray, but next to Boris Nabiyev's face, the color seemed warm, vibrant.

I couldn't think of any way to get close enough to Nabiyev and Sturlese to eavesdrop. Besides, I was sneezing so loudly I'd drown out their conversation. I pulled my wet jacket collar around my neck and stumbled back to the Subaru.

35

FAMILY TIES

It took me the better part of an hour to drive across town to my apartment, snuffling and sneezing the whole way. I'd have to have a decontamination specialist clean the Subaru before I gave it back.

I wanted a hot bath, a hot drink and bed, but Mr. Contreras saw me dragging my way up the sidewalk and came to the door, clucking over my wet clothes, my rheumy eyes, my snuffles. "Bernie's fine, doll. You go change into something dry."

Bernie was alarmingly fine—post-traumatic stress was taking the form of a ramped-up belligerence. She wanted to drive down to South Chicago, hunt down Insane Dragons—*We will know them by their tattoos, Vic, didn't you see last night? All those boys had dragons on their arms, the biggest one, he had a dragon on his face!*

"It was on his neck," I said dryly. "Bernie, your dad is coming to collect you. The police will shake the names of the guys who jumped us out of the one who's in the hospital. When they've made an arrest, I will testify at any legal proceedings."

"And until then, what will you do?" Her small vivid face flooded with color. "You will make out with Jake and murmur, oh, law and order will prevail if we wait a thousand years or two."

I couldn't help laughing, which turned into a wheezy cough. "Bernie, the people who we're up against are so much bigger than we are—not just a bunch of street thugs, but someone from the Uzbeki Mob. Law and order may prevail at a snail's pace, but me letting you get killed isn't going to speed the process."

"Those people you took me to see last night, the lawyers, the insurance man and so on, are they involved with this Uzbeki Mob?"

"I don't know." Peppy came over to me, rubbing against my damp jeans, but Mitch stayed close to Bernie. "After I've had a bath and warmed up I'm going to see if I can dig up who owns whom."

"We need to go to South Chicago ourselves, to confront these Dragons and also this mother who murdered her child. It's what you would have done with Uncle Boom-Boom when you were my age. Or have you gotten too old to take risks anymore?"

I couldn't help laughing. "Dr. Lotty and Jake say I take too many risks. Anyway, although your uncle and I had some hair-raising adventures, none of them involved the Mafia or large street gangs."

I looked at Mr. Contreras. "Will you please chain her to a radiator while I take a bath?"

Mr. Contreras followed me to the hall. "She needs something to do, doll. She slept until noon and I took her over to see the doc, like you asked, but she's bouncing off the walls."

"Yeah, I can tell. Think you can hold her for another hour or two? The Stanley Cup playoffs start tonight—that should keep her settled while I rest—I feel like original sin right now."

The climb up the stairs to my own place seemed as hard a journey as the drive across the city. When I got there I sank into the tub, pouring in eucalyptus oil for my aching eyes and nose. Maybe Bernie was right, maybe I was getting too old to take the risks I needed as a private eye. Surely I could compensate by getting craftier, but when I thought of Jerry Fugher's death, suffocating in the pet coke, I felt only scared, not crafty.

"The sun's not yellow, it's chicken," I sang as I finally emptied the tub. I made myself a toddy, whisky with lemon, honey and hot water, and curled up in my big armchair in the fluffy gold robe Jake had given me for my last birthday. I logged into LexisNexis and started doing ownership searches, for Scanlon, for Nina Quarles's firm, for Sturlese Cement. I ordered family records through Genealogy Plus. I ordered personal records on Brian Sturlese and Nina Quarles, along with Fugher, Sebastian Mesaline, his sister, Viola, the Guzzo family. Even the Reverend Umberto Cardenal.

I found a container of lentil soup in the freezer and thawed it to eat with another hot toddy, got dressed, sat at the dining room table with my printouts.

Sturlese Cement was family owned, third generation with three brothers in charge: Darius, Lorenzo and the one I'd met, Brian, the youngest. Looking at the P&L statements, I could see the brothers had gotten in over their heads: right before the collapse in the construction industry, they'd put $150 million into a building going up near Navy Pier.

Ajax Insurance had supplied the surety bonds on the project, but Sturlese had been left holding the bag when the bottom fell out of the market. The cement company seemed on their way to Chapter 11 when someone—angel or devil—bailed them out.

None of my reports could tell me who'd bought a controlling share in Sturlese—it was privately held, so they didn't need SEC filings. Obviously Nabiyev played a role, but he looked like an enforcer, not a money man. The Uzbeki Mob is an amorphous entity, not one whose profit-and-loss statements will show up in LexisNexis, so if the

Mob now owned Sturlese, it was through a shell company, but no shells were washing up on the beaches where I was looking.

Between my injuries, my cold and the second toddy, my brain was getting sluggish. I was putting all Sturlese papers away when I did a double take on the address where Sturlese's consortium had planned to build. After that project folded, it had been replaced by Virejas Tower. And one of the investors in Virejas was Illinois House Speaker Connor "Spike" Hurlihey.

Hurlihey might not be connected to the Uzbeki Mob, but he ran the Illinois legislature as if he were a Mafia boss. That didn't mean he hired people like Nabiyev to snuff out people like Jerry Fugher, mostly because he wielded so much power no one ever tested how far he'd go to win.

He had a right to invest in a building if he wanted to, as long as there wasn't a conflict of interest with bills he'd put through committee. I went back to LexisNexis to look up any special legislation that affected Virejas Tower.

Two years ago, right before the public announcement of the project, the legislature voted to grant Virejas an exception to performing an environmental assessment, on the grounds that the previous project proposed for the site—the one that nearly bankrupted Sturlese Cement—had been approved by the city. However, as I discovered going slowly through the paperwork, the zoning permission had been granted "pending an environmental assessment," which never took place.

This was a problem, because all that land on the west side of Lake Shore Drive, across from the big Navy Pier Ferris Wheel, had been a dumping ground for thorium-based gas lanterns a century earlier. Getting an environmental exception meant the Virejas consortium didn't have to check thorium levels in the soil or take precautions against aerating them during excavation for the tower's foundation.

That was slimy, but it also seemed to be a way of shooting the project in the foot: anyone buying or leasing at Virejas could look up the same information I had and order an environmental study before plunking down money. Virejas was going to be a mixed-use, residential and business building. Maybe a family wouldn't think about an environmental report before buying a condo, but most corporations would. Even so, I sent Murray an e-mail with the file about the legislation attached—maybe he'd be able to do a story. Assuming his corporate masters didn't cave in to pressure from Spike Hurlihey to keep the environmental hazards under wraps.

Rory Scanlon's insurance agency and Vince Bagby's trucking firms were also family owned, closely held companies, without a lot of information available. Scanlon, in his seventies now, had inherited an agency started by his grandfather during the Depression, when people used to put aside a few pennies a week for their funerals. He lived modestly, not flaunting wealth with exotic cars or multiple homes. He'd never married, but an unmarried sister lived with him. Three other sisters, who'd all left the neighborhood, had children and grandchildren. No one had ever accused him of sexual misconduct, or any other kind—which didn't mean it hadn't happened.

As Conrad and Bobby and Father Cardenal kept insisting, everything in Scanlon's life seemed to revolve around the South Side—he was a frequent sponsor at fund-raisers for St. Eloy's, for the widows and orphans of the police and fire departments, for Boys and Girls Clubs, and a slew of other civic-based charities. He also was a steady contributor to local political campaigns. I couldn't find any records of giving to presidential or senatorial candidates, but he did his part as a Tenth Ward committeeman to keep the alderman, the state reps and the mayor well oiled.

Vince Bagby's profile was similar—hard to get access to company reports, but lots of public good deeds in the community. No wonder both Conrad Rawlings and Father Cardenal wanted me to stop look-ing for dirt under either guy's nails. In an area with 40 percent un-employment, a pair like them kept a lot of machinery oiled.

I quickly scanned Bagby's personal history. He'd married young, been divorced five years. Delphina was his only child, apparently named for his mother, Delphina Theodora Burzle.

Burzle. I'd heard that name recently, but where? I put a query to my computer, and it came back with the file from the Guzzo case. Nina Quarles's mother had been Felicia Burzle.

I stared at the screen and then slowly put my pen down, as if it were a heavy, fragile object. I went back to Genealogy Plus for Rory Scanlon's full family tree—the first time round I'd only gone back to 1920.

I find genealogy tables hard to follow, but I painstakingly wrote down all the names and dates of births and marriages of the Burzles, the Scanlons and the Bagbys. The enormous families people had be-fore World War I made it a tedious project, but in the end, I could see that Vince Bagby and Nina Quarles were first cousins. Vince's mother and Rory Scanlon were cousins as well. Vince, twenty years younger than Rory, had grown up within two blocks of the Scanlon house.

I sat back, picturing Vince at eight or nine, trotting around after his big cousin. Rory, who liked to look after the neighborhood, would have paid special attention to a young cousin. Taken him to ball games, to the beach, to the bank, whatever the magnificent big cousin wanted, the little cousin would sign on for as well.

I checked the Sturlese, Previn and Guzzo genealogies as well, but no Burzles or Bagbys or Scanlons appeared. I'd expected Stella Guzzo to show a connection to one or the other families—it might explain why Mandel & McClelland had agreed to represent her—but the Irish family she'd grown up in didn't connect to Scanlon, Burzle or

Bagby, even when I traced them back to their first generation in America.

I couldn't find a connection for Sebastian and Viola Mesaline, either, nor for their Uncle Jerry's adoptive family. As for Boris Nabiyev, I dug up a meager file on him in a Homeland Security database. He had arrived in Chicago from Tashkent, Uzbekistan, eleven years ago. He had a green card. That was all the computer could tell me about him—not his address, or even his age.

On the other hand, when I looked up Spike Hurlihey, he turned out to be a cousin of Rory Scanlon's. Hurlihey, Scanlon, Nina Quarles and Vince Bagby all grew up in the same pack. One for all, all for one. Maybe they hadn't deliberately kept the relationship a secret from me, but I could feel them giving each other a nod and a wink on their side of the fence: we're keeping her chasing her tail, while we write the script.

A cold anger began to build in me. I could rewrite this story. Maybe not tonight, but soon. I had learned one of their secrets and I would uncover others.

I'd lost track of the time and of my cold. It was midnight when Bernie bounced into my apartment, Mitch at her heels, announcing that the Blackhawks had lost the first game of the Stanley Cup playoffs in triple overtime.

"The Canadiens won their first game, so it's not so bad. Papa will be here the day after tomorrow, but you have to tell him I'm not going back to Canada, not until we've cleared Uncle Boom-Boom's name, and anyway, I have summer camp at Northwestern, so what's the point? I'll just be coming back in July."

"Bernie, if it were up to your mother and me, I'd be packing you in a box to ship to Quebec tonight. I'll be happier seeing your father walk off that plane than I would be looking at Stanley Cup celebrations in Grant Park. And I want you back down with Mr. Contreras tonight. It's safer than it is up here."

Her lips twitched—she wanted to argue back but realized in time she was out on an unsupported limb. She gave a rueful smile, an endearing Gallic shrug. We rounded up the stuffed animals she slept with, I found her cell phone charger under the sofa, retrieved her retainer from its burial ground in the sofa cushions, and loaded everything into a backpack with a change of clothes for the morning.

I got dressed myself to escort her back down the stairs to Mr. Contreras's place. The old man was standing in the doorway, keeping a watch over the street door.

"We thought you'd be back down for dinner, doll, but then I thought maybe you'd gone to sleep. You should, with that cold and everything, but we have a plate of spaghetti for you if you're hungry."

"Sorry." I kissed his cheek. "I lay too long in the bath, but I should have called."

I wrapped up in one of his old coats to take the dogs out back for a last time. Jake was coming in the front door when I got back. I walked upstairs with him, but repeated what I'd said to Bernie.

"I don't want to huddle alone in my place, but these people scare me. I don't want anyone I love caught in their crossfire."

He looked at me quizzically. "You think if they firebomb your apartment the rest of the building will escape unscathed? I'm more afraid of catching your cold than I am of Uzbeki hit men or Insane Dragons."

"That's because you never saw the hitman."

"I never saw a germ, either." He put his free arm around me for a moment before going into his own place to park the bass. "But I know what they can do to my sense of hearing."

When I went back inside my own place, I saw a coaster from

Weeghman's Whales on the floor. I frowned over it—it's a Wrigleyville bar that I never go to. It must have fallen out of the sofa when we were collecting Bernie's animals, but what had Bernie been doing there? Another problem for another day. I went into my closet safe to take out my gun storage box.

Jake came in behind me, unfortunately: he hates guns, he hates to know I even own one. The sight of the weapon made him back away from me.

"Call me when you've put that thing away, V.I. I can overcome my terror of the rhinovirus, but a gun is a total antiaphrodisiac."

36

CHANGEUP

When I finally woke up, a little after nine, my clogged sinuses were putting painful pressure on my sore eye—not to mention my broken nose. I wanted to take enough sleeping pills to put me under until at least my cold had passed, if not until every member of the Guzzo family died, but I forced myself to my feet.

My face in the bathroom mirror would have done Picasso proud: the left side held a creative mix of yellows, purples and greens. Just as well the Smith & Wesson had driven Jake away last night: Romeo would have vanished without a single metaphor if Juliet had appeared on her balcony looking like this.

While my espresso machine heated up, I huddled over a ginger steam pot. After fifteen minutes of that, and a few shots of caffeine, I didn't look any more beautiful, but my left eye was working; I would make it through the day.

I went down to the ground floor where Mr. Contreras was feeding Bernie his staple comfort breakfast of French toast. She agreed to a walk over to the lake with me and the dogs. She chatted about North-western's hockey camp, wondering if it had been a mistake to commit to their program without seeing Syracuse and Ithaca.

My gun was in my tuck holster inside my jeans waistband. As we walked along Belmont, I wondered how much of the rest of the city was armed. I didn't blame Jake for hating guns; they make you twitchy, make you see the world around you as dangerous, as if you wanted an excuse to pull your weapon and fire.

Every half block or so, I'd pull Bernie and the dogs into an alley or doorway to see whether the same people were around us, and if they, too, were halting. Bernie made a few scornful remarks about imaginary Uzbeks, but when we returned home, she assured me she would spend the day pulling her things together for her return to Canada.

"Is this one of your things?" I held out the coaster from Weegh-man's Whales.

"Oh!" She turned red and stuffed it into her backpack. "I went there with friends the other night. I *am* eighteen, you know, or at least, I will be in five weeks!"

"Darling, the legal drinking age may be eighteen in Quebec, but here in Illinois it's twenty-one. Don't tempt the fates again, okay?"

She accepted the reprimand without argument, to my surprise, just gave me a puckish smile and announced she was going to use my bathroom before she went back to Mr. Contreras. "Your tub is so big, I love lying in it."

I hoped she couldn't get in trouble in a midday bath, because I needed to go to my office. Although it was Saturday, I was too far behind in my work to stay home with her.

I resolutely put the Guzzo-Bagby-Scanlon world out of my mind while I caught up on client business. Murray called as I was crossing Milwaukee for a coffee. He was exuberant, taking the e-mail I'd sent him yesterday about Hurlihey's involvement in Virejas Tower as a sign that we were once again best friends forever.

"What do you have on Spike that you're keeping to yourself, Warshawski? You know this environmental exception only looks serious if you live in Vermont or Oregon."

"Nothing, Murray, just fishing in very murky waters."

"Come on, Warshawski, something's going on: I read the police reports, and I know you tangled with Insane Dragons the other night. I know Spike comes from the same slagheap you do, so if you've been digging up skeletons in the land of your youth, tell me now, while I still feel I owe you one. If you sit on the story too long, I'm going to be peevish and make you look bad on air."

"Spike didn't come from my slagheap—he was across the Calumet on the East Side, back when that was the tony part of Steel City," I objected.

I put him on hold while I ordered a cortado. My frustrations with Murray, for letting himself look ridiculous on cable TV, or for trying to pretend he wasn't fifty by dating women half his age, were outweighed by our long years of working together.

He was still on the line when I came back. "There's no novel, Murray, at least not yet, but there are a whole lot of unconnected chapters."

I gave him a thumbnail. The number of names and relationships were so complicated Murray decided he needed to see my reports firsthand. As a further sign of renewed friendship, we agreed to meet at the Golden Glow around seven.

Thinking about the control Spike had over the legislature made my head ache again. In my own lifetime, four Illinois governors have gone to prison for fraud. As has the mayor of Cicero, numerous Cook County judges, Chicago aldermen, and state and federal representatives. What a place. Maybe I should move to Vermont or Oregon, where people are still shocked by violations of the public trust, and are willing to take action to stop them. Moving would also get me far away from the Cubs. I couldn't see a downside.

Back in my office, I had an alert on my computer, reminding me that I owed one of my regular clients a report on an internal auditor suspected of skimming. Senior staff were meeting on Saturday so they could get together without alerting the suspected auditor. The company had let me insert keystroke software into the suspected skimmer's computer, which showed him sending a penny on every hundred dollars to an account in Liechtenstein. I took a heavy-duty decongestant and was pulling together the final report—with ten minutes to get it to the client—when Stella Guzzo phoned.

I stared at the caller ID in disbelief, but let the call go to voice mail while I did a final proofread and e-mailed the report to the client. We were handling the meeting via videoconferencing, so I got myself hooked up to the meeting room before playing Stella's message.

"You need to come to South Chicago this afternoon to see me." The recording accentuated the harshness in her deep voice.

My impulse was to phone her back, but I thought of all the changes she and Frank—and Betty—had been putting me through. She could summon me, and then have me arrested for violating the restraining order. I copied the message and e-mailed it to my lawyer's office.

Is there some way to find out what she wants? Is she vacating the r.o.? Going into a meeting; will call back in an hour.

I sat through the meeting in profile, good eye to the camera, answering questions more or less on autopilot, trying to imagine what Stella wanted. When I'd finally fielded the last of the financial VP's questions—he kept asking the same thing, hoping for a different answer—I checked my messages.

Freeman Carter had called to say that the restraining order was still in place. "Her lawyer is doing a very annoying dance. The short answer is don't go near the Guzzo family until I tell you I've got a document signed by a judge lifting the order. Call or e-mail me to confirm that you will not go down there."

The urge to drive to Stella's house, to burst in on her and turn her house inside out, was strong, but even more than dismembering Stella, I wanted to sleep. I called Freeman to confirm that I was following his advice. Between the decongestant, the injuries and the pain meds, I could barely keep my eyes open. I staggered to the cot in my back room and was asleep almost before I was horizontal.

The phone dragged me awake an hour later. It was Natalie Clements, the young woman in the Cubs media relations department.

I felt drugged, but Natalie was bright and peppy and delivered a breathless monologue. "Your name came up last night when Mr. Drechen and I went to visit his old boss. Mr. Villard is the gentleman who had the pictures we showed you of your cousin. The day after our press release, his house was broken into and somebody stole a lot of his photographs. They took Billy Williams's first home run ball, oh, a lot of treasures. It's horrible—they're his memories!

"Anyway, he's cleaning out his house, or his daughter is—he has to move, which is really sad, but he has diabetes, same as Ron Santo, and it's getting hard for him to walk or climb stairs. He asked if you were still interested in photos of the day your cousin came to Wrigley Field. I said I didn't know how far along you were with your book, but I'd ask you."

"Not very far," I admitted.

My voice came out as a thick croak. I carried the phone with me to the bathroom and tried to gargle in a discreet and soundless way while Natalie went on.

"Well, his daughter came on a box of photos up in the attic, and some of them are from the day your cousin came to the open tryouts. Mr. Villard would love to show them to you."

I told her I was a little under the weather but would be glad to visit Mr. Villard early next week.

"I'm sorry if you're not feeling well, but it would be best if you could come today. His daughter is packing up his baseball collection, what the thieves didn't steal—she's going to auction it off to give to Cubs Care. He's afraid if you wait, she'll get rid of all those photos."

That threat gave me enough of an adrenaline boost to say I'd be at Villard's place within the hour. I held an ice cube over my eyes for a few minutes to make my sinuses retreat, washed my face, decided makeup would only make my green-and-purple eye more lurid, and headed north, to the Evanston address Natalie had given me.

Pierre Fouchard called while I was driving. "Bernadine called me. She seems well, but what do you think?"

"She's very resilient but she's showing some delayed shock," I said. "Even though she's saying she doesn't want to go home, she'll probably feel a lot better when she's back in Quebec."

"*Oui*, yes, I mean. But this is the story, Vic: the Canadiens, they are playing the Bruins tomorrow night in Boston. The Canadiens want me to go to the game. I have scouted many of these Bruins, you see, and the management, they think my opinion can help the team. Arlette says no, but—Bernadine will be all right for two more nights, do you think?"

My heart sank: until that moment I hadn't realized how much I was counting on unshouldering my caretaking burden. "I hope so. I hope so, but maybe I'll hire some extra protection, just to be on the safe side."

"*Bien.* I will be in Chicago for sure by Monday afternoon."

I pulled over to a side street when Pierre hung up. Between the gang attack, Stella's message and the threat about my dad, I was unusually nervous about how to look after Bernie. I called Mr. Contreras to double-check on her. To my dismay, she'd gone off to meet with the girls from the peewee league she was coaching.

I bit back a sharp remonstrance: the old man was easily wounded, and I knew how hard Bernie was to keep in check. I hung up and called her cell. She was well, she was impatient with me, yes, her dad had phoned her, she was happy to stay in Chicago as long as possible.

"I'm not the scaredy-cat," she said.

"Yep, that's me, meow, meow. Don't leave the rink alone, okay? Seriously, Bernie, word of honor or I'm driving straight there to collect you."

"Oh, very well. Word of honor." She cut the connection.

I didn't have the time or energy to bird-dog her. I needed backup. The Streeter brothers, whom I'd called on to help get access to Stella's bank account, do body-guarding, furniture hauling, anything that takes a lot of muscle. They are quiet, they are smart, and fortunately Tim, whom I most often work with, was free. He'd go to the rink where Bernie was working, he'd make sure she got back safely to Mr. Contreras's apartment. He'd keep an eye on the street until midnight; his brother Tom would cover the midnight to eight A.M. shift.

Mr. Contreras was huffy when I phoned with the details—maybe he was ninety-something, but he didn't need some kid showing him how to look after Bernie. Bernie herself was even huffier: I was *une lâche, beu platte*, it was surprising I didn't have spiders weaving webs in my hair I was so old.

"Yep, my precious one, and those spiders are attached to you until your dad gets here, so you'll have to put up with the sticky webs for the duration."

I texted Tim's picture to her, texted hers to Tim. He'd let me know when he'd connected with her. I looked up *beu platte* and *lâche* in my online dictionary. I was not only an antique fuddy-duddy, but a coward. As I turned back onto Sheridan Road, I realized I was hurt by the accusation. I was the risk-taker, the person who skated close to the edge—how could she possibly think—until I had to laugh at my own absurdity. The next time Lotty got on my case, I'd put her in touch with Bernie Fouchard.

37

HIGH SPIRITS

When I saw Villard's house—mansion—on a cul-de-sac overlooking Lake Michigan, I realized why a man having trouble walking needed to move. An old stone building with graceful lines, on a bluff over-looking Lake Michigan, it was three stories tall, with a high staircase to the front door. Even with the ramp he'd installed over the marble steps, just getting into the house would be a challenge.

Villard's daughter, a brisk woman of sixty or so, let me into the house. "I hope you're going to take some of Daddy's memorabilia with you—he's an impossible packrat—he still has all of Mother's clothes in their bedroom closet and she's been gone over twenty years now! When he had the break-in, he finally realized how vulnerable he is out here. I don't even know how the thieves had the patience to dig through his baseball memorabilia to steal anything of value!"

She flung these remarks over her shoulder as she led me to a sitting room on the Lake Michigan side of the building. Villard was in an easy chair facing the lake, but he struggled to his feet when he heard his daughter and limped over to greet me. Although he had bedroom slippers on his swollen feet, he was dressed as he must have been all the years he went to work, in trousers, a white shirt and a sports jacket with a large Cubs logo pin in the lapel.

He politely didn't look at my face while shaking my hand. "It's a pleasure to meet you, Ms. Warshawski. Like everyone else in this city, I was a big fan of your cousin's."

His daughter turned the chair around to face me and bundled him back into it. "Daddy, I'll get Adelaide to bring you and your guest something to drink, but I have to get back to the papers in your den. I've left all the photographs you were interested in on the table here, and Adelaide will find me if you need anything else."

"It's a pity my daughter didn't want to go into baseball," Villard said. "She's such a brilliant organizer, she'd have whipped the Cubs into a World Series or two by now."

His daughter kissed his cheek. "Daddy, it's enough I take flak for wearing my Cubs gear in Diamondback country. Anyway, someone has to stay on top of getting you packed and moved." She looked at me. "I live in Tucson and I can't stay away too long; I'm the associate dean of the nursing school down there. My sister's flying in from Seattle next week to finish up."

She was off, her jeans making a rustling sound that conjured an old-fashioned starched white uniform. A few minutes later another woman came in—Adelaide, who was Mr. Villard's attendant, not, as I'd supposed, another daughter. She was as unhurried in her movements as the daughter had been brisk, but she managed to make Mr. Villard comfortable without taking anything from his dignity.

Besides his diabetes, Villard's fingers were swollen and distorted by arthritis. Adelaide brought over a table that fitted onto the front of the easy chair and opened the box of photos for him. I pulled up a chair next to him and helped him start turning over pictures.

They were all taken either at Wrigley Field, or were candid shots at players' homes or on trips to away games.

"My girl found these in the attic yesterday. I don't really want to leave this house, so I'm having trouble concentrating on the job. My wife and I, we lived here together for forty-seven years. We raised our family here. We used to have magnificent Christmas parties—you can see here—this was the year before she died—it was so sudden, cancer of the pancreas, it came like a grand piano crashing down from the sky onto our heads—this was her last healthy year and she was in magnificent form."

I admired the pictures of his wife, a handsome woman in her older age, who was laughing joyously with Andre Dawson and another man—a neighbor, Villard said.

Adelaide brought ginger tea for me, gin and tonic for Villard. We went through Christmas photos, and grandchildren photos, and finally came to the spring day that Boom-Boom and Frank had gone to Wrigley Field. The pictures I'd seen at the ballpark had all been with the would-be prospects, either in the dugout or on the field, but these were more candid shots, some in the stands or the locker room. Boom-Boom was in many of them.

The official photos in the dugout had been in color, but this set was in black-and-white. It wasn't my cousin's face that made me stop and carry one to the window for more light, but the young woman in the frame. Annie Guzzo, in jeans and a man's white shirt, grinning up at Boom-Boom from the bottom row of the bleachers, a look that dared him to chase her.

I had forgotten what she looked like, and anyway, I'd never seen her like this, face alive with high spirits, with sexuality. I'd never seen her with my cousin, either, not like this, I mean. Maybe Boom-Boom had been in love with her. Maybe she'd been in love with him.

She'd been seventeen the day they were at the park together. Seven months later she would be dead. I wanted to be able to go inside that picture, that day, and warn her—stop, don't look so carefree, your mother (your sister-in-law?) is about to murder you.

Villard saw my face. "That young lady—she's someone you know?"

My mouth twisted involuntarily. "Her older brother was one of the guys who came to try out that day. I didn't realize she'd been there, too—no one ever mentioned it to me. She's been dead a long time; it's wrenching to see her looking so vital. She wasn't in the dugout shots."

"No," Villard said. "Family weren't allowed in the dugout or on the field. She'd have been watching from the stands. The photographer took a liking to her, or maybe he was a fan of your cousin, because he seemed to follow the two of them around the park."

There were nine shots that included Annie and three more of Boom-Boom alone, two seen from behind in what looked like a narrow passageway. Villard picked these up, shaking his head over them in puzzlement.

"I don't know why I never noticed these before. Maybe because that was the spring my wife . . . I thought I was so tough, unbeatable, coming in to work every day, but I couldn't pay attention to much of anything, I see now.

"You can tell from the overhead pipes that those two kids got into one of the restricted sections of the ballpark. The bowels of Wrigley Field are unbeautiful space. You can see in this shot—too many dangling wires, unsealed conduits—it's worse now because they've added more wiring for the electronics the media folks have to have, but it was bad enough back then. Maybe your cousin . . . But the photographer worked for us, he should have had enough sense to stop them."

"When Boom-Boom had a full head of steam he was hard to stop," I said. "But from the looks of these, it was Annie who was leading him on a dance."

She'd been playing hide-and-seek, I guessed, from that daredevil grin she'd been flashing at Boom-Boom. *Find me if you can, follow me if you dare.* Seventeen years old, feeling her powers start to unfold. Whether she'd cared for my cousin or just been enjoying being alive didn't matter.

I sat back in my chair, wishing my head weren't quite so clogged. For a week I'd been arguing with Bernie that the putative diary didn't matter, but now it started to feel important to me again.

Annie had flirted with the lawyers at Mandel & McClelland—maybe even had sex with Mandel. There was no sin or crime in her flirting with Boom-Boom, too, but how had he responded? Someone else—Joel Previn, or Spike Hurlihey, or Mandel himself, maybe would have gotten angry enough to threaten her with the classic male complaint: You led me on, how could you have been playing with me?

Not Boom-Boom: my cousin would not threaten any woman for having multiple strings to her bow. Or for any other reason. Even on the ice, where he was fast and cunning, Boom-Boom did nothing out of malice.

Mr. Villard was studying the prints, trying to figure out where Annie and Boom-Boom had been. He put them down with a rueful smile. "I haven't been underneath those stands for years now and I don't remember them clearly. Some of the boys used to go down there to smoke marijuana before the game—I pretended not to notice and they assumed an old fart like me wouldn't recognize the smell."

"Would you let me take these home with me?" I asked. "I can scan them and get them back to you."

Villard laughed. "Take them, keep them. My girls want to sell all my memorabilia for charity, so if you bring them back, chances are they'll sell these, too."

Adelaide brought me more tea, and a second gin for Villard, although a moment later I heard his daughter in the hall upbraiding her for encouraging his drinking—a no-no with diabetes. I lingered with him, watching the lake while Villard talked to me about his wife, his son who died in Vietnam, the baseball players he'd known and loved. I left him regretfully so that I could make my appointment with Murray.

"When you get that book about your cousin finished, you be sure to come back and give me a copy. Get Adelaide to tell you the address where I'll be moving."

I definitely had to write the wretched biography, I thought, bidding Villard a reluctant farewell. He was an attractive guy, and for a brief time I'd forgotten my wounds and my worries. I wasn't eager to get back to them, but once in my car, my uneasiness about Bernie, myself, the whole situation returned.

I had a text from Tim Streeter, saying that he'd connected with Bernie, who'd decided that he was cool enough to tag along for lattes with her and her friends. At least I didn't need to fret about her for the moment.

I stopped at my office before heading to the Golden Glow to meet Murray, since I'd left all my papers there. I had half an hour, too short for a nap, but instead of returning e-mails and phone calls, I spread the photos of Annie and my cousin out on my worktable.

In the second of the pictures of my cousin in the hidden passageway, I thought I could make out the shadow of Annie's face in the background. I got out a magnifying glass and she appeared more clearly, an elfin ghost with curly black hair, the outsize white shirt hanging over her jeans halfway to her knees.

I held the glass over each of the pictures and saw one where her shirt was smudged with dirt. So, taken after she'd been in the tunnel. An obscure impulse made me try to lay them out in chronological order, starting with the first print I'd seen, with Boom-Boom looking down at her from the top of the bleachers.

In the next one she was facing the camera full on, apparently talking to the photographer. She had a black oblong in her left hand that I'd originally assumed was a clutch purse, but under the glass it turned out to be a notebook bound in leather or plastic.

The room seemed to heave around me. I clutched the edge of the table, waiting for the dizziness to pass. Annie had kept a diary. She cherished it so much she brought it with her on a date to Wrigley Field.

I put the magnifier over the notebook, but it didn't tell me anything. Dark leather or vinyl, could be brown or black, or really any dark color. No lettering, no embossed letters proclaiming *Annie Guzzo, Her Private Thoughts on Boom-Boom Warshawski and Sol Mandel*.

I went back to piecing together the rest of the collection. There were several shots whose place in the order I couldn't figure out, but in the one where Annie's white shirt was dirty, she no longer had the book. I studied her face for a long minute, saw the streak of dirt on her forehead and along her right forearm. Her expression was a mix of guilt and glee—she'd done something she shouldn't have and gotten away with it.

Whatever that book was, she'd left it somewhere in the bowels of the ballpark. What was in it that she couldn't keep at home, but thought she could retrieve if she left it at Wrigley? She didn't know anyone there, unless she was taking for granted that Frank would get the nod from the Cubs that he so desperately wanted.

Boom-Boom couldn't be bothered with things like journals and diaries; there wasn't a hope that he'd written about the day, even if Annie's behavior had meant something special to him. And I doubted he would have paid much attention to the book, not unless it was his, and she was teasing him by running off with it.

I looked at it again, wondering if it might be something else, not the diary that Stella had hammered into my head. A dossier, perhaps? I put the magnifying glass down in frustration—it was impossible to make out any detail. All I could say was that it wasn't a conventionally shaped diary or book, which was why I'd thought at first it was a clutch purse.

That break-in at Villard's house. My head was so thick today that I only just put that incident together with Annie.

Thieves had taken some valuable baseball memorabilia, but they'd also stolen photographs. And they'd done it after the story appeared about my bogus biography project. Maybe it was coincidence— maybe the story told random thieves that Villard had valuable Cubs memorabilia in his home. But maybe whoever was pulling the strings in South Chicago knew Annie had taken something to the park that they wanted to make sure stayed buried there.

I felt cold suddenly, and found a sweatshirt on a hook behind my door to wrap around my neck. *"Boom-Boom, what were you involved in?"* I whispered, shivering. I thought I knew him inside and out, but there was a piece of his life about which I knew nothing.

"You didn't kill Annie Guzzo, I know that much," I said to his face on the table. "But what secrets died with you?"

I pulled the pictures together and laid them between sheets of acid-free tissue paper for protection until I had time to scan them. I placed them in the wall safe in my storeroom, looked longingly at my cot, but reminded myself that duty was the stern daughter of something or other. Anyway, Murray was a good investigator, and I was definitely at a point where an extra head would be useful. For the first time in a long time, I was looking forward to seeing him, working with him.

38

SUICIDE SQUEEZE

I was shutting down my system, stowing one backup drive in the safe, the other in my briefcase, when the building front bell rang. I looked at the monitor: Conrad Rawlings, with an acolyte. I took my time, closed my safe, walked deliberately down the hall to the front door, trying to gather my energy: it is not easy to be at your witty and alert best, which you need in a police encounter, with a broken nose and a head cold.

"Good evening, Lieutenant," I said formally, stepping into the street and closing the door behind me.

"I need to talk to you," Conrad said. "Can we do it inside?"

"Can I have a hint?" I asked. "Is this the kind of visit where you hurl abuse at me and threaten to cuff me, or is it information gathering?"

It was hard to read Conrad's expression in the fading light, but he told his companion to wait for him in the car. I typed in my door code and led him back to my office.

"Wagner got you good, didn't he," Conrad said, inspecting my face.

"Wagner?" I repeated.

"How many fights you been in lately? Look in the mirror in case you've forgotten."

"Is Wagner the Dragon's name? He hadn't been ID'd when Bernadine Fouchard and I made our statements."

Conrad thumbed through his iPad. "That's right. We didn't know him then, but we printed him this morning when he came out of surgery. He'd been arrested a good few times and did a nickel in Joliet for assault. I need to know if you were anywhere near him today."

I backed away, astonished. "Any special reason you're asking?"

Conrad took my shoulders in his hands so he could look directly at my face. "Can you prove where you spent the day?" He spoke with an unsettling urgency.

"What is going on?"

"Arturo Wagner is dead."

I sat down hard. Not that I would shed a bucket of tears over him, but it's hard news to handle, the news you've killed another person. "They told me his jaw was broken and he was concussed, but no one suggested his life was in danger."

"No one thought the boy was going to die. Which is why I need you to tell me how you spent your day."

I stared at him. "Could you please tell me what's going on? Your bangers beat me pretty hard and I'm not up to solving riddles."

"Answer the question and then I'll tell you."

"You know, I think I'm going to record this conversation," I said.

"I'm trying to keep this from being a police matter, or a state's attorney matter, Vic."

"And a recording will help." I brought my system back up and turned on the recording software before I spoke again. In the background my cell phone barked: Murray texting, wanting to know where I was. I ignored Conrad's growl to let it keep and wrote back, *Soon. Cops in my face.*

"Does the state's attorney plan to give my name to a grand jury?" I asked Conrad.

"Vic, please believe me—this is for your sake: tell me where you were this afternoon."

"He was murdered this afternoon? Not as a result of our fight?"

Conrad nodded. "He was too doped up to answer questions this morning, but when I sent one of my guys over to the hospital this afternoon, Wagner was dead. The hospital pathologist says he was suffocated. You know Saint Raph's—it's almost as big a warren as County. Nurses are stretched thin, no one keeps a regular eye on the wards, and our only worry was having a violent perp there, so he was cuffed. And the state's attorney will fry my guts if she knows I told you all this. Where were you?"

Prisoners are always handcuffed to the bed when they're hospitalized. It's inhumane, makes it hard for people to recover from gunshots and other debilitating injuries, but in Arturo Wagner's case I didn't find myself minding too much.

"I was videoconferencing at one-thirty; at two-thirty I was driving to Evanston. I spent the afternoon with a retired member of the Cubs front office, so it would be hard for anyone to make a case that I was forty-five miles the other way. Okay?"

Conrad's shoulders sagged in relief. "Thank God for that, Ms. W., thank God for that. Someone sent an anonymous message to the state's attorney saying you had an animus on account of the Fouchard girl being related to your cousin, and that you went over to Saint Raph's to finish off Wagner."

I was silent for a beat, remembering Stella. I told Conrad about her lunchtime call, ordering me to South Chicago.

"You didn't go?" he said. "And I can believe this?"

"That's my rap, isn't it," I agreed. "I drop everything and gallop off in all directions at once."

I played the voice mail for Conrad.

"The Guzzos have been so unpredictable and so angry that I thought they might be trying to get me to violate the restraining order so they could have me arrested. Only—now it looks as though they were trying to frame me for murder. But on whose command?"

"Don't gallop in that direction without proof, Ms. W.," Conrad said. "My big worry is your alibi. For safety's sake, get me the names of the people you saw this afternoon. Sooner rather than later."

"I hear you, Conrad, but—killing Arturo Wagner, that was done to silence him, which means that the attack on Bernadine and me wasn't random street violence."

"That isn't the only possible reason," Conrad objected. "They might have tried to get you down there to frame you for his murder and pull you totally out of the picture."

I grinned at him. "So glad we're getting onto the same page at last, Lieutenant. Why do they need me out of the picture, and who is the 'they'?"

Conrad couldn't come up with an answer.

"Someone paid the Dragons to attack us," I repeated. "Rory Scanlon, Vince Bagby, Thelma Kalvin, Umberto Cardenal. They were all at the youth club meeting. Any one of them could have—"

"Don't, Vic," Conrad said sharply. "I'm not going to believe Father Cardenal would sic the Insane Dragons—"

"Don't tell me priests are above heinous behavior! That bird doesn't fly any longer."

"Vic, you can't toss this kind of accusation around, especially not in South—"

"I know," I interrupted again. "Bagby and Scanlon keep the neighborhood afloat. If either of them gets indicted for major criminal activities, everything from Frank Guzzo's mortgage to the Chicago Skyway will collapse. People keep telling me that, which means everyone down there has a stake in turning a blind eye to anything those guys might be doing."

Conrad's scowl was ferocious. "You'd better not be accusing me of turning a blind eye to any criminal activity on my turf, no matter how high or low the perps sit."

"No, Conrad. I know that, absent my father, you are the most honest, steadfast cop in Chicago. But I've lived my whole life in this city, and I know too much about how business gets done here. Yesterday morning, someone called to warn me away from this case, told me what happened to my dad when he 'got the wrong people' pissed off. I called Captain Mallory. He assured me it wasn't Scanlon, but still . . ." My voice trailed off, remembering Tony's refusal to ride in Scanlon's bus to Boom-Boom's debut all those years ago. And Scanlon's jibe about the Warshawskis—what had it been? Was I upholding justice the same way my dad had? Something like that.

"Mallory's word isn't good enough for you?" Conrad demanded. "I came here for a one-on-one out of concern for you, but you are always Almighty God, knowing more than us mere mortals."

"Conrad, please: it's not that, and you know it. But Bobby is going on decades-old information, he's not in the Fourth every day, and you are up to your eyeballs in gang shootings and drugs and garbage—you don't have a reason to be looking at these people, not the way I do. So cut me some slack, don't assume I'm doing what I'm doing in an effort to make you look bad, or to thumb my nose at my dad's oldest, staunchest friend!"

Conrad breathed heavily, paced to the wall where my outsize map of the six counties hung, studied it long enough to memorize all the streets. "Anyone else in your sights, besides the local power players?" He spoke to the map.

"I've crossed paths with Boris Nabiyev, who hung out with Jerry Fugher, and I've seen the Sturlese brothers, whose cement company Nabiyev has a stake in. Or his masters have a stake in, anyway. Bobby assures me that Judge Grigsby and Stella's new lawyer wouldn't be in the threats business. I don't know about Stella's current lawyer, but Grigsby is connected to Democratic politics, all those years he was going to fund-raisers for his campaign war chests—he had to scratch a lot of backs. And all these people circle around and tie back either to Scanlon or Bagby. And Scanlon and Bagby and Nina Quarles are cousins."

"Nina Quarles?" Conrad turned around.

"She's the absentee owner of the South Chicago branch of Mandel & McClelland. And Spike Hurlihey is related to Scanlon."

Conrad groaned. "I should have known you wouldn't think a couple of homeboys were big enough targets. Still and all, Ms. W., even though you're the biggest pain in this copper's ass, I don't want to see you on a slab. You moved north; do yourself a favor and me in the bargain: stay north."

39

PINCH HITTER

I watched Conrad on my security monitor, made sure he was leaving the building, getting into his car and driving off, before I once more shut down my computer. Before leaving, I checked in with Tim Streeter. All was quiet on the northern front—he was eating spaghetti with Mr. Contreras and Bernie. The three of them were going to watch the Bruins-Canadiens game; face-off was in ten minutes.

When I got to the Golden Glow, Murray was on his second Holsten, eating a rare hamburger and flirting with Erica, Sal's head bartender. Erica was a vegan and a lesbian but she enjoyed teasing Murray.

Time was when Sal didn't serve food at all—her core clientele, the traders from the nearby Board of Trade, tended to blow off steam over vodka or bourbon without wanting to eat. But the South Loop has come back to life; the old industrial buildings from a century back, when this area housed printing presses for many of the nation's magazines, phone books and the like, have been converted to loft apartments. Young professionals and retired couples have moved in. They want poached salmon with a glass of Sancerre, not a shot and a beer with a pretzel.

Sal cut a door in a wall of the bar that backs onto the kitchen of one of those trendy South Loop restaurants. Sal supplies their booze and they feed her drinkers from an abbreviated menu.

What hasn't changed are the Tiffany lamps over the mahogany tables, giving the room the soft glow of its name. Sal came over with the bottle of Johnnie Walker as I was laying my papers out under one of the lamps.

"I hope the cement truck looks worse than you do, girl. What happened?"

"You know how it is. I was jumping over a tall building and forgot that it takes me two bounds these days."

"Bet you can't see the color of my underwear anymore, either," Sal said.

"You'd be wrong about that, but only because your décolletage is revealing black lace, not because I still have my X-ray vision."

It felt good to be in the place where everybody knew my name. I ordered a bowl of soup, although trendy restaurants only serve designer soups, perhaps lotus blossoms pureed with chives and a whiff of liquid nitrogen, not the hearty minestrone I was longing for.

I waited for Murray to finish his raw meat, then brought him to my table. He studied my documents carefully while I ate my soup, which I had to admit was pretty good, despite its delicate ingredients—good enough that I ordered a second bowl.

I told him everything I could think of, including the business about the break-in at Villard's place, and my concern about what Boom-Boom might have been up to.

"All his papers are in Toronto at the Hockey Hall of Fame, but I looked at them before I sent them up there; if he'd been protecting some scandal under cover of a trustee account, I'd have seen it then. And he never kept a journal that I ever discovered."

"Yeah, but the secret could be something that doesn't look like anything." Murray waved to Erica for another beer and ordered a basket of French fries—fried, of course, in duck fat, not in something dull like safflower oil. "Could be something that Boom-Boom himself didn't know was explosive. You know con artists are always trying to get a sports star's money. And their old friends are always trying to get a piece of reflected glory."

"That suggests Frank Guzzo," I said.

"I could go up to Toronto and take a look at Boom-Boom's papers," Murray suggested.

"It might be worthwhile," I agreed doubtfully. "You'd have to pay your own way, though—I haven't seen a dime from the Guzzos and I'm likely to be in the hole for legal fees to get this wretched restraining order lifted. But before booking a flight, why don't you comb the *Herald-Star*'s archives. Your old gossip columnist, Freda Somebody, might have had a few titillating hints about Boom-Boom."

"It's the Spike Hurlihey part of the story I want most," Murray said. "There's a lot here, but it's all vague. Before looking at Freda's old columns, I'm going to double back into what we have on Spike, The Early Years. He wasn't born with the Speaker's gavel in his hand, he muscled his way into the job. Nobody can write anything about him now, he's so goddam powerful, but twenty years ago, when he was first starting to gobble up the smaller fish, it was a different story. Of course, my current owners love him. They like oligarchs and he is the consummate protector of the oligarchy, so Global isn't likely to let me print dirt in the *Herald-Star*, but *Salon* or even the *New York Times* might be interested."

"If you expose his dirty underwear you could be unemployed," I said.

He grinned, the old Murray grin. "Won't be the first time. What will you be doing, Girl Wonder?"

I played with my soup spoon, drawing a design in the bottom of the bowl with the remains. "I'll talk to Pierre Fouchard. He's flying in on Monday to collect his daughter before anything disastrous happens. If Boom-Boom confided in anyone besides me, it would have been Pierre."

"Too many unknown unknowns," Murray grunted.

"The one I'm worried about is Nabiyev," I said. "The unknown I want clarified is who he's working for, and if they think I'm as much a threat as—as, I don't know—Jerry Fugher, for instance."

"Nabiyev! How the hell did you get yourself tangled up with him?"

"I've been delving in genealogy." I pulled out the page that dealt with Sturlese and showed Murray, but I realized I'd never told him about Sebastian and Viola. When I explained that story to Murray, including how terrified Viola was, he frowned in worry.

"Crap, V.I.—that doesn't have anything to do with whose ma was whose grandfather's second cousin five times removed. If this Viola is frightened about Nabiyev, you shouldn't go near her without full body armor, and even then you'd be pushing your luck. What I hear about Nabiyev is he's a freelance enforcer, but he gets legal help from the attorneys who manage the Grozny Mob's affairs. No one knows if the Uzbeks bought a cop or a state's attorney, could be either or both: Nabiyev has been arrested a bunch of times but never charged. If you haven't made a will, better get to it before you do anything else."

"Yeah, I don't think it's very funny, either. I wish to God I could shift Bernie tonight—I could go underground if I didn't have to worry about her."

Having reminded myself of that worry, I signaled Erica for the check: I wanted to get back north to make sure Bernie and everyone else I cared about was safe. As a sign of goodwill, I split the bill without looking to see how much more four Holstens cost than one Johnnie Walker.

Murray and I exchanged those meaningless hugs and agreed to check in with each other at the end of the day tomorrow—unless we uncovered something dramatic beforehand. We didn't vow never to let the sun go down on an anger again—we knew each other too well to believe a promise like that.

I could hear Jake moving around his apartment when I came up the stairs. I wondered if he'd brought a violinist home with him, someone who carried a Strad, not a gun. I put the Smith & Wesson in my nightstand drawer with the lock on and texted him that I was home.

When he came across our shared porch to the kitchen a few minutes later, he couldn't help staring at my hips, so I turned my waistband inside out to show him it was empty.

He was still a bit stiff and circumspect, but after we'd had a glass of Torgiano, he kissed my bruised eye and gave me a shoulder rub while I told him about the meeting with Villard—the one part of my day that I figured he'd genuinely enjoy.

"You are going to have to write that book about your cousin, V.I.: you've got too many people excited about it. Or write an opera. Of course, this town loves sports more than music, if High Plainsong could put together a hockey opera, that might solve our funding problems."

We agreed that Boom-Boom should be a baritone, not a tenor, and spent a happy hour debating which leading singer should have the privilege of debuting, "With my slap shot I am invincible," while Jake improvised an accompaniment on my piano. His *boom! boom!* in the bass clef was tremendously convincing.

He went back to his own place for the night—it's no fun trying to sleep when your partner is snuffling and coughing—but I had my first peaceful night's rest in several weeks. No dreams of being beaten up or having the people who love me turn their backs on me.

On Sunday, I luxuriated in doing nothing. Bernie came with me for a long walk up the lakefront with the dogs. She didn't bring up Boom-Boom or Annie, and we ended the day with a movie, a pizza and a sense of goodwill.

By Monday morning, both my cold and my bruises were fading. I did my routine of stretches and weights—longer, because I'm at an age where laying off for two days means it takes twice as long to get in shape—and took the dogs to the park for a good workout. Tom Streeter stayed inside Mr. Contreras's place while we were gone, but when I returned the dogs, he went back to his post on the perimeter. Bernie was still asleep in my neighbor's guest bed when I headed to work.

My good mood soured somewhat at my office: my insurance adjuster had left a message. The Mustang wasn't salvageable, and, given my high deductible, all I'd get from them was five hundred thirty-seven dollars. I called Luke and told him to sell it for scrap; he could keep whatever he got in exchange for letting me hang on to the Subaru a few more days.

"You wreck it, Warshawski, and the deal is off," he warned me.

"Right you are, Eeyore."

I hung up on his demand to know what in hell I meant by that. I needed a car, I needed a vacation in the Umbrian hills, I needed a wealthy benefactor. Instead, I scanned the photos Mr. Villard had given me on Saturday. When I had them stored in the Cloud and on a flash drive, I felt a little easier about doing other errands.

I trudged across North Avenue until I came to a branch of Global American, where I opened an account. Back in my office, I repeated the steps I'd gone through with Stella's account at Fort Dearborn Trust, noting the security questions GA asked.

Before trying to bypass GA's security to get Fugher's account number, I called the guy who owned the garage where Fugher had lived. If he'd taken a security deposit, he might give me the information without my needing to squirm my way through another round of illegal data gathering. Unfortunately, the rent was cash only. And no, he'd never had occasion to need Fugher's Social Security number.

I looked involuntarily at the Uffizi engraving, the avatar of my mother's ethical standards. "Sorry, Gabriella," I whispered, logging onto my LifeMonitor search engine. It didn't care if I was a creep as long as I paid the five-thousand-a-year subscription price. It gave me all the information I needed to look at Fugher's bank account.

Armed with that, I called Global American, repeating my tremulous pitch, this time about my brother with dementia. The bank was regretful, but someone had closed and emptied the account on Friday.

"That's not possible: I have his power of attorney," I exclaimed. "The scam artists must have drained his assets and closed the account. This is terrible—his bill at the nursing home is due tomorrow."

Because I had the Social Security number, along with his adoptive mother's birth name and the street he'd grown up on, they finally told me the account number. I promised I'd take it up immediately with their security office in Atlanta.

When I hung up, I wondered if I might be a sociopath, I lied so glibly, so easily. At least I'd gotten what I needed. When I went back to Stella's accounts, sure enough, the account that had covered her bills while she was in prison had belonged to Uncle Jerry.

I stared at the screen for a long time. Fugher was connected to Stella, but who was pulling those strings? Except for the money he got from Viola and Sebastian through their debt to Sleep-EZ, and the occasional payout from his betting account, all his deposits had been made in cash, some in the high four figures.

I made up a spreadsheet, showing both Fugher's and Stella's accounts, with a paragraph summarizing where Fugher's money came from, and sent it to Murray. I didn't like being the only person to know something about a man with ties to Nabiyev.

I was pacing around my office when my phone rang, an unknown caller.

"Is this the detective? . . . I'm Aliana Bartok. At the Virejas Tower project."

Oh, yes, the promising young engineer with beaded braids. "What's up?"

"You know how we were all trying to figure out what Sebastian was doing here so early in the morning the last day we saw him? I think I know. It's—I can't explain it on the phone. Can you come to the job site?"

40

SOUND CHECK

Aliana met me at the entrance to the hoist. She'd refused to answer any questions on the phone, just saying that I had to be at the computer to understand it. While we waited for the hoist, she fiddled nervously with the ends of her braids, looking aslant at my bruised face.

The hoist operator remembered me. "You go ten rounds with Nabiyev?" he asked jovially. "He was in early this morning looking same as always, so you must not have landed any of your punches."

"I hit the kidneys," I said. "My face looks spectacular but it's blows to the kidneys that leave the other person limping for a week or two."

The operator laughed more heartily than the comment merited, expanding on the fight theme all the way up.

They'd poured three more floors since I was last here. When we got off at twelve, the rough work on the walls was done and carpenters were marking off spots to start building interior walls. As she led me across the floor to the engineers' room, Aliana asked if I'd really been in a fight with Nabiyev.

"No. Your hoist operator seems to have a one-string guitar that he likes to keep plucking. I was jumped by some street punks and fortunately the cops drove up before they murdered me. You know Nabiyev?"

"Not personally, but when he's on the job site everyone gets tense." She knocked on the door to the architects' and engineers' room, which had a sign on it that read "Temporarily Off-Limits to All Personnel."

A couple of the engineers I'd seen the first time I was here were hovering nearby and were infuriated when Tyler, the senior man, unlocked the door for Aliana.

"Hey, man, what gives?" one of them demanded, trying to muscle past us into the room. "I need to get to my machine. There's an array whose specs I have to check—"

"The room will be open in fifteen minutes, Clay. I'm sure you can do the calculations on your tablet, right?" Tyler pulled the door shut behind Aliana and me, and slid the dead bolt home.

"Aliana brief you on what she found?" he said.

"I didn't think I could explain it on the phone," Aliana said.

She took me to one of the computers set up on a work counter that ran the length of the far wall. "We each have our own laptops, of course, but these are machines we can all access during the project to see what everyone is doing—the files are shared pretty much among the design and structural people. The computers aren't assigned—anyone can use any machine—but we all get in the habit of sitting at one particular spot, set up our coffee mugs there, that kind of thing."

The cloth board that lined the wall behind the computers was filled with photos and cartoons. Personal items—coffee mugs, pencil cups, action figures—sat on the shelf that ran the length of the counter. A faded photo of Cubs legend Ryne Sandberg, signed to Sebastian, was pinned behind the computer where Aliana was standing.

"So this was the machine that Sebastian mostly used. And this morning Tyler asked me to go through the files, make sure anything Sebastian worked on was, well, was correct and to get it uploaded to the project database if Sebastian hadn't already taken care of it."

She tapped the keyboard and the monitor came to life. "It all looked straightforward, and then I found this audio file in a hidden sector. When I heard it, I got Tyler and he said I should get you."

She clicked on the play icon. The recording was scratchy; two men were talking, but the mike had been fairly far from their mouths. The recording was too muffled to follow well; I had Aliana replay it several times but still couldn't get it all.

"*All we want is a chance to bid [words unclear],*" the first one said.

"*We're not talking to new [players?] now,*" the second man said.

"*[Unclear] permits are [unclear] and even for this job there can be [unclear] obstacles. We can [unclear] for you.*"

"*Is this a threat?*"

"*Of course not, but everyone has to pay to play. No one gets something for nothing.*"

A pause, then the second man said, "*I don't make these decisions. I'll have to get back to you.*"

Another pause, longer, then the first speaker said, so quickly that he was even harder to understand, "*You work with us and we work with you. You don't want to work with us, just remember we gave you [unclear—maybe 'a chance'].*"

That was the end of the file.

I looked at Aliana. "Was that Sebastian?"

She shook her head. "I don't know who either of them was."

"Would you know Nabiyev's voice?" I asked.

"He has a very heavy accent, Russian, Uzbeki, whatever," Tyler said. "And his voice is deeper."

"Where could this have taken place? Is there some project your engineering firm is trying to bid on?"

"I don't know either of those guys," Tyler said sharply. "And my firm doesn't do business that way, not with threats. There's plenty of work for construction engineers in this city. We don't get one project, we go after a different one."

"Any idea where the original of the recording is?" I asked.

"It's not in this room—it would be on a thumb drive, likely, not in the Cloud," Tyler said. "Otherwise, Sebastian wouldn't have been in here early to upload it. But after I heard it, I shut this office. Aliana and I scoured the place. While she was waiting for you, I checked the contents of all the drives we found."

He pointed at a carton that held a good thirty or more USB drives. "I discovered that some of our architects and engineers are too bored—I saw a staggering amount of porn as well as video games—but not the audio file."

It hadn't been in the gym bag he'd left in his locker, so either someone had taken it from the room, or Sebastian had been carrying it when he disappeared. Or it had been taken by the person who ransacked his and Viola's apartment last week.

Uncle Jerry had promised if Sebastian did something difficult for him, he'd make sure the debt was forgiven. Fugher and his handlers hadn't asked Sebastian to deliver the threat, but they must have had some assignment connected with the threat, otherwise why had he recorded it? Or had the assignment been to record the conversation so that someone—Fugher? Nabiyev?—could use it for blackmail?

"I can't figure out background noise on this," I said, listening to the recording again. "Was Sebastian in the room with a device, or did he plant a bug, or was he eavesdropping?"

"I don't give a rat's ass if he was standing on his head juggling beer bottles while he recorded it." Tyler's expression was fierce. "He's a punk. As of this morning, he is barred from this job site. If he's smart, he will find a new line of work, because I will make sure no one hires him again as an engineer."

I had an uneasy feeling that Sebastian wasn't ever going to work at anything again, but I only said, "It would help to know what project they're talking about, even if it isn't one that your firm, or the contract firm Sebastian works for, cares about."

Tyler said, "This is a needle in a haystack, Warshawski. Too many projects, too many building and zoning permits in play all over the Metro area."

He turned to Aliana. "Make a copy of the file for Warshawski. Put another on a thumb drive for me and then delete it from the hard drive. And then we'd better stop wasting the Virejas project's money and get back to work."

While Aliana uploaded the recording to a couple of clean drives, Tyler unlocked the door. Angry—and vocal—young architects and engineers crowded into the room.

"Easy, boys and girls," Tyler said. "Aliana discovered a security breach in one of our machines this morning. We called in this woman here to try to sort it out. We're good to go now, so let's get going."

I put the drive into my hip pocket. All the way down to the ground, all the way across the pockmarked dusty ground, I felt as though the device were burning through my jeans into my butt. I drove quickly to my office, keeping a jittery eye out for tails, and got the file uploaded to the Mac as soon as I was in the door. It wasn't until I'd stored it both in my backup drives and in the Cloud that I finally stopped to think.

Pay to play. That is the phrase that defines Illinois politics. The speaker was threatening to block permits for some kind of project. The recording was unclear, but the word might have been "zoning" or "building."

Zoning permits are the fiefdoms of Chicago's aldermen. Pay isn't great for service in City Hall, but contractors put campaign donations into the pockets of their alderman in exchange for zoning permits and zoning exceptions. Rory Scanlon was the Tenth Ward committeeman, which meant he played a role in routing those donations to the Tenth Ward alderman's nest egg.

Uncle Jerry, down there on the South Side, he could have been doing dirty work for Rory Scanlon. I tried to imagine a big project in South Chicago that some crony of Rory's needed to bid on, something big enough that it was worth threatening the project owner. There was a lot of talk of putting housing, offices and even a theme park on the two thousand acres where the old USX Works had stood, but if Scanlon wanted friends of his considered for those jobs, he'd go directly to the project owners himself. No threats necessary, just his friendly offers to make people feel at home in the Tenth Ward.

And if a project was outside the Tenth Ward, Scanlon wouldn't have any power to block permits, not unless he was involved in a conspiracy with the city or with the other ward's officers. I didn't know if Scanlon was a crook, or a pedophile or neither or both, but whatever he was, he was too savvy a player to put himself at the mercy of a lot of weak links—the other aldermen, or Sebastian Mesaline himself.

Pay to play. Spike Hurlihey, Speaker of the House, was the consummate paymaster. He couldn't help or hinder a Chicago building project, unless it was through the shenanigans he'd pulled on Virejas Tower—getting a special law passed exempting the project from an environmental assessment. But he wouldn't have needed intermediaries to threaten the Virejas project. He was an owner himself, for one thing, so he had a say in who bid on the work, and besides, work was too far along to add new players. It had to be a project where work hadn't started yet.

Looking for a big project not yet underway seemed like a really good way to waste a couple of months. It might be easier to start at the other end: Uncle Jerry had promised Sebastian he'd clear the debt forever if Sebastian did something connected to this meeting.

It was frustrating not to know whether Sebastian had been in the room, secretly recording the conversation on behalf of one of the threateners—or the threatened—or hovering outside, trying to get a version of events he could use for his own purpose.

I took out one of my burn phones to call Viola. She didn't want to come see me: it was the middle of a workday, she couldn't keep taking off, she was a clerk, not a manager, she could lose her job.

"Sebastian recorded a meeting and loaded the file onto one of his computers at work; they found it this morning and gave it to me. I'm hoping you can tell me who's speaking, and what they're talking about."

I hooked my speakers up to the computer and played the file through for her, twice. At the end, when she didn't respond, I realized she'd ended the call. I took that as confirmation she knew who was speaking, although maybe it merely meant her supervisor had walked by. I turned off the speakers with an angry twist—Viola was at least as tiresome to work with as the Guzzo family.

41

LAND OF THE DEAD

I sat for a while, staring at nothing. My office phone roused me from my stupor some minutes later. Stella Guzzo. This time, I answered the call, instead of sending it to voice mail and alerting my lawyer.

"Is this the whore's daughter?" she demanded.

"Nope. Wrong number," I said, and hung up.

An instant later, she phoned again. "I'm looking for Warshawski."

"Right this time," I said. "But you have an order of protection against me. You can't be calling me."

"I can do whatever I goddam well want. I told you to come down here Saturday and you never showed up."

"The order of protection," I repeated. "I come see you, you get me arrested, and then I'm in jail and lose my license."

"But I *needed* to see you."

I knew Freeman would kill me for not hanging up, but instead I said, "You didn't have anyone left to insult?"

"I can say what I want to whoever I like, and if you and your family—" She cut herself off mid-rant. "Frank came to see me last week."

"He's a good son." I kept my voice neutral.

"Maybe he is, maybe he isn't. You look at him, and he's the image of my dad and my brothers, but inside, he's just as soft as his own old man."

I couldn't imagine any way to respond to that.

After a moment, Stella went on broodingly. "I could tell he had something on his mind, but it took him all night to spit it out. What's this you're saying about Betty?"

"Nothing." I was astonished.

"Don't lie to me! All you Warshawskis lie faster than you talk. Frank told me you thought Betty killed Annie while I was at the bingo."

"No, ma'am. I thought *if* you hadn't actually killed your daughter when you punched her in the head, there was only one person you might have taken the fall for, and that was Frank. If you thought his wife had killed your daughter, there was a sliver of possibility you wouldn't have said anything so that his children's mother stayed out of prison."

"Listen, you. You know as well as me that you're trying to cover up for your old man stealing evidence from the crime scene. You want this to be about my family, but you won't admit that it's really about yours."

She hung up.

Every time I talked to Stella, I felt about a hundred years old. I leaned back in my chair, eyes shut. I was paying an awfully high price for the brief comfort Frank had brought me all those years ago.

I started to call him, then decided to go see him in person. Enough of this idiocy.

Using one of my burner phones, I called Bagby Haulage. Fortunately, not only did Delphina answer the phone, but Bagby's dispatcher wasn't at her elbow to guide her away from people like me. She accepted my spurious story, that we'd given the wrong package to the truck Frank Guzzo was driving, and even let me know that he was in the Midway Airport area.

"Great," I said heartily. "We're at 5236 Sixty-seventh Street. Sanjitsu Electronics."

"You're not in my system," she said.

"We may be there under a different name; we recycle for a lot of different electronics companies. Tell Guzzo someone from shipping will meet him on the loading bay in thirty."

I hung up before she could say anything else. As I closed the office door, the burner phone started ringing. At least she was calling back, a good double check. What a pity I hadn't thought to record voice mail.

The address I'd given Delphina was almost sixteen miles southwest of my office. By pushing my luck with cops and speed limits, I got there within half an hour.

The short runways at Midway bring the planes in low and slow overhead. Driving down Cicero Avenue, I kept wincing as the Southwest wheels skimmed the treetops along the route. They've never actually taken out a building, but it's an unnerving flight path.

The address I'd randomly chosen for its closeness to the airport belonged to a giant cardboard manufacturer. The parking lot was packed, but I found an open space in the middle and walked over to the loading bays.

There wasn't any sign of a Bagby truck. Maybe Frank had come and gone, maybe Delphina decided the call was a prank and didn't tell him about it. I walked across the lot to the road and waited twenty minutes. Just as I was deciding my luck was out, Frank turned into the parking lot.

I stood in front of his truck. He leaned on the horn, and then opened the cab door to swear at me.

I walked over. "Hey, Frank."

"Tori!" He was so startled that his foot slid on the clutch and the truck shuddered. "What the—and what happened to your eye?"

"Vince didn't tell you?" I said, smiling affably. "He was right there when it happened. You and I have so much catching up to do, and neither of us has much time. I'm going to follow you until you take a break."

"The lawyer said—"

"Yes, we all know what the lawyer said. Stella violated the order herself this morning, calling to tell me to stay away from your family. Since I'm already hog-tied by the order, it's hard to know what she's referring to."

His sunburnt face turned a richer shade of sienna. "Maybe it was Betty talking to her about you showing up at Frankie's game. You have to stay away."

"And I will. She's not a pleasure to talk to, and nor, at the risk of hurting your feelings, is Betty. Both of them slug first and listen second. I hope Betty doesn't beat you, but I can give you the number of a domestic—"

A short queue of trucks was trying to get into the lot. They honked loudly. Frank slammed his cab door shut and drove forward. I sprinted to where I'd left the Subaru and wove my way around the lines of parked cars. Frank had to drive all the way into the yard to find a space where he could turn around out of the way of the trucks that were pulling in. I caught up with him easily as he exited onto Lavergne Avenue.

Frank made another pickup at a warehouse a few blocks farther west, saw me in his rearview mirror when he left and pulled into a Wendy's.

"Make it fast, Tori, I got fifteen minutes, and they monitor every leak we take."

I climbed into the cab, over his protests—he wanted to shout down at me from his window.

"So your mother thinks I'm doing something to wreck Frankie's chances?"

Frank's shoulders slumped. "Nothing in my goddam life ever works out for me. My shot at the show, Frankie's, whatever it is, it always falls apart."

"Yes, your shot at the show, that's something else I wanted to ask you about. The day of your tryout at Wrigley, when Boom-Boom was there and made you so angry you whiffed the curve, Annie was there as well. Why did she come along and why didn't you tell me?"

His lip curled in disgust. "Are you my fucking parish priest? Am I supposed to confess every detail of my life to you?"

I grinned savagely. "Only the ones relevant to why you involved me in the Guzzo melodrama. Annie had something with her. She lost it, or deliberately hid it, inside Wrigley Field. Was this her diary, for real, and did someone dig it out and put it back in your mother's house when Stella got out of prison?"

He was bewildered. "I don't know. I don't know what you're talking about. I mean, the diary, I told you already, Ma says she gave it to someone for safekeeping, so I can't tell you. Are you saying Annie had it with her at the ballpark?"

"If I knew I wouldn't be asking you," I said. "She was holding something about the size of a clutch purse."

"Yeah, I carry one of those all the time so that tells me a lot."

"About four by eight inches, say, and maybe an inch thick. I only saw it in an old photo, so I don't know what it is. It was dark, maybe black or navy, but didn't seem to have any writing on it."

"Tori, I had way more important stuff on my mind that day. I didn't even remember about Annie being there until you told me just now."

"Why was she there in the first place?" I asked. "I assumed she came to cheer you on."

"Cheer me on?" he jeered. "You're thinking of a different family. God, I hope my girls turn out for Frankie when he needs them. And him for them, come to that."

"Did Annie drive up with you?" I repeated.

"Vince's old man ordered a limo for the five guys from Bagby's team who were going to the tryout. I didn't want Boom-Boom riding with us, everyone would have been all over him."

I didn't say anything, out of sympathy, but Frank took it as a criticism. "Okay, I was jealous. Are you happy? I was so fucking jealous of Boom-Boom. He always was so fucking lucky! It was like some old fairy tale Ma told us when we were little, some Irish thing about a boy who got taken up by elves and everywhere he went, the sky opened up and gold fell down. That was your goddam cousin."

"He got murdered, so not so fucking lucky," I snapped. "Annie went with Boom-Boom?"

"Yeah, I guess. She was a brat sometimes, you know. She wanted to see the tryouts, or to be with Boom-Boom, I don't know what. The night before, when Boom-Boom stopped by the house to give me some last-minute advice, she heard us and came in demanding to go along. It was like when she was five years old and wanted to play baseball with me and my friends, *Why can't I, you can't stop me, Daddy will bring me.* Only this time, our father was dead, so I guess she got Boom-Boom to take her."

"Were they dating?"

"I don't know! Why does it matter? Maybe she wheedled him into taking her to the park and then charmed him into going to bed. Why do you care?"

"I'm trying to find out what your real reason for coming to see me was. What did you or Stella hope to gain by involving me in your problems—was this some revenge Stella fantasized about all those years in prison—bring the only living member of the Warshawski family back down here so she could humiliate me in public?"

Frank turned on the engine but didn't put the truck into gear. "Believe me or not, my mother didn't know I was coming to see you. She had a shit-fit when you showed up the next day. I hadn't had time to tell her, and afterwards, the fury she was in! It took me back to all those times—she tried to slug me one last time, but she wasn't strong enough to, anymore."

"But what did you think I could do? Why involve me at all?"

Frank pounded the steering wheel with his right fist. "The exoneration claim. Scanlon, he's taking an interest in Frankie's future. He told me, baseball isn't like the old days, they look at the family, not just the kid, and if Ma involved the press in this exoneration claim, then Annie's murder would be on everyone's minds, and it could hurt Frankie's chances. I was hoping you could stop Ma, but it's like so much in my so-called life, nothing works out the way I want it. I call you, Ma goes postal, Scanlon's annoyed because the press is all over us."

He covered his face, his voice dropping so low I had to lean over the steering wheel to hear him above the engine. "I—if all this derails Frankie—I don't know what I'll do."

The driver behind us leaned on her horn. Frank saw he'd done the unpardonable—left a big gap in front of him. He drove up to the mike and ordered a double cheeseburger with extra-large fries and a super-sized shake.

"Scanlon told you to stop your mother?" I asked.

"Not like that. He said no one cared about a crime that old any-more, unless she made them care, don't you see? He came up to me at Saint Eloy's when I was watching Frankie and said he'd heard through the grapevine what Ma was doing. He was going to get one of his lawyer pals to look after her interests so she wouldn't feel like we were giving her the brush-off, but if I could talk her into letting it lie it would be better for Frankie. And then, everything got out of control. Like it always does in my life."

He pulled over to the curb with his order and started eating mood-ily, shoving a great handful of fries into his mouth.

"What did Scanlon say after all the press brouhaha began?"

"I was sweating bullets. I talked to Vince and asked him what I should do, but he spoke to Scanlon for me, and he told me Scanlon saw I wasn't to blame; he still is willing to sponsor Frankie."

I turned sideways in the seat to look at him squarely. "Frank: someone sicced a trio of Insane Dragons on me when I left Scanlon's office the other night. Do you know anything about that?"

"What the fuck are you trying to say?"

"Bagby or Scanlon or Thelma Kalvin, they were all there when I went up to visit his youth program, and so was Father Cardenal. Did any of them talk to you, tell you that *I* was bringing too much atten-tion to your family?"

"Crap, Tori." He set his box of food on top of the dashboard so violently the fries jumped out of the box onto the gearshift. "You cannot go around accusing people of stuff like that. There are so many gangbangers in South Chicago I bet every person you pass on the street has at least one in their family. You were in the wrong place at the wrong time. Don't go accusing Scanlon of this: everyone knows your old man couldn't get along with him, but he's the person who—"

"I know," I cut him off. "Believe me, I hear that script every time I cross the border."

He gaped at me.

"Only making a feeble joke. So many people have told me I don't know anything about the South Side that it's starting to seem like you guys think you live in a different country than the rest of the city."

"We do," Frank said. "We live in the land of the dead."

That shut me up for a moment: it was poignant, but also an unexpected image to hear on his lips. I couldn't let his previous comment rest, though.

"What do you mean, everyone knew Tony couldn't get along with Scanlon? When I saw Scanlon last week, he passed a comment about my dad—what does the whole neighborhood know that I don't? Did Rory get Tony shipped off to Englewood?"

"You are like a goddam squirrel trying to get into a birdfeeder, Warshawski. I don't know who did what to whom, but everyone knows that Tony wouldn't ride to Boom-Boom's first game in Scanlon's buses. Everyone talked about it, back at the time, I mean. Don't ask me what that was about because I fucking do not know."

"If Tony didn't trust Rory Scanlon, then Scanlon was up to something. What was it?"

"Why can't you grow up? Everyone else learns their parents are human, that they make mistakes. Your father wasn't a saint. He wasn't a moral bloodhound, either, who could smell good and evil in people. He was wrong about Scanlon."

My left eye was starting to throb, fatigue and anger pushing too much blood to my face. I massaged the bruise with my fingertips. What would Scanlon have been up to that Tony didn't trust? I kept coming back to the sex that swam around this history, Annie with Sol Mandel, the old priest from St. Eloy's making Frank pull his pants down, no one wanting to rock Scanlon's boat for fear he'd cut them loose.

I let the atmosphere in the cab calm down for a minute, then went back to the day of the Wrigley Field tryouts.

"Do you remember anything Annie said that day? Anything that might give me a hint about what she was carrying with her? At first I wondered if it was something to do with your baseball career, press clippings or something."

He curled his lip. "Annie never gave a rat's ass about my baseball career. So-called. Your ma, music, her college life, that's all she thought about. Sometimes you or your dad. Anyway, that day she was higher than ten kites—I couldn't bear to be around her! She had no sympathy for the fact that I'd blown my shot at the big time. No interest. No wonder I blocked it out of my head that she was there.

"I'm doing my best not to burst into tears in front of Warshawski—Boom-Boom, I mean—and Annie keeps saying, 'No one can touch me now, no one can touch me now.' It's a horrible thing to say, knowing what Ma did to her, but I came close to whacking her myself. Only good thing out of it is that I remember that afternoon every time I come close to hitting one of my own kids. Remember where that led with Annie and Ma. Remind myself to act more like my dad, keep it calm."

"And Boom-Boom? How did he react, to you or your sister?"

"I don't know! I couldn't bear to be near him! I didn't want his fucking sympathy—Chicago's golden boy, can't you understand that? He wanted to drive me home, go out for a beer in that damned 'Vette he was hotdogging in at the time. I couldn't fucking bear it.

"Bagby's had the car waiting to take all us losers home, but I didn't want to be with them, either. I snuck off to the L and got myself back to the South Side. Back to the slime where I belonged."

"Sounds like a day in hell, Frank. Sorry to make you revisit it . . .

On a completely different subject, I'd like to play a recording for you. Tell me if you know either of these voices."

While he ate his way through three thousand calories, I took out my cell phone and downloaded the recording from the Cloud.

"God, who is that scuzzball?" Frank said at the end. "Who's he trying to threaten?"

"I don't know. I hoped you would recognize one of the voices."

"Wish I could help you, Tori, because then maybe you'd let go of that goddam bill your lawyer put through my mailbox."

I was feeling sorry for Frank, but not sorry enough to say I'd forgive the bill. I jumped down from the cab and walked back to the Subaru.

42

STICKBALL

I drove north in a melancholy mood. *Nothing in my so-called life,* Frank had said. Nothing worked out the way he wanted it to.

That might be true, but how much else of what he said could I believe? His forgetting that Annie had been at the ballpark for the open tryouts, that sounded credible. He'd needed support and sympathy, but he didn't want them from Boom-Boom, and his sister was so wrapped up in her own affairs that she didn't have room for her brother.

Growing up, like so many only children I'd fantasized about siblings, someone to confide in, play with. Boom-Boom had been a kind of surrogate brother, but we saw each other only once or twice a week. It seemed painful that Frank and Annie had squandered their relationship in the short time they'd had together, but perhaps that had been the inevitable outcome of growing up with a mother as turbulent as Stella.

While I waited at the long light at Damen and Milwaukee, I

dictated a summary of the conversation for my files. As an after-thought, I sent a copy to Freeman.

Sorry to violate the r-o, but I had to ask him about the pix.

You did not *have to ask him about the pix,* Freeman typed back sharply. *You don't need to know about the damned pictures. Unless you want to spend 30 days in County, you will respect the order.*

I made a face: he was right, but I was tired of having to admit everyone around me was right.

The grease from Frank's lunch had gotten in my hair and skin; I could wash off under Tessa's shower and start on a project for Darraugh Graham. Like Frank, sometimes nothing in my life worked as planned: when I reached my office, Viola Mesaline appeared in the doorway of Tessa's studio.

"What happened to you?" she wailed. "As soon as I heard that recording, I told my supervisor I was sick and ran over to see you, but you'd disappeared. I went to your apartment and they didn't know where you were, so I came back here."

I was losing my grip: I'd forgotten that I'd been on the phone to her about her brother's recording. "You hung up on me. If you'd let me know you were coming, I'd have waited for you."

"They're going to fire me, I can't keep running away from work pretending to be sick. Why did you call me and then disappear?" She was going to blame me for her troubles no matter what.

Tessa appeared in the doorway behind Viola and beckoned to me, leading me to the cubbyhole where she handled the business end of her work. "She's scared of her own shadow. I couldn't leave her out on the street, but I didn't know what to do with her—you weren't answering your phone."

I'd turned off the ringer when I was talking to Frank and had forgotten to turn it back on; I looked down at the screen and saw I'd missed nine calls, most from clients. One from Vince Bagby. Great way to run a detective agency.

"And what did you do to your hair?" Tessa wrinkled her nose. "Can't say I like your new shampoo."

"It's called *Grasso de Sud-Chicago* and only Yuppie snobs are put off by it," I said with dignity. "I was planning to wash it, but I guess I'd better deal with this poor little kitten. I sprang a thunderbolt on her this morning."

I ushered Viola into my own office, moving the bouquet Vince Bagby had sent me so I could watch her face. She looked genuinely distressed as she rehashed her fears. I made her sit still, take some deep breaths, drink a glass of water.

"Viola, who was that on the recording? Your brother?"

"No, no, it was Uncle Jerry, it must have been what he wanted Sebastian to do, but—"

"Which one was Uncle Jerry?"

"The man who was speaking first."

I played the file again for her. It was Uncle Jerry who said he wanted a chance to bid, that everyone has to pay to play. Viola had no idea who the second speaker was.

"And what does this have to do with Sebastian?" she sobbed.

"He recorded the conversation, then, the day he disappeared, he went in early to work and loaded it onto a computer there. Think, Viola: Where could this have been taking place?"

"I don't know, how can I possibly know? How can you be sure Sebastian was involved?"

I repeated what I'd just said, about his loading the file onto his work computer. "Does your brother have some kind of secret recorder?"

"I don't know, why would he? He isn't—he doesn't listen in on people if that's what you're trying to say. You're making him sound like some kind of pervert, but he's a sweet boy who doesn't want to hurt people."

I changed the subject. "Have you heard from anyone about your loan since Sebastian disappeared?"

"Like what?"

"Like anything. Like, you still owe Sleep-EZ money, or threats about your loan, or promises to forgive it."

She shook her head, the fear lines around her eyes and mouth deepening: I'd handed her another thing to worry about.

"Do you know if the company Sebastian worked for was trying to get access to a big project, something where they thought they hadn't been given a chance to bid?" I asked.

"I told you before, Sebastian wouldn't say anything about what Uncle Jerry wanted him to do. I don't know, I don't know!"

I looked at the wall clock; time was running short and my brain wasn't functioning. "What else did your brother work on before the Virejas project?"

Viola was having a hard time focusing as well, but she made a valiant effort. Sebastian had helped with part of the city's sewer restoration, he'd done work on a couple of playgrounds for the park district.

"Any of this in South Chicago?" I wondered if he'd been on Scanlon's turf, but Viola couldn't remember.

"I think he did something for a cement company. Would it be stress tests? Something like that. I only remember because Sebastian is afraid he may have to go work for them—he's afraid he'll get fired by Brentback, and the cement people kind of promised him a job if he needs one. He doesn't want it, he says he'll never get to do design work, just stick probes into batches of cement, and how boring is that? He did his degree, he loves engineering, he's good at it."

This wasn't the time to tell her that her brother was barred from the Virejas site. "Would this be Sturlese Cement?"

"That's right. How did you know?"

"Your uncle had a connection to a guy named Boris Nabiyev, who's involved with Sturlese Cement. Did your uncle ever mention Nabiyev?"

"No. What does he have to do with Sebastian?"

"I'm trying to figure out who Sebastian made the recording for," I said with as much patience as I could summon. "In fact, the second time I saw your uncle—"

I broke off, mid-sentence. The second and final time I'd seen Jerry Fugher had been outside Wrigley Field, where Boris Nabiyev was terrifying him.

If you wanted to name a big project that the Illinois legislature had a say in, it was the rebuilding of Wrigley Field. There were endless proposals for state and city aid to make the five-hundred-million-dollar price tag less onerous for the owners—tax breaks, state-sponsored bonds, a special levy. If Sturlese wanted a piece of the Cubs action, and had been cut out of the bidding, they might have sent someone to try to threaten the team.

But why send Uncle Jerry to try to shake down the Cubs? Why not let Nabiyev do it? He was the pro at threats and enforcement.

For that matter, why would Spike care whether Sturlese got a contract or not? Unless he, or his pal Rory, was the mysterious angel who'd bailed out the cement maker.

"In fact, what?" Viola wrung her hands. "What's wrong, your face, you know something, you know what happened to my brother, don't you?"

"No, Viola, but I may finally have a starting place for my search. You're going to have to leave now; I don't have any more time today. Go to your doctor and get a medical form to take to your supervisor, and then try not to worry if you don't hear from me for a day or two."

Her nervousness about being seen at my office returned, exacerbated by her realization that she'd run here without taking any precautions: the people her brother was involved with could have been following her.

I didn't argue with her, just forcibly led her out the back way and into a cab.

I'd only talked to one man at the Cubs, Will Drechen in media relations. I didn't think he was the other speaker, but I couldn't be sure. I needed expert help.

I took the time to go back into the warehouse to shower the French fry grease from my hair and skin. I had a clean T-shirt in the back; it would have to do. I didn't want to stop at home for a change of clothes.

I knew I should call ahead, but I had a superstition that doing so would bring me bad luck. When I got to the Villard mansion in Evanston, I breathed more easily: old Mr. Villard was still there, and Adelaide, the empathetic caregiver, answered the door, not the brisk, brusque daughter.

Oh, yes, she remembered me; my visit had brought Mr. Villard a lot of pleasure; she'd see if he felt strong enough to see me. She left me in the foyer, which was stacked high now with packed boxes, some labeled for his new home, others for charities or to what I assumed were his daughters' addresses in Seattle and Tucson. It felt sad, a full and happy life reduced to cartons.

Before I descended too far into melancholy, Adelaide returned to take me to the room overlooking Lake Michigan where I'd seen Villard on Saturday. He was in his easy chair, the custom table that fitted into the arms holding a book and a glass.

"You finish writing that book already, young lady?" he asked as I bent over to shake his hand.

"Right now, that book is about as remote as a Cubs championship," I said ruefully. "I have a favor, I guess yet another favor to ask. I want to play a recording for you and ask whether you recognize any of the voices you hear."

He was pleased to help out; it would take his mind off the impending move.

"It's not necessarily going to bring you pleasure: it's a recording someone made of an attempt at extortion."

I stepped him through the background of the recording before I played it. He was old, as old as Mr. Contreras, and he needed time to absorb the story, so I told it in small steps. Adelaide gave little gasps of horror at the description of Jerry Fugher's death.

When Mr. Villard seemed to have the details under his belt, I took out my cell phone and played the recording for him. He had trouble hearing it, so I asked Adelaide to hold it to his ear.

At the end, he stared hard at me, eyes troubled. "You knew who it was before you played it for me, didn't you?"

"No, sir," I said quietly. "The first speaker is a man named Jerry Fugher. He was murdered last week, but I have no idea who the second person is. I thought it might be a politician, but now I'm thinking it's someone connected to the Cubs."

"I'm old. It's easy to con the old." He looked up at Adelaide. "Should I believe her?"

"Why did you think Mr. Villard would know who it was?" Adelaide asked.

"It was a guess, a leap, but Sturlese Cement plays a role in this, and there's a mobster who has a stake in Sturlese. I saw him outside the ballpark almost two weeks ago. I'm wondering if they were meeting with someone in the team's organization."

She didn't like what I was doing, but she told Mr. Villard I was telling the truth. "Probably telling the truth," she amended.

He picked up his glass with his distorted fingers and took a deep swallow. "I'm old. My hearing is crap. Can you leave that recording here? I want to check with someone else before I say for sure."

I hesitated. "There are a lot of ugly players in this game, sir. The way they disposed of Jerry Fugher is proof of that. Quite possibly this unusual makeup I have on my left eye came from them as well. I can't let you put yourself in danger."

Adelaide nodded. "She's right, Mr. Villard. You know what your daughters would say."

"My daughters, God love them, think their job is to swaddle me in baby blankets so that nothing bruises me between now and my funeral." He put the glass down with a snap. "I'm ninety-one. I'm tired of no one thinking I'm good for anything besides being a grinning ornament at Cubs CARE dinners. Give me the recording and I'll get it back to you tomorrow."

I explained that I needed to copy it to an electronic device—I couldn't hand over my cell phone. Adelaide didn't have a smartphone, but the daughters had given their father one and Adelaide knew the basic technology; she'd help him listen to it if I forwarded the file to his e-mail.

43

DINNER PARTY

By now I was cutting it close for collecting Bernie so we could meet Pierre's flight at O'Hare. The Subaru was a sturdy beast, not built for speed. That didn't really matter, given the thick traffic, but I missed the Mustang's ability to maneuver.

I found Bernie and Mr. Contreras having a sad farewell. The old man tried to persuade me that he and Mitch could take care of anyone who came after Bernie.

"Her parents are the ones who are summoning her home," I said, "and after the attack last week, I agree it's the right decision.

"Let's go," I added to Bernie. "Your dad's flight lands in under an hour and he will be very disappointed if you're not there to meet him."

We stowed her backpack and suitcase in the Subaru along with her hockey stick. She and Pierre were spending two nights at the Trefoil Hotel. They would detour back to Florida for the Canadiens' next playoff game, then fly to Quebec.

Mr. Contreras brought the dogs out to see us off. While Bernie knelt on the sidewalk to clutch Mitch's neck, I told Tom Streeter, who was on duty this afternoon, that the brothers could end their surveillance for now.

"No one's been sniffing around that I could see, Vic, but a young woman tried to get into your place this afternoon—"

"Right, Viola Mesaline. Kind of a client."

"Yes, Mr. Contreras told me. There may have been someone on her tail, someone on a Hog. I wasn't a hundred percent sure, and I didn't want to follow them in case they'd been sent to smoke out Bernie's protection detail."

My stomach turned to ice. If someone was tailing Viola—Nabiyev? Bagby? Scanlon?—it was because—how could I know why? Not because they thought she'd be easier to track than me—I had done nothing to cover my trail lately. Then because they thought she'd lead them to someone? To her brother? Which meant he was probably still alive.

"Do you want us to check in with her, see if we can spot the Hog again?" Tom Streeter asked.

I didn't like to think how much the Streeters' bill might run. The last few weeks, all I'd incurred was overhead, not income, but I couldn't leave Viola naked if the Grozny Mob was after her. I agreed, but said they didn't need to stay on her during business hours, assuming she went to her job at Ajax.

"Got it, Vic. I'll cover you as far as the expressway."

That was helpful, too: once we were on the glue called the Kennedy, it would be impossible to check for tails.

We seemed clean, unless the pursuit was doing it with multiple vehicles, which implies both a security team with a lot of resources—think NSA—and a target worth spending them on. The Uzbeki Mob's finances might rival the NSA's, but I wasn't that kind of target. I'd be easy to take out the old-fashioned way, a good marksman with one bullet to the head. I rubbed my forehead reflexively.

I glanced over at Bernie, but she had her earbuds in and the volume turned up. She was texting friends, ignoring me, leaving me to send my brain uselessly around a maze that didn't seem to have a center.

Where did Sebastian and the Cubs fit into this scenario? Villard had been briefly angry when I played Sebastian's recording for him, accusing me of knowing who was on the other end of the conversation before I played it. Someone I'd met when I'd been at the ballpark? Will Drechen in Media Relations was the only man I'd talked to, and it didn't sound like his voice.

"What are you thinking?" Bernie asked as we finally reached the airport exit. "You look angry."

"Not angry, frustrated."

"Are you glad I'm leaving? Uncle Sal told me I was making you worried."

"I worry because I can't keep you safe. When you come back in July for Northwestern's hockey camp, I hope all this Guzzo business will be resolved so you can run from my home to the lake without my worrying that someone might hurt you."

"And me, I am sad to leave without clearing Uncle Boom-Boom's name. And of course, I am happy that we have met," she added as a formal afterthought. "Also the dogs and Uncle Sal. And Jake. I know Uncle Sal is sorry I'm going."

"Yes, you've brightened his life," I agreed.

When we reached the O'Hare parking garage, I passed up the first few open spaces to make sure that none of the cars following us up the ramp was sticking with us.

Pierre's plane was on time, a miracle on the route between O'Hare and the Northeast. He ran through the revolving doors at the security exit, bag over his shoulder, and scooped his daughter into his arms.

As soon as she saw him, Bernie's animation returned. Father and daughter exclaimed in French for a moment until Pierre turned to embrace me. "Ah, so good to see you, Victoire, much too long since we were last together. Thank you for caring so tenderly for our *tourbillon*."

He brushed Bernie's hair from her forehead, saw the fading bruises where she'd scraped her face against the concrete. "Yes, *petite*, you've had far worse injuries on the ice rink, that is for sure. As for you, V.I., you look much more like Boom-Boom with that nose and your face all green, but it's a badge of courage. Arlette and I, we don't forget that you saved our darling's life."

"After putting it at risk," I said dryly.

He made a dismissive gesture. "Bernadine has a gift for mischief, so enough of that. Now—you must be my guest for dinner. Not much of a thanks—for that, as soon as the hockey season ends—as soon as the Canadiens defeat the Blackhawks for the Stanley Cup—you will come for a week or a month or a summer to the Laurentians, right?"

"Canadiens beating the Hawks?" I said. "Not only Boom-Boom's ghost but the Golden Jet will come for you, you renegade."

"Americans are so greedy," Bernie said. "The Blackhawks have won for *years* and the Canadiens not since 1993, before I was even born! If Vic is coming downtown to dinner, then can we ask Uncle Sal? He's so very sad that I am leaving and I am sad to be going."

The upshot was that we collected both Mr. Contreras and Jake on our way into the city. I changed out of jeans into gray silk trousers and my favorite rose-colored top and the five of us went into the Loop in a festive mood. The bartender at the hotel restaurant, who remembered Pierre from the Blackhawks glory days, sent over a bottle of wine, while the hostess, who knew Jake's playing, put together an off-menu meal.

The first bottle disappeared quickly, the second one only slightly less so, and we were partway through a third by the time the hostess presented us with a cart of artisanal cheeses. Bernie was drinking her share and more besides, but her father didn't object, and thankfully she was no longer my worry.

As Jake sliced a pear, twirling it around and laying uniform sections out on the cheese board, Bernie brought up her complaint, or perhaps concern, that I was letting Boom-Boom down by paying too much attention to that "dreary woman's missing brother," and not enough to the slander against my cousin.

Jake said he was just as happy if something had taken my mind off getting beaten up in South Chicago. "Dreary is good. Dreary is low-risk."

I decided it would be prudent not to mention that the dreary woman's brother might have a connection to the Uzbeki Mob.

"But what is happening with this history of Boom-Boom?" Pierre said. "His name has not been in the news since ten days. I thought this *tracasserie* about a girl being terrified of him had died down."

"It has, in a way," I said. "And up until two days ago, I'd become convinced that Stella Guzzo, or maybe her handlers, had invented her daughter's diary. Then I saw some photos that made me think the diary might actually have existed."

I pulled out my phone and showed Pierre the photographs from Mr. Villard's collection. "This is the young woman who was murdered. Did you ever see Boom-Boom with her? Or did he ever talk about the day he went to Wrigley Field with his boyhood friend?"

Pierre beckoned to the hostess to bring over a better lamp. "Vic, you know this is many years in the past. What do I remember of the thirty thousand times your cousin and I spoke? The camaraderie, not the details. Especially no details of Boom-Boom's love life. Me, I was always with Arlette, but for Boom-Boom, in those early years, it was a new love every three or four months."

Still, he took his time going through the photos, tilting the phone so the light hit the screen at the best angle. When he put the phone down, Bernie snatched it and looked through the file herself.

"That man, the drunk one with the soft hands, he thought I was this girl, but me, I don't see it at all."

Mr. Contreras leaned over her shoulder. "No, I see what he meant, Peanut. You both have a kind of liveliness in you. Reckless, maybe."

I looked at Mr. Contreras with respect. He was right: it was that quality that Joel Previn had been responding to, not the fact that the two had the same coloring or were the same age.

"And this was the girl whose mother murdered her?" Bernie said. "And now I see, she was playing hide-and-seek with Uncle Boom-Boom—where? At the baseball stadium? And she is holding—*quoi?*—*pas une pochette*. A little book, no? You didn't tell me this, Vic, you didn't tell me you saw this girl with the diary in her hand."

"I'm not sure that's what it is," I said. "It's not clear—"

"When it quacks, and waddles, and drops white feathers on the grass, you still say, it is not a duck?" Bernie slapped the phone back on the table, throwing up her hands to emphasize her sarcasm.

"Bernadine! You are jumping to conclusions like a kangaroo. *Pas plus de vin.*" Pierre moved the third bottle out of her reach, adding to me, "As for this poor girl—so terrible to think she was soon to be dead, she is so—so *vivace* in the photo. But I never saw her with your cousin."

He tapped the screen. "In these pictures, if anyone was afraid it was Boom-Boom, after all. Look at his face—it's not a game for him. She's leading him in the dance all over this stadium."

Mr. Contreras and Jake took their turn to look at the pictures.

"Whatever she was carrying, she don't have it when she comes out of that tunnel, or wherever she went off to," my neighbor said.

Bernie grabbed the phone again. "Uncle Sal, you are right. This Annie left the diary behind, and then the mother saw the pictures and went back and found it as soon as she got out of prison."

"Nobody knew the pictures existed until after the story about the diary surfaced," I objected. "And then—"

I stopped.

"What are you thinking?" Bernie demanded.

"Mr. Villard's house was burgled and some of his Cubs memorabilia were taken. I was going to say, maybe the thieves were looking for these pictures. Well, not these specifically, but the break-in happened soon after the story ran about Boom-Boom being at Wrigley. Maybe I'm wrong—maybe the break-in was random and not connected to Boom-Boom or Stella's quest for exoneration."

"These pictures prove the diary!" Bernie cried, cheeks flaming.

"This conversation proves that you cannot have more than one glass of wine, Bernadine," Pierre said. "You are behaving as if you were with your teammates, not at a dinner party. You and I, we are going up to our room and let these people have some peace and quiet."

He took my hand and kissed it. "Tomorrow, Bernadine and I will see the sights of Chicago, including a chance to watch the Blackhawks skate against St. Louis. You must come, too. The Blackhawks, they will be thrilled to have Boom-Boom's cousin in the house. And these gentlemen?"

Mr. Contreras was torn, but decided he needed a night at home. Jake seemed thankful to plead a rehearsal, but I accepted happily.

44

HIGH AND INSIDE

Between the wine, my cold and my lingering injuries, I was ready for bed within minutes of getting home. It was a luxury to stretch out in Jake's clean sheets, not to have my brain on partial alert for Bernie sliding out of the building.

Jake had recently been selected to play the Martinsson Double Bass Concerto with the Chicago Symphony and wanted to practice fingering. I fell asleep to the soft rumbling of his playing and for once managed a full night with no intrusions from Guzzos or mobsters or tar pits.

I woke to yet another cold cloudy day in the city that spring forgot, but finally felt well enough to run the lakefront with the dogs. My muscles were loose, I was moving easily, I was happy.

At the Fullerton Avenue beach, I returned phone calls while the dogs swam after their tennis balls. I was just finishing a conversation with one of Darraugh Graham's financial officers when Vince Bagby phoned.

"How's the nose?"

"Almost well enough to smell the peonies you sent."

"And the girl you're looking after?"

"Back in Canada with her parents. Why?" I kept my voice friendly, but I didn't trust him with the truth.

"I'm a friendly guy, Warshawski, who's trying to make conversation. I'd be glad to show you face-to-face—you free for dinner?"

"Not until after I find Sebastian Mesaline, and even then, no guarantees." I found myself checking the gun in my tuck holster.

"Come on, Warshawski, you can't be interested in a wussy kid like him."

"I've never met him," I said. "Tell me what's so wussy about him."

Mitch and Peppy, sensing my attention was elsewhere, started wandering up the beach. I whistled to them sharply.

"You have to do that into the mike? You damn near broke my eardrums."

"What's so wussy about Mesaline?" I repeated.

"Word on the street. When you meet him, you can let me know. I hope it happens soon—I'm going to hold you to that dinner date."

I pocketed my phone while I went after the dogs. Why had Bagby called? To see how much I knew or because he actually had taken a liking to me? I guess there was no reason it couldn't be both; he was a friendly guy, as he himself agreed: he got along with everyone, from the security manager at the Guisar dock to me.

Mitch was cleaning up after the Canada geese. I brought him to heel and jogged the rest of the way to the car.

It was interesting that Bagby knew about Sebastian Mesaline. I'd never mentioned Sebastian around him, but Bagby also knew Jerry Fugher, Nabiyev and, presumably, the Sturlese brothers, the people on the Virejas Tower project, perhaps even the contractor who had placed Sebastian there.

"Too wide a field to analyze," I told the dogs, unlocking the Subaru. "But Bagby is definitely playing with a very rough crowd."

They showed their agreement by shaking hard and covering me with wet sand. I guess that was a good thing—it meant less sand for me to vacuum out of the Subaru before I returned it to Luke.

Back home, I changed into office clothes and brought espressos over to Jake's. He was still asleep, but when I sat cross-legged on the bed, he stuck a hand out from under the covers for one of the cups.

"Trucker who might have Mob ties invited me to dinner," I said.

Jake propped himself up on an elbow. "You want me to play while you eat? Those gigs are *so* depressing. You get to measure 113 of the Martinsson, for instance, where the bass goes into an upper register that sounds like a cello, and at table nine, the trucker with the oil under his fingernails starts telling a crude joke, and the detective next to him, who you thought at first had some understanding of you and your music, in fact you were imagining what her skin might feel like under that red thing she has on, this detective laughs so loudly no one can hear—"

"You make it sound so romantic." I put my cup down and curled up next to him. "I didn't know the detective had such a disruptive laugh."

"When she's genuinely happy, it sounds like champagne fizzing out of the bottle, but when she's faking it, like laughing at a mobster's vulgarities, it's more like a barnyard cackle."

To protect my relationship, I'd left the gun at my place, but my phone was in my hip pocket. I ignored it when it started to ring, but the terrified voice leaving the message made me forget laughter, whether fizzy or cackling.

"This is Adelaide, you know, from Mr. Villard. Someone shot him, it's really bad, I'm calling his daughters, I'm calling the hospital, but you're a detective, I need you to come."

Jake sat up. "Who was that?"

"Caregiver to an elderly gentleman I met with yesterday." I rolled over and off the bed, tucking the red thing I had on back into my slacks.

Jake pulled on a pair of jeans and walked me to the door. "Be careful, V.I. Whoever your elderly gentleman is and whatever happened to him, don't risk your life, please. I hate that way worse than people telling jokes while I'm playing."

I squeezed his fingers and ran across the hall to put on shoes and collect my gun. While I tied my laces I called Adelaide to let her know I was on my way. Her phone went to voice mail, which sent me to the car at double-speed, worried that if someone had attacked Villard, she might be in danger, too.

When I reached the cul-de-sac in Evanston where the mansion sat, police sawhorses were blocking the road. I didn't bother trying to argue my way past the cops, but turned left, away from the lake, and found parking on a through street a block away. I jogged back to Sheridan Road and cut across the garden of a house north of the barricade. This section of Evanston sits twenty or thirty feet above Lake Michigan. A high rock fence runs about a quarter mile up the coast here, more to keep kids and dogs from tumbling down the bluff to the water than to keep out miscreants like me.

I scrambled to the top of the fence and started walking down toward Villard's place. The top was only about as wide as one of my feet, and there were places where a thin iron rail had been inserted. As I skirted the grounds of Villard's neighbor, a woman came to the door, shouting at me. I smiled, waved, which made me teeter and grab the overhanging branch of a tree. The woman opened the door and let out one of those Hungarian hunting dogs, which roared over to me, yelping in a high-pitched, indignant tone. Using the branch, I swung over the edge of the wall into a corner of Villard's garden.

"Nice doggie," I said as it stood on its hind legs to bark across the wall at me. Probably playful, since it was a house pet, but you never know.

I was screened from the road by a thicket of bushes and spiky prairie grasses, but I could make out a clutch of Evanston squad cars, as well as an officer at the bottom of the marble steps. I watched the woman who'd sicced the dog on me cross the drive and begin talking urgently to the officer on duty.

I did not need to be picked up by the Evanston cops. I faded behind a giant ash to text Adelaide. Mercifully, she came out through the back door a moment later. Her skirt and shirt were stained with blood.

"What happened? How badly is Mr. Villard hurt? Did they get you, too?" I demanded.

Her usually calm face was crumpled with worry and fear. "He was alive when the ambulance came, I hope he still is. I didn't know, if I'd known I'd never have left him on his own, but my gentlemen and ladies, they need respect, you shouldn't treat them like they're little children, only the daughters don't believe me."

"Of course they need respect," I assured her, "and I've watched you with Mr. Villard. He told you to leave him on his own because he was meeting someone he wanted to be private with?"

She nodded, miserable.

"After you left last night, he was very troubled. I was blaming you, to say the truth, for upsetting him in his mind. He sat looking at his old pictures from the baseball team for hours, letting his food get cold. When I came in to help him up the stairs to his bedroom, he was on the phone and motioned to me to leave, so I only heard a little bit of the conversation."

"Which was?" I prompted.

"Something about of course he'd listen to the other person's side of the story. Then this morning he told me someone would be coming to see him. He asked me to help him out to the garden and then to leave him on his own. I brought out a tray with coffee and cups and the little cookies he likes, but I went inside, only I stood with the door open, so I could hear him if he needed me. I could only see his back, or the back of the chair where he sat, but not the driveway, or anyone who might be sitting with him."

She took me through the kitchen to an enclosed porch that opened onto the garden. I saw what she meant: only one chair and a bit of the wrought-iron table where Villard had been sitting could be seen from here. The scene looked peaceful, no overturned chairs or coffee cups, none of the blood that Adelaide had gotten on her clothes. I started down the steps so I could see the rest of the setup, but an officer held up a hand, warning us to stay inside.

I went back to Adelaide, who was twisting her hands over and over. "The police, they act like I knew these people, like I could have stopped them, but it happened so fast, I couldn't see them, just heard their voices."

"How many were there?" I asked.

"I think it was two, I think they were both men, but I can't be sure. Anyway, one of them talked to Mr. Villard, and Mr. Villard, he played this recording you gave him, and the one man tried to laugh, but the other—he—I couldn't believe it—he shot Mr. Villard, then the two of them ran around to the front. I could hear the car taking off, but I was in the garden helping my gentleman and calling for help and calling you."

As if on cue, a plainclothesman came into the sunporch. "Who are you?" he demanded of me.

"V. I. Warshawski. A private investigator."

"Let's see some ID."

I hate being cooperative, but the law has so much enforcement going for it these days I didn't want to protest enough to be detained for questioning—I didn't have time today for heroics. I showed my licenses, driver's, investigator's, gun permit.

"You follow the sirens?" he asked.

"You mean, am I cruising the streets, hoping for clients? No, Officer. Mr. Villard was sharing some of his old photos of Wrigley Field with me."

"You the woman who climbed the fence next door? That how you always arrive at your contacts' houses?"

"When the cops are blocking access I have to get to my clients as efficiently as possible."

"And how do you know this gal?" He jerked a thumb toward Adelaide.

I was white, so I was the woman who climbed the fence. Adelaide was dark, which made her a gal. Was that a step up or down from being a girl?

"This *woman* is a professional caregiver whom I've talked to when I've met with Mr. Villard. Did anyone get a look at the car that the shooters drove?"

"We're taking care of canvassing the neighbors and asking questions. We're looking for this *woman's* contacts."

"Mr. Villard made an appointment with someone for coffee this morning. Rather than wasting your time harassing people who never heard of him, you might check his phone records, see who he called last night at—what time was it?" I asked Adelaide.

"It would have been around ten o'clock, right before I came to help him get ready for bed."

"It's a good story," the detective said, "and the two of you have had plenty of time to rehearse it."

Instead of answering him, I called Murray Ryerson, who fortunately picked up. I cut short his sarcastic greetings. "A situation in Evanston. Stan Villard, used to be head of media relations for the Cubs, has been shot, taken off to the hospital. Evanston cops are trying to frame his caregiver, but smart money is wondering where Boris Nabiyev or Vince Bagby were when the shots were fired. Also, call Freeman Carter for me, in case we get too crowded here."

The detective took the phone from me. "Call is over." He pressed the off button.

"Murray Ryerson is a reporter with Global Entertainment," I said. "He'll get the rest of the details from his connections at the state's attorney's office. And my lawyer will be ready to help Ms.—" I realized I didn't know Adelaide's last name.

"Trimm," she said.

"Right. Ms. Trimm, as well as me."

The detective stared at me, then called over to one of his patrol officers to come get some names from me.

"This gal seems to know a hell of a lot about what was happening here. Take down her details, and get the names of the people she thought we should be talking to. And then get the Trimm woman's personal phone book and see where her friends and relations were this morning."

Being confrontational had transformed me from a woman into a gal. Interesting.

"You'll want to check Mr. Villard's phone," I prompted, as the officer came over. "He set up this meeting around ten last night; see whom he called."

"The day I need a private dick to tell me my job is not coming anytime soon," the detective said. "You can leave when you've given your details to my officer, but you stay close, real close."

He was saving face, so I didn't push him further. I gave his officer my phone numbers, gave him Murray's number to call for more information, and texted Freeman Carter's contact information to Adelaide's phone in case the detective decided to arrest her as soon as I was gone.

For the time being, the Evanston police were willing to leave her sort of alone, although when I asked her to show me the pictures Villard had been looking at last night, the detective sent his officer along with us. Who knows what might happen if two gals were alone together.

The photos didn't tell me anything, except that Villard missed his wife and wished she'd been there for him to consult—he'd been going through an album of family pictures, mixed together with some of the players and staff who apparently had been close to him over the years: these were candid shots, not the posed press pictures.

Adelaide asked me to stay with her until she'd talked to the daughters. The movers were supposed to come in three days, and she thought they should be canceled, but that was the family's decision.

"I hope my gentleman will recover and be happy, but—" She let the sentence finish itself.

Talking to the daughters was an ordeal. They were distressed, they had questions Adelaide couldn't answer, and, as she'd predicted, they blamed her for letting their father go outside on his own to meet with a stranger. I tried to help Adelaide talk to them, but the daughters felt I had introduced an element of sorrow or perhaps instability into their father's world. It was hard to argue with that—if I hadn't come up yesterday with Sebastian's recording, he wouldn't have made the appointment he'd set up this morning.

The nurse, calling from Tucson, relented near the end of her conversation, at least toward Adelaide, if not me. She knew her father was a stubborn man who liked to do things his way, and how could

Adelaide possibly have known he'd be meeting with someone who wanted to shoot him.

"But you're a detective; you should have known better," the nurse told me.

My superpowers don't include predicting the future, I started to say. It's true I had tried to warn him, but I hadn't really pictured this kind of attack. It was best to say nothing: her father had been shot and she was twenty-five hundred miles away. I turned her over to Adelaide, who needed to know whether the sisters wanted her to remain in the house for the present.

45

BEHIND IN
THE COUNT

About half an hour later, Murray called back. He had a contact in the ER at Evanston Hospital, who told him that Mr. Villard was in surgery, but the prognosis was hopeful.

"Whether he was cocky, or afraid of witnesses, the hitman only took one shot. Turns out Villard had a Cubs doodad on his jacket that saved his life—slowed down the bullet, deflected it, so it went into his chest but missed the heart. Of course he's an old guy and getting shot is never good for you, but if the creek don't rise he'll live long enough to see the Cubs in the cellar for at least another year. If they haven't arrested you in suburbia, I'll meet you in your office in an hour."

Adelaide was calmed by the better news about Villard's condition, which she quickly passed on to the daughters. Before I left, I put my lawyer's and my numbers on speed dial for her, making sure the Evanston detective knew I was guaranteeing her high-end legal aid.

"If worse comes to worst," I said, loudly enough for the cops to hear, "do not say one word to the police without your lawyer present. Anything you say will be twisted into a shape that will have nothing to do with what happened, so best keep completely quiet. Don't even say you are exercising your right to remain silent; that will make them think they have a lever they can use to pry on you. Believe me, I've heard them all, starting with, 'Only a guilty person would want a lawyer,' or 'An innocent person wouldn't be afraid to talk to us.' Got it?"

Adelaide pressed her lips together, bottling in her fears, and gave me a convulsive hug. "Got it," she whispered.

I smiled cheerfully at the detective. "The reporter and I will follow up on Nabiyev's whereabouts this morning. Also, if you're not going to check Mr. Villard's calls, why don't you give me his cell phone. The person he was trying to reach at ten last night will likely know who was coming to breakfast."

The detective's scowl would have dug craters in the few pot-hole-free roads left in the city.

Murray reached my office almost an hour after me. He'd made a detour to the Villard mansion, but the cops hadn't let him past the roadblock. He was envious of my strategy for getting into the house and pelted me with questions about the scenery, the photos Villard had been studying last night, his eating habits, his children.

"Murray, I don't know his waist size, but I'm guessing boxers, not briefs, okay?" I glared.

"Give me the gal's number who's looking after him, she'll tell me that."

"You're talking like a cop. Just because she provides elderly people with intimate care does not turn her into a child. And she also has the ordinary person's right to privacy, so no."

"Come on, Warshawski, I'm doing—"

"Whoa. I'm the one who got you your scoop."

"I'm getting rusty—I have to practice badgering someone, might as well be you," he said. "Do you think Bagby and Nabiyev are involved in this?"

I told him about Bagby's phone call this morning, although I left out the bit about the dinner invitation. "Have you found out anything that links Bagby or Scanlon to the Dragons, or the Mob?"

Murray pulled out his notebook. "I've found the ties between Scanlon and Spike Hurlihey, but they aren't a surprise. Scanlon has been a big money tree for Spike for years, helped bankroll his first campaign for the Illinois House when Spike decided to leave Mandel & McClelland and go into politics. Pretty much nothing in Illinois fund-raising is illegal, so it doesn't seem to be much of a story.

"The cousin, Nina Quarles, seems willing to be a front for both Bagby and Scanlon. The best guess is that lets both of them qualify as a woman-owned business—her name appears as a co-owner of the insurance agency, and as a trustee for Bagby's daughter as owner of the trucking company. Even though Nina's voting address is in South Shore, her real residence seems to be Palm Beach in the winter and Long Island in the summer. With lots of months in Europe or Singapore in between."

"What a life, when your name does the work for you and all you have to do is spend the profits," I sighed. "What about Nabiyev?"

"That's been a more fruitful search, because it's harder for foreign nationals to funnel U.S. funds to overseas shell companies. I can't prove the Grozny Mob bailed out Sturlese Cement, but I have found a trail between one of Nabiyev's accounts and Grozny. What do you know that I don't? Besides Adelaide's phone number."

"Jerry Fugher was the conduit for covering Stella's bills while she was in prison, but I can't find out where that money came from. Everyone who paid him gave him cash, including his unfortunate niece and nephew. I also don't understand who would underwrite

Stella, or why. But it has to be connected to her decision to go after an exoneration, because all this other stuff began boiling up after Frank Guzzo came to see me."

I told Murray about yesterday's conversation with Frank. "I think he was telling me the truth, about coming to see me because he was worried about his mother, and that she blew up at him for doing it, but there's still something not right about the story. Joel Previn, who handled Stella's defense twenty-five years ago, knows something, but I can't figure out a way to make him tell me. And whoever shot Villard this morning, that person must have some connection to the Cubs, or why would Villard have wanted to talk to him privately first?"

"Please, Warshawski, don't try to connect the Cubs to the Mob— if they had that kind of protection, they'd be winning more."

"Yeah, you could hardly accuse them of fixing games," I agreed. "They lose through grit and hard work. The connection has to be to Scanlon, or through Scanlon to Spike Hurlihey. In the recording, Uncle Jerry says 'everyone has to pay to play,' which is the defining sentiment of Spike's life."

Tom Streeter phoned as Murray and I were deciding we couldn't come up with any new ideas. Villard's shooting had completely knocked Viola Mesaline out of my mind—I'd forgotten the Harley that might have been following her when she left my place last night.

"The Harley buzzed around her apartment last night," Tom told me, "but there was mud on the plate and I couldn't get the number. This morning a kid on a bicycle seemed to track her as far as the bus stop. What do you want me to do?"

"Pick her up after work this afternoon," I decided. "Tell her it would be good if she left town. Or went to a safe house, which I do not happen to possess."

"We could put her up in the back of the warehouse," Tom suggested doubtfully. "There's a kind of apartment there we use for Airbnb. Bed, bath, kitchenette. We can keep her safe there, but not at work."

"It doesn't make sense to me," I fretted. "If someone wants to kill her, they've had plenty of opportunities. If they're simply following her around town—"

"They hope she'll lead them to someone, or to something," Tom finished the sentence.

"She led them to me," I said, "and they've left me alone. At least, I think they have. Or maybe I haven't yet found whatever it is they're looking for. My only guess is that they want Sebastian Mesaline. That's why Viola is scared every time I try to see her: they've been to her, threatened her, but believed her when she said she hired me to find him. And now I'm the stalking horse who's supposed to lead them to her brother!"

Murray had only been able to follow the conversation from my end, but it was enough to put him in the picture. When I'd hung up, he said, "You know, Warshawski, I'm not any fonder than you of letting the Feds or the cops get between me and an investigation, but if the Grozny Mob really want Sebastian dead and they think you can find him, you should talk to your pals in blue."

I didn't like it, but he was right. I spent much of the rest of the day talking first with Conrad Rawlings and Bobby Mallory, and then with an array of officers in Organized Crime. Of course, the hit on Stan Villard had happened in Evanston, not Chicago, but the two cities share a lot of streets, so they have protocols for sharing leads and even resources.

Because Villard had been with the Cubs, the team was breathing down the necks of both forces. Powerful citizens get more police attention than people like the Guzzos. Fact of life, not a nice one, but it meant that both Bobby and Conrad tried to be cordial, instead of snarling at me for keeping Sebastian's recording from them. They snarled a little, but that was just a reflex.

They also needed to talk to Viola and didn't really believe me when I said I'd been trying to talk her into going to them.

"Vicki, you need to take us to her, or her to us," Bobby said. "No dodging around, no sleights of hand."

We were meeting in a conference room at the CPD headquarters on South Michigan, me, Conrad, Bobby, three officers from Organized Crime, and another trio from Evanston. Also a couple of junior officers to take notes and make coffee runs.

"There's a guy on a Harley who's been keeping tabs on her," I said, "and at least one on a bicycle. The Harley seems to pick her up after work, but they probably have somebody on foot, since she takes the Green Line home. We haven't spotted any cars, but that doesn't mean the trackers aren't using them."

"We'll try to keep an eye on Nabiyev," an officer from Organized Crime said, "but he's gone to ground for the time being, may even have left Chicago. If we'd known he was a person of interest in the shooting, we could have taken steps at the airports right away."

All ten officers glared at me in unison. They had a good choreographer.

"I suggested it to the detective in charge at the crime scene," I said. "He was so eager to pin the blame on Mr. Villard's caregiver that he wasn't interested in anything I had to say."

"Yeah, well, when you're with us poor dim-witted coppers, you have a habit of making your suggestions sound like sarcasm. It's a good trick," Bobby said, "because it means we don't take you seriously and then you get to go off and pull your own rabbits out of your own hats and make us look ineffectual. And that also is annoying."

"Put it in my file," I couldn't help saying. "'When she's most annoying, she's on to something worth paying attention to.'"

Bobby made a sour face. "I'd love it if just once you'd act your age. You can go—we'll take it from here."

He followed me into the hall. "Vicki, if you see or hear or even smell anything from Nabiyev, you call me or Rawlings at once. Don't try to tackle him on your own because you can't. I don't want your ma greeting me at the Pearly Gates, telling Saint Peter not to admit me because I let you run headfirst into danger, but that's what will happen if you keep thinking you're smart enough to handle thugs like Nabiyev. *Capisce?*"

"*Capisco,*" I said. I felt my age plus another decade as I walked to the elevator.

46

IN THE MADHOUSE

My seat used to be up near the rafters, where the noise shook one's bones. Seventeen thousand fans slamming our chairs up and down, stomping, screaming, whistling, while the foghorn under the scoreboard bellowed whenever Steve Larmer or Boom-Boom scored. The Madhouse on Madison, it was called, and rightly so—decibel level around 130 on average, up to 300 when all the noisemakers were turned on. The sound coming from the rafters could push skaters to their knees.

They tore down the old Stadium about the time injuries forced my cousin into retirement. Just as well—he was superstitious about his success and hadn't wanted to play in the fancy new place. Tonight, sinking into a plush red seat, I kind of agreed with Boom-Boom. I didn't want my eardrums shattered, but I missed being right on top of the ice the way you were at the Stadium. The brightly smiling attendants, poised to bring us everything from name-brand cocktails to lobster rolls, made me perversely long for the Stadium's cheap beer and pretzels, even though I don't like beer.

The teams were skating warm-ups when I got there. Pierre had invited me to a pre-game dinner with his daughter and some of his old pals from the team, but I'd had to skip that: I'd gone with Conrad and one of his officers to talk to Viola before she left Ajax for the day. We'd done it the right way, gone through corporate HR, corporate security, explained she was dealing with a stalker and we wanted to guarantee her safety to and from the workplace.

Her supervisor turned out to be helpful, even supportive: Viola's twin might not shine on the job but Viola worked hard and seemed to be a popular member of her unit, at least until the last week or two when she'd become erratic. If she was dealing with a stalker, that explained everything and the company would be glad to help.

Viola wasn't quite as grateful. She accused me of betraying her trust, then, when I told her I knew she'd received threats of reprisals if she didn't reveal her brother's location, she accused me of listening in on her phone calls.

Conrad, at his gentlest, most avuncular, was finally able to persuade her to tell what she knew, although it wasn't much. He coaxed her into describing the threatening phone calls, but Viola didn't know who'd been making them. She kept insisting that she knew nothing about what Sebastian had agreed to do for Jerry Fugher, and no idea where her twin might be. She also resisted a police escort to her apartment.

"Don't you see? They'll know I went to the police if they see you. They already know I went to Vic. No police, they keep telling me, or they'll kill me, and what's to stop them murdering me now? They know where I work, they know where I live."

She looked at me, her amber eyes once again flooded with tears. Just keeping her in Kleenex was going to bankrupt me.

"You want me dead," she sobbed. "You're not really trying to find Sebastian, if I'm dead you won't have to look for him anymore."

"She has a point," I said to Conrad. "Unless you can put a twenty-four/seven detail on her, she'll be vulnerable as soon as your officer leaves."

Conrad smacked his thigh, frustrated. "And you can afford to guard her?"

We hashed it over for some time. The only solution we came up with was cumbersome and highly dependent on luck, but in the end, I drove Viola home to pack a suitcase. Conrad trailed us discreetly and hovered a few blocks away until Tom Streeter picked up Viola.

Once they were gone, I drove back to Conrad, who got out of the car to say that a Harley had buzzed the street a few times, but he hadn't been able to pick up the plate without revealing he was watching.

"You look after yourself, Ms. W. That broken nose doesn't help your looks any, and a bullet in the chest would definitely reduce your sex appeal, okay?"

The morning had started with Vince Bagby inviting me to dinner. Now Conrad was admiring my sex appeal. Despite the day's traumas, I drove to the United Center in a cheerful mood.

Pierre was surrounded by old friends and old fans when I got there, while Bernie sat listening to music and texting, looking up only when Pierre pulled out one of her earbuds to introduce her to someone. She gave me a nervous smile, but pulled herself together to ask after Mr. Contreras and the dogs. She was wearing one of Boom-Boom's jerseys—I'd given it to Pierre after my cousin died, and Bernie was swimming in it. To show that her loyalties lay with her father and her home country, she'd put on earrings with the Canadiens' logo—the flattened *C* embracing an *H*—done in red and blue enamel.

Once the game got under way, father and daughter both focused on the ice. I didn't recognize the current crop of players on either team—I hadn't paid much attention to hockey after Boom-Boom's death, although the Hawks were always generous with tickets whenever I wanted to come.

I tried to focus on the action, but about halfway through the first period, I realized Bernie was paying more attention to me than the game. As soon as she saw me looking at her, she turned red and picked up Pierre's binoculars to stare at the ice.

"What's up?" I asked her as Toews and the rest chased the puck to the far end.

She pretended to be too focused on the game to hear me, but the tightness in her shoulders told a different story.

At the end of the first period, Pierre took her with him down to the Blackhawks bench. Since he was scouting now for a rival team, he couldn't go into the locker room, but I watched him talking to the front office staff, introducing Bernie, who flashed the family's famous smile.

Someone handed Bernie a stick. She walked out onto the perimeter of the rink and showed off her form. After a certain amount of confabbing and gesturing, someone escorted Bernie to center ice to play the game of "Shoot the Puck": a board is placed in front of the goal with three slots in the bottom and contestants—usually drawn randomly from the crowd—get three chances to put the puck through a slot.

A woman from media relations was there with a mike, talking to each of the contestants before they addressed the puck. When it was Bernie's turn, the woman said, "I see you are wearing Boom-Boom Warshawski's number, even though your dad is with the Canadiens."

"Boom-Boom was my godfather," Bernie announced into the microphone. "I wear his number tonight and dedicate my shooting to his memory. Some ignorant people try to deface his reputation, but me, I am proud to show my support of him in public."

The remark was so pointed, I figured it explained the tenseness she'd been exhibiting in the stands—she must have been planning to toss this barb my way.

The crowd went wild over Bernie when they caught on to her connection to Blackhawks royalty. The cheering and catcalls grew almost to old Stadium decibels. Bernie waved a quick, shy hand, but looked at her feet, not the audience, while the other three contestants took their turns.

When it was Bernie's time to shoot, she treated the matter with total seriousness, adjusting her stick as if it were a golf club. The puck sailed through the center slot as if someone were pulling it on a string. Bernie permitted herself a small tight smile, bowed briefly to the cheering audience and scurried off the ice, where Pierre was waiting to hug her. The Blackhawks brass slapped her on the shoulders. I could imagine the threadbare comments: too bad the NHL doesn't let women try out, we'd put you on one of our affiliate teams right away.

I left the stands to join a line for the women's toilets. By the time I got back to my seat, the second period had started. Pierre and Bernie apparently had accepted an invitation to sit with the Blackhawks officers: their seats were empty, but I saw Pierre in the row of seats right behind the players' bench. I picked up the binoculars that he'd left on his seat. No Bernie. Bathroom break, maybe. I sat uneasily for half a minute, then texted her.

About halfway into the second period, when she hadn't responded to that or to my second text, I headed to the ground floor. The entrance to the floor-level seats was blocked by security staff who demanded a ticket that gave me the right to enter. I opened my mouth to argue, decided that was futile and gave a small scream instead.

"A rat! A rat just ran right over my feet—oh, horrible—look—look, it's over there!"

I pointed dramatically. The three guards couldn't help following my arm, which gave me a second to duck around the barrier and run into the stands. I pushed and shoved my way past annoyed fans and squawking security staff to the row of seats behind the Blackhawks bench.

"Pierre! Pierre!" I had to shout his name a half dozen times before someone heard me over the fan noise. The guards had caught up with me and were trying to wrestle me away when he turned and saw me struggling in their arms.

He tried to come to me, couldn't get by the glass barrier separating the team from the crowd, and shook one of the manager's arms. By this time, the guards had managed to drag me past the excited spectators to one of the aisles. What a wonderful night of violence, even better than a fight on the rink, guard versus berserk fan right in front of them.

Before the guards could turn me over to the Chicago police, Pierre arrived—he'd had to go through the tunnel into the dressing room and then up and around behind me. Someone from the Hawks was with him, explaining to the guards that I was a friend of Pierre's.

"Vic, what is it? Bernadine, she is ill?"

"Where is Bernadine?" I demanded.

"But—with you. She is saying my old friends are *trop ennuyants*, she is wanting to watch the game—"

"No," I said flatly. "She's gone."

"But—where? Maybe she is in the toilets?"

"She hasn't been around since the second period started. It's been a good twenty minutes, maybe more."

"No," he whispered. He grabbed his binoculars from me to inspect the section where we'd been sitting, but the three seats remained empty.

I looked around despairingly: twenty-one thousand fans, another thousand or more guards, press, you can't search a building like this. Not much in the way of security cameras, either.

"Get the head of security," I said to the guards who'd just been holding me. "Let's see what we can do. She was on camera for 'Shoot the Puck,' and everyone paid attention because she's Pierre's daughter. If she left the building, or someone took— Anyway, you can alert everyone in security to look for her, or report whether they saw her, right?"

The man from the Blackhawks management who'd come up with Pierre nodded at the guards. "Get that going now, guys. Pierre, if she's here, we'll find her."

I called Conrad Rawlings on his personal cell. "We don't know what happened to her, whether she left on her own, or if Nabiyev or Bagby had someone here waiting for a chance to get her on her own."

Conrad took the few details I had, promised to call Bobby to see what resources the department could put into a search. "Don't beat yourself up, Ms. W.," he added. "Slows down the investigation. You got a current photo you can text?"

"YouTube. Tonight's 'Shoot the Puck.'"

The next hour was a blur of frantic, useless activity. The security crew did a crowd scan with their fan cams, trying to match Bernie's face to anyone in the stands. I joined two women staffers to search the women's toilets. I felt dull, empty, while my body moved to staircases, ramps, hidden elevators, dark spaces under the rafters, all against the backdrop of the organ, the screams from fans, the blare of foghorns. My injured eye and nose were aching. The pain forced me to know this was happening now, in the body, not some dream from which I might mercifully awaken.

The woman from security I was working with got a call on her radio: they'd found a gate attendant who was pretty sure he'd seen

Bernie leave. We all rushed down to the security office, where the Stadium's staff had been augmented by members of the Chicago police, including Conrad, who nodded a greeting when he spotted me.

The attendant was flustered, not used to this kind of spotlight. Conrad took the questioning away from the security chief.

"You're not in any trouble, son, but the girl may be in danger, so we need you to think calmly. How sure are you?"

He was pretty sure, yeah, well, during the game not much happened at the gates, you reminded people that once they left, they couldn't come back in, and other than that, he and his buddies, they kind of hung out.

"Right," Conrad said as the security chief started to demand what "hanging out" meant. "What time would you say you saw the girl leave?"

The attendant couldn't pinpoint it, more than to say around the start of the second period. "Because by the third, with the Hawks on cruise control, you start to get a lot of people leaving, trying to beat the traffic."

"She seem to be leaving under her own steam, son, or was someone forcing her?" Conrad asked.

The attendant hesitated. "She left alone, for sure, but maybe a minute or two later two guys left, too. I started telling them the policy, you know, no reentry, and they told me to shut the f— up."

Conrad and the security chief tried a dozen different ways to get the attendant to describe the two men. The attendant became more and more flustered: he saw so many people every night, it was a miracle he even remembered this pair. Conrad finally let it go, his shoulders sagging.

47

OLYMPIC TRYOUTS

One in the morning, sitting in the cold walkway at the United Center. Conrad and the cops had taken off, Pierre had called Tintrey, one of the biggest of the private security firms, and was out in a car with them, driving the streets around the Stadium.

The security staff were getting ready to shut down the building for the night. The security chief was sympathetic: everyone felt devastated by Bernie's disappearance, but she wasn't in the building; I needed to leave.

I got up, my legs so stiff I lost my balance. I clutched the handrail along the wall, my bleary eyes not registering what I was looking at, the shuttered food stands, the garbage that the cleaning crew was shoveling into bags, the aisle numbers going dark as the interior lights were shut off. I was standing near 201, which was blinking at me, the bulb inside getting ready to die.

"Know how you feel," I muttered.

I had a feverish urge to join the cops and Tintrey Security in driving the city's streets, the way one does in hunting a missing wallet: it could be here, have you looked there?—even if the police organized a search by quartering the vicinity and fanning out from there they couldn't cover the buildings, the bridges and tunnels. You need some kind of hint or clue and I had nothing to contribute.

My day had started with Mr. Villard's shooting. My encounter with the Evanston police seemed part of the dim past, as if it had happened to someone else many decades earlier. I was so worn that I would be more of a hindrance than a creative help in a search. I drove home. Maybe I'd sleep, maybe I'd wake up with an idea.

"Don't beat yourself up." I repeated Conrad's advice as I climbed the back stairs to my place. "Plenty of time for that later. Anyway, Pierre is doing it for you."

He had looked at me with something akin to hatred, cursing me in two languages for involving his daughter in my criminal affairs. I was so tired that even fear and self-recrimination couldn't keep me awake. I fell into those fever dreams, where your eyeballs feel scratchy and you only skim the surface of sleep. Viola was chasing me on a Harley . . . Nabiyev was pouring cement over my head . . . Vince Bagby invited me to dinner, then stuffed me into the middle of a mound of pet coke. As the dust closed over me, I saw the light over aisle 201 blinking on and off.

I sat up, completely awake. The slip of paper I'd found in Sebastian's gym bag had the number "131" scrawled on it with the time. Aisle 131. Be there at 11:30 P.M.

The United Center was on my mind. I stopped in the middle of dialing the phone number for the security chief. Sebastian had been going to see the Cubs, not the Hawks, the day he vanished. Aisle 131, that was Wrigley Field. He'd been meeting someone at Wrigley Field in the middle of the night.

The coaster Bernie had brought home from a Wrigleyville bar. It wasn't underage drinking that had put those mischief lights in her eyes a week ago—she'd been scouting the ballpark. It didn't make sense—a week ago, she hadn't seen the pictures, she didn't have any reason to think Annie had been there. Maybe she only wanted to emulate Boom-Boom's and my old bravado in climbing into the park and then after she saw the pictures, decided that was where Annie had hidden her diary.

I dressed in black: T-shirt, warm-up jacket, jeans. Rubbed mascara over my cheekbones to keep them from reflecting light, pulled a black cap over my hair. I tucked my pencil flash and picklocks into my pockets, put on a shoulder holster. Maybe I should leave a message for Jake. Everything I could imagine writing made my errand sound embarrassingly stupid at best. In the end, I scribbled,

> *Bernie Fouchard disappeared midway through the game. There's a slim chance she went on her own power to Wrigley Field; I've gone off to look for her. Please let Mr. Contreras know as soon as you get up. Also Conrad Rawlings.*

I went out the back way, slipped the note under Jake's kitchen door, then ran down the back stairs as quietly as possible. The dogs still heard me. They were lonely for me and for Bernie; they started barking, demanding that I take them with me. I ran on tiptoe down the walk and was opening the back gate before the light came on in Mr. Contreras's kitchen. As I jogged down the alley, I heard his gruff voice demand to know who the heck was out there, he had a shotgun, keep your distance.

When I reached Racine, the adrenaline that had propelled me out of bed drained away and I slowed to a walk. My legs felt thick and heavy from the hours of climbing around the United Center and I couldn't force them into anything faster than a kind of shuffling jog.

The predawn air had a bite in it. The calendar said spring, but under the streetlamps I could see the mica in the sidewalks glinting with frost. I should have worn gloves. My fingers were numb and I needed them to be flexible. I thrust them deep into my jacket pockets and tucked my fists around my thumbs.

The bars along Clark and Addison had finally closed for the night. I had the street mostly to myself. I passed a man inspecting bottles that had been dropped along the street, drinking from any that still had a little something left in them. A squad car slowed, shone a light in my direction. My heart beat uncomfortably—not good to be stopped with a blackened face and picklocks. They played their spot along the street, rested it on the guy on the curb, decided he was harmless, turned south onto Clark.

I walked to the back of the bleachers. Gate L stood invitingly near me, but the wooden doors opened inward, with the lock on the inside, no handles, no place I could insert a pick.

I went back to the wall under the bleachers. Boom-Boom and I had made this climb a dozen times, but never in the middle of the night. And not with the overhang from the new rows of bleachers they'd added. Sometime between my reckless childhood and today they'd also put in new bricks, new mortar. No toeholds.

I used my flash sparingly. Even if I could get to the top of the wall, which was about six feet above my head, I couldn't crawl past the cantilevers that supported the new bleachers. So near and yet so far.

A rattling in the wire mesh around the stands made me flinch. Night nerves, not good, but I risked a quick look upward with the flash. A piece of newsprint had been blown against the fence. Every time the wind gusted, the edge would slap the chain links.

I walked slowly along the street, studying the wall. Right beyond the gate, the shuttered ticket windows offered the only chance for entry. Not a great chance, but if I could coerce my frozen fingers and tired, middle-aged legs into action, it would do.

I studied the layout carefully, memorizing the distances: I'd have to put the light away and judge it all by feel.

I stuck the flashlight back in its belt holder, rubbed my hands together. The palms were tingling.

I can climb this wall. I am fast, smart and strong. I repeated the sentences, tried to pretend I believed them, grabbed the ledge under the ticket window and wedged my toes against the wall, shifted my hands to bring up my right knee, lost my hold, dropped to the sidewalk.

I am smart, fast, but big. Size is not always an advantage—if Bernie had figured out this route ahead of me, her lithe little body would have floated up like a gymnast's.

I grabbed the ledge, swung my legs up and fell again. My shoulders and hamstrings were already feeling the strain. Turned around, palms on the ledge behind me, pushed down and jumped at the same time, got my butt inserted into the deeper space left by the window, swung my legs over.

Four inches of ledge supported eight inches of thigh, unstable. I moved fast. Balance beam, yes, we used to jump on a beam no wider than this in high school. I straddled the ledge, pushed myself standing. You can still do this, girl, even if it's been thirty years.

Light from the streetlamps on Clark provided a dim glow, enough that I didn't need the flashlight to see where I was going. I started a heel-to-toe walk along the narrow ridge, heading for the brick wall underneath the bleachers.

Headlights appeared, reflected in the glass of the building across the street. A squad car making its rounds. I froze, my shape a dark silhouette. If they looked up—they shone their spot on Gate L, some ten feet in front of me, decided it was secure, moved on. The shirt under my warm-up jacket was wet with sweat. The cold wind began turning it into an ice pack against my back. Get in motion, warm those muscles up again.

Someone was coming up Waveland toward me, but I couldn't stop now. I walked up the wall until my knees were at squat angle, got a hand up, grabbed the clay tiles at the top of the wall. One last hoist, come on, Warshawski, you fast smart detective, do it.

"What you doing up there?"

I was lying on top of the clay tiles, a beached whale. The drunk I'd passed earlier, or maybe a different drunk, was standing underneath me.

"Practicing for the Olympics," I said. "The wall-climbing event."

"Seems kind of a funny place to practice."

"Yeah, I can't afford a gym."

I got to my hands and knees. My muscles were wobbly, not good, since I had a lot more stadium to cover. Right hand forward on the sloping clay tile, left knee, left hand, right knee.

"You fall, you gonna crack your head open, no Olympics, no medals," my companion said. "They got those places on the Internet where people give you money, you say you need to join a gym, they pay your membership."

I grunted. Crowd-sourcing, what a great idea. Way better to be in a gym than creeping along the clay tiles of Wrigley Field in the dark.

"You ain't the first to be up here practicing, case you interested," my friend said, as if the memory had just pinged a neuron. "Other person didn't say nothing about no Olympics. Maybe they stealing a march on you, or maybe you ain't no Olympic athlete yourself."

I sat up, banging a knee into the edge of one of the tiles. "When was this?" I tried to keep my voice casual.

"Oh, tonight. Don't have me no watch, can't tell you exactly when, but when I called out, he moved fast, way faster than you, missy. If he's your rival, you better get your faster moves worked out."

"He? It was a man?"

"Didn't ask for an ID. Small kid, might have been twelve or thirteen. Wore one of those big sweatshirts, got caught on the tiles. He moved like a crab through the sand with a kingfisher after him and if you'd a asked me, I'd a said he was breaking in, not training for no Olympics. What about you?"

"I think he was breaking in, too." Bernie, Boom-Boom's jersey hiding her breasts, small, agile, looking like a twelve-year-old boy in the dim light.

"Meaning, maybe you breaking in, too. Like the older guys coming after the boy."

My heart skipped a beat. Two beats. "They climb up after him?"

"They not as spry as you and the boy. They saw him go over the wall. One stood on the other's shoulders, but he fell over, they both swore a blue streak, then they tried using a crowbar on Gate L here, only then the *po*-lice drove by, they took off."

"I'll tell you a secret," I said. "I'm not in the Olympics. That's my kid, running away from home, and I've got to find him before he hurts himself. Thanks for the tip."

The drunk sat on his haunches, watching me. "Yeah, I didn't figure you for no Olympic athlete," he said under his breath.

Ignore the grinding pain in the knees where the tiles cut through my jeans. Force the numb fingers to cling to the tiles. Inch by inch, until I felt the metal of the staircase next to me, a sharper shape in the shapeless night. I swung the right leg out and over the stairwell fence bar, slipped, fell backward onto the bleacher stairs.

"Hey! You in the ballpark now!" my cheering squad shouted. "You don't belong in there, they gonna arrest you, give you fines."

I didn't bother responding.

"Hey, you still alive?" the drunk shouted. "You find any beer, you drop it over the wall, you hear?"

I sat up, rubbed my tailbone. Everything in one piece. I'd done the easy part.

48

RUNDOWN

I skirted the bleachers and clambered into the right-field stands.

"Bernie!" I shouted. "Bernie!"

The wind whipped my voice away.

I called Conrad, message went to voice mail. I texted him and Pierre: *Bernie was seen scaling the bleachers at Wrigley Field around one a.m. Two guys on her tail, my source a drunk.*

Pierre replied as I was trotting along the gangway: *I'm coming. Conrad, you will meet me there.*

The aisle doors loomed as darker holes against the darkness of the green seats and concrete. I went into the nearest one and turned on my flash again: it was impossible to see inside. In the dark, the place smelled of stale beer and popcorn, of damp concrete.

I stopped every few yards to call her name again. My voice bounced around the concrete columns; the echo was the only reply I got.

It was no warmer inside the cement walls than it had been dangling from the brickwork outside. I swung my arms, slapped my sides, tried to restore circulation to my arms and legs, even if not in my fingers, jogging in a great circle past the closed concession stands, the locked doors in side walls that led to the stadium's guts. It would take a hundred cops to search this place thoroughly.

Where had Bernie gone? Had she overheard me talking about the scrap of paper in Sebastian's bag? But even if she had, she wouldn't have known it meant—possibly meant—a meeting outside Aisle 131.

Fatigue and fear were stirring a great soup in my gut. Because I couldn't think straight, or think of anything else, I went on down the gangway, following the ramps down to the field box level, toward Aisle 131.

I climbed the short flight of stairs that led to the stands. After being inside in complete darkness, I could make out the field and the seats in the grayer light outside. I held myself completely still, heard nothing, saw nothing move except a few stray pieces of trash.

I went back inside, trying to figure out what place Sebastian might have been meeting someone. Men's room, smelling thickly of disinfectant layered over urine. I banged open the stall doors but the room was empty. Women's room, empty as well. The concession stands were locked tight. I pried at the shutters, but not even a skinny street urchin could wriggle through the cracks.

There were several side doors, also locked. One door had two industrial mops wedging it shut. I took them out, but the door was locked. Maybe a janitor had been fooling around.

Bernie didn't have picklocks, and using them was a skill I'd prudently kept to myself. She could not have opened this lock on her own.

I was close to weeping. I needed a plan, a thread to follow, but I had nothing. The men who'd been after her, who had they been, had they found another way in and grabbed her?

I shone the flash around one more time. Light glinted on metal. I knelt and saw an earring in a crack in the concrete just outside the doors with the mops through the handles. I used the edge of my pick to pry it free. A design in red and blue enamel of a flattened *C* embracing an *H*, logo of the Canadiens, inlaid in a reddish gold circle.

A chill deeper than the cold of the stadium froze my bones. I couldn't move, couldn't think.

You are frightened now, my darling one, and that is as it should be as we prepare to say good-bye. Gabriella's words floated into my panic-stricken brain, her comfort to me when she told me she was dying. *The brave person isn't the one who feels no fear, but the one who continues to act, even in the middle of fear. I know your brave heart and I know you will not let fear disable you.*

My brave heart. Open the damned door, stop whining, start acting.

I knelt in front of the door, flashlight in my mouth so I could use both hands on the picks. The lock was tricky and my frozen fingers kept dropping the picks. When I finally got the last tumbler in place and heaved open the heavy door, it was to see the outsize pipes and cables that ferried water and power through the building.

I tried shining the light into the depths of the room, but my flashlight was puny and the space was vast. The entrance looked like the one I'd seen in one of Mr. Villard's photos, the tunnel where Annie had emerged, grinning cockily, empty-handed after leaving her book inside. How had Bernie known to come here?

As I played the light around, a movement overhead made me jerk my neck back: red eyes stared down at me, then turned to saunter a short distance off along the pipe: *We own this space, we own the night, we're leaving because we want to, not because you scare us.*

I jumped back involuntarily, then stomped forward, loud. "Bernie, are you in here? Come out, it's V.I.! You're safe now, let's go home."

I shut my eyes, concentrated on sound. Creaks and clanks in the ancient pipes. Feet whispering overhead, those were the rats. Gurgles and clangs along the pipes, all the sounds of an aging building.

A hard hat was hanging on a hook inside the door. I pulled that over my wool cap and started into the tunnel.

The pipes curved away in front of me, following the shape of the stadium. I rounded the first bend and heard the door slam shut behind me. I turned on my heel, jogged back to the exit, turned the inside knob. The door had been locked again from the outside. I took out my picks, worked the tumbler, shoved hard. The door was wedged shut. Those mops, they had been put there to keep someone inside.

I drew back my hand to pound on the door, stopped. I'd been locked in here on purpose. Begging would waste time, energy.

I turned back into the tunnel and called Bernie's name again, again heard nothing but the grunts of the pipes, the dripping of water along the route.

I put the flashlight into my belt, pulled out my phone. No signal in here, of course, but it had a brighter light than my pencil flash. I kept it in my left hand, the Smith & Wesson in my right, safety off. I kept my mind on small things: overhead pipes, flooring, shelving. Tried not to breathe too deeply around the sheets of asbestos that had unpeeled from the overhead pipes. I sidestepped the cables snaking along the floor, looked behind pillars, little things to keep bigger things like rats, or Uzbeki mobsters, at bay.

I paused every few yards and called Bernie's name. I thought I heard noises louder than vermin would make, steps retreating from me up the tunnel.

My fingers had lost all feeling, my forehead ached with cold. I couldn't tell if I was moving forward or if the damp, slime-coated walls were sliding past me. Time had disappeared, everything, my life, the planet, the Universe, all compressed to this tiny point, numb body in a cavern.

The wall angled past me again and great steel cantilevers slid into view, bracing wall and ceiling. I looked up and saw steel nets holding slabs of concrete. Above them more pipes, joists, a faded box of Cracker Jacks. Water dripped past the slabs of concrete and spread along the floor. I turned to shine the light farther ahead of me, wondering how much farther the tunnel stretched, moved too quickly, slipped and fell into the slime. Gun and phone skittered away from me. The light went out. I fumbled for the flashlight in my belt loop and cut my finger: the plastic shield and the bulb had cracked in my fall.

Near me I heard creaking, the ceiling net or the joists or the wood panel, they all could be giving way. I imagined an army of rats gathering on the overhead pipes, preparing to hurl themselves onto my head. I drew my knees up to my face, arms clutching them, sweat coating the slime on my face.

Lâche, Bernie had called me. I was a coward if I was going to give in to night noises. A coward to let a few rats drive me to gibbering. Let loose your fingers, spread your arms, ignore the jolt of pain through the right shoulder, take in a breath, a slow deep breath, let it out, unlock the brain. The phone and gun had slid away from me. Reimagine the sound, figure out the direction they'd gone. In front of me. All I had to do was go forward on hands and knees and feel the ground; I'd come to them.

Deep breath in, deep breath out, hand patting sludge, hand touching snakes, hand recoiling. Not snakes, V.I., cables.

"Vittoria, vittoria, vittoria, mio core," I started to sing.

My voice came out in a reedy quaver. Not good at all. Gabriella and Jake would be so disappointed, all their careful coaching coming to nothing. I sat up on my haunches, took a deep breath and belted it out. *Victory, my heart! No more weeping, no more vile servitude!* My voice bounced against the walls and pipes, creating a tinny echo.

Back onto my hands and knees, a hand out, patting the slime. And a crash, and a cry of pain somewhere behind me. No rat created that noise.

"Bernie?" I said. "Are you there?"

No response.

"Are you alive? Can you move your arms and legs?"

Muffled groaning. I moved cautiously toward the noise. Banged into a steel panel. The sounds were coming from behind it. I felt my way around. Ran into the soft warm body that was Bernie.

"Hey, girl. Hey, I'm here." I was so sick with relief I could hardly speak.

I felt along her body. Her hands were tied behind her and there was duct tape across her mouth. I pulled that off. She gave a little whimper of pain, swallowed it.

"Vic? Vic? Is it you? Oh, help me, help me. He's crazy. Where is he?"

"Let's see about getting you untied, *carissima*. Let's make that happen. I don't know who 'he' is or where he is. I think he locked us in here, but one thing at a time."

The knots were tight. My numb fingers kept slipping on them. "You're going to be okay, girl, it'll be all right," I crooned. I took out my picks and finally managed to pierce the heart of one of the knots. Hours went by or perhaps minutes—in the cold dank dark it wasn't possible to count—but the threads came loose. I moved Bernie's arms to her sides and began chafing her forearms and wrists, get the blood moving.

"We need to get out of here," I said, "but it will help if we can find my phone and my gun."

Bernie's teeth were chattering. She was clinging to me, smelling sickly sweet, the symptom of shock.

"Who is he? Did you arrange to meet him here?"

"Non! Non, j'ai été stupide—"

"Bernie, my French is primitive. Tell me in English."

"I don't know what I was thinking," she whispered. "That I would show you—but I didn't imagine—and the stadium, it's so big and so dark. And then I saw the open door, and it was like the photo you brought home, and I thought, I will prove to her—to you—that she was a coward and a fool, I will find the journal of this Annie. And then he jumped on me, out of nowhere. I tried to fight, but he was too strong. He lives in here, he tied me to this shelf where he is living. He said no one looks behind here, even the men who come in every day to check on pipes and valves, they don't know this little space exists, that I will die here."

She gave a hysterical gulp and clung more tightly to me. "Then I heard you calling and I tried to get free, tried to call to you, I was so frightened, I thought you would leave and never know I was here, and then I fell off the shelf where he tied me."

A homeless man in the bowels of Wrigley Field? Not so strange, maybe: I've encountered homeless families camping in the bottom of elevator shafts and in cardboard shanties by the river. Why not underneath a baseball park?

"Where's your flashlight?" I asked.

"He stole it from me. He said his own flashlight is dead and mine is a good one."

If he had set up housekeeping back here, he had to have some source of light. I gently removed Bernie's clutch on my arms, moved her into the circle of my left arm, used the right hand to grope amid the detritus on the shelves. Something sticky, a mess of cloth that stank of stale grease. A matchbook. Yes, a matchbook.

I struck a flame and saw a jumble of partially eaten food, cups of beer, stadium seat cushions, a filthy blanket with the Cubs logo still showing faintly blue against the dirt.

The match went out. I lit another. In its brief life I saw a row of makeshift torches, rags wrapped around wooden spindles. I gave one to Bernie to hold and lit it with another match, lit a second for myself.

Bernie was trembling and weeping, but she obediently followed me into the body of the tunnel.

"Your homeless man locked us in and barricaded the door," I said, "but I'm betting there's a way out at the other end. I sent a message to your dad and to the police, that you'd been seen climbing into the stadium, so I'm hoping they'll be here looking for you. But you and I are not going to wait around for someone else to rescue us."

49

BEANBALL

Under the flickering light of greasy rags, we finally found my phone and gun. They had landed in the sludge under one of the cables, a couple of yards away from the perimeter I'd been patting. It would have been a long night in here with the rats. I wiped the phone on the underside of my jacket. It seemed to still be alive, but showed only 29 percent battery. I put it in airplane mode so it would stop wasting energy looking for a signal; I wouldn't use the flashlight unless I absolutely had to.

I tore a strip of fabric from my underpants—the cleanest garment I had on right now—so I could clean the gun barrel. Bernie wrung her hands, demanding that we get going, oh, why stand there playing with your weapon?

"I know, darling, I know, but if worse comes to worst and I have to shoot, I don't want this gun jamming or blowing up on us."

I gave her small tasks, things she had to concentrate on, working to bring her back from the edge of terror: Hold her torch over the gun barrel. Rewrap the rags around my torch. Tie her shoelaces. It's amazing how much you can steady yourself by tying your shoelaces.

By the time I'd finished with the gun, Bernie was calm enough to tell me what she remembered of the night. She'd been imagining going to Wrigley for more than a week—my guess about her scouting trip to the ballpark, the night she'd said she was going out with friends from the peewee hockey league, had been correct.

"That time, I just wanted to see if I could do what Uncle Boom-Boom and you did, you know, see if I could climb up the bleachers. It looked like fun. Only then, when I saw the pictures, I *knew* this Annie, she must have left her diary here. I would have done that."

Of course she would have. She was seventeen, with a high sense of adventure and a low sense of consequences.

Today, when Pierre took her to a camping store to get a few things for their mountain cabin, she'd bought a high-grade pocket flashlight—that made her feel confident she could navigate the stadium in the dark. Taking advantage of Pierre's involvement with the game and with his old friends, she'd slipped out of the United Center and caught a cab.

"The driver, he asked me, am I sure I want to come here, since I am leaving a hockey game and there is no baseball game, and then when we got here—I saw how big this ballpark was in the dark, almost I called to him, wait!, but—" She broke off, shamefaced.

I skirted another pool of dank water dripping through the steel nets overhead. "But you didn't want to admit you were no braver than I was," I said matter-of-factly.

She nodded miserably. "He drove off. I felt very small and stupid. You said you and Uncle Boom-Boom used to climb over the back of the bleachers and I looked at them last week, but tonight—they looked so big—oh! Why did I think I needed to show off to you?"

Rats were skirmishing over something bleeding in a corner. I put an arm around Bernie to shield her from the sight.

She described her climb up the wall behind the bleachers—the same route I'd taken. A drunk had been watching her, which had scared her into swallowing her fears and scrambling over the wall.

"But when I was inside the park, I didn't know where to look or what to do. I should have just gone back over the wall. Only the drunk man, it was dark, I didn't know if he would attack me."

"Let's concentrate on being here now," I said. "How did you find this tunnel?"

"I went inside the stadium, through the open aisle door. I thought, just one look, to prove I'm no coward, and then back outside, over the wall, and ride a cab to the hotel. I ran through the hallways, shining my flashlight around, not opening any doors. But then I came to the door to this tunnel. It was open, and I saw how she—it, the door, how it looked like the door in that photo. I stepped inside and the homeless man jumped me. He kept yelling at me, like he thought he knew me, or that I knew something I don't know."

"That's typical of someone with a mental illness who's been living on the streets," I said. "Their reality is all they can process. Homelessness exacerbates the problem."

"No! It wasn't like that. He said that he was tired of tricks and people not believing him, that it was empty, there wasn't anything here, but he wasn't going to die for it. If anyone was going to die it would be me. And then he could be left alone."

"That what was empty?" I started to ask, but I was interrupted by a loud clang, a sound vibrating along the iron pipes overhead, and then shouts, heavy footsteps.

"Is it Papa?" Bernie's face was eager.

"I don't know. I don't like it." Pierre would have been calling Bernie's name.

I stuck our torches into holes in the concrete walls and pulled her back, away from the light.

"Stay here," I murmured. "I want to see who's here."

I started up the tunnel, gun in hand.

"Don't leave me," Bernie cried. "I can't be by myself in here, I don't care if I'm a *lâche* myself, it's too—"

The voices came through clearly.

"They're further along, I can hear them. *Papa*!" Bernie called joyously. *"J'y suis, je t'attends!"*

Footsteps pounding, slipping, men shouting. I tried holding Bernie: "Wait, wait until we know," but she broke away from me and ran toward the voices, calling *"Papa, Papa."*

I lumbered after her, heard her scream, rounded a corner to see her struggling in the arms of a masked man. A second masked man loomed over him, gripping a third man, who wasn't masked. Oily unwashed black hair hung over his forehead, almost joining with a week's growth of beard. Jeans, a sweatshirt. I could just make out the Illinois Institute of Technology logo on its filthy front.

"Come one step closer and we shoot the girl," the second masked man warned.

"Sebastian!" I shouted. "Sebastian Mesaline. Give it up. The police are on their way."

"I told you," Sebastian shrieked to the two goons. "I left the girl tied up in here, she's the one you want, not me, she came in here, she stole the diary, she has the pages."

"No," I shouted. "We don't have a diary. There is no diary."

"Don't lie to me, bitch," the larger goon said. "I saw the cover to the diary. This worthless piece of shit"—he shook Sebastian—"says it was empty when he found it."

"You found a book in here?" I stupidly asked.

"Yeah, Fugher, he fucking double-crossed us. He said this pansy of a nephew here did. Or you did. Which is it?"

I couldn't recognize the voice. Not the heavy accent of Nabiyev. Not Bagby's lilting baritone.

"Stella doesn't have it?" I asked.

"Oh, the Guzzo broad—she's so crazy she sees double whatever she's looking at. No, what she has isn't what we're looking for. Which one of you is telling the truth—the boy or you?"

"I am," Sebastian wailed. "I told you, I told you last week, when I gave it to Uncle Jerry the pages were already gone. Someone else was in here ahead of me. It had to be her."

Sebastian wrenched himself free of the thug holding him and fled toward the exit. Big Goon turned and shot. I leapt over and smashed my gun stock into Small Goon's jaw.

He roared in pain, loosed his grip on Bernie.

"Go, go, go!" I screamed.

She almost made it, bending her slight frame low, to slide under Small Goon's arms, but she was too tired, too shell-shocked for the speed she needed. Big Goon grabbed her. Small Goon slugged me. I kicked his shins, hard, and he jumped back. Small Goon fired at me, missed.

I felt the heat as the bullet zinged past. I ducked down, scooted under a pipe, shot back, high, over Bernie's head. The sound was unbearable, echoing, reechoing. Smoke filled the air, the stink of sulfur. Big Goon fired again.

"Don't fucking kill her until we know where the goddam pages are!" the smaller creep yelled.

"We'll get little missy here to tell us where she lives and search her place. I'm tired of fucking bitches thinking they own the universe." Big Goon shot again.

Eyes watering, coughing, ears ringing, find a target that wasn't Bernie. Edge forward. A sharp shock, and I was plummeting over a cliff, bouncing down rocks into the tar pits.

50

WILD PITCH

Tar was in my nose, my lungs. It sucked me under, I couldn't move my arms. Someone had been sick in front of me and the smell mixed with the tar was so terrible it made me vomit. I wanted my mother but Stella Guzzo and my aunt Marie appeared.

The tar poured over me and I blacked out. I woke in the modern epoch, into darkness so awful that I thought for a moment I actually was buried in tar. I flung my arms wildly trying to swim to the surface. Hit my hand on metal, heard it clang. Not tar. Tunnel. The smell of sewage and vomit. I'd been sick.

I struggled to sit up. My head knocked into a pipe and the jolt made me throw up again, a trickle of bile that left me panting for water.

Test for concussion: Can you remember the day, the president, the geological epoch? What's your name? *V. I. Warshawski.* What's your occupation? *Idiot.*

Bernadine Fouchard, she'd been with me. And then—masked

men. Sebastian Mesaline. We'd fought, I could still smell the acrid gun smoke through the stench in my nose. Don't think about what you've inhaled, sit up, move, slowly, but move! Phone in pocket, still working, turn on the light.

I'd been in the dark too long, I'd become a mole, couldn't handle the stabbing shapes, colors. My head ached, my left eye was tearing, but I forced myself to keep blinking, looking, hoping for Bernie.

I was alone except for the rats. They'd gathered where I'd been lying, insolent, unconcerned, eating my vomit. Good thing I'd been sick, they'd have gone for my nose and cheeks first without it. The hard hat I'd borrowed had rolled off. My gun, nearby, I wanted to shoot the rats, but I only had one magazine and I'd already fired twice.

I bent slowly, not wanting to challenge my head, picked up the Smith & Wesson and the hard hat. I must have fallen heavily: the hat had a dent in it. I started to put it on, then looked at the dent. I'd been shot. The hat saved my life. The impact had knocked me out, but the men must have thought I was dead.

Move, V.I. Don't be feeble, get out of here. I moved up the tunnel, got to the entrance. Locked in, no time for finesse. I shot out the lock, put my shoulder to the door. Damned mops were holding it shut. I backed up, shot at a hinge. The bullet ricocheted, but before I could find a cleverer strategy I heard shouting from the other side.

"What the hell are you doing in there?" Noises, mops scraping back, the door opened. I stood in the shadows, put away my gun when I saw who was on the other side. Five in the morning, game day. The grounds crew was there, getting the field ready for play.

I left through the doors in the outfield wall while the grounds crew were waiting for the cops to pick me up. The crew hadn't been able to follow my story, or at least they didn't believe my story—how could someone have been living inside the ballpark without the security detail noticing? They didn't want to go into the tunnel to see the squalid nest Sebastian had built behind the steel panel, they didn't have time for this kind of BS. No, the best thing was to have me picked up for trespassing and shooting a weapon inside the park.

I didn't try to argue, just said I needed to use the washroom. While they stood guard at the entrance they'd unlocked, I picked the lock at the far end and slipped out, back hugging the wall, until I'd rounded a bend in the stadium wall. I went out through the first open aisle door, staggered down the seats and shuffled along the perimeter of the field to the exit. At least it was still so dark that they didn't see me until I actually opened the door beneath the ivy. I heard them shout, but I hobbled over to Clark without stopping to look.

I didn't contact Conrad until I was clear of the park, but as soon as I was sure I wasn't being followed I texted a full report of my night. *Terrified,* I finished. *They have Bernie and I don't know where they're taking her. Check Sturlese Cement, check Virejas Tower and Bagby's truck yard.*

Conrad wrote back at once: he'd sent a team into Wrigley as soon as he got my first message—he'd taken an hour off for sleep—but they hadn't checked the locked doors. And now where was I and what evidence did I have that would allow him to apply for a warrant to any of the three places I'd mentioned?

My phone died as I was dictating a response. Squad cars were passing me, lights flashing, presumably on their way to Wrigley to arrest me. I turned down Racine, my legs quivering, waves of nausea overtaking me. My body wanted to go to bed.

"Permission denied," I said out loud in my sternest voice. "They have Bernie and you must find her."

A woman out walking her dog in the early dawn turned to stare, called the dog to heel and scuttled into her building. I sounded as crazy as I smelled and looked.

My legs were two numb trees plodding down the street, untethered from my mind, which floated between Racine Avenue and the tunnel. *We'll get little missy to tell us where she lives.* The thug's words floated back into my memory.

Don't hold out, Bernie, don't hold back. I prayed that she had blurted out my address as fast as possible, but what they might be doing to her—I would not think about it. Could not. I couldn't fix it by taking time for fear. Focus on what you can do, move your damned legs.

The building floated up in front of me, no one casing the front, good or not good? How could I tell? No one in the back, don't be holding out on them, Bernie.

My front door didn't show any signs of forcible entry. Maybe I should have checked the back as well, but the thought of going down all those stairs and coming up to the kitchen entrance was more than I could bear.

Once again I stripped before going inside, once again left a heap of foul-smelling clothes outside my door, took just enough time in the bathroom to scrub sewage and asbestos from my hair and skin. Hurry, hurry. Two pairs of jeans destroyed, I had one left, not quite clean, but it would do. I'd sacrificed both pairs of running shoes, time to move on to my work boots. I plugged my phone into the charger. Reloaded the clip for my gun, stuck two spares in my fanny pack. While the coffee machine heated, I went downstairs to rouse my neighbor.

Once Mr. Contreras grasped the crisis, he stopped fussing over my own corpse-like appearance. He sent me out back with the dogs while he dressed, and was huffing up the stairs to my place in pretty quick order. I typed up some talking points for him, which he studied and practiced a few times.

When Mr. Contreras thought he was ready, I dialed Vincent Bagby: I'd captured his number when he'd called yesterday morning to ask me to dinner. Bagby answered his cell phone on the fourth ring.

"You missed me so much you had to get me out of bed, Warshawski?" My ID showed up on his screen as well.

"This ain't Warshawski," Mr. Contreras said. "I'm her neighbor and a good friend. Vic's been in an accident, they ain't sure she'll make it."

"Where is she?" Bagby demanded. "Was she shot?"

I grimaced: Lucky guess or did he know?

"Cops don't want nobody knowing where she is, case they try to finish her off. But she talked to me before they put her under. Said you was looking for some special papers Annie Guzzo hid underneath Wrigley Field all those years back. I'll give 'em to you once I see the girl Bernie is safe."

"I don't know what papers you're talking about, or who the girl Bernie is."

He knows, I quickly wrote. *He gave us a ride after we were attacked by the Dragons.*

"You got Alzheimer's already at your age?" Mr. Contreras said. "You forgot you give her a ride when her and Vic was beat up last week? I see Bernie walk into her pa's arms and I give you the papers."

"Was that her name? I didn't know, and I don't know about the papers. Don't play games with me, old man; I'm not even sure I believe Vic was hurt last night."

"Maybe you know what I'm talking about, maybe you don't. You tell your friend Rory Scanlon what I said, maybe he'll take it more serious. You know the Coast Guard station out by Calumet Park? You, or him, or the Sturlese boys, they bring Bernadine Fouchard out there in two hours and I'll get them the papers they're so hot after."

"How come you have Warshawski's phone?" Bagby demanded.

"She gave it to me."

I made the kill sign and Mr. Contreras hung up.

"Sure hope this works, doll."

"Sure hope it does, too," I agreed grimly.

I went into my subscription databases and found a cell phone number for Brian Sturlese, but not for Rory Scanlon or Nabiyev. Mr. Contreras repeated the conversation with Brian Sturlese.

Sturlese was surlier than Bagby, and not as smooth: he paused too long between his lines. "I don't believe you. Warshawski went on the warpath because she said there never was a diary."

"Yeah, what she said, and what she knew, they're two different things," Mr. Contreras growled. "I'm giving you a chance, but I'm gonna let the cops take over if you don't show up with Bernie. And if she has so much as a scratch on her, I got the whole machinists' local gonna make you sorry you ever left your ma's womb."

"Now what?" the old man fretted when he'd hung up.

"Now we need to get you out of here in case they think they can break in and beat you up."

He didn't like it: he was more than a match for a cement mixer half his age and twice his bulk, he knew tricks that the Sturlese boys never heard of. I let him rattle on, bravado, while we went back down to his place to pack an overnight bag. I also took a large bottle of Coke from his fridge. I don't normally like sugary drinks, but the Coke would settle my stomach and the sugar might give me an illusion of energy.

Before we left the building, I gathered up copies of Mr. Villard's Wrigley Field photos, then went to check on Jake. He was deeply asleep, his wide, humorous mouth slack. I wanted to get into bed with him, I wanted to move into the safe world of music and walk away from kidnappers, crimes, fraud, assault, but I went to the kitchen to change the note I'd left him:

> *Bernie's been kidnapped. I don't know when or how I'll be back and won't be easily reached, but I'll try to get you a message before the end of the day. Conrad Rawlings will know where I am if you get worried. I love you.*

I wanted to ask him to play the CD of my mother's singing at my funeral, but he would know to do that. I jotted down Conrad's cell phone and lumbered back down to collect my neighbor. The Subaru had become a liability; too many of the wrong people knew my Mustang was a total loss and it would have been easy to spot Luke's car in the parking lot by my office. My neighbor and I took a cab to the nearest rental place, where he got us a beige Taurus, one of a hundred thousand on the roads at any given moment. We got them to supply an in-car charger for my phone—my own car charger had vanished with the Mustang's wheels last week.

We stopped at the apartment to pick up the dogs and headed south. We were passing the Jackson Park boat harbor when my cell phone rang. Caller ID blocked. I pulled over to the curb and handed the phone to Mr. Contreras.

"How do we know you're telling the truth?" the caller demanded without preamble. "We need to see a sample before we do a deal."

Want me to post it on Facebook? I quickly wrote. My neighbor nodded and repeated the question.

"Salvatore Contreras, right?" the caller said. "You're Warshawski's neighbor, right? You get a sample up in ten minutes."

Mr. Contreras looked at me in alarm. I jotted a couple of suggestions.

"Screw that," my neighbor sputtered. "I gotta dig up the paper and get me to a copy shop to scan it and everything. It'll take me pretty darn near all day."

The caller said he'd have two hours and cut Mr. Contreras off mid-protest.

I texted Conrad, told him I was pretty sure the Sturlese brothers were the ones who'd been in the tunnel last night. He wrote back,

The SA doesn't think your hunches are enough to base a warrant on. Get me something concrete.

Put a trace on my cell, I wrote, *they're calling me with threats.*

Where are you right now??

South Shore but I'm on the move.

51

RIGGING THE GAME

The Previns lived in one of South Shore's elegant old condos on Sixty-seventh Street, right on the corner. We found a space on the street without any trouble—the hard part was keeping the dogs in the car: they smelled the lake and were desperate for exercise.

Ira and Eunice owned the penthouse, with Joel on the sixth floor. At least he'd been able to put eleven stories between himself and his parents.

It was seven in the morning now, but I didn't imagine Joel was an early riser. In fact, I had to lean on the buzzer to his apartment for three minutes before I roused him.

"V. I. Warshawski," I said into the security phone. "We have to talk."

"Go to hell." He hung up.

Other residents were walking their dogs or leaving for work; we had a very short wait before someone came out and obligingly held the door for us. Elderly man, white woman, we might not live in the building but we must be harmless.

I put a finger on Joel's front doorbell and held it down until he opened the door, his face the color and texture of putty. He was wearing silk pajama bottoms and a T-shirt.

"I'm calling the cops. You can't harass me in my own home."

"While we wait for the police, I need some answers." I pushed past him into his apartment, Mr. Contreras on my heels.

The space was unexpectedly clean and tidy, its severe white walls hung with what looked like important art. An antique cabinet clock chimed the quarter hour as we came in. A grand piano stood in a corner.

I pulled the stool out and sat down. "You'll never guess where I was between one and four this morning."

Joel swayed on his bare feet. "I've always hated playing games with the wiseasses of the planet, and I'm not going to play yours."

I pulled a photograph from my bag, Annie at the mouth of the tunnel, and held it out. "I spent a chunk of time right inside this tunnel."

Joel's skin changed from putty to ash. "Where did you get this?"

"From a man who used to work with the Cubs. Annie hid something in this tunnel, but she'd been so clever, she had to brag about it to someone. Maybe she told Boom-Boom, but I'm betting not. I'm betting she chose you, the person in the office who was in love with her, the one who could appreciate her cleverness. When did you go to Wrigley to take the pages out of the album? Before or after she was killed?"

Joel grabbed the edge of the piano. His forehead was beaded with sweat. He looked around, from me to Mr. Contreras, from me to the door. He couldn't flee, not in his pajamas and no shoes.

"Before," I said with certainty. "Annie was crowing at the end of that day in the park, 'No one can touch me now, no one can touch me now.' She told you where she'd stashed the book, and you were itching with curiosity. You had to know what she'd hidden at the ballpark."

Joel didn't say anything, but his shoulders slumped farther.

"Must have taken a certain amount of courage to go into that tunnel, broad daylight," I said.

"Don't patronize me," he panted. "I'm not the man Ira was, I'm afraid of my own shadow, you can't believe I could actually go to Wrigley Field and sneak into a tunnel the way you did, or—or Annie."

Mr. Contreras cleared his throat, but I shook my head at him: waiting was the only useful strategy here. I tried not to listen to the ticking of the clock. *Tick*, Bernie, *tock*, grievous bodily—no.

"All right, I was in love with her," Joel burst out. "Who wouldn't be, such a beautiful bright girl. And then I heard she was hanging around with Warshawski. I knew I didn't have a prayer. They laughed at me, Spike and his buddies, telling me she'd been seen with him. 'Why would she care about an overweight nerd like you? And one who usually likes boys better than girls, anyway.' Spike. That was his line, but all the others copied him."

His lips were flecked with white and his breath stank.

"Get him a glass of water," I said to Mr. Contreras, keeping my eyes on Joel.

"I don't want water. Get me the hair of the dog. You'll see it easily enough," Joel said.

"So you went up to Wrigley," I prodded.

"Yes, I went up there, she'd told me where she'd put it, inside some loose asbestos tape around one of the pipes, and I found it."

"What was it?" I asked sharply.

"A photo album that she'd stored papers in. I couldn't make sense of them: canceled checks, an accounting statement for the Scanlon Agency, a statement for the law firm and also one for Scanlon's youth club—his obnoxious *Say, Yes!* program that everyone who worked at Mandel & McClelland had to donate to."

"What did you do with the documents?" I asked.

"I was flipping through the pages, so bewildered I didn't leave the damned tunnel, and then I heard somebody coming in, so I taped the book back up against the pipe, only I was so rattled all the pages fell out onto the muddy floor. Ira or Spike or Sol Mandel, any of them could tell you that's my normative state."

"Never mind that. Did you take them with you?"

"I was trying to pick them up when this maintenance man came in, wanting to know what the fuck I was doing in there. I said I got lost looking for the men's room and he marched me out. I only managed to save part of a bank statement. When I got home, I saw another page had stuck to it—someone had torn it in two and taped it back together and the tape stuck to the bank statement."

He licked his dry lips. "Where's the old man with my drink?"

Mr. Contreras came out with a glass of water. "You don't need alcohol to get you through the day, young man. You drink this and start pulling yourself together."

Joel knocked Mr. Contreras's hand away. "What, are you another goddam friend of Ira and Eunice's sent to make me take the pledge?"

Joel left the room. I got up to follow him but collapsed as a wave of dizziness swept through me. I half fell onto the piano. By the time I'd steadied myself, Joel had returned with a half gallon of Grey Goose and a glass.

"The papers," I said sharply. "What about the torn-up note?"

"It said—never mind, I have it someplace."

He put the vodka and glass on a side table and went into another room, where we heard him opening drawers and rustling through papers. He came back with a tattered, yellowed page. At the top, someone had written in a tidy hand: *FYI, Law and Order Man*. The text was also handwritten, by a different person:

> *Thanks for the $7500 to our Widows & Orphans Fund. You know by now that your boys have been released—the SA agrees that youthful high spirits aren't grounds for arrest. Our overzealous officer will be moving to the Seventh, where you can count on the unit's hostility to snitches to keep him from bothering you again.*

"Whose writing is this?" My voice came out in a croak: I was sure I knew who the overzealous officer had been.

"Don't know. Someone in the police, I guess. I asked Annie and she said some of the boys from *Say, Yes!* had been picked up on assault or extortion. She said she was working late and overheard Scanlon talking to Sol Mandel about how to get the charges dropped. She wasn't sure what the boys had done, but she guessed it had to do with 'persuading' local businesses to buy their insurance from Scanlon."

"When did you talk to her about this?" I demanded.

"The night she died." He poured vodka into the glass, but stared at it, not drinking, seeing a past that made him twist his mouth into a grimace of self-loathing.

"I tried figuring out what was so important about the things she'd hidden up at Wrigley. All I had was that one page of a bank statement, but it was from Continental Illinois, not Ferrite, where Mandel and Scanlon's insurance agency and all of us banked—neighborhood solidarity, you know. It showed the balance from *Say, Yes!* but it was before the Internet, back when you still got your canceled checks sent to you in the mail. The page I found showed the closing balance, which was big for such a small neighborhood organization, I think it was ninety-three thousand."

"You didn't keep it?" I asked.

"No, I left it at Annie's."

"What? The night she died?"

He swallowed half the vodka in the glass, winced as the alcohol jolted his body.

"Yes, the night she died," he mumbled. "I tried to figure out what the deal was with the *Say, Yes!* bank statement, why she thought it was worth hanging on to, and I thought it had to do with the fact that Scanlon kept the funds downtown, in the biggest bank in the state. I started working late—Ira was so pleased, he thought I was finding a vocation for the law. He didn't know all I had was a vocation for Annie. One night, Scanlon came over to see Mandel. I don't know if I'm such a negligible part of the landscape he couldn't see me, but he told Mandel they had the fund up to where they could flex some serious muscle. 'Get your boy Hurlihey ready for the front line, Sol,' Scanlon said. 'I think we're going to get us a friend in Springfield.'"

"So they were using the *Say, Yes!* foundation funds to bankroll elections, or at least Hurlihey's election?" I asked.

Joel shrugged. "Maybe, I suppose."

"Why didn't you turn them in?" Mr. Contreras asked. "They sound like a room full of crooks!"

"Turn them in to who? Rory and Sol's cronies?" Joel jeered. "They were players, the SA was a player, they probably all played together. Anyway, what evidence did I have? A piece of a bank statement and an ambiguous conversation. I went to Annie, instead."

Mr. Contreras was watching the clock in agony. He tugged on my arm, but I needed to get as much as I could from Joel if we were going to construct any kind of file that would persuade the thugs to release Bernie.

"I knew what nights her mother played bingo over at Saint Eloy's. I waited across the street until Stella had taken off, then I went to the door. Stella had beaten her: Annie's lip was bloody and swollen, she had a black eye and a cut on her forehead.

"I was so upset at seeing her all messed up that I forgot at first why I'd come. She laughed off her injuries, she wouldn't let me take her to the hospital: she said she was going to be rid of all of us soon. I put my arms around her, I said something stupid, like, you don't want to be rid of me, I'm the one who understands you, I helped you with your music composition that got you into Bryn Mawr. I even tried to kiss her. She put my face aside. She tried to cover up what she was feeling, but I could see the disgust in her face." He rubbed his cheek, the spot where he could still feel her hand on him.

"'You're sweet, Joel, and I appreciate your help, but I don't like you, not like that.'" He raised his voice to a savage falsetto in imitation. "No one ever 'liked me like that,'" he added bitterly, in his own voice.

"I asked her if it was the jock—Warshawski—your cousin. 'His career will be over by the time you're thirty, he'll get fat, too, believe me,' I told her, but she said she wasn't interested in love, not with any of us. 'I've got a future of my own, my own life, not slaving for some man, whether he's a lawyer or a hockey star or just a mill hand like my dad,' she said.

"I showed her the Continental bank statement page, and the torn-up letter. She was startled, that was one thing—I completely took her off guard. She wanted to know where I'd got them. I said we could make a team, we could take Sol and Scanlon down, I'd start my own law firm, don't ask me to remember every crazy thing I said, 'but I need your help,' I told her. 'I need to know where they're getting the money that they're putting into the foundation account. Is it coming out of client accounts, or is Scanlon shaking people down? Once I know that, we can take them down—I'll go to the federal prosecutor, we won't be dependent on some corrupt state's attorney.'"

He finished what was left in the glass and poured another tumbler full. "Here's the part that will make you split your side laughing: Annie said she didn't want to take Mandel down. 'I won't tell you what I know, I don't want you hurting him. He's my meal ticket, Joel. I didn't get all those scholarships I bragged about. I got some, but not enough to go east, he's paying me to go, I told him I have proof in a place so secret no one will ever find it, and he's giving me the money to get me to Bryn Mawr. If you go snooping around, he'll think I told on him. You'll cost me my future.'

"'What about this?' I asked her, waving the letter. 'That's not from Mandel.' And she said no, she was over at your house, playing on Mrs. Warshawski's piano, and she saw your dad take it out of the mail and read it. He looked upset, sick, I think Annie called it, then he tore it in half and threw it out. She picked it out of the trash and took it away because she realized Scanlon had written the line at the top, that 'FYI, Law and Order Man.'"

He looked at his feet and mumbled, "I hate to say it about her, but I think she thought she could use it to get more money."

So that was why Tony had been sent to cop hell, all those nights on patrol with no one at the station backing him up. Beneath my fatigue and woozy concussed brain I could feel anger starting to burn, a fury with Rory Scanlon. The stress of that assignment, on top of my mother's death, had easily taken a decade, maybe more, from my father's life. That's why he wouldn't ride the buses Scanlon hired to take the neighborhood to Boom-Boom's debut. It's why Scanlon made that snide remark to me about another Warshawski upholding law and order for the neighborhood.

The clock chimed the three-quarter hour.

"Doll," Mr. Contreras was frantic. "We gotta get going."

He was right. I would sort out Scanlon when we had Bernie safe. I got up.

"You didn't kill Annie, did you?" I asked Joel. "That isn't why you defended Stella, is it?"

Joel gave a mirthless laugh. "I don't have that kind of—whatever it is. Initiative? Vanity? Annie didn't want me, but it didn't stop my feelings for her. Maybe it would have, if she'd lived. I dropped the bank statement, but I held on to the letter and walked out with it. I walked all the way back to this place. I forgot I'd driven down there. I am a useless fuckup from the beginning of the story to the end. I had to take the bus back down to pick up my car, and when I got there, Stella was walking up the street, coming home from the bingo. I ducked down and fell over onto the curb, but she didn't see me.

"Then, the next day, I learned Annie had died. And I told myself, all the hateful things she'd said, she hadn't meant them, she said them because she had a brain injury from Stella beating her."

I stayed long enough to ask about the bank statement. "Why didn't Stella say something about it during the trial?"

He shook his head. "She didn't know anything about it. I asked her, I asked her what she found in Annie's room, or in the living room, anything that was connected to the law firm, but she didn't seem to know what I was talking about."

"Why did you represent Stella? You'd seen Annie's injuries, you must have known she was guilty."

Joel shot me a resentful look. "Mandel saw my car outside the Guzzo house. He said they needed someone to represent Stella, and either I would do it, or he'd tell the state's attorney that I'd been there and had a chance to kill Annie."

The clock hands seemed to swoop and bend. "Joel." My voice was so gentle he had to lean his stinking mouth close to hear me. "Joel, don't you see. Mandel only knew you'd been there because he was there himself."

52

SWINGING FOR THE FENCES

Joel's clock started to chime the hour. Sixty minutes to get something up on Facebook. Sixty minutes to save Bernadine. If she was still—of course she was still alive. She was the terrorists' bargaining chip.

We left Joel standing in the middle of his living room, the half gallon of Grey Goose in one hand, a half-drunk glass in the other. He tried to keep us there—he wanted to talk about Mandel, did I really think Mandel had killed Annie, but I brushed him off.

"The only thing I care about this morning is saving Bernadine Fouchard. We'll worry later about Spike and Scanlon and whether Mandel killed Annie."

As we walked out the door, he called after me that he wanted me to talk to Ira. "Tell him his old pal Sol was a criminal and a murderer."

I shut the door, pushed the elevator button over and over.

"He only thinks about hisself," Mr. Contreras fumed when the car finally arrived. "Don't he care about Bernie?"

When we were back on the street, I took a precious minute to phone Conrad. He'd gotten a search warrant for Sturlese but they hadn't found Bernie.

"What about the Sturlese brothers? Were they all there?"

"Two were on job sites, at least according to dispatch. One claims he was home with the flu, but his wife said he felt so sick he'd gone to the hospital. We're trying to track them all down."

"Anything on Sebastian?"

"No one's spotted him yet. We went to the sister, what's her name? Viola? Told her where you'd found him, tried to get her to cough up someplace he might be hiding. I don't know if she's scared stupid or really doesn't know. I had my guys take her in, but all she does is sit and cry. Give me a bright idea, Warshawski."

"Scanlon," I said. "He's got a slush fund under cover of his *Say, Yes!* foundation. He's connected to this—"

"What I meant was a smart idea." He hung up.

I put the car in motion. I'd come up with only one idea and it wasn't necessarily bright or even smart, but I talked it over with Mr. Contreras and he agreed to try it.

We found the nearest copy center, down on Jeffery, and dug up photos of Scanlon and Sol Mandel online. We used free software to create a new website that we called "Annie Guzzo's Murder."

Stella Guzzo spent twenty-five years in Logan Correctional Center for killing her daughter. In the words of the Chicago Mob, she wore the jacket. Only she never agreed to. She didn't know she was covering up for two smooth operators: Sol Mandel and Rory Scanlon.

> When a police officer tried to put an end to a campaign of terror
> against South Chicago's small businesses, Scanlon sent money
> to the police widows and orphans fund and got the officer sent
> to Chicago's highest-crime district, with a target painted on his
> forehead for his fellow officers to aim at. Here's the cocky note
> Rory Scanlon sent to the officer when the old Fourth District
> watch commander got rid of the meddlesome cop.

We scanned the letter and added it to the site. I also e-mailed it to Freeman Carter, my own lawyer, with the login and password for the website. *Do your best, Freeman, in case I'm not around to do it for you*, I wrote. *I'm putting the originals in the mail to you.*

We posted Scanlon's and Mandel's photos, spun a narrative based on my guess about the use of *Say, Yes!* funds, to send Hurlihey to the state legislature, and finished by writing, *Stay Tuned for More Details.*

We finished at 8:56. At 8:57, while we were still at the copy center computer, my phone rang again.

"Not seeing anything on your Facebook page, Contreras," the ugly voice growled.

"Not there," my neighbor said. "Got a website. You check it out. For the next hour, you can only get to it with a password. You turn over Bernie—Bernadine—and if she ain't been hurt, I'll take it down. You screw up, the whole world will see it and I'll be adding details. Password is 'ScumbagYes.'"

There was a pause while the caller went online. "We won't meet you in Calumet Park, too exposed, too easy for you to get cops into the Coast Guard building. We'll wait for you on Stony, where it dead-ends at the river. Be there in thirty with that letter you're saying Scanlon wrote."

"Sixty," Mr. Contreras said. "I'm ten miles away from you."

We heard muted talk in the background. "Forty-five. We see cops coming, the kid goes over the retaining wall into the Cal."

"They're already there," I said flatly to Mr. Contreras when he'd hung up. "It's the perfect ambush spot: there's only one way in."

I put the original of the "widows and orphans" letter into an express pack and sent it off to Freeman.

"Don't be calling the cops," Mr. Contreras begged as we hustled back to the car, "'cause they won't know to come in quiet and next thing you know, these bastards'll toss little Bernie overboard."

"We can't drive in," I said.

"You gonna hijack a chopper?" my neighbor said. "We don't have time to joke around."

He was right. The clock kept ticking. I drove fast and dangerously, running red lights, weaving around traffic on two-lane streets, earning fingers, honks, even a brandished weapon at Eighty-third.

At 103rd, the top of the marshes along the Calumet River, I crossed over to Stony Island. We were at the start of a stretch of swamp, park, golf course, waste dumping and heavy industry, dotted with ponds made by the overflow from the big lake and Lake Calumet. If the thugs were in place, they were three miles to the south.

Move, move! I ordered myself savagely. Mr. Contreras was almost weeping with anxiety. My own state: sick, terrified, head a balloon bouncing ten feet from the ground, body in motion, body in motion will stay in motion, at rest—will rest forever.

I spied a canoe in the underbrush, jumped out of the car, saw the canoe was chained to a log. The old man still had enough strength to shatter the lock with a rock. I took the paddle stuck in the mud underneath it.

Stealing, no, borrowing, stuffing it any old way into the Taurus's trunk, bouncing it down the road to the top of Dead Stick Pond, smashing through the fence around the pond, launching the boat. Mr. Contreras watching while I climbed into waist-high filthy water, fanny pack around the neck to keep my gun dry. He scrambled back through the brush to the car while I began to paddle, paddling for life, not a beautiful stroke, not knowing how to do it except by gut feel. Herons watched me with malevolent eyes: I was frightening away their lunch. Geese squawked indignantly, took to the air.

At the south end, I climbed out again into water brown with waste, purple-green with industrial oil, boots soaked, squelching through mud, up the bank to the wall separating the road from Lake Calumet. I could see the smokestacks of ships on the far side of the wall. The dredges and cranes at work on the hidden docks covered the noise I was making.

I used to walk that wall with Boom-Boom, while we dared each other to jump off under the noses of the freighters in Lake Calumet. We used to boost each other up. Back then, we wore dry clothes and shoes, but I could do it alone today in sodden jeans and mud-caked boots.

I found a place where the concrete had crumbled, exposing rebar. Put a toe in, hoisted myself into place. This was so easy, my third wall in twenty-four hours, I could join Cirque du Soleil. I straddled the wall, crabbed across, lay flat when I got in squinting distance of the road. The goons' car was on the shoulder, tilting downward into the ditch, hidden from street view by the shrubs and tall marsh grasses.

Fifteen minutes from launch, five over our limit. I pulled out the Smith & Wesson, took off the safety, placed the spare clips on the wall in front of me. Right on time, the Taurus engine roared as Mr. Contreras floored it and drove headlong toward the wall. He swerved a second before he hit it and fishtailed, knocking the rear end against the wall.

The doors facing the wall opened and the dogs jumped out.

Gunfire rattled from the underbrush. The Taurus's windshield shattered. I aimed at the flash of light in the weeds, emptied half a clip, saw movement in the brush, fired again, reloaded, slid from the wall, jumped across the ditch to the enemy car, shot out the tires. A savage growl behind me: I turned to see Mitch fling himself against a thug sneaking up behind me. Mitch knocked him to the ground. I stomped on the man's arm, forced him to drop his gun, kicked the gun away, kicked the thug's head hard enough to knock him out, hit the road as more gunfire erupted.

"Down," I ordered Mitch, panting, "down!" He loped off instead, heading across the road to Dead Stick Pond.

I didn't know where Peppy was, didn't know where Mr. Contreras was, had to concentrate on the gunfire still coming from the thick grasses.

Furious shouts from behind the retaining wall. Heads appeared— men in hard hats, men with walkie-talkies, cell phones. The gun roar filled my head; I didn't know what they were saying, kept my eyes on the car, on the underbrush. Saw movement in two places, ducked low, shot at the feet as they appeared. And then the hard hats were over the wall, moving into the brush, surrounding the punks.

Police cars screamed in. Pierre arrived with a team from the private security firm Tintrey, the FBI alongside them. By then we had found Bernie, where the thugs had tossed her bound body. It was Mitch and Peppy who led me to her: the goons had dumped her in the mud along the edge of Dead Stick Pond. Mr. Contreras tried to follow us to Bernie, but he was too dazed and exhausted; he collapsed onto the backseat of the Taurus. The hard hats, guys who'd been working on the barges below us on Lake Calumet, were talking excitedly to the cops, helping them hoist the thugs into squad cars.

Bernie was still alive, but with a very weak pulse. My own exhaustion was overwhelming me; I fumbled at her bonds with thick clumsy fingers until one of the hard hats saw what I was doing and came to my aid. A sheet of gray water seemed to envelop me, making it hard for me to move or think. I could see Mitch and Peppy anxiously lick Bernie's face and hands but couldn't decide if that was good or bad and couldn't move my arms to stop them.

Pierre appeared and pushed the dogs away, lifted Bernie. I saw his mouth move but couldn't hear any words. A helicopter materialized and Pierre and Bernie shimmered away into it. The water pulled me down, into the grasses, the mud, the rusting cans. No more responsibilities. How good it felt to drown.

53

FIFTEEN-DAY DL

I was out for the better part of two days. The concussion I'd suffered under Wrigley Field, the lack of rest, the more-than-strenuous race around Chicago had me unconscious long before an ambulance drove me to Beth Israel Hospital. Lotty's anesthesiologist gave me a cocktail that kept me deeply asleep while the worst of my wounds healed.

For once, I slept dreamlessly, no nightmares about tar pits or Stella Guzzo. It was only when I woke the next night, feeling Lotty's fingers on my wrist, that the fears came tumbling back in on me. Bernie, Mr. Contreras—I'd watched him collapse—but I'd passed out instead of helping him. The dogs, the thugs.

Lotty looked at me with wry sadness. "I'm tempted to put you under again, *Liebchen*, if you're only going to wake up to frenzy. Your neighbor is recovering. He was dehydrated and exhausted—he went through a heavy workout for a man his age. For anyone of any age, even for you. As for Bernadine, she, too, is on the mend. She isn't my patient, but the doctors at the University of Chicago who have been treating her tell me she is tormenting herself with guilt over putting you and your neighbor in peril."

Lotty sat on the edge of the bed, brushing my hair back from my face, her black eyes glittering with unshed tears. "When you come to me like this, wounded, my heart stops: I don't want to be the one to outlive you. But if you hadn't torn yourself apart, Bernadine would be dead. I'll never be able to balance what you do to yourself to save others with my own need for you to save yourself, but I promise to stop adding to your torment by chastising you for it." She stopped, smiled wryly and added, "I will *try* to stop."

I squeezed her fingers. "What happened to my dogs?"

"The dockworkers who saved you before the police arrived seemed to have taken charge of the dogs, as well. Your neighbor wouldn't let me hospitalize him until he knew they were safe. Jake went to South Chicago to collect them. He's boarding them in the place he says you always use." She made a face. "He said it's called doggie day care— because you are convalescing, I will spare you my opinion of that."

I laughed weakly and fell back into sleep while she sat next to me. When I woke again, Lotty was gone; a nurse had roused me to warn me that the police and an FBI agent were on their way up to my room.

I felt at a disadvantage in my hospital gown, grubby and unkempt. I made them wait while I wobbled into the bathroom and rinsed my face and hair. Jake had brought over some clean clothes, a pair of his own jeans, since I'd trashed all three of mine, and a rose cotton top, which made me look almost soft, graceful—a useful piece of misdirection in speaking to the law.

Conrad looked ostentatiously at his watch when I emerged. "You can spare a few minutes now? Must be nice to take off for R and R when you feel like it, instead of sleeping standing up the way I've been doing."

"Like an elephant." I sat cross-legged on the bed.

Derek Hatfield, from the FBI, looked startled. "Elephant?"

"They sleep standing up. I expect if you'd been shot in the head and kept going so you could rescue a kidnap victim, the department would let you take a break. At least twenty minutes. Take it up with Captain Mallory. What can you tell me?"

"Wonder Woman saves the city again." Conrad was only half jeering. "You got some major bad boys way out on a limb they can't climb back from. The Sturlese brothers and Boris Nabiyev, they were the goons who tried killing you and the Fouchard girl. Their alibis—the flu, being on job sites—unraveled like my mother's knitting, once we flashed some warrants around. They didn't really have any interest in any ancient papers, just wanted to get a couple of meddling women out of the way."

"Did they reveal who paid them?" I asked.

"The Sturlese boys say it was all about the muscle they tried to put on the facilities VP at Wrigley. They were deep in debt after the downturn, Nabiyev got money for them from the Grozny Mob, but they had to earn it out. The Grozny goons wanted to pour all the new concrete in the Wrigley reno, and when the Cubs wouldn't talk to them, the Uzbekis sent Fugher in to try to bribe or batter a guy named Brineruck in the Cubs organization. He was the person talking to Fugher in the recording you turned up."

"How'd you smoke him out?" I asked.

Conrad yawned. "Your friend Villard, the guy who was shot up in Evanston, he made it through surgery. He ID'd the punk speaking to Fugher. Villard called him after you played the recording and the creep panicked, called Brian Sturlese for advice. Sturlese and

Nabiyev weren't going to take any chance on being named in a potential bribery case; they drove up to the Villard mansion with Brineruck, used him as their stalking horse, and shot Villard. The Cubs fired Brineruck on the spot, of course, but we arrested him for conspiracy to commit murder. Bribery, too, but attempted murder always plays well with a jury."

"What about Sebastian Mesaline?" I asked. "Did he ever show up?"

Conrad made a face. "Punk was hiding in his uncle Jerry's garage down in Lansing. He dissolved like the soggy piece of Kleenex he is. Sniveled about the loan he'd been forced to take out to cover his embezzlement. His sister, who must have 'Born to be a Martyr' tattooed on her someplace, is insisting that he didn't do anything wrong— even though he locked the Fouchard girl behind a steel barricade and left her to die there. Sis is putting aside money for his legal defense. She tried hiring your mouthpiece, but Freeman Carter apparently told her there'd be a conflict of interest."

"Was there any sign that Vince Bagby was involved in the Fugher murder?"

"You have a hard-on—"

"Disgusting expression, especially when talking to me," I said. "The Sturlese brothers didn't have an interest in anything Annie Guzzo may or may not have hidden under Wrigley Field. I'm trying to find out who planted that in their tiny minds, or in the Grozny Mob's brains. If it was Vince Bagby—"

"I'm not digging into Bagby on your say-so," Conrad said coldly.

"He was at *Say, Yes!* the night that Bernadine and I were beaten up, and he's been popping up every time something dramatic happens. I don't know if it's coincidence, or because he's keeping an eye on me for Scanlon."

"I can't help you there. Maybe he knows you're an unguided missile and he's trying to make sure you don't land on his trucks."

Derek swallowed a grin.

I curled my lip. "I suppose mocking me is the easiest way to assuage your guilt over not getting to the Sturlese brothers before they dragged Bernadine Fouchard to South Chicago. Thank goodness Mr. Contreras and I rescued her before she died."

Conrad shifted in his chair. "Sorry. Out of line. But I'm still not going after Scanlon, or Bagby, because you have an itch you want to scratch."

I sucked in a breath, held it for a count of ten, waited for the red to fade from in front of my eyes. "There's the business of Annie Guzzo, and what she was hiding in the tunnel at Wrigley, and why she was murdered. And all of that leads back to Rory Scanlon."

"There's no connection to Scanlon. And definitely not one to Bagby, who wasn't even running the trucking company when Annie was killed."

"Bagby and Scanlon are cousins, and Bagby is the younger one. He wanted the big boys to let him play with them when he was little, so he'd do whatever they said. It got to be ingrained. Now that they're all grown, Bagby still does what the older boys want so he can be part of the gang."

"What, now you're a family therapist? They're cousins, they do things together, so Bagby helps support *Say, Yes!* I'll admit you were a big help two days ago in South Chicago, but I've got enough real crime in the Fourth to keep me going until my granddaughter's in college—and I don't have a kid of my own yet. I'm not going to start inventing crimes where the system is running smoothly."

"The system is exactly what runs smoothly only for the people running it!" I cried, exasperated. "Scanlon is funneling money through that *Say, Yes!* foundation to stuff that's either illegal or would get his insurance license revoked. Back when Annie Guzzo worked for Mandel & McClelland, she uncovered evidence that Scanlon was using the kids in his *Say, Yes!* foundation to beat up local businesses and push them into buying their insurance through his agency. Joel Previn overheard Scanlon and Mandel talk about using foundation funds to bankroll Spike Hurlihey's first political campaign."

I told them what I'd learned from Joel, from Frank Guzzo, from Mr. Villard and from the photographs themselves.

Conrad rubbed his forehead. I could see past my anger to the fatigue lines gouged in his face.

"I am not a fan of Stella Guzzo," I added, "but the night Annie Guzzo was murdered, two other people came to the house while Stella was off playing bingo: first, Joel Previn, and after he left, Sol Mandel."

Conrad sat upright. "What? What crystal ball spat that detail out twenty-five years after the fact?"

Derek interrupted to ask who we were talking about.

"Joel told me he was there," I said after Conrad and I had explained the Guzzo murder story. "I never could understand why Mandel & McClelland took the case, or why poor Joel, who had a crush on Annie, agreed to represent Stella, but he told me Mandel saw his car outside the Guzzo house and threatened to turn him over to the cops if he didn't defend Stella. It had never occurred to him that Mandel could have been Annie's killer."

"Maybe because Joel had already killed her himself," Conrad snarled.

"Yeah, right, that's a possibility. I don't believe it after spending a lot of time with Joel."

"Convenient to blame it on the dead partner." Derek chipped in his two cents.

"Yes, but there's a living person who had a stake in what Annie had uncovered," I said. "I'm betting he came along for the ride, if not for the deed."

Conrad stared at me. "You're back on Scanlon's ass. God *damn* it, Warshawski—"

I bared my teeth in a ferocious grin. "I have a handwritten note to my dad, rubbing his face in the fact of his transfer to West Englewood. Whoever wrote it implied that he put word out that Tony snitched on his brother officers—in order to make sure Tony was in maximum danger on the street. My father was almost killed, not once but many times, because the boys at the Seventh didn't get him backup. The stress—he might still be part of my life today if it weren't for whoever made sure he got put there!"

Conrad said, "And you think it was Scanlon? What proof, Ms. W.? What proof?"

"The letter! I've sent it to my lawyer for safekeeping, but—"

"We could run forensics on it," Derek offered.

"I don't want to risk it evaporating while it's out of my custody," I said coldly. "But I'm betting Conrad can at least ID who wrote it, even if not the taunting message to my dad. A facsimile is up on the Annie Guzzo's Murder website."

Conrad's copper skin darkened to mahogany. "You did what? You set up a murder site on your own without talking to the police? And you complain when I say you take the law into your own hands?"

"We were working against the clock. I was keeping in touch with you, but the police apparatus, you couldn't move on this as fast as I could."

Conrad gave me a withering look, but buried himself in his smartphone, looking up the URL. I gave him and Derek the password Mr. Contreras and I had created.

Conrad looked up after reading the letter, anguish in his eyes. "I know that handwriting: Oswald Brattigan. He was my watch commander at the Fourth when I was first transferred in there. If that sentence to your father was written by Scanlon—" He broke off, his chin collapsing against his chest.

"I don't want to believe this, or deal with it," he mumbled after a moment. "Rory Scanlon—if he's been using the kids in *Say, Yes!* to extort or intimidate—my God—it's going to be an unholy war down there. He's so connected, Vic: he's got the Speaker in his pocket, the local parish—"

"But if Joel's report on what he overheard Scanlon and Mandel talk about is correct, they were using both client accounts and foundation money to fuel political campaigns. Spike Hurlihey owes his Speaker's gavel to illegal money."

Conrad smacked his thigh. "That doesn't mean he knew the money was illegal. Assuming it was illegal, which is a big 'if.' An overheard conversation twenty-five years ago by an alkie who couldn't cut it at the firm? I don't believe it and neither will a jury."

"The prosecutor for the Northern District is going to want to take a look," Derek said. "If the paper trail is there—we can subpoena records from Continental Illinois. Do a handwriting check on this 'FYI, Law and Order Man' scrawl. Maybe we can roll on one of the *Say, Yes!* kids to wear a wire."

"They're used to prison," Conrad said. "It doesn't frighten them. They build new gang networks there, they learn new street skills."

"Okay, someone in the law office, or someone in Hurlihey's office," Derek said. He looked sympathetically at Conrad. "I don't have to work there every day, it won't bother me any."

"And Annie's murder," I said stubbornly.

Conrad thought it over. "There's no forensic evidence, Vic. I told you I had the files sent up when the story broke about Boom-Boom. It looked so cut and dried, girl dies from bleeding into the brain after mom beats her on the head, we didn't look for other prints at the scene. There's nothing to tie anyone—not even Previn—to the murder scene now."

I let it go at that. He was right, for one thing, and for another, I was too exhausted to argue any further.

Conrad held the door open for Derek, but came back to my bed after the Fed had left. "You know that call, warning you away from South Chicago after the Dragons attacked you? I found out that Sid Gerber did it."

"Sid?" My dad's old pal who was the desk sergeant now down in the Fourth. "Conrad—no, he can't have been part of—"

"No, he wasn't, stupid old goat. He was worried about you, thought he'd be doing your old man a favor by scaring you away. When he saw what had happened down in Dead Stick Pond, he talked it over with one of the boys, who came to me with the news. I decided to pretend I hadn't heard about it—guy is six months from retirement. I just told him that the quickest way to get you stung by a thousand wasps was to tell you to stay out of their nest."

He turned on his heel and marched out before I could respond. I went back to sleep, but was awakened an hour later by Murray Ryerson, who'd bullied or charmed his way past the nursing staff, demanding an exclusive. He'd found photos from Mr. Contreras's and my rescue at Dead Stick Pond that one of the hard hats had posted on Facebook and wanted my story.

I gave him most of what I knew but didn't tell him that Derek might get the Feds to look into the *Say, Yes!* foundation accounts—I didn't want to short-circuit a potential investigation with a media broadside. Instead, I told him my growing doubts about Stella's guilt in her daughter's death. For Murray, an old crime reporter, this was like a gazelle wandering in front of a lion. He agreed there wasn't enough to print yet, and also no way to get evidence linking either

Mandel, Scanlon or one of the juniors in Mandel's firm to Annie's death.

"Why did Previn have to be reckless enough to go up to Wrigley to find the papers and then such a twitcher that he fled as soon as someone confronted him?" Murray grumbled.

"Doesn't matter," I yawned. "The documents wouldn't have survived the damp, let alone the rats, after all this time. The unbelievable thing is that the binder itself was still there for that prize idiot Sebastian to discover."

Jake arrived after lunch to bring me home. I spent the afternoon listening to him rehearse the Martinsson concerto, and in the evening went with Lotty and Max to hear him perform.

All my houseplants had died from neglect. The next day, I went to my office so that my practice didn't suffer a similar fate. In the evening I went back up to the hospital to collect Mr. Contreras, and to bring the dogs home from the doggy B&B where they'd been boarding. While we rehashed our glorious rescue mission over a picnic supper, Pierre and Bernadine showed up.

"We're flying home tomorrow," Pierre said, "but—I called you a lot of bad names when this *petite monstre* was cracking my life apart. I need to say that I am sorry."

Bernie flushed and drew a semicircle on the floor with the toe of her boot. "I'm sorry, too, Vic, I—I almost died. Twice in one night and two times you almost died to save me."

Mitch bounded over, pushed his big nose between Bernie and me, turning the awkward moment into a laugh.

"You had a horrific time," I said. "Does it mean you're going to turn your back on Northwestern's scholarship?"

Bernie made a moue. "Cornell, Syracuse, they want me, too. I will decide after I visit them, but—"

"But only with Arlette," Pierre said. "This *tourbillon* goes nowhere alone until she is forty."

"Papa!" Bernie protested.

"Very well. If you behave and endanger no one's life for ten years, I will reduce the sentence to age thirty-five." Pierre smiled, but he pulled his daughter to him in a ferocious hug.

54

LOADING THE BASES

Life began returning to a semblance of normal: clients, concerts or dancing with Jake, helping Mr. Contreras get his handkerchief garden in shape. TV and Web media rushed in to cover the drama of Bernie's rescue, but it was easy to deflect them to the dockworkers who'd come to our aid.

The spring continued cold and wet, but I ran the lakefront with the dogs, played basketball with my friends on Sunday mornings. I spent time with Mr. Villard, visiting him first at the rehab place where he went after surgery, and then in his assisted living apartment when he was strong enough to go home. Adelaide continued to look after him: the daughters had tried to fire her, but Mr. Villard insisted that he was to blame for getting shot:

"I should have told Ms. Warshawski it was Gil Brineruck's voice on that recording, instead of thinking I could confront him alone. He was a terrible disgrace to baseball and to the Cubs. Adelaide knows how to look after me without turning me into a three-year-old. Adelaide stays."

I even went back to working on my voice. My mother had once presented me with a music list for my birthday: songs about Victoria or Victory or music by women named Victoria. I was trying to learn madrigals by the Renaissance composer Vittoria Aleotti, with Jake playing the counterpoint. Love songs often ended with a practice session in bed, which helped make my hellish twenty hours in tunnels and swamps recede to the background of my brain.

Jake and Lotty both urged me to stop thinking about South Chicago, despite the many open ends to the business. I knew I didn't have the time or the money to dig into the *Say, Yes!* foundation's records, or Scanlon's old accounts at Continental Illinois. Perhaps the federal prosecutor for the Northern District was doing so, as the FBI's Derek Hatfield had suggested. No ripples were surfacing on the street yet, so either the Feds were moving very cautiously, or they weren't moving at all. I didn't have any way of finding out.

The problem that gnawed at me—that made me so restless that Jake sent me home to my own bed more than once—was Annie's death. I could let Scanlon's and Mandel's financial skulduggery go—almost.

But much as I disliked Stella Guzzo, much as I knew she'd beaten her children many times, and Annie on the last night of her daughter's life, I couldn't stop trying to imagine a way to prove she was innocent.

I'd become convinced she'd been set up. It wasn't only Joel's revelation that he and Sol Mandel had both been at the Guzzo house the night that Annie died, but the whole load of laundry that unfolded after I started asking questions. Every time I got close to a piece of the story, a new drama erupted, forcing my attention elsewhere. The diary implicating Boom-Boom, that had been designed to keep my attention away from Stella. The beating Bernie and I had experienced had roused my suspicions, but in a different direction.

Conrad was right: no physical evidence existed to prove one way or another if Mandel or Scanlon, or even Spike Hurlihey, had been in the Guzzo house the night Annie died. But there was another route, actually two other routes, and in the end, I decided—against Freeman Carter's advice, and to Jake's dismay and Lotty's fury—to pursue both of them. The fact that both Mr. Contreras and Murray Ryerson supported me didn't improve the atmosphere with Jake and Lotty.

I started with Frank Guzzo; he and I had already violated the restraining order, so I figured I could do it again without risking arrest.

We agreed to meet in Grant Park—halfway between north and south—next to the Christopher Columbus statue. Chicago's Italian community had raised money for the statue; maybe it would make us remember Frank's Italian father, my Italian mother, and bring us closer together.

Frank arrived half an hour after me. He was nervous, demanding I show whether I was recording him, looking around to make sure no one was videotaping him. He finally stood still long enough for me to say I'd come around to thinking his mother had been railroaded.

He was suspicious, not gratified. "What are you trying to trick me into saying?" he demanded.

"I'm trying to talk sense to you, Frank," I said.

I told him about Joel Previn coming to the house and seeing Annie alive with all her wits about her the night she died, and he finally started paying serious attention to me.

"That means that Previn killed Annie?"

"Could mean it, but I doubt it. Sol Mandel and Rory Scanlon were the people who had the most to lose if Annie kept on the way she was going, and Mandel at least was at the house after Joel left. He had other people with him, possibly Spike Hurlihey, possibly Scanlon—"

"No, Tori! No, don't you see—you cannot go around accusing Scanlon. You can't, you mustn't!"

"Or what?" I demanded. "He'll send Stella back to prison? He'll get Bagby to fire you?"

"I—oh, *damn* you, Tori, why can't you leave well enough alone? The diary, that was supposed to make you go away, the mugging, nothing would stop you. Do you want them to kill you?"

"Frank, what is it? What have you done that has you doing whatever they want?"

"It's not me," he burst out. "It's Frankie, my boy!"

A couple out walking their dog stared at us with open curiosity. I waved at them and they scurried on.

"What has Frankie done? Is he running with the Insane Dragons?"

"No. It's baseball."

"Baseball?" I repeated. "Oh. Scanlon has told you that if you rock the boat about Stella, he'll make sure Frankie doesn't get a shot at the big time."

Frank didn't say anything, just looked at his hands, his face holding such a naked display of helplessness that I had to look away.

"Frank, why did you come to me to begin with, then, if you were worried about Frankie? As soon as you asked me to investigate what your mother was up to, that whole string of lies was likely to unravel."

"I didn't know," he said. "I came to you for the reason I said, I didn't know what Ma was up to or what she was going to do. I was afraid if she started acting too wild in public, it would hurt Frankie. You know, baseball today, the family has to make a good impression. Scouts see there's a crazy grandma bouncing around in public, they got a thousand other talented boys they can look at whose grandmothers didn't beat or kill their own kids. Mr. Scanlon, he had promised he'd make sure no one found out about Ma killing Annie, but when you started asking questions, he got mad."

"He came to you, told you this?" I asked.

"No, I'm too far down the food chain. He talked to Bagby. Bagby came to me, said Scanlon had a bee in his bonnet about you digging up old dirt, that you look down on the rest of us, you think people like me are idiots or fools for staying on in the old neighborhood.

"And then, the lady at the law firm, Thelma, she found Annie's diary in an old desk. Vince told me maybe stick it in Annie's dresser and have Betty go over and suggest to Ma that they get rid of Annie's clothes. They thought if there was evidence against Boom-Boom, you'd want to bury it, and so you'd stop asking questions."

"Oh, Frank. The law of unintended consequences. It turned up so conveniently that once I stopped seeing red, white and blue, I was sure it was a fake. The diary goaded me into asking more questions."

"They told me it was the real thing. They said they wouldn't ask me to plant a fake in my own ma's house," Frank said.

"But when you looked at it—you must have known it wasn't Annie's writing."

Frank flung up his hands, exasperated. "I don't know Annie's writing. She didn't write me letters, we lived in the same house! I wasn't reading her school homework and even if I had been, it's so long ago I wouldn't know if it was her or you or the Pope who wrote it."

He had a point. Besides, he'd wanted to believe in the diary: it was an easy way out of his problems. And given his lingering jealousy of Boom-Boom, he'd probably felt a certain Schadenfreude at the thought of fingering my cousin.

I pulled out a photocopy of the condolence letter Annie had written my dad when Gabriella died. "Does this look like her writing to you?"

He read it, hunched a sullen shoulder. "I guess, if you say so."

"Yep. I say so. The original is in a safe, but if I can get a subpoena, I am going to force your mother to produce the book you hid in Annie's dresser drawer. And then it will be an ugly court battle."

"Just leave it alone. Ma, her doctor made her start taking lithium. She's not going to bother you anymore."

I glared at him. "I am not going to let the boys in the old Mandel & McClelland office get away with framing your mother for murder. I don't know which one killed your sister, but I'm going to have a shot at forcing him—them—into the open. However—" I held up a hand, demanding silence, as Frank started to protest.

"I'll make sure they know you didn't have anything to do with it. I promise you that I will not leave you and Frankie out to dry."

"Oh, your promises, you can promise anything, your life isn't going to be hurt by you digging up dirt left, right and center."

"What do you mean, my life won't be hurt?" A red mist swam in front of my eyes. "I was nearly killed by the Sturlese brothers and their gorilla. You cost me weeks of income, asking me to work for you and then not paying me. I have legal fees from dealing with this insane order of protection your mother filed. Boom-Boom has been slandered. And all so you can protect the remote chance of Frankie making it to the show. I have bills, just like you. I work for a living, just like you. You're lucky I don't sue your sorry ass."

"Yeah, well, you can't get blood out of a turnip."

"Maybe not, but you can get enough turnip juice to make soup."

Frank kicked a hole in the grass with the heel of his work boot. He muttered something that might have been an apology, but when he had started back toward his truck, he couldn't resist turning around to yell, "If you'd ever had any kids, you'd know you do anything to protect them."

"Yeah, Frank, right, whatever."

I watched him drive off before I got into my car—actually Jake's Fiat—and headed north to Rafe Zukos and Kenji Aroyawa's home in Rogers Park.

55

MONEY PITCH

"Today's top story, Chicago—who has the real diary written by murder victim Annie Guzzo on the night she died? V. I. Warshawski or Stella Guzzo? They call Warshawski Chicago's premier investigator for a reason: she's thorough, she's good and she's lucky. When she almost lost her life to save Blackhawks star Pierre Fouchard's daughter, the news galvanized an anonymous citizen into mailing her pages from the diary of a long-dead Chicago girl, Annie Guzzo."

It was a great story, and Murray made the most of it. While he narrated, the production team ran footage from South Chicago, from Pierre's and Boom-Boom's days with the Hawks, from Wrigley Field where Annie had hidden her diary.

"You can see a copy of the diary Warshawski received in the mail on our website: globalentertainmentnews/Annie-Guzzo-Diary. No one knows how the handwriting or content compares to the diary Annie's mother, Stella, claims to have found, because no one, not even our lawyers, has been allowed to view that version."

I went to the website. Sure enough, the pages of Annie's diary that I'd given Murray were posted there, the sprawling schoolgirl hand-writing difficult enough to read that Murray had put a typed transcript underneath.

September 10

Ma is out of control. Mr. M, ditto, Frank and Betty are so *depressing*, nothing but babies and diapers and looking down their nose at anyone who thinks there's a life outside St. Eloy's. Joel looks at me like a sheep that wants to break through the fence and nibble on me but is too scared to. Oh, I can't wait to be FREE, FREE, FREE.

September 14

All Frank can talk about is stupid fucking baseball. There, I said it, at least in here. Can't wait to get away. Bryn Mawr, that's where I want to be, pictures are SOOO gorgeous. Ma thinks Frank walks on water, all she talks about is how he'll be with the Cubs and then I'll see how stupid my college dreams are. She doesn't hit Frank anymore. She broke my front tooth yesterday, dental bill is HUGE. Have to work more overtime.

Boom-Boom is getting Frank in shape for tryouts. Says Frank has good hand-eye coordination but out of practice. Frank loves B-B, Frank hates B-B.

September 18

Going to Wrigley for Frank's tryout. Frank said, no Boom-Boom, he doesn't want the Star to take the shine away from him, but B-B wants to watch. Told B-B I wanted to come along.

September 24

Boom-Boom so angry with me for running off, he didn't watch Frank fuck up on the field (my good deed for my brother, kept the Star from seeing him "whiff the curve"). Ma hit me again, mad at me because Frank lost his chance. Didn't even feel it. Now all the papers showing what Mr. M and Rory Scanlon are really doing with the foundation money are safe, inside a kind of tunnel, wrapped inside insulating tape around some big pipe. Cubs photographer, maintenance guys, they were cool, they saw it as a big joke I was playing on the hockey star, they helped me out.

October 13

Mr. Warshawski says criminals feel an urge to share their cleverness, that's how the police catch a lot of people. Now I know what he means, I'm aching to tell someone else, about the papers, and how I hid them, but who can I trust?

October 27

Mr. M tries to wheedle the papers out of me. Says I have a BIG Christmas bonus coming. I said I thought Jews didn't celebrate Christmas. He said it's a secular society, I'll realize when I get out of the St. Eloy's orbit.

December 20

Joel helped me with my college applications. Spike and the other guys make fun of him. If only he didn't SWEAT so much I'd let him kiss me, he's so sweet and vulnerable in a puppy kind of way.

He helped me write a piece of music to use in my college applications. I played it on Mrs. Warshawski's piano; Mr. W said it sounded like Verdi, and that he was sure his wife was listening in heaven and loving it. I loved Mrs. W, I wish he hadn't said that, if she's listening in heaven she knows I didn't do most of the work myself. Fail on your own merits, that was always her advice to me. Work hard and fail on your own merits, don't succeed on someone else's. Now—I'm disobeying her. Feels 1000 x worse than disobeying Ma. Who hit me AGAIN for bragging about the music. Maybe that evens it all out.

January 21

Joel was working late tonight, accused me of having sex with Mr. M, with Boom-Boom, said he thought I was too precious a person (can you believe that? Precious a person?) to sell myself even for college. Finally told him I found these financial papers about what Mr. M and Mr. S are doing with the client accounts. Told him I hid them in Wrigley Field and they can't touch me. I'm free.

April 13

Learned today that Bryn Mawr accepted me. Told Ma and everyone at school, full scholarship, but they only gave me half of what I need. I'll still have to work, but even with that, it's SO expensive—need Mr. M's support. I AM GOING TO PHILADELPHIA IN AUGUST & NO ONE CAN STOP ME!!!!

April 15

Told Mr. M I know what he and Rory Scanlon are up to, told him I'd found the bank statements from Continental for the *Say, Yes!* foundation. Said I hoped the foundation could help pay my college tuition when I go away next year. He said he'd talk to R.S.

He asked, what did I do with the papers, told him they were in a *very safe* place. Scary look on his face.

April 18

Ma beat me so bad tonight I want to kill her! Betty, busybody hypocrite Betty told her I'm on the Pill. Ma said I was stabbing the Blessed Mother through the womb. Went through my private things! Found the money Mr. M gave me, stole it, said it was immoral, time I learned she would never let me leave Chicago for college. I picked up kitchen knife, said, "You want to see what it's like to stab someone through the womb, try this!" and she went insane, hit me with a frying pan. I blacked out. Came to with goose egg on head, woozy, throwing up.

Mr. W keeps saying I can stay in Vic's room until it's time to leave for college. Maybe I will, Ma will go insane, she hates all the Warshawskis, most of all my beloved Mrs. W.

Joel came over. I was in bathroom cleaning sick off my face. He saw my goose egg and freaked, begged me to let him marry me so he could protect me against Ma. Told him I don't need protecting, just need to leave Chicago!!

Then he said he'd gone to Wrigley Field and found my book of papers, but he freaked when a maintenance man came in. He dropped them in the mud! They're gone. All but one page from the Continental Bank which doesn't mean shit on its own. I sat down in the middle of the floor and bawled my eyes out. He tried to put his arms around me and kiss me, tried to say he was in love with me. I told him to leave, to leave me alone, he ruined my plan. Anyway no man will ever own me. Not him, not Mr. M or Rory or Spike, none of them.

Joel looked so sad, slouching off down the sidewalk, almost forgave him for losing my papers, but what will I do without them?

I saw Rory Scanlon's Buick across the street. I'm watching Joel, R.S. is watching the house like he does two or three times a week, maybe he thinks he can find something to blackmail me with. Like, if he said Joel was sleeping with me, I'd give him and Mr. M their papers back.

56

CLUTCH HITTER

Dead teen, and beautiful at that, life cut short, missing documents, sex with powerful men. It was a story made for TV; it went viral in an hour. By mid-morning, I was once again fielding media inquiries from as far away as Kazakhstan.

How and where had I found the diary?

It had come to me in the mail, in an anonymous envelope, no return address and according to the private forensic lab I use, no fingerprints.

How sure was I that this was really Annie's handwriting?

I had the condolence letter Annie had written to my father; I was willing to let an independent lab compare that to the diary I was looking at—but only if Stella Guzzo would submit her diary to the same lab for the same tests.

The Kazakh media, obsessed with hockey, were more interested in Boom-Boom—did my copy of the diary vindicate him?

Other reporters had other questions, of course, about the drama at

Dead Stick Pond, about the Sturlese brothers, but the main focus was on Annie's death. Did I believe Rory Scanlon was responsible?

"I don't know who killed Annie Guzzo. Twenty-five years ago, it seemed obvious that Stella Guzzo murdered her daughter, so no forensic evidence was taken from the crime scene. Now it's a wide-open field. We know Annie was alive when her mother left to play bingo, but we only have these pages to suggest other names. It's tantalizing, but we probably will never have the truth."

In the middle of the media push, a cop came to my office, one of Bobby Mallory's personal staff. The captain would like a word; could I ride with him to Thirty-fifth and Michigan.

Bobby had Conrad and a forensic tech with him. "I need to know about these documents, Vicki."

Bobby was getting old; his jowly face had deeper lines around the mouth and eyes. At least he was no longer so red in the face—Eileen and his doctor had finally persuaded him to change his diet, take some blood pressure meds.

"I don't know anything about them, other than what's up on the *Herald-Star* website. They came to me in an anonymous envelope, and I don't know if they're real or fake. And they are in a vault right now until Stella Guzzo produces hers for comparison. Or you produce a subpoena."

"The envelope?" Bobby held out a hand.

I took it from my briefcase: a plain manila 10x14, available at every office supply store in America. Postmarked three days ago, date-time stamped "Received" by me yesterday.

"What proof do you have that this is the envelope that held the so-called diary?" Bobby asked.

I shook my head. "I don't open my mail expecting to have to prove I got it. When I saw what was in the envelope, I drove up to Cheviot Labs with it. They checked for fingerprints, and for DNA on the gummed label, but whoever sent it used tap water, not saliva, and apparently handled it with gloves."

I held out the notarized report from Cheviot's fingerprint specialist. Bobby grunted and handed it, with the envelope, to his forensic tech.

"A written receipt, please," I said. "Or I can photograph your expropriation."

I switched on my phone camera, but Bobby, with an exaggerated scowl, called to his secretary to bring me a receipt. I was supposed to feel guilty for making them do extra work while seizing my property.

Conrad and Bobby exchanged glances; Bobby nodded at Conrad.

"Vic, whether what you've put out is really Annie Guzzo's diary or if it's a forgery, you could be lighting a fuse on a powerful piece of dynamite," Conrad said.

Meaning, I was in serious danger. "You think it's a forgery?" I asked.

"With you, I think anything is possible," Bobby said. "You and the law know each other well, but you don't always respect the acquaintance."

"Unlike people with money and with access to the Illinois Speaker," I said. "They are *sans reproche*. That's comforting."

"I'm not going to argue that with you," Bobby said. "You know Illinois politics better than you know the law. Rawlings and I are just saying, it would have been better to bring those pages to us, instead of publishing them first."

"Got it." I stood to leave, but Bobby asked Conrad and the tech to step outside.

"Vicki, Rawlings told me about the letter the old Fourth District watch commander wrote, saying he'd sent someone off to the Seventh District. He said you assume that was Tony, right?"

"Right."

Bobby fingered the fold of skin above his necktie, as if the knot were too tight. "It might have been. Say it was, say Brattigan did send your dad off to face the danger of—well, the dangers he did face in the Seventh. Say it was Rory Scanlon who put him up to it. This diary you've conjured wouldn't be payback for that, would it?"

"Conjure. That is a very loaded word. No one used it when Stella burst forth with a diary of Annie's that mysteriously appeared in a drawer twenty-five years after her sister-in-law had been pawing through the same place looking for cash."

"Tap-dance around, clown around, but did you hire someone to create a forgery so you could try to get at Rory Scanlon? If you're framing him as punishment for upending Tony's life, you are playing a dangerous game."

"Tap-dancing, clowning and playing a dangerous game? Way more energetic than I'm up to after getting my nose broken and a whole lot of other injuries." I leaned forward and kissed Bobby's cheek. "You know my parents' memories are sacred to me, Bobby, so anything is possible, but I'm more concerned about someone getting a green light for murder just because he put a new piece of stained glass over a church altar."

Bobby's staff officer drove me back to my office. It wasn't until he dropped me off that I started to feel that prickle along the back of the neck, that fear you get when someone is following you or is training a sniper's rifle on your neck.

I went through the day with as much focus as I could manage, met with Darraugh Graham and a couple of other Loop clients, took the dogs to the lake, borrowed Jake's Fiat to go grocery shopping—Luke Edwards had reclaimed the Subaru after our shoot-out near Dead Stick Pond—he'd seen the damage to the rental Taurus on YouTube and hadn't wanted to risk the Subaru in my hands a day longer.

They struck in the middle of the night. Fast, ruthless, jimmying open the building door, hydraulic ram on my apartment's steel front door, thugs at the kitchen exit when I tried to escape through the back. The dogs were barking ferociously from Mr. Contreras's place, but the goons had me bound, gagged, a hood on my head, and flung into a pickup bed before the old man could get them outside. I'd gone to sleep in my clothes, just in case, but they'd moved so fast I didn't have time to put on shoes.

Three in the morning, couldn't tell where we were going. Expressway, maybe. South, maybe. Wind whipped underneath the hood, rubbing against my face. After a time I smelled the lake through the sack, and then my eyes were tearing, I was coughing and choking behind the gag. Pet coke dust. We were close to the Guisar slip.

The air changed overhead. A closed space. Hands dragged me from the back of the truck, thumped me down onto a chair. Tied me to it.

When the hood was unbuckled and pulled off, the light blinded me. I blinked and a wall of metal filing cabinets came into focus. Metal desks. A locked grate with a pay window and a safe behind it. The office for Bagby & Family Haulage. Vince Bagby was leaning against one desk, Rory Scanlon was seated in the chair where Delphina Bagby had been playing solitaire. Three solid-looking youths in the green T-shirts of *Say, Yes!* lounged by the door, faces blank.

"So those flowers and dinner invitations and stuff, they weren't because of my beautiful eyes," I said.

Bagby squirmed, shrugged, gave a fake-hearty laugh.

"One last Warshawski," Scanlon said. "One last person thinking they don't have to play by the rules."

"Depends on the rules," I said. "I guess Tony's mistake was thinking the law meant something besides pay to play."

Scanlon nodded at one of the *Say, Yes!* youths, who walked over and hit me in the face. I was able to move my head away from the blow, but it still hurt.

"Where did you get that diary you put out?" Scanlon asked.

"Funny," I said, "Captain Mallory asked me the same question only twelve hours ago. You probably have your own stooges inside the CPD, although I hope they don't include Conrad Rawlings. But in case the information is slow drifting south, I'll tell you the same thing I told the captain: someone mailed it to me. No return address, no prints, no DNA."

"I don't believe it's real," Scanlon said flatly.

"It's on the Global Entertainment website," I said. "It looks pretty real."

"I want to see it," Scanlon said. "I think you hired someone to forge it."

"If it is a forgery, I bet it's way better than the one you had Frank put in his sister's underwear drawer. It actually looks like Annie's handwriting, at least like the one letter of hers that I still have."

"Pretty convenient, how it showed up," Scanlon said, his lips a flat, ugly line.

"Yeah, that's how I felt when Stella's version showed up. It will be fun to get both diaries vetted by experts."

"Not any kind of fun you'll ever have," Scanlon barked. "You could have died in your bed if you'd kept your goddam nose out of my business. But no, just like your parents, all of you thinking you were too good for this neighborhood. I do a lot for people down here, I did a lot for your family, but I never got any gratitude."

"Thank you," I said. "Thank you for getting my dad transferred to the Seventh, for putting a bad rap out on him so that he was sent without backup into gang shootings. Does that help?"

Scanlon nodded again at his pet, who smacked me again. I didn't move as fast this time; my nose started to bleed. Bagby winced. He didn't like seeing me beaten? Maybe my beautiful eyes had played a small role.

"Your precious cousin." Scanlon was panting. "I got him his chance, but Tony, high-and-mighty Tony Warshawski, bad-mouthed me in the precinct."

"My cousin's talent and drive got him where he needed to be," I snapped.

"I made the connections that brought him to the attention of the Blackhawks organization. Otherwise he'd have been like Frank Guzzo, another loser wannabe driving a truck."

"Is that the only kind of employee Bagby has?" I asked, looked at Vince. "Frank Guzzo works hard, he keeps his family going. That isn't a loser's behavior. A loser is someone who can't operate without a lot of people in his pocket to do his dirty work for him."

"Yeah, well, you've cost Frankie Junior his chance to go to ball camp," Scanlon said. "I warned Guzzo to keep you away from here, but he's such a useless piece of quivering jelly he couldn't even manage that. His ma is twice the man he is. Twice the man old Mateo was, too."

"You've been watching too many Clint Eastwood movies," I said. "Mateo was like Frank: honest, quiet, hardworking. Twice—no—ten times the man you and your cousin are. Although ten times zero is still zero."

Another blow. My mouth started to fill with blood and I spoke with difficulty. "On the night she died, Annie wrote in her diary that she saw your car outside the Guzzo house. Was it you who killed her? Or did you already have enough thugs on your team twenty-five years ago that one of them gave her the last blow?"

"I need to know where you got the diary," Scanlon said. "I need to know if there's more out there."

"You mean, did Annie send a message through a medium to say

you murdered her?" Blood dribbled down my chin and pooled on my neck. "I haven't seen any ectoplasm shimmering through my office. If she wrote your or Sol Mandel's name on the living room floor, the cops kept that detail private. Of course, Oswald Brattigan, watch commander at the Fourth, he was your boy, he could have disposed of any evidence you left, to make sure Stella Guzzo carried the can for you."

The circulation was starting to go in my hands. I would have been worried about them, except I was more worried that I was going to die soon. I curled and uncurled my fingers. My wrists scraped against the rope.

"Mandel was soft," Scanlon said. "He let that little bitch bleed him, instead of taking care of her from day one. As soon as he told me what she was up to, he agreed something had to be done, but he couldn't bring himself to do it. I made him go to the Guzzo's front door, on the pretext of reasoning with the girl about her demands. We let Spike do the honors, since it was his career we were helping build."

Vince made a restless gesture.

"You think I shouldn't say anything, little cousin?" Scanlon jeered. "Don't tell me you're soft, too. Warshawski isn't going anywhere, isn't going to tell anyone anything. Mandel and McClelland both knew Spike was tough enough to do anything, and he's proved that over and over again in Springfield."

"Yes, all you cousins," I said, proud that my voice was steady, despite my terror and my aching mouth. "You and Vince, and Nina Quarles, who owns that law firm. Did you have her buy it in case Mandel had left any loose bits of evidence lying around in his old files?"

"Never mind why we did what we did. You wouldn't understand that kind of loyalty, to family and to shared values. I'm giving you one chance to let me have the original of any other papers that came into your possession."

"And if I give them to you?"

"Then your friends will survive to say prayers over your grave. If not, all those people, the old man, the dogs, the doctor, the musician, we will eliminate them one by one, and they will die cursing you."

"Then if I had any papers to give you, I would do so in an instant. I don't."

More questions, no answers. More blows, no defense. Time lost meaning, voice lost meaning, body lost feeling.

We ended where we all knew we would, back in the pickup, out onto the docks, the hood on my head, truck driving up an incline, someone tossing me over the side, a smear of dust coming under the hood, choking me. I was on the coal mountain where Jerry Fugher died.

"That's over with," the smooth white voice said. "The last of the Warshawskis. They all thought they were too good for this world, and by God, they were."

"Hey, man, you ain'tcha gonna bury her?" one of the green shirts asked.

"No need," Scanlon said. "She'll choke to death soon enough."

"You're making a mistake." It was Bagby, his voice urgent but somehow supplicating. "You don't own Rawlings and he won't let her death go."

"There's no evidence, at least not if you do a good scrub-down in your office." A pause. "Oh, Vince, Vince, don't tell me you had the hots for her? It wasn't an act? You ever get inside her pants? Want the boys to bring her back to the loading bay for some action before she dies?"

Bile rose in my throat.

"You're an asshole, Rory."

"Hey, I look out for widows and orphans and helpless cousins."

Feet thudding on concrete, getting more remote. I burrowed hard with my butt, made a ledge in the coke. Shifted buttock to buttock, worked my hands down behind my thighs, bunched forward in a ball, slid my hands up over my legs. I lifted my bound hands to my face and the blood pounded painfully in my fingers. I tried pushing the hood away from my head, but it was buckled behind me. I couldn't budge it. I stood on quivering legs, fell heavily.

Hands grabbed mine. Some action before I die, you'll see action before I die. I kicked hard.

"Hey, *Vittoria, mio core*. Easy does it: I play with these fingers."

57

STEALING HOME

I sat on the ground, leaning against Jake's legs while he unbuckled the hood. When he'd freed me, he helped me down the hill, our feet sliding and sinking to their ankles. I kept coughing up balls of black phlegm and at the bottom, I was hit by such a violent paroxysm that I fell again.

Jake squatted, pulling me to him, stroking my filthy hair. "I was so afraid, *mio core*, so afraid I wouldn't be in time."

The dogs had roused the whole building, he said. He'd run first to my apartment.

"I saw that the door had been broken open, but my brain wouldn't work. And then I saw them carrying you through the gate, that foul thing on your head. I ran to the alley, but their truck was already rattling away."

He pulled me closer. "I was afraid if I took time to call the cops, the truck would disappear. I didn't have any phone numbers, anyway, just nine-one-one, which I called while I was driving." He'd been frantic, trying to keep an eye on the Bagby truck, trying to explain what was happening to the emergency dispatcher.

"I hung up—I couldn't talk and follow you, but I thought of Max. He knows everyone. He told me he'd locate your police pals. He tracked down Frank Guzzo, too, and got him to explain the likely places Bagby or Scanlon would take you. Max talked me through the route. He was way better than any GPS." Jake gave a laugh that bordered on the hysterical.

He helped me back to my feet, waited out another coughing attack.

"So you got to the Bagby office?" I asked. "Where were you?"

"They'd left a window open. I stood under that and recorded it all, but it was agony, listening to—never mind that. I—I wasn't brave enough to go in after you. Forgive me, Vic, but I just couldn't do it."

It was my turn to squeeze his shoulder reassuringly. "You made the right choice. If you'd gone in, you'd have been a hostage; we'd both be dead."

Conrad roared up just then, six squad cars flashing in his wake.

"Five men in a truck," Jake said to Conrad when he bounded over, roaring commands through a loudspeaker. "Two first chairs and three pit members. I stood under a window at the Bagby office and recorded their words."

"Scanlon," I coughed at Conrad, spitting out a mouthful of coke. "Scanlon and Bagby."

Conrad sent his squads out to find them. He tried to question me, there on the Guisar slip, under the searchlights he'd turned on, but I couldn't speak. Wouldn't speak. Too many questions, too many blows. No more.

"I'm taking the lady home, Rawlings. I'll e-mail you the recording from my smartphone."

Jake guided me off the Guisar slip, drove me to Lotty, who'd been warned by Max that I might need reconstructing. She tucked me into her own guest bed. Over the next few days, her doorman and a private nurse kept cops and reporters at bay, even Murray, who thought he was entitled to a front-row seat.

Jake stayed close by. Even later, when I was back on my feet, resuming my workload, there were times when he thought I might have disappeared on him and he'd race to my office to check on me. He started practicing in my big workroom. The acoustics were good, so good that his High Plainsong group began rehearsing there.

"Remember I told you I'd pull you out of the tar pits if you got stuck in them?" he said the day he drove me home from Lotty's.

"You said you'd use your bass strings," I reminded him.

"From now on I'll keep a spare set in the glove compartment," he promised.

Eventually, of course, I did talk to the cops. According to Conrad's off-the-record report, Spike had been using his many connections in Chicago to short-circuit any indictments, but the media storm for once was bigger than the Speaker's power. The state's attorney wasn't able to indict Rory or Vince for Jerry Fugher's murder, but he had enough from Jake's recording and my own testimony to charge them not just with attempting to kill me, but framing Stella Guzzo for Annie's murder.

When the SA subpoenaed the diary extracts that Murray had posted online, I handed them over without a murmur. Even if a lab decided they were forgeries, there wasn't any way to trace them: they had indeed come to me in the mail, with no return address, postmarked from the Loop postal station that saw so much traffic no one could remember one manila envelope. And I had never claimed they were Annie's, simply that I had them and was willing to submit them to tests.

The diary Frank had helped Scanlon or Bagby or Spike plant in

Stella's house was also subpoenaed. It turned out as Bernie had been insisting—Stella had given it to Father Cardenal. Having to guard Stella's secret was probably why Cardenal's attitude toward me underwent such a major shift.

When I finally got to see the document, I felt a certain satisfaction: Scanlon hadn't made any effort to get old paper or to disguise the handwriting; the diary was declared fraudulent.

Kenji Aroyawa was ecstatic when two labs—my private one and the State of Illinois's crime lab—decided my pages were authentic. He and I shared a bottle of champagne while Rafe Zukos sulked downstairs in front of his geese-in-flight painting. Zukos had bitterly opposed Ken "prostituting his art" to help anyone in South Chicago, but Ken had loved creating Annie's diary.

"It's an art project, Rafe, it's what art students do—they copy the masters to learn their craft. It takes me back to my own sensei's studio, copying someone else's calligraphy—not that poor little Annie's handwriting would have been allowed in Sensei Yamamoto's atelier."

I'd found paper for the project by going to garage sales until I came on an empty journal of about the right vintage for Annie to have kept. Ken took three days over the writing. I didn't tell anyone, not even Mr. Contreras or Jake, about the project. It's the kind of story people like to repeat, and it wasn't one I wanted to hear in a courtroom.

There was some positive fallout. Ira and Eunice Previn's chauffeur drove them to my office one morning to give me a backhanded thanks for making Joel's role in Stella's trial look less inept, or at least more explicable.

"I let my ties to Sol and the temple blind me to all the holes in the case. You were better than us on this one, young lady," was all Ira said.

"It was more than that," Eunice said. "We didn't know—we didn't want to know. Sol was one of the only people at the temple who took me—took our family—for what it was. Not me being the stereotypical black sexual animal ensnaring Ira, but a man and a woman who respected each other. And Joel—my only child—we wanted so much for him and—"

She broke off, squeezed her eyes shut as if she could blot out the pictures from the past. Ira tried to take her hand but she shook him away.

"I had three miscarriages, and then Joel, and—I wasn't ready for such a sensitive boy. I—his music, I wish I'd let him follow his music."

She stood, head erect, spine straight, marched to the door with Ira following more slowly in her wake. I wished I could believe the resolution of the story would send Joel into rehab, but his drinking was such an entrenched part of his life now that I wasn't optimistic.

There was another, better outcome to the story: Murray decided it was high time someone actually wrote my cousin's biography. He got a nice advance from Gaudy Press—with Boom-Boom back in the headlines, they thought it was a worthwhile project, assuming Murray could give them a quick turnaround.

As the cold spring turned into summer, I found myself taking refuge in singing. I would play a recording Jake made of counterpoint to Vittoria Aleotti's madrigals, trying to match my voice to the intervals, sometimes succeeding. Even when I failed, the music, the muscles, the voice brought me a kind of connection to my mother that made the night in the coal dust seem like one more bad dream, nothing more.

In June, Jake came with me to Wrigley Field to see St. Eloy's play in the Catholic League championship game. Stella, who was there with Betty, Frank and their daughters, looked at me with loathing, but the lithium seemed to be holding—at least she didn't try to punch me.

Mr. Villard sat on the first-base side so that he could watch Frankie at short. Adelaide was with him, helping him in and out of his seat. At the end of the game, he beamed enthusiastically at Frank and Betty: no promises for the future, a lot can change in a boy's life, a talented kid at fifteen may have developed as far as he ever will, but he liked what he'd seen; he'd make sure Frankie Junior got a spot in one of the league's premier talent camps this summer.

A few days later, Mr. Villard came to High Plainsong's last concert— High Plainsong's Swan Song, they'd billed it, with medieval songs and music about swans dominating the second half, and me performing a duet with Jake from Vittoria Aleotti's "Garland of Madrigals," to end the first.

A few days later, I got a letter from Mr. Villard.

Dear Ms. Warshawski,

I've always liked players with guts and determination. They dig deeper, often outlast flashier players. You did a major service to baseball and to the Cubs by exposing Gil Brineruck; you saved my life, and now, your visits bring me a lot of pleasure.

I heard through the grapevine that you lost your car and lost a lot of income this spring. This check is from me, no strings attached, but maybe you can get yourself a nice little car. The other check is for your friend. The only song I can sing is "Take Me Out to the Ball Game," but he and his musician friends are major leaguers, I can see that, and they deserve to keep their own playing field green.

Two checks fluttered out. Mine would buy me a very nice little car indeed. I wrote Mr. Villard a thank-you note, then sat daydreaming in front of car websites. Muscle car or getting-around-town car?

The front bell roused me. I looked at my security camera monitor: it was Frank. I almost didn't let him in, but he looked so uncomfortable that I finally released the lock.

Just as it had been when he first showed up in April, it was hard for him to find a way to talk. I sat quietly until he blurted, "Tori, I'm so sorry. You saved Ma. You saved Frankie. I know you almost died because of me, and I can't even pay your bill."

"It's okay, Frank." I couldn't meet his eyes.

"I made a big mistake, letting you go."

"You did the right thing, letting me go. You brought me great comfort when I needed it most, but we weren't right for each other."

"Yeah, but—" He broke off, but I could see all the unsaid words on his face: if he'd stayed with me, it all would have turned out differently, he wouldn't have whiffed the curve, it would be him in Cooperstown, just as Boom-Boom was in Toronto.

"No, Frank," I said, my voice gentle. "I would have made you a lot unhappier down the road than you ever made me. My dad never cared much for men who rated success by how much money or power they had. To him, a successful man was honest in his public and private affairs. You have four beautiful children, and that's something I will never have. You're a good dad to all of them. You go home and remember to feel proud of that."

"Yeah, okay, yeah."

I walked him to the door and stood on the sidewalk until he climbed into his truck.

THANKS

Bill and Eleanor Revelle showed me V.I.'s route into the Villard mansion in Chapter 44. Fay Clayton gave generous advice on payday loan companies. Cheryl Corley and Elizabeth Brackett's coverage of the pet coke in South Chicago, for Public Radio and PBS, respectively, first alerted me to the existence of these dust mountains in Chicago. Tricia Rumbolz drove me as close as we could get to them as ordinary tourists. Kathryn Lyndes stepped into the breach to help me finish the final rewrites.

This book is a bit of an anachronism: part of the action takes place under the stands at Wrigley Field, but starting in the fall of 2014, the field has been undergoing major demolition and reconstruction. I first heard about Wrigley's underground spaces from Brian Bernardoni and thought they would be a perfect setting for a crime novel. Although I tried for over a year to see these spaces firsthand, I was never able to get calls or e-mails to the Cubs answered, and so I relied on my unfettered imagination to describe them.

As for climbing up the bleachers into the stands, as V.I. says she and her cousin Boom-Boom used to do, when I worked in advertising many years ago, one of my clients told me about doing this as a young man during the Great Depression, when he couldn't afford the price of a ticket. He also used to shinny up the L girders so he could ride the trains to Wrigley Field for free.

I've also taken a few liberties with how Bernadine Fouchard handles the college admissions process.

Thanks to Karl Fogel for explaining how easy it is to hack into someone's bank account online.

Aimee LaBerge gave correct Québécois idioms for the French in the novel, in particular the insult *"ostie de folle."* Heather Watkins confirmed this phrase.

Readers interested in how Boom-Boom ended his life under the screw of the *Bertha Krupnik* can find out by reading *Deadlock*.

READ ALL THE
V.I. WARSHAWSKI BOOKS

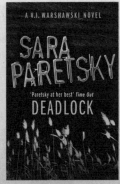

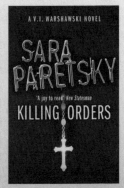

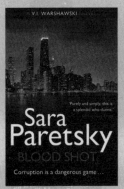

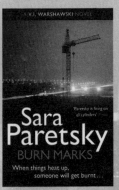

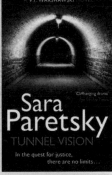

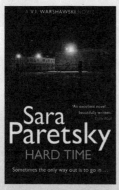
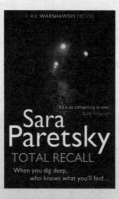
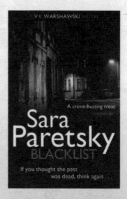

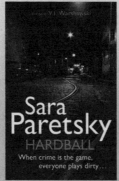
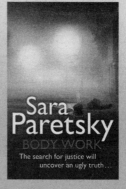
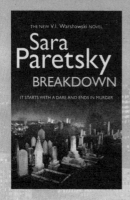